"I didn't get you a pie. I *made* you a pie."

Her eyes were dancing in the low light, and he could see the golden highlights in her hair. Forget the damn pie. He wanted to taste *her*.

Whoa there, Colton. Friends, friends, friends, he repeated to himself. What had happened to all that animosity between them? The desire to tease her, to make her blush? To keep her at a distance, which was what all that bickering had done. Now he found he did want to make her blush. But for a completely different reason.

"Better hurry and wish before it fizzles," she said, gesturing to the candle, which really did seem to be on its way to flickering out.

Oh, he wished all right, while she did a speedy rendition of "Happy Birthday." She couldn't hold a tune to save her life, but he loved it just the same. Then he blew out the candle.

As it sat there smoldering, a thin wisp of smoke curling elegantly into the wooden slats of the porch ceiling, Sara jumped up. "Do you like warm pie? I'm going to nuke some pieces and put ice cream on them, is that OK? I've been waiting for this all ni—"

Before he knew what he was doing he reached up for her arm, tugged her back down beside him, and planted his lips on hers. Then he curled his hand around her neck and pulled her in deeper.

then
there
was
you

MIRANDA
LIASSON

FOREVER

New York Boston

Copyright © 2018 by Miranda Liasson

Cover design and illustration by Elizabeth Turner Stokes
Cover copyright © 2018 by Hachette Book Group, Inc.

Forever
Hachette Book Group
1290 Avenue of the Americas, New York, NY 10104
forever-romance.com
twitter.com/foreverromance

First Edition: May 2018

Forever is an imprint of Grand Central Publishing. The Forever name and logo are trademarks of Hachette Book Group, Inc.

The publisher is not responsible for websites (or their content) that are not owned by the publisher.

The Hachette Speakers Bureau provides a wide range of authors for speaking events. To find out more, go to www.hachettespeakersbureau.com or call (866) 376-6591.

ISBN: 978-1-4555-4180-5 (mass market), 978-1-4555-4179-9 (ebook)

Printed in the United States of America

OPM

10 9 8 7 6 5 4 3 2 1

*For anyone who must walk the
Alzheimer's journey with a loved one.*

then
there
was
you

Sometimes the last person on earth you want to be with is the one person you can't be without.

—Tagline for the movie
Pride and Prejudice, 2005

Chapter 1

♥

Dr. Serafina Langdon stood in the Angel Falls Community Hospital ER before the door to exam room three, squeezing her eyes shut, struggling to be a better person. Clearly a higher power was telling her she'd made the wrong decision, returning to her hometown of Angel Falls, Ohio. Because the name on the sheet of paper in her hand said that the patient occupying the room in front of her was *Colton Bentley Walker*.

Not him. *Anyone* but him. She'd hoped to ease back into town, get herself established, and then confront—on her own terms—the man who'd helped ruin her engagement a year ago. Who'd been a burr in her side for years—since she was fourteen, really. She'd known this day would come; she just hadn't expected it during her first ER shift.

Sara sucked in a deep breath. She could handle this. She reminded herself again of the reason she'd returned to this sleepy small town to join her dad's medical practice after her high-powered Ivy League training at

Columbia. Her sweet, precious grandmother had recently been diagnosed with Alzheimer's disease, and Sara wanted to do all she could to help the woman who'd been her rock, her support, her unwavering cheerleader her whole life. She could face the demons of the past for Nonna's sake.

Sara opened her eyes. Slid the sheet of paper back into the metal pocket on the wall. She couldn't do it. Not today, and maybe not ever. She turned on the soles of her Dansko clogs and walked at a fast clip back to the nurses' station.

The ER was just as white bright at two on a Saturday morning as it was at high noon. And just as busy. Even the administrative assistant was on the phone. Sara peeked around the corner to find the doc she was sharing this shift with. Sara was a primary care doctor, but in a town as small as Angel Falls, the primary care docs worked alongside the ER docs to help staff the ER. Brian Graves, a guy from the next town over whom she knew from residency, was her partner this shift. He had one claim to fame: he'd bedded more women than an eighties rock star.

She hated to approach him, but what was worse? Asking a favor of a guy who wanted to get her in the sack or inflicting irreversible pain and suffering on the man she blamed for ruining her chance at happily ever after?

An unwanted flash of herself in her mother's wedding gown passed before her, pivoting slowly in front of the big mirror at Katie O'Hara's bridal shop, while her sisters and her grandmother and her stepmother oohed and aahed. Sorrow over the future that had come crashing down around her stabbed her in the gut, as it tended to do at the worst times. She didn't want to be reminded of all that pain, and she could *not* see Colton without wanting to kill him. All righty then. Brian it was.

She found him sauntering down the hall to an exam room, eyeing the butt of a nurse as she made the usual two a.m. pot of coffee.

"Trade me a patient?" Sara asked.

He reached out and took the electronic tablet she carried in her hand. "Oh, Chief Walker." He looked from the tablet to her. "You running away from the law or something?"

He chuckled at his own joke and trained his baby blues on her. Many women found them mesmerizing, but she was definitely immune to his slithery brand of charm.

Brian handed her back the tablet, but when she made to take it, he continued to hold on. "Can't do it. Sorry. Although it's an easy case, not sure why you're worried. A few stitches and a tetanus shot and you're done. Unless you're afraid you'll fall for the cop. You'd be better off with a hot doc like me. I love danger too, by the way, if that's what you're looking for."

She rolled her eyes. "I *know* it's an easy case, and I do *not* have a thing for him. What are you working on?"

"Potential cardiac arrest. Or maybe the guy just has bad heartburn from eating at that new Mexican place off Route 44. I already saw him and ordered tests, or I'd trade. Next time I'd be happy to accommodate." He let his gaze drag up and down, as if she were wearing a boob-uplifting cocktail dress instead of blue scrubs, a white coat, and a stethoscope adorned with a little fuzzy koala bear. Her best friend Kaitlyn had given her the koala as a welcome-home gift, so that the kids Sara saw wouldn't be so afraid.

"Um, OK. Thanks." He was still eyeballing her with that yucky I-want-you-babe look.

"Speaking of accommodating…"

"Not going to happen, Brian." She yanked hard on the tablet. "Thanks, though," she called over her shoulder as she walked away.

Oh, what the hell. If she could handle horny Brian, she could handle He-Who-Must-Not-Be-Named. So she knocked on the exam room door and walked in.

There, lying on the gurney watching late-night Spanish soccer, was Colton, his long lazy frame sprawled out, one elbow behind his head as he inclined toward the wall-mounted television. The hospital gown fell away from his arm, revealing its sinewy, tanned glory for all the world to see.

All that manly muscle distracted her momentarily from his problem, which she now saw clearly. His left arm was laid out straight, exposing the jagged edges of a bloody wound that curved around his biceps.

His very toned biceps. He was a fit man, lean but muscular. Not that she was noticing in any other manner but that of a physician evaluating her patient.

He would be handsome, if not for the fact that he was the world's biggest jerk. That he was tall and strong and broad shouldered only mattered from the standpoint that if you had him with you in a dark alley, you'd totally be covered. His hair used to be longish and thickly layered but was now cut in a no-nonsense buzz. He flicked his eyes—cool, devastatingly blue, with too-long eyelashes—from the TV to her. She saw the moment recognition set in, and hey, was that *fear*?

She certainly hoped so. After all, she would be the one wielding the needle. This was *her* territory. And Sara was not going to allow him to forget that, not for one second.

He looked her over in that bored, detached way he had, as if she were far beneath his notice. Before she could stop herself, her hand flew up to her glasses, which she suddenly remembered she was wearing for her middle-of-the-night shift. She caught herself from adjusting them in time. Reminded herself that high school was eons ago, that she wasn't that gawky, awkward girl with blazing-red frizzy hair he used to mercilessly call *Sara Jane the Brain*. Followed by more years of being mostly ignored and patiently tolerated, which made it especially awkward as he was her ex-fiancé Tagg's best friend.

Tagg was at the Cleveland Clinic an hour away, working as a neurologist, while she was back home in Angel Falls trying to carve out a life for herself that looked nothing like the one she'd envisioned a year ago. On the bright side, being back home with family reminded her of how much she'd missed them, although the fact that her dad was less than thrilled at having her as a partner at his practice still stung.

Sara had opened her mouth to utter what she hoped

would be a professional greeting when the door opened behind her. Brian stuck his head into the room.

"Hey, Colt, great to see you, buddy," he said. "Wish I could stitch you up myself, but I'm busy with a critically ill patient. You know how that goes."

"Yeah, he needs two Tums stat," Sara said. "Better hurry."

Brian laughed. "Very clever. I like my women with spunk."

"And I'd like to get going on my work." She held the door open and gestured for him to exit. Which he did, unfortunately winking at Colton first.

"I didn't know you and Brian were an item," Colton said. Of course his first words would raise her blood pressure, his favorite pastime.

"We are *not* an item," she said.

"Well, I just assumed. Judging by the lovey-dovey looks you two were exchanging just now."

Lovey-dovey looks? Was the man out of his mind? "I guess you don't need great powers of deduction to be the police chief in this town."

"Ouch," Colton said, pretending to be offended. "Well, excuse me for assuming. You're a little too wild for him anyway, huh, Red?"

Sara felt her cheeks heat, the curse of the redhead. No one called her that ridiculous nickname but him, and she hadn't heard it for years. No one poked fun at her for being buttoned up and uptight except for him, and he'd taken great pleasure in doing it ever since high school.

"Grow up, Chief." She washed her hands at the sink

and pulled suture materials from the drawers. "I just want to remind you that I'm going to be wielding a needle here shortly, so you might want to restrain your mouth. If you're capable."

He held up his good hand. "Hey, more than capable, Doc. You just do your job so I can get back to work, OK?"

She walked over to the exam table. "You also might want to pull a bullet out of your holster and bite on it while I'm stitching you up." He suddenly looked a little pale. She should have felt guilty, but instead she was just glad it shut him up for a minute. "So you got gashed by a rusty fence?"

"I was crawling under it to catch a perp."

"Did you catch him?" She forced her focus on the jagged bloody wound. And away from the biceps.

"I'm surprised a well-educated lady doc like you is so sexist," he said in a deep baritone that seemed to reverberate right through her. "How do you know it wasn't a *she*-criminal?"

"Because we sewed *him* up a half hour ago. What took *you* so long to get here?"

He grinned, but she remained totally unaffected by his bright, broad, and just-imperfect-enough-to-melt-panties smile. "Paperwork at the station."

"You were bleeding like this and you stopped to do *paperwork*?"

He leveled big blue eyes at her and shrugged. Which she interpreted as an "I can handle it all even if I am bleeding like a stuck pig" gesture. His arrogance didn't seem tempered even after all these years.

Her eyes flicked to his too-handsome face. Colton had been blessed with angel-kissed good looks that had been turning the heads of females since he was a boy. He'd been popular, a stellar athlete, and quarterback on the football team until an injury had sidelined him and caused him to lose his college scholarship. He was the guy who'd sat on homecoming and prom courts, and who'd always had his pick of women.

Bringing her focus back to the task at hand, she prepared a soapy solution by squirting a bottle of antiseptic scrub into a bowl and brought it over to his bedside.

"Maybe I should wait for the nurses to do that," he said, sounding a little nervous.

"They're all tied up," Sara said sweetly, holding the curved suture needle up so he got a good view of it. "Better if I do it all and get you out of here quicker. I'm going to soak your arm in the antiseptic now."

"Will it sting?"

"The last patient cried for ten minutes, but he was six. Since you're a tough guy, I'd anticipate you'd be fine in half that time."

His dark gaze met hers, his thick brows knit together. Under all that bravado, Mr. Arrogance did seem a little worried. Which made her unconscionably happy. To his credit, when she lowered his arm into the soapy tub, he didn't even flinch. Truthfully, he didn't have to, because the solution they used didn't sting at all.

As she irrigated and scrubbed, she felt his gaze on her, quiet and assessing. She didn't usually get unnerved when people watched her, but she didn't like being this close to him, smelling his spicy, woodsy smell, feeling his eyes drill a hole through her.

When she glanced at him, he steered his gaze quickly away. "Um, not to question your professional ability," he said, "but are you sure you can see out of those things? I mean, I wouldn't want you to screw up. My arm is one of my better features."

Her cheeks burned, and for an instant she was back in ninth grade, feeling the same acute anguish. *You ever think about getting contacts, Brain? There just might be a pretty girl under all that glass.*

He was the kind of man who used his charm and good looks to get away with acting like a jerk. *Still.*

She couldn't believe she'd ever expected him to have her back last year, when he'd failed to keep her fiancé from "celebrating" so hard he fell face-first into his bachelor party cake—*and* the woman in it. Valerie Blake had always had a thing for Tagg in high school, a fact everyone knew. Especially Colt, who'd hired her for the party.

Tagg had been Sara's first boyfriend, and he'd loved her despite her ugly duckling phase. He'd seen who she was and loved her for her brains, not despite them. She'd often wondered why someone as good-looking as Tagg would want her, and sometimes that had kept her up at night. But he'd proposed, and suddenly everything she'd ever wanted was about to come true—a great job, a loving husband, a home of her own.

Until Colton had gone and waved a half-naked Valerie in front of him. Colton had always had a way of knowing her deepest fear and shining a spotlight on

it. And his actions last year hadn't just shone the spotlight, they'd blown up her entire life.

Yes, Tagg was to blame. She understood that. But
Colton had lit the match. If he'd been a good best man
and contained the party, Tagg would've gotten over his
last-minute panic without incident. They'd be married
now, all settled and enjoying life in the house they'd
picked out in a pretty suburb of Cleveland. The one
that Tagg was now living in with his girlfriend, aka
Cake Girl.

Sara stood up straight. She couldn't afford to wallow
in the past. "My glasses may not be attractive," she said,
"but I can see twenty-twenty out of them. Of course, if
I miss a stitch or two, the scar will just make you look a
little tougher. Because you're kind of a pretty boy now."

He threw up his hand in defense. "Hey, no offense,
Dr. Einstein. Just making a joke. I trust you."

He was looking at her oddly. For a moment she wondered if he felt bad for the glasses joke. Or maybe he'd
made it on purpose to throw her off-kilter. It didn't
matter.

Some people never grew up, never changed. Colton
was obviously one of those people. But she had. And he
couldn't hurt her anymore. She wouldn't let him.

* * *

Colton shouldn't have ribbed her about the glasses. He
immediately saw that in her eyes. To be honest, he'd said
it because he felt...uncomfortable. A little too close to
Sara Langdon, who was all grown up and nothing like

the shy, homely girl she'd been in high school. But to her he was still an emotionally stunted adolescent who needed to grow the hell up.

Surely Sara had to know how attractive she was now. All that thick hair the color of copper and those stunning green eyes. Not to mention her killer curves. She was Dr. Knockout, nothing like the Coke-bottle-bottom-glasses-wearing fourteen-year-old he'd known so long ago when he was a smart-mouthed hotshot and she was an easy target. Lest he soften, he reminded himself she was still the most type A personality he'd ever met. And Colt didn't do type A.

"Lie back," she said, flicking off the TV.

"Hey! Game's on," he said, but he hadn't really been paying attention to it. He knew he shouldn't be so difficult at every turn, but he couldn't seem to help himself. Irritating her was too much fun.

Warm soapy water flooded his arm and trickled into a basin she placed under it. She worked quickly and competently, and he felt his eyes closing. He was finally coming down from the adrenaline rush and it was, after all, the middle of the night. He even got pretty close to falling asleep, until he felt the sting of a needle.

He opened one eye and looked at her. "Warn a guy, will ya?"

She didn't respond, all concentration and focus. Whatever she'd injected had numbed him, so he watched her loop the needle in and out, suture and cut. Repeat. In and out, suture and cut.

"Is it bad?" he asked.

She turned her gaze on him. Even behind the big

glasses he could see the soft moss green of her eyes, just as pretty as he remembered. "I think you'll live. And I'm no plastic surgeon, but the scar will be minimal."

She worked in silence for a few minutes. The ticking of the old wall clock was the loudest thing in the room. Outside in the hallway there sounded a scattered symphony of beeps and alarms, intercom noises, and even the crackling fuzz of an EMS radio announcing another ambulance on its way.

When she bent her head he could smell her hair. *Lemons.* Nice. It made him recall a time, long ago, when things could've been different, when the animosity that gaped so large and wide between them might've turned into something else. But then Tagg had moved in and swept her off her feet.

Sara's life had been full of choices Colton had never had. After he'd busted up his knee in high school, he'd lost his football scholarship to Penn State. The policemen who'd worked with his dad—who'd started out as an Angel Falls cop before moving to Chicago, where he'd died in the line of duty—took him under their wing and helped him get to college. After college Colton had returned home to take care of his grandmother and sister, end of story. Whereas Sara had left town to conquer the world, attending Princeton on scholarship and medical school in New York City.

The opportunity for anything more between them had long passed, and the intervening years had cemented their relationship as antagonistic. He also understood she was furious at him. That ass Tagg had gotten drunk the night of the bachelor party despite

Colton's best efforts to cut him off. Colton had arranged for the cake stunt but had no idea the woman the company would send to pop out of the cake was someone Tagg had had the hots for in high school. And apparently still did.

Sara blamed Colton. After all, he'd been the best man. He was supposed to keep order and prevent things from getting out of control. What Sara didn't know was that Tagg had been nervous as a teenage shoplifter the entire week before the wedding. Colton had tried to quell his doubts and calm him down the best he could, had even driven Tagg home himself to keep him out of trouble the night of the bachelor party, but Tagg had still figured out a way to break Sara's heart.

Finally Sara was done, and he sat up, looking over her handiwork.

"Fifteen stitches," she announced, walking over to the counter.

"Thanks. Am I done?" He got ready to hop off the gurney.

"Not just yet," she said, coming to stand in front of him, blocking his exit. She pulled a syringe from her white coat pocket and uncapped it, displaying a needle that seemed to be the size of a quarter-inch drill bit. "Bend over and drop your drawers."

"No." As in, there was no way in hell he was going to drop trou in front of her.

She raised an elegant brow. "What do you mean, *no*?"

"I don't want it in my ass."

"Well, unless you want your arm to fall off, you

probably want to do as the doctor orders." She flicked the syringe with her finger. Put her finger on the plunger.

"I've never seen a needle that big for a shot. I'll just wait until Monday when my *usual* doctor can see me." She didn't have all the control here...did she?

"As you like. Except by then lockjaw will have set in and you won't be able to swallow or breathe." She bit back a smile. "Oh, and did I mention the drool? There will be lots of it."

She was enjoying this way too much. But the picture her words conjured was enough to keep him planted. "You're serious, aren't you?"

Tapping the syringe with her finger, she said, "Dead serious. Drop 'em, Officer Walker."

"*Chief* Walker," he mumbled as he stood up and dropped his pants, leaning over the gurney.

He smelled the antiseptic scent of alcohol, felt the rub of a cotton ball on his ass cheek.

That was when he decided not to let her get the best of him. At the last minute, he cranked his head back and gave her his most charming grin. Sara glanced up, maybe even looked a little startled.

"You can turn around now," she said, cool as a cucumber.

"I'd rather watch," he said, not backing down.

"Suit yourself," she said, drawing back and stabbing the needle into his flesh.

Son of a bitch. Charm got him nowhere with her. It never had.

The needle sliced through his muscle, burning and

stinging. It felt like an ice pick boring into his flesh. He bit down on the insides of his cheeks to take the pain.

Then she was talking again. "The most common side effect of a tetanus shot is pain at the injection site. You'll be fine in a week or two."

He pulled up and belted his pants before she could inflict more damage. Blew out the breath he'd been holding. "A *week* or two?"

"You just won't be able to sit comfortably for a while. Stitches come out in a week to ten days. Come back if anything looks red or swollen." She discarded the syringe in the red sharps container on the counter, pulled off her gloves with a snap, and tossed them in the trash. Then she wrote a few things down and handed him a clipboard. "Sign out here."

He took a step forward. His butt cheek hurt like he'd just been bitten by a yellow jacket. Still, he signed on the dotted line and managed a smile. "See you around, Doc."

She shot him a wide, innocent smile. "See you."

Chapter 2

♥

A light summer rain was pattering on Nonna's old slate roof when Sara awakened the next morning in her mom's old bedroom under the eaves of Nonna's little craftsman bungalow. The sound of the rain on the shingles above the sharply slanted ceiling brought her back to her childhood, when she used to snuggle and giggle with her sisters under this same patchwork quilt her grandmother had made when she was a young bride.

Desperate to know the mother they'd lost to cancer when Sara was just thirteen years old, her sisters and she used to carefully sift through her mother's childhood possessions—classic books like *Little Women* and *Gone With the Wind*, award ribbons for track and basketball, literary awards for writing and English. Air Supply and Journey posters pinned up on the closet door, endless balls of yarn and colorful handmade scarves. Every empty perfume bottle, every old notebook filled with notes and doodles was an endlessly fascinating clue to who their mother had been, a tiny piece of her to hold on to just a little bit longer.

But waking up in a shrine was lonely. She thought of Tagg, waking up under the eaves next to his girlfriend in the brand-new house he and Sara had meant to call home.

His rejection still hurt, but now her grief was more for the life she would've had rather than for Tagg himself. Being married, decorating their new home, planning a family... *that* was the life she mourned. After all, she was almost thirty-one years old. She'd wanted that life, dammit. A happy life with a partner she loved, settling down. Being able to do all the things she'd put off for years because she was too busy studying, working, and being broke while all her other friends already had great jobs and had started their real lives. She was tired of delayed gratification. And she wanted a dog.

For ten years she hadn't thought of her life as being any other way but with Tagg. And then suddenly... everything had changed. She'd gotten over the shock, yes. But she felt adrift, unmoored. Bobbing around in the middle of the ocean with no compass.

Her grandmother had always been her guide, and now Sara was losing her too. All the more reason to make every moment with Nonna count. To be there for Nonna the way her grandmother always had been for her.

Sara dug under the bed for her fuzzy purple slippers and tiptoed down the hall. The wooden floors creaked a little, but Sara wouldn't trade this old house for anything. She'd always dreamed of someday having a quirky house with a lot of charm, but Tagg had preferred a brand-new house in a cookie-cutter subdivision that looked like all its neighbors, and she'd gone along with it. How much else had she gone along with, not really wanting to?

It was definitely too early for soul-searching. Nonna wasn't up yet, which meant Sara had time to start the Sunday routine, one Nonna had followed without deviation for fifty years. First up was starting the coffee and homemade cinnamon rolls, then getting ready for Mass at St. Alfonso's, followed by coffee and doughnuts and socializing in the church hall, followed by a trip to the grocery store and an afternoon of cooking for Sunday dinner.

Sunday dinner was a tradition that had been going on for generations. During her years of medical school and residency, Sara had missed everything about it—the food, the easy camaraderie, the squabbling—typical family stuff that made anything else the world had to throw at you bearable. Gathering at Nonna's every week was nonnegotiable; unless you were overseas or serving a life sentence, you showed up, on pain of death.

Sara loved cooking alongside Nonna, spending time with her and learning to make the special Italian dishes that had brought her family together for generations. Not for the first time since she'd been back, it hit home hard that time with anyone was not an endless gift. Today would be the first time she'd see her entire family since she'd been back, and though her crazy family came with its own set of challenges, they loved each other a lot, and she never would've made it through the last year without them.

As Sara descended the stairs, she was greeted by the familiar clicking of Nonna's dog Rocket's toenails as he raced to her across the old pine floors. Rocket was a bull terrier with brown ears, a brown patch encompassing his left eye, and another on his right flank. A combination of pirate and Guernsey cow. His personality was definitely more on the pirate side; he was charming, sneaky, and a trickster.

"You got up early this morning, didn't you?" Rocket usually slept curled up against her back, since Nonna often shoved him out of her bed, claiming she couldn't sleep well. But he'd left her room sometime before dawn. Maybe he had insomnia too. Sara could relate. The events of the past year had kept her awake many a night.

"Oh, I bet you want some bacon, don't you?" she crooned as she scratched behind his ears. "Because it's Sunday, yes it is. Want to go get the paper?"

At the word *bacon*, the dog's ears perked up and he started jumping up and down, practically levitating with glee.

"OK, let's go."

She couldn't find a robe, but when she got to the front hall, she found Nonna's purple raincoat with a row of ducks along the bottom and slid it on over her pj boxers and T-shirt. Rocket, true to his name, darted out the front door into the wet morning to do his business.

The mid-June rain was steady but not pouring. The dark clouds and the fact that it was still quite early—

before seven—cast the day in gray. The smell of clean fresh air mingled with the scent of roses in crazy, brilliant bloom along the driveway. Sara located the paper in the grass near the road and, kicking off her slippers, ran barefoot to where it lay, encased in bright-blue plastic. Just as she bent over to pick it up, Rocket swooped in and grabbed it up in his mouth.

The dog was quick, but Sara was quicker. She clamped on to one end of the paper and tugged. Unfortunately, Rocket seemed to think she was playing his favorite game. As she tugged, he tugged harder. Her hood fell off, sending a cascade of cold rainwater spilling down her back.

With one wrenching pull, the dog sidestepped away, bolting for the yew hedge that separated her grandma's property from the street. Sara ran through the wet grass after the dog. He teased her by showing her the paper, an arm's length away, but as soon as she reached for it, he dashed into the hedge.

He emerged a few seconds later, wet and leaf covered...without the paper.

Oh, bollocks.

There it was, lying in the mud under the hedge, surrounded by prickly branches that rivaled Sleeping Beauty's briar patch. Sara walked around to the road side, having no choice but to get down on her hands and knees and dig out the paper. Ugh, and all this before coffee. She stuck her arm into the tangle of branches and was trying to capture the bag with her fingers when she heard a car idling behind her. And something that sounded suspiciously like a whistle.

Sara immediately popped her head up and turned around. A spotlight with the wattage of the noontime sun beamed on her. Through the glare she could make out a police cruiser. There sat Colton behind the wheel, his arm sticking out the window. The arm that she'd stitched up just a few hours ago. Clearly healing well, due to her excellent care, thank you very much.

"You can turn the floodlight off," she said. "And did you just whistle? Because that would be completely unprofessional."

"Of course not." But he was biting down on his cheeks to keep from laughing. "I just happened to be driving home, minding my own business, when suddenly there it was...plain as day."

"There *what* was?" Sara asked, lifting a brow. He'd better not mention anything about her behind. That would be...inappropriate. But, she couldn't help thinking, completely par for the course as far as their relationship went.

He swept his hand in her direction to demonstrate. "A roadside distraction."

She rolled her eyes.

"Need some help?"

"Thanks, but I'm fine. I was just fishing the paper out of the hedge." Rocket sat next to the cruiser at full attention. Colton reached under his seat and tossed him a dog biscuit. Clearly something he'd done before, judging by Rocket's expectant look and the fact that his tail was wagging faster than the speed limit.

As if on cue, the front door of the house opened and her little gray-haired grandmother stepped out on the porch. She was wearing a bright flowered apron and waving excitedly. "Colton! Yoo-hoo, Colton!"

Yoo-hoo, Colton?

"Hey there, Rose," he called back. "I'll be right up."

Sara shot him a startled glance. *Right up?*

"Hurry up, dear," Nonna said. "I'm just going to put some cinnamon rolls in."

The thought of Nonna baking sent a stab of fear through her. Dad and her stepmom, Rachel, had already gently and painstakingly taken away Nonna's car...Surely operating an oven was just as dangerous as driving.

Colton gave Sara a satisfied grin and backed up the cruiser, pulling it into the driveway while she dug around in the hedge and rescued the soggy paper. They walked silently to the house, the dog trailing happily at Sara's heels. She felt aware of Colton in an uncomfortable way—a way that prickled the hairs at the back of her neck. Extreme irritation could do that to you, she supposed. It had nothing to do with that white, just-short-of-perfect smile that lit up his face and made little crinkles appear around his striking blue eyes, which were filled with amusement. These traits might make him seem like a warm and caring person, yet she reminded herself he was not. "After you," he said, holding open the door.

It took the willpower of the ages not to roll her eyes again. Once they were inside, she took off her grandma's rain jacket and shook it, then hung it on a hook in the foyer to dry. When she turned around, she saw Colton quickly avert his eyes.

Realization dawned, sending heat blazing to her cheeks. She was wearing pj boxers and a black T-shirt with a rib cage on it that read "I Got an 'A' in Anatomy." She grabbed Nonna's long gray sweater off a hanger and tugged it on, along with the purple slippers she'd left on the foyer floor.

Nonna appeared in the doorway. "Come in, you two. I just put coffee on."

Sometimes Nonna amazed her and seemed completely unaffected by the disease that had crept up so insidiously. It was a cruel thing, the dementia. Even though Sara was a doctor and knew the course, the moments Nonna acted exactly like herself made hope soar, as if this whole thing were a nightmare and she would wake up and Nonna would be...Nonna again. Then the next moment her grandmother would repeat a thought for the tenth time, and hope would come crashing down.

"Here you go," Colton said, handing her grandmother a nice dry newspaper. Sara looked at the soggy blue bag in her hand, pierced with multiple fang marks.

Ass kiss, she mouthed behind Nonna's back.

"Oh, you are a dear," Nonna said, patting Colton's hand. "I bet you worked all night too."

"I did have the night shift, yes, ma'am," Colton said, grinning widely. His charm knew no bounds, affecting women of all ages. And dogs, as Rocket had no reservations about accepting Colton's friendly scratch behind the ears as an invitation to glue himself to his side.

"You must be starving then."

Was this what had been going on while she'd been

gone? Colton had insinuated himself into her grandmother's good graces. For free meals and other grandmotherly services, no doubt. Like socks-darned, buttons-sewed, shirts-ironed kinds of things.

In the kitchen Sara was surprised to see her younger brother Rafe sitting at the heavy oak table, still in his firefighter uniform. He rose, walked over, and kissed Nonna. "I let myself in," he said, gesturing to the back door. "I see I'm just in time for breakfast. Hey, Colton. Hi, Sis." Sara hugged her baby brother, who was around three years younger than she but was also a broad-shouldered, muscular six two, so *baby* probably wasn't quite the right term. Colton and Rafe shared some kind of complicated handshake that made it clear they were on friendly—*fist-bumping*—terms.

"Tough night?" Colton asked, sitting down with Rafe at the table. Rocket flopped down at his feet and promptly fell asleep.

"Big three-alarm blaze in the next county. Took us most of the night to put it out. Fortunately it was an abandoned warehouse, so no one was hurt." Rafe spoke animatedly with his hands, and his whole face lit up.

"You firefighters can't wait to rush to a great fire, can you?" Colton said.

Rafe laughed. "At least no one's shooting at me. Or making me chase them under barbed wire fences. Your arm OK?"

Sara helped Nonna put the rolls in the oven, then watched Nonna disappear into the dining room to fetch a platter. She sneaked a glance at Colton, whose response to Rafe was a shrug and a smile. Today, as in the ER, he seemed to take pains to downplay the danger of his job. She wasn't sure if he was just cavalier or if maybe time had humbled him a little. Probably the former. He always had been Mr. No Big Deal.

He sat there talking shop with her brother, looking the picture of masculinity in his navy-blue uniform, his hands grasping his coffee mug. Sara couldn't help but notice the sinewy muscle that ran the length of his tanned arms, and the elegant, long fingers curled casually around his cup.

"I heard you were in the ER," Rafe said. "Hopefully your doctor did a nice job fixing you up." Rafe gave Sara a wink.

"Yeah," Colton said, "my doctor did a nice job but also gave me a nice pain in the ass. But I guess that's OK, because she also complimented me on it."

Sara dropped the mixing bowl she was carrying into the sink. "I did *not* compliment you on your ass." There was no way she was going to let him get away with that in front of her brother.

"Maybe not, but I could tell you wanted to."

What an ass. Literally. "That is the most ridiculous—"

Nonna shuffled back into the kitchen. "Sara, be a dear and pour Colton some coffee, would you?" Nonna asked.

"Can I put arsenic in it?" she mumbled as she took the coffeepot out of its holder.

"I heard that," Colton said quietly as Nonna proceeded to wipe off the counters. "So much for the Hippocratic oath."

"That only applies to patients," Sara said.

Colton slid his cup toward her as she approached the table. "You did sew up my arm, so I guess you *are* my doctor."

"A one-time visit to the ER does *not* make me your doctor."

"You're right. I'm not a one-night stand kind of guy."

Rafe laughed. "That's not what I heard."

Colton's face turned red. Sara was surprised he was capable of a good strong blush. "I could tell stories about you, Rafe," Colton said, "but out of respect for your grandma I'll refrain. Besides, you're listening to too many rumors."

Rafe patted Colton on the back. "They're not rumors, Colt my man, they're legend."

Sara made an involuntary gagging noise.

"Sara, are you choking on something?" Nonna asked.

"Just the thought of all those poor women," Sara said so only the men could hear. "I'm fine, Nonna," she said louder.

"Don't feel bad for those women," Rafe said. "They were all very...happy."

Colton gave Rafe a cease-and-desist look. "Rafe, so help me God, if you do not shut up, I'm going to tell everyone about the time we all went out for your birthday and you decided it would be fun to take a little dive into the river buck naked with that—"

"Hey, Nonna," Rafe said loudly, "those rolls ready yet? I sure am hungry."

These guys and their fish stories. Sara found it interesting that Colton seemed so eager to downplay his reputation. Rafe had told her once that the firemen and the town's one deputy police officer jokingly referred to Colton as the Revolver, and it wasn't because of his gun.

"Oh, you boys go out and have fun together, do you?" Nonna asked, bringing the sugar bowl to the table.

"Yes, Grandma," Rafe said. "Colt and I go out all the time."

Sara was happy to take a seat at the far end of the old oak table and tune out their banter. Since she'd been gone, it seemed Colton had become part of the family. She hadn't counted on negotiating that now that she was home to stay.

A big bay window overlooked her gran's backyard and a giant old oak tree that she and her siblings used to climb. In the years when her grandpa was alive, they used to swing on a swing he'd hung from the lowest branch, which was now much higher than she remembered. The swing was long gone. Even the dirt patch underneath, worn by little feet pushing higher and skidding to a stop, had filled in with grass.

Sara supposed she'd have to get used to such change. After all, this was not the world of her childhood, or even the world she'd left behind when she left town for college and med school. Or, for that matter, the world she'd left last year when her engagement went bust.

"I can't find that darn pot holder," Nonna said, rummaging through a drawer.

Sara got up to help, found the pot holder on top of the toaster, and pulled the rolls out of the oven.

"Would you like some cream, Colton?" Nonna asked.

"No, thanks, Mrs. Faranaccio. I take it black," he said.

Sara helped Nonna ice the cinnamon rolls. When she returned to the table, she noticed a full, steaming cup of coffee sitting at her place.

Nonna couldn't have poured it. Rafe was at the other end of the table, near the back door. That left Colton.

She must have looked a little puzzled. He passed her the cream, chatting to Rafe about some kind of potluck the police and fire departments were going to host.

How did he know she took cream?

"Colton, would you like cream, dear?" Nonna asked again as she brought the rolls to the table and sat down.

"I'm good, thanks, Mrs. F," Colton said politely.

Sara caught his gaze across the table. He hadn't embarrassed Nonna or pointed out that she'd asked twice. Still, Sara got busy stirring her coffee, unwilling to let him see her concern.

Every little slip-up Nonna made caused a little trickle of dread to churn in her stomach and gave her a tip-of-the-iceberg kind of feeling. Nonna, however, was in a great mood, laughing and joking with the guys.

After polishing off half the cinnamon rolls, Rafe said, "I gotta run."

"I'll walk you out," Sara said, following him out the front door and closing it behind her.

"What's the deal with you and Colton?" he asked as soon as they were out of earshot. "You were busting his chops."

"You *know* what the deal is."

Rafe's brows pulled down as he frowned. "He's a good guy."

Sara crossed her arms. "Legends? Antics with women? And you pal around with him."

"You certainly seemed amused about his dating history," Rafe said. "Maybe you're a little jealous?"

"Jealous? Of the Revolver? You're... you're nuts!"

"Right. Well, you know how I feel about things," Rafe said. "Tagg got his just deserts, if you pardon the cake pun. All he thought about was himself. Good riddance."

"God, Rafe, I wish you'd have more conviction about things," Sara said, smiling. He'd always been a straight shooter, and he'd always been quick to stand up for her, even when they were kids. She had to admit it felt really good to have her grown-up little brother defend her. But that didn't mean she was going to agree with him about Colton.

"Anyway," Rafe said, "give Colton a chance. He might surprise you."

"Um, last time I checked you were my *much* younger brother, and therefore it goes against natural sibling order for you to offer me advice. You're forgetting I've known Colton longer than I've known Tagg. Once a jerk, always a jerk."

"Geez, give the guy a break, OK? People can change."

"Dad swears most of his patients still have the same personality they had when they were thirteen."

"That's fatalistic," Rafe said.

"So is dating a different girl every week," Sara said, tossing him a pointed look.

"I said people can change—if they want to. I, however, have no reason to, seeing as I'm in my sexual prime. See you tonight for Sunday dinner?"

"Yeah." She kissed her brother on the cheek. "See you." Sara couldn't be too critical of her brother's dating habits. His longtime girlfriend had died in an accident when he was just twenty-one, and for years he'd barely dated at all. She supposed the fact that he was dating now and joking about it was a big improvement. She just wasn't sure how much of his attitude was bravado.

She watched from the front porch as Rafe got into his shiny black F-150 with custom chrome rims and drove away. Colton came out of the house carrying two rolls in a baggie. No one ever left Nonna's house without a full doggie bag.

"Thanks for letting me stay for breakfast," he said.

She shrugged, although she was secretly surprised he'd bothered with a thank-you. "Not my choice. It was Nonna's."

Colton was standing very close. So close she couldn't help noticing the vibrant blue of his eyes, a cross between summer sky and Caribbean ocean. Man, the guy had been kissed by the gods in looks. A real heart-stopper.

Not that he stopped *her* heart or anything.

"Bye, Mrs. Faranaccio," he called to her grandmother, who was still in the house. "See ya, Red." His gaze flicked quickly up and down Sara. "I tend to agree with your shirt. You do get an A in Anatomy. But it's a shame, because the rest of you is a little salty." He gave Sara one last sweeping look, put on his hat, and headed out into the rain.

Chapter 3

♥

At four forty-five p.m., Nonna's kitchen smelled like spaghetti sauce and freshly baked bread. As Sara pulled the homemade rolls out of the oven, she silently declared Nonna's house ready for Sunday dinner.

"Nonna, where's Gabby?" she called to her grandmother, who was in the dining room setting the table.

"Oh, I don't know, dear," she said as she set two forks by one plate. Before Sara could intervene, Gabby's voice called from afar.

"I'm up here!"

"I'll grab Gabby and be right back to help you finish setting the table," Sara said.

"Take your time," Nonna said, lining up yet a third fork near the other two.

"Here" turned out to be the attic, up the pull-down ladder at the top of the stairs to a space under the dormers lined by old crossbeams and layers of fluffy pink insulation. A solitary light bulb hung on a chain from the central roof beam.

Sara climbed halfway up the ladder, her head at floor level, debating going the rest of the way up. "Hey, Gabs, dinner's in fifteen minutes. Can you come down and help? Nonna needs some help setting the table."

"Oh, sure," Gabby said, crinkling up her cute nose. Gabby was Sara's closest sister, in age and in bonding. They were only fifteen months apart, and they told each other nearly everything. Gabby was one of the big reasons being back home was tolerable.

"Come up here, I'm scared," Gabby said, exuberantly holding out her arms. Did Sara mention she was the dramatic sister as well as the imaginative one? "I need my big sister. Especially since I've barely seen you since you've been home. Besides, Nonna sent me up here to look for those pretty dessert plates with the white scalloped edges, and I can't find them. Remember those?"

Sara hauled herself up the remaining rungs and sat down near Gabby on a couple of stacked wooden crates.

"This place always creeped me out," said Gabby, who was sitting in the middle of the wooden floor surrounded by open boxes. "Rafe used to tell me terrible stories about families forced to live in the attic—like in those novels everyone was reading years ago, remember?—and I believed every word. I never wanted to come up here as a kid."

"You always had the biggest imagination too," Sara said.

Despite being a wills and trusts attorney, Gabby was a dreamer, and Sara wouldn't be surprised at all if she'd gotten caught up in rifling through Nonna's stuff, completely losing track of time.

Sara took a glance around under the dim light of the solitary bulb. For an attic it was pretty meticulous: Boxes lined up and tidy. Rolls of fabric propped in one corner, covered in plastic. An old wooden rocker and a baby bassinet hanging from hooks, plastic zipper bags containing old curtains, an old aluminum washtub that they used to wash their dog in.

"Maybe while you're at it you can find my thirteenth-birthday present."

"You still haven't given up on that, have you? God, we looked everywhere for that."

Sara shrugged. Her mom had been very sick on her thirteenth birthday and had died just a week later. "Mom was really good about that. She never forgot a birthday. Maybe she just hid it so well we never found it."

"Well, I'm happy to keep looking. And while we're at it, you can help me find Mom's journals." Gabby dug into a nearby box and took out something wrapped in yellowed newspaper. "Wow, look at this." She held up a ceramic flamingo standing on one pink foot. "Fabulous. I might need this for my apartment."

"Nice," Sara said. "Mom had journals?"

"She was always writing in spiral notebooks, do you remember that?" Gabby said. "They have to be here somewhere." She pulled out another box. Also filled with newspaper-wrapped objects.

Sara reached in and unwrapped one. "Oh, Nonna's Fiestaware!" She dug through the box. "In all colors of the rainbow. I remember this stuff!" A thought suddenly occurred to her. "Does Dad know where Mom's journals are? Maybe he'd have them instead of Nonna."

Gabby shook her head. "I'm checking here first. I mean, when Dad married Rachel, he probably gave most of Mom's stuff to Nonna. That makes sense, doesn't it? You wouldn't keep your dead wife's personal belongings in your attic, would you?"

Sara had no idea. What she did know was that even now, her dad said very little about their mother. He never talked freely, and when questioned gave the briefest answers possible.

Sometimes she longed to sit down with him and have a heart-to-heart. Ask him about their mom, their childhood, happy memories. With Nonna's memory fading, she wished her dad would share more about her mother.

Actually, she wished her dad would share more, period. With her mother gone, her dad had turned into a man who was very involved in guiding and shaping their life decisions as he saw fit. Without their mother's more relaxed and intuitive attitude, her father sometimes pushed for things he felt strongly were right but weren't necessarily so.

"Have you asked Nonna?" Sara asked.

"All she says is, 'Your mother was always scribbling in those notebooks of hers.'"

"Maybe someone got rid of them. Jane Austen's sister burned two-thirds of her letters, did you know that? Presented to the world only a certain scrubbed version of events. Some people claim she ruined her sister's legacy."

"I'd call that a good sister," Gabby said.

Sara laughed. "Maybe so. But Gabby, journals are private. Maybe Mom wouldn't want us reading them."

"I need them," Gabby insisted. "Don't you ever feel you wished you knew her? Not how we knew her as children, but how she was as an adult?"

Sara got up and hugged her sister. It was a relief to know she had as many questions about their mom as Sara did. "I wish that all the time." She sat down next to her on the floor, pushing aside a box of recipe clippings. "I wish Dad would talk to us more about her."

"Dad has a different life now. He hates talking about Mom, and I always feel uncomfortable bringing it up in front of Rachel."

"Well, I think looking for her journals is a great idea, and of course I'll help." Sara examined the old box of cut-out recipes, for sure Nonna's doing. "So, everything going OK with Malcolm?" Gabby had reconnected with her college sweetheart, who was a hedge fund manager they'd all been very relieved she'd stopped dating years ago. At the time he'd spent more time exercising than being with Gabby, and that about said it all.

Gabby flashed a bright smile. A little too bright, but maybe that was just Sara's imagination. "Things couldn't be better. Malcolm is awesome. He showers me with gifts and never fails to tell me how much he loves me. In fact, he's planning to come out to dinner with the whole family sometime soon. Are you free some Friday or Saturday?"

"For you, I'm free anytime."

"Great. You know, we've gotten pretty serious."

Sara raised a brow and tried hard to put a nonjudgmental expression on her face. "Really?"

Gabby nodded. "I know you didn't like him that much, but he's changed. Grown up. I think you're going to really like him."

Sara's recollection of Malcolm was that he was always into *things*. Bigger, better, more expensive things. One look at Gabby's face and Sara realized her sister was waiting expectantly for her to say something. Screaming *Get out while you can!* probably wasn't what she wanted to hear.

"Gabby, my main objection to Malcolm back then was that he was really into himself. He spent a ton of money on you, but it seemed like that was all part of his image. I hope that's changed."

"Malcolm's very ambitious. Dad would love that. He's a hard worker but he still finds time for me. He doesn't beat children or kill cats. Plus I'm twenty-nine. He's not perfect, but who is? Maybe he's as close as I'm going to come."

"Oh, Gabby." Sara hated the idea that Gabby seemed to be talking herself into believing how great this guy was. "You're not over the hill yet."

She shrugged. "Not yet. But it's getting really hard to meet nice guys who aren't already taken, going through nasty breakups, or who aren't just plain weird." She paused. "Oh, and who also meet Dad's criteria for a good spouse: educated, makes good money, worthy of his daughters."

Sara laughed but had to admit Gabby was right

about their father. He definitely had certain expectations about the men he wanted them to marry.

"Also, I have one more bit of news: I just got promoted to partner, but that's less thrilling. Overall, life is great!" Gabby worked for a law firm in downtown Cleveland and had a gorgeous loft apartment there.

"How come you didn't tell us about the partnership? That's fantastic! Another reason to celebrate."

"The money's good, but it's dullsville, Sara. I'm working eighty hours a week, and every single minute, I feel like pulling all my hair out one strand at a time."

"God, Gabby."

"I know. Please don't tell Dad, but I'm working on an exit plan. Besides, for now, Malcolm makes up for how crappy I feel about my job."

Worry riffled through Sara like a good strong wind before a storm. Their father had urged Gabby, wonderful, artistic, creative Gabby, to go to law school. It had probably saved her from becoming a hippie. It also appeared to have made her very unhappy.

Despite the bad vibes, Sara put on a cheery smile. "Well, we can't wait to see him again." She pulled something out of a box. "Oh, look what I found!"

"Is it the dessert plates?" Gabby asked.

"No, it's my beat-up old copy of *Pride and Prejudice*. Look." She held up the battered book with curled edges and yellowed pages, which looked as if it had definitely seen better days. The first thing she did was to put it to her nose and sniff it. God, she loved the smell of real books. Especially old and beloved ones, and this one had been—and still was—her favorite.

"Oh, you carried that thing around for years," Gabby said.

Sara grinned. "I love it. I just never thought *Pride and Prejudice* would become my life."

"What are you talking about?"

"Oh, just Tagg. I mean, I thought he was my Darcy." She sighed.

Gabby sat down beside her and gave her a squeeze. "Tagg would definitely play the role of the perfidious Wickham in your life. But then who would be Darcy?" She tapped a finger against her lips. "Oh, I know. Colton!"

"I was just going to tell you how much I missed you and how happy I am to be home because you're here. But after that comment I can't." Sara paused. "And besides, Colton would have to be Mr. Collins," she said, pulling a face.

"First of all, he can't be Mr. Collins because he's not our cousin." Gabby laughed. "Plus he's nowhere near hideous."

"Not in looks, but in personality he is." Sara rose and headed to the stairs. "Come down and help me fix Nonna's creative table setting before everyone gets here." There were definitely no Mr. Darcys on her horizon. She certainly hoped for Gabby's sake that Malcolm had transformed during the intervening years from a Wickham to a Darcy, but she seriously doubted it.

Chapter 4

♥

When Sara and Gabby returned from the attic, Sara helped Nonna set the old Duncan Phyfe dining room table with the pretty floral bone china passed down from Nonna's grandmother, quietly subtracting extra forks as necessary.

Sara took a plate from Nonna. "I've always loved these," she said, smoothing her finger over the intricate pattern of pink roses intertwined with English ivy. They reminded her of being a child, sitting at this very table with her mom and dad. She used to study the flowers and the twists and turns of the ivy as she waited impatiently for all the big Italian dinners they'd eaten every Sunday, every holiday. She always called them the rose plates, not just because they had roses on them but because that was her grandmother's name too.

"My mother's mother brought these dishes from Italy," Nonna said. "They were a gift from her parents for her wedding. Then my mother gave them to me for my wedding." They were beautiful and old-fashioned and delicate, yet they'd withstood many years of wear.

Although Sara loved them for another reason too. "Remember the bullies?" It had never been easy being the fair redhead among a bevy of dark-eyed, dark-haired siblings: her older sister Evangeline, her younger sister Gabriella, and Raphael, their baby brother. Kids at school loved to tease them for having all been named after angels. The story went that after Evie, their mom couldn't get pregnant, and prayed and prayed for a child. Four years later, she found herself pregnant with Sara, then Gabby was born just fifteen months later, and Rafe came along two years after that. "I'm the luckiest mother in the world to have four beautiful angels," her mom had said. Sara loved the story, and her name, but it was just one of the many things that had made her a target at school.

It didn't help that their parents had chosen their names despite the fact that Angel Falls had an angel legend of its own. The centerpiece of downtown, beautiful cascading falls that used to power paper mills in the 1800s, were flanked by a quaint bridge guarded by a bronze statue of two angels. Any couple who kissed in front of the angels (and had their picture taken) was supposed to have true love forever. People came from all over to see the falls, shop along the quaint Main Street, and of course get their photo taken in front of the angels.

Despite being the only redhead, Sara was also the only sibling with glasses, which she'd worn from the age of four. Every year it seemed they got thicker and thicker. One afternoon in fourth grade, after she'd been made fun of by some kids on the playground, her mother had sat her down at this very table and told her how special she was, and how loved. "We wouldn't want any of you kids to be the same as anyone else. You're all unique, on the inside and out," her mom had said.

Nonna had pushed a glass of milk and one of these very plates, full of warm chocolate chip cookies, in front of her. Sara hadn't been hungry until she'd smelled the cookies. Nonna had sat down beside her and put an arm around her. "My little Serafina, the ivy is very different from the roses, yet they're still wrapped around each other tight. They still belong together. That's how families are."

That's exactly how her family was, thank God. In some ways she and her siblings couldn't be more different, but they were all bound by an unalterable I've-got-your-back mentality.

And that family bond had been in full force over the last year after Sara's wedding imploded and she'd taken a position as a temporary physician out west, getting as far from Angel Falls—and Tagg—as she could. Nearly every day that she'd been gone, one of her siblings, Nonna, her stepmother Rachel, or even her father had called her to tell her crazy stories about their days, to entertain or amuse her, or just to ask how she was. They must've had a rotating schedule, and she'd worried that she was becoming yet another to-do item in their already busy lives. But those calls had gotten her through a really rough time, and the knowledge that her family stood behind her had helped give her the courage to come back to a town with a long memory for mistakes.

Sara ran her finger around the delicate pattern on the plate before her. She could almost see her mom sitting here. What would she say about the state of Sara's life now? The humiliation of an embarrassing failed engagement with no romantic prospects in sight, and going AWOL from academia to work in their tiny town?

All of Nonna's memories connected her to her mother. Now Nonna was unable to offer her usual loving advice, but she still had a great reserve of memories. If Nonna lost that thread, would Sara lose it as well?

"You always did love these plates."

"They're very special, Nonna," Sara said.

"That's why I'm leaving them to you. Because you're very special too, Sara Jane." Her grandmother's voice cracked with emotion as she wrapped her arms around Sara.

Sara spoke past a tangle in her throat. "Nonna, please—let's not talk about that. I don't need the dishes."

Nonna grasped Sara's hand and pierced her with vivid blue eyes. "It's important. I've got something special for each of you girls. But the china is yours. Now that's that."

That's that. One of Nonna's favorite sayings, and an excellent way of cutting off all further discussion.

"Is Tagg coming for dinner, dear?" Nonna asked.

Sara's stomach seized up. The comforting smell that

had made her so hungry a moment ago now made it churn sickly. "Tagg and I broke up, Nonna," she said quietly. "He won't be coming."

"Oh yes, of course!" Nonna said, nearly dropping one of the dishes. "I meant to say *Rafe*. Is Rafe coming?"

"He'll definitely be here," Sara said just as they heard the front door bang open.

Rafe walked into the dining room, placed a big white ceramic bowl and a brown paper bakery bag on the sideboard, and immediately wrapped up their tiny grandmother in his big arms. Gabby came out of the kitchen to greet him carrying a giant bouquet of orange tiger lilies and set them in the center of the table. Rocket, never good at being ignored, leaped up and down until Gabby broke down and petted him.

"Those are beautiful, sweetheart," Nonna said to Gabby.

"Thanks, Nonnie," Gabby said. "I picked them in the field next to the grade school this morning."

"You're not supposed to pick the flowers at the school," Evie said, walking in behind them. She was the oldest and the stickler of the family, the only one married or with kids, whom she'd quit her job as a pottery artist to stay home with. In practical mom style, she'd brought a bagful of paper plates and cups for easy cleanup. Sara took them and hid them in Nonna's pantry. They'd be using the rose plates, even if she had to stay up until midnight doing the dishes.

Gabby shrugged. "I just took a few of them. No one will notice."

"You look extra beautiful tonight, Nonna," Rafe said, grinning his handsome smile. He looked around at the food that was already spread out on the table—pork tenderloin, antipasto salad, rolls wrapped in a linen towel to stay warm, some prosciutto and cantaloupe sliced thin, a pasta dish with chicken, and the massive bowl of pasta waiting for Nonna's favorite sauce front and center.

"What, only five courses today, not six?" Rafe asked.

"I'm glad you're hungry," Nonna said, patting Rafe's stomach. "We missed you last week." Funny how Nonna could be forgetful about a lot of things but certainly remembered dinner attendance.

"There was a fire last Sunday, Nonna."

"Fire, schmire. You have to eat, don't you?"

"Yes, and I'm very hungry now." He sneaked an olive.

"Where's that nice girl you bring sometimes? The one who owns the coffee shop?"

"Kaitlyn?" he asked. "We're just friends, Grandma. And she's busy baking this afternoon. Oh, I almost forgot. She wanted you to have something." He walked over to the sideboard, picked up the white bowl, and set it on the table, then presented Nonna with the brown bakery bag.

"Rafe, you made salad!" Evie said, inspecting it. Romaine, cut-up veggies, grated cheese, croutons. And a cruet of homemade dressing to boot.

"Hey, I can cook now," he said. "Have to at the station."

Gabby pinched his cheek. "Some little woman is going to be so happy because of those culinary skills."

Rafe gave her a little push on the shoulder. "Number one, I have many other skills that women would find far more appealing than cooking, and number two, only Nonna's allowed to pinch my cheeks."

"Kaitlyn sent something with you?" Sara asked.

"Yeah. I ran into her at the coffee shop and she handed me this."

Sara made a mental note to call Kaitlyn ASAP. Between Sara's getting settled at Nonna's and starting work and Kaitlyn's busy schedule as owner of the Bean, the coffee shop downtown, they hadn't had a moment to sit down and catch up. Sara and Kaitlyn had been best friends since third grade, and yet it was surprising to hear Kaitlyn had been coming to Sunday dinner, something Sara would have thought her friend might have mentioned. The fact that she hadn't made Sara wonder if Kaitlyn still harbored her long-standing crush on Rafe, which, given Rafe's theories on "dating," could only end in disaster.

Nonna peeked inside the bag Rafe handed her. "Blueberry muffins. My favorite. Tell Kaitlyn I'll enjoy them with my coffee tomorrow morning." She pinched Rafe's cheek. "Sara and I baked brownies and made extra for you to take to the station. I have them all wrapped up for you already."

"Thank you, Gram," he said, kissing her on the cheek and shooting his sisters the I'm-her-favorite look.

Rafe walked over and made Sara the next object of his bear-hug affection. "Anything else exciting happen last night in the ER besides stitching up our heroic police chief?"

"You stitched up Colton?" Gabby asked, unwrapping a plate of some kind of orange-colored dip and chips and placing it on the table. "And he made it out alive?"

Sara made a face. "I'm a professional, Gabby. I'm capable of doing my job, no matter what my personal feelings are."

"Yeah," Rafe said, chuckling. "You did a nice job with the fifteen stitches, but the tetanus shot in the butt was a little over the top."

"What do you mean over the top?" Sara asked, then regretted not changing the subject entirely when she felt her face heating up.

Gabby's mouth fell open. "You saw Colton's *ass*? How'd it look?"

"Gabby! He needed a tetanus shot. I gave him one. End of story."

Rafe gave her a look. She tried to signal him with her eyes to please shut the hell up. "I'm a paramedic, remember?" he said, clearly not taking the hint. "You don't usually give tetanus shots in people's butts."

Busted. "Well, I did, OK? His left arm was all messed up and bloody and he's right-handed. So that left giving it to him in his butt." *Or his leg*, but she didn't have to say that.

The door opened again, thank God, bringing Dad and Rachel and Evie's husband Joe with their two little kids, Julia, who was five, and Michael, who was three.

The kids ran over to their mom—or tried to, until Rafe scooped them up and ran around the living room with them, eventually tossing them onto the couch, where they landed laughing and squealing. Rocket, never one to miss out on the action, ran over to join the fun.

Julia tumbled off the couch and came running over. "Aunt Sara," she said, holding up a pink furry purse, "I brought barrettes. I'm going to fix your hair after dinner."

Julia loved Sara's long red hair, and Sara had missed playing hair salon this last year. "Can I fix yours too?" she asked, bending down to kiss and hug her niece.

"Mine too," Michael said. "I want my hair fixed too."

Joe looked a little wary.

"Don't worry," Evie said, patting her husband's arm. "It's all right."

"Sara, you're a doctor," Joe said. "Your sister thinks it's fine if he plays with Barbies and baby dolls. I just don't like it."

"Oh," Sara said. Evie was drilling her with a look, as if she'd better be on Evie's side *or else*. "Well, of course it's fine. I mean, boys and girls should be able to play with anything they want."

"Sometimes Julia dresses him up in Disney princess skirts," Joe said.

Sara laughed. "Once we made Rafe wear ballet tights. And then Mom took pictures."

"Hey, someone better have burned those photos," Rafe said.

"You had nice legs, Rafe," Evie said. "That's what Mom said, anyway."

"The point is," Sara said, "Mom wasn't too concerned. I wouldn't be either."

Just then her dad, a tall, soft-spoken man with gray hair and glasses, walked over and hugged Sara. "Hey, sweetheart," he said.

"Hey, Dad," she said.

"The girls are very excited to see you tomorrow at the office."

Sara tried not to cringe. Or notice that her father hadn't said *he* was excited. "The girls," as her father called them, were actually two women close to retirement age who'd been working in her father's office since before she was born. They were both really sweet, but she had a feeling they, like her father, were very set in their ways.

Rachel placed a pie on the sideboard. This made Sara feel a little bit bad. Cake had been a part of every Sunday dinner since forever, but her stepmother knew that after the bachelor party incident, the sight of cake—any cake—still made Sara sick to her stomach.

"Hey, Daddy," Gabby said, giving him a hug. "Sara gave Colton a tetanus shot in the butt. I think he could have a case for malpractice."

Their dad raised a brow, and Sara glared at her sister. Gabby had always been the sister she told her secrets to first. Perhaps she should start rethinking that policy.

"Colton's such a nice young man," Nonna said. "He takes out my trash every week."

"He's also really arrogant," Sara said. "Still a first-class jerk. Some people never change, you know?"

"I always liked Colton," Gabby said. "I know he had a tough upbringing, and maybe he wasn't all that nice when you knew him in high school, but he comes in sometimes to testify in the hearings for family court and always sticks up for the kids."

Rachel scooped up some of Gabby's dip. "When UPS leaves my shipments at the door of the antique shop, he always helps me carry them in. Plus he's a great police chief. Everyone in town loves him. And he's very kind to the library ladies. Always hauling books back and forth every month for the sale. He tells them that's how he keeps himself in shape."

"All the ladies love him, Rach," Evie said. "And he loves them back. That's the problem—he goes on more dates than Rafe. I'm with you, sweetie," Evie said to Sara. "Avoid him and all men like him like the plague."

"I don't know," Gabby said. "I'm sort of liking this enemies vibe. Lots of sexual tension. It's like watching a rom-com."

"One that will end like a Stephen King novel," Sara said darkly.

"Well, don't forget your blind date next Friday," Gabby said.

"Gabby, we've gone through this. I don't think now's the time—"

"Sure it is. There's no better way to show everyone in town you've moved on."

Sara'd had a few dates in the past year, but nothing serious. She just hadn't had the heart.

"I'm so happy you're back, honey, and joining your father at the practice. I think it's going to be a wonderful partnership," Rachel said, clapping her hands together. As always, her stepmother was quick to jump to her rescue. "And maybe now your dad will be able to slow down just a little and enjoy some golf and more time with me."

"Now, Rachel," her dad interjected, "you know it's only temporary. Sara's going to reapply for her infectious disease fellowship next year." Sara had given up her spot in the prestigious program at the Cleveland Clinic after the wedding that never was. Tagg had gotten a position there as well, and there was no way in hell she could have seen him every day. Not without losing her mind, anyway.

"Well, maybe she'll fall in love with Angel Falls and stay."

Rachel was endlessly optimistic. And her dad clearly hadn't changed his expectations about the kind of future he saw for Sara, and it wasn't as a hometown family doctor.

"Honey, are you all set to start tomorrow?" her dad asked.

No. Absolutely not. The thought of working side by side with her dad brought on as much trepidation and dread as excitement.

She tried to channel a bit of Rachel's optimism. "I think so, Dad."

"How about we meet over at the office later and I'll go over how I run the practice?"

Disappointment riffled through her. Her father had agreed to their working together to placate her need to be near Nonna. He didn't want to hear her ideas about improving his office, of bringing it into the millennium. He didn't want her as a *partner*. "Sounds great."

"We can talk about your fellowship applications. Maybe you should go more Ivy League again, what do you think?" Sara's heart fell. Her dad had always wanted her to be an academic, a nationally recognized expert in her field, and it didn't seem he was going to stop pushing until she accomplished that. And at one time she'd wanted that too. The problem was, Sara wasn't exactly sure what she wanted anymore. All she knew was she was happy to be back home and looking forward to things in a way she hadn't in a long time, since even before the wedding disaster.

Gabby tapped their father on the shoulder. "Dad, your grandson wants a pony ride and he's requested you be the pony. Career decisions can wait till after dinner, OK?"

When he left to do his grandfatherly duty, Rachel turned to Gabby. "How's that boy you said you're dating?" she asked. "I want to hear more."

"You remember Malcolm, don't you? From college?" Sara didn't miss the sudden look of concern that appeared on Rachel's face. "The hedge fund guy?"

Oh God. They all remembered Malcolm, an egomaniacal, self-absorbed guy. Even the fact that he had a job her dad approved of could not save him.

"We reconnected," Gabby said, and her smile said it all. "He wants to take us all out to celebrate my promotion, so you'll all get a chance to see him again next weekend."

"Is this the guy with the Bugatti that he wrecked the same day he got it?" Rafe asked.

"That wasn't his fault," Gabby said. "The car was just really...fast. I'm going to check on the brownies," she said cheerily, escaping into the kitchen.

All this and dinner hadn't even begun yet. Yep, it was great to be home.

Just then the doorbell rang. Nonna rushed to get it, Rocket zooming at her heels. Sara followed them, just in case.

But it wasn't Nonna who was at a loss for words when she opened the door. Standing there with an enormous package in her hands was Claire Milhouse, Tagg's mother.

"Hello, Rose," Claire said, smiling her practiced doctor's wife smile. Her stylish blonde hair was perfectly in place, and she was dressed as if she'd just walked out of a Talbots window, in a cute navy sailor's dress and pumps. Sara had not seen her for a year, this woman who had been just shy of two days from being her mother-in-law. And yet she'd not heard a word in all this time. Nada.

"Sara, you look wonderful," Claire said, giving her an air kiss on the cheek. "Taggart told me you were back in town. How are you doing, dear?"

"She's doing great," Rose said. "She's a doctor now. Going into practice right here in Angel Falls with her father." Nonna patted Sara's shoulder, and she shot her grandmother a grateful look.

"Is that right, dear?" Claire asked. "Taggart didn't mention that to me."

Sara bit back the urge to ask how Tagg was. She wondered how he'd known she was back, if he missed Sara, and if he felt any remorse at all. Not that she would take him back, of course. But still it was odd, how one day your life could be sailing along as usual, and the next, the person you'd talked to every day for ten years was simply...gone forever. Cut out like a friend on the edge of a cropped photo.

"Anyway," Claire said pleasantly. "This box arrived from Australia. It's a wedding gift. I thought I would bring it over so you could mail it back to whoever sent it."

"Mail it back?" Nonna said. "That son of yours is so smart, Claire. It's a pity you never taught him to mail a package."

Sara took the package, but Nonna lifted it right from her hands and took it into the kitchen.

"Sorry, Claire, you'll have to excuse Nonna," Sara said, but didn't really mean it. Last summer, after the wedding that wasn't, it had taken her an entire week to ship all the gifts back. Tagg couldn't take care of one gift? And who lived in Australia? Not anyone from her side, that was for sure.

Claire lowered her voice to a whisper. "It's the dementia, isn't it?"

"Yes, yes, of course," Sara said. "Well, thanks for stopping. Have a nice day."

As soon as she closed the door, Nonna was back. "That box rattles. It's something cheap, I can tell," she said and made a gesture as if she were dusting off her hands in good riddance. "Imagine the nerve. Asking you to return more wedding gifts after her son was the one to call the wedding off."

"Hey, Sara," Gabby called from the kitchen. "Could you come help?"

"Coming!" Sara called and gave Nonna a kiss on the cheek.

In the kitchen Gabby was frantically opening cabinet doors. The box that Claire had brought was sticking conspicuously out of the trash can. The dementia or not? Sara wondered. She liked to think not. At least she wouldn't be returning anything to Australia.

"What's going on?" Sara asked.

"I snuck some icing," Gabby said. Nonna's home-made brownies sat stacked on an old-fashioned milk glass cake holder, looking pretty and perfect.

"So what else is new? You've been doing that since you were three."

"Sara, the icing tastes terrible. I'm no baker, but it tastes like Nonna must've put flour in it instead of pow-dered sugar." She gestured to the bag of flour sitting next to the icing bowl. "I'm looking for the powdered sugar so we can make more really quick."

Sara swiped her finger into the bowl and tasted it. "Oh my God," she said, making a face.

Then she joined her sister in the search.

The powdered sugar was not in the cabinet reserved for baking supplies. They finally found it shoved on top of some canned goods in the pantry.

"Do you remember the recipe?" Gabby asked, then pulled out her phone. "We can Google it."

"I remember it. Powdered sugar, cocoa, butter, vanilla, and a little milk." Sara whipped up another batch while Gabby scraped all the bad stuff off each brownie. They'd just finished re-icing and restacking every brownie when Nonna walked in.

"I came in for the sauce. Oh, I thought I iced those already."

"Gabby licked one and so we just repaired it a little," Sara said. "Right, Gabby?"

Gabby shot Sara a dark look.

"Gabby! My goodness, dear," Nonna said. "Poor thing, you must be starving. Dinner's ready. Come eat some real food." Nonna linked elbows with Gabby and tugged her toward the dining room. "Bring the sauce, Sara, sweetie. It's time to eat."

Sara took a deep breath. She thought about a hospitalist position in New York City she'd been offered by one of her mentors. She could've been very happy taking that and telling her family it was too good an offer to pass up. She could have avoided her opinionated dad and the fact that her sisters, even Gabby now, seemed settled in relationships. She'd never have had to face Colton or Tagg's parents or even Tagg himself, or the fact that she'd never find anyone in this one-horse town.

Yet she loved Nonna fiercely. And Nonna needed her help. Her gut told her in a way she'd never experienced before that she'd made a difficult decision, but the right decision.

As she carried the old aluminum pot into the dining room she realized it was the first decision she'd made for herself in a very long time.

Chapter 5

♥

It was early evening when Colton pulled up the driveway of the little pale blue cape where his grandmother and eighteen-year-old sister Hannah lived. The teenage boy he'd hired to paint the house, Aiden Cross, was still here, judging by the once-red-but-now-faded-to-rose, somewhat rusty Toyota Corolla parked in the driveway. A ladder leaned against the side of the detached garage, which Colton could see was already half-scraped. The kid was a good worker, and apparently still hard at it on a Sunday evening at seven p.m.

Colton parked his police cruiser in the driveway and walked toward the garden. On his approach, Cookie, his paternal grandmother, rose from where she was kneeling, tying up a row of tomato plants, a bright-red fisherman's hat over her gray hair, matching red garden clogs on her feet. "Hello, sweetheart," she said, kissing him on the cheek. "I'm sorry about not fixing dinner tonight. Hannah's in the kitchen grabbing something between her waitress shift and dance class. Did you eat?"

"Hannah and I are capable of fending for ourselves, Cook." Cookie deserved a break after caring for him and his sister all these years, and he didn't want her to feel guilty for going to lunch with her friends. "I grabbed a pizza with a couple of the kids at Lou's, and there's leftovers for Hannah if she wants them."

Colton believed in keeping a heavy presence at Lou's, a local pizza joint with a couple of pool and Ping-Pong tables that tended to attract a lot of teens. It was a fun place where the kids could hang out and stay out of trouble, and he wanted to keep it that way. It also happened to be where Hannah worked, so he was able to pop in and keep an eye on his little sister too. Which she didn't much appreciate, but hey, curse of the big brother.

"You need to get off the clock some too," Cookie said. "It's Sunday."

"Yeah, yeah."

"Don't tell me, young man." She gave him a shrewd once-over, noting his ball cap, his sweaty appearance, and his grass-stained clothes. "You spent the afternoon clearing that plot of land, didn't you?"

"I've got plans for it, Granny," he said, smiling. "Besides, it's not work. It's...fun."

"I wish you'd just move into our house, Colton, once I move to the condo and Hannah leaves for college," Cookie said. "It's a nice house, and the yard is fantastic. Isn't that better than living in that apartment all by yourself?"

Colton had moved into his own place after he'd gotten the chief job a year ago. Not that he didn't love Cookie and Hannah, and he did try to spend nights off with his grandmother as often as he could, but he was thirty, and he didn't want to have to explain his comings and goings to either one of them. But even the idea of living in Cookie's house alone didn't appeal. The house was dated in a seventies-ranch sort of way. He didn't mind that it needed work but the seventies vibe just wasn't his thing. Even if the yard was great and had played host to many a ball game when he was younger.

"I'm sorry, Cookie." They'd been through this before. The land he'd bought six months before was in the middle of town, next to the park, surrounded by woods, and it had become available when the grandchildren of an elderly couple had decided to sell off a couple of parcels of a twenty-acre allotment. The adjacent plot, which was also for sale, held a dilapidated century-old colonial that looked like something out of *Hoarders*. He had no use for the disaster of a house but for a guy with a job that sometimes made him feel like he was living in a fishbowl, that hidden plot of land seemed like a magic oasis. Even if it was a wild mess.

"Well, OK, but don't say I didn't offer," she said.

"You're not going to be thinking much of this place in January when you're basking in the sun in Palm Beach while we're up to our butts in snow here." That was her plan. A little condo across town, snowbirding in Florida for the cold and icy months. No one deserved it more.

"So Sara Langdon's back in town. Have you run into her yet?"

Of course it had taken Cookie about ten seconds to change the subject and mention Sara. "Sure did. She's the one who stitched me up last night." He stuck out his arm, which he was keeping wrapped with gauze, just like Sara had instructed him. As far as he could tell, things were healing up pretty well. Unlike their relationship, which was just as prickly as ever.

Cookie glanced at the bandage. "So did you ask her out on a date while she was stitching you up?" His grandmother would never give up on this topic. She'd always had it in her head that Sara was the one for him. He would never understand the vagaries of granny matchmaking.

"No, Grandma, I did not. That would be a little awkward, seeing as the woman can't stand me." He called her "Grandma" when he was a little irritated, and "Granny" as an endearment. Other than that, even though her name was Charlotte, she was Cookie. To everybody.

"Oh, pish," Cookie said, waving a hand dismissively. "Now that she's free of that idiot, you'll make her see what a real man is like."

For once he didn't jump to defend Tagg. Which said a lot, because Tagg and his family had taken Colton under their wing when he was an unruly teenager and shown him that he could succeed despite his messed-up past. Tagg had helped him study in high school and catch up after the years when he'd lived with his mom and school had been hit or miss. His family had taken Colton places like amusement parks and on vacations that Cookie could never have afforded, plus Dr. Milhouse, Tagg's dad, had counseled him about college and helped him apply for the police officers' scholarship after he'd busted up his knee and his football scholarship fell through.

He'd always be grateful for all of that, even though as adults, Tagg and he lived very different lives. Besides, in the last year, Colton had truly come to believe the idiot remark was accurate. He'd only talked to Tagg a few times, and had gone out with him even less, making excuses when he could. "Thanks for the encouragement, but I'm not looking for a relationship."

"Nonsense. Everyone's looking for love, and you're not immune. Sara may be a little angry right now, but you've got to make her understand what really happened. Sometimes it's hard to believe people you love are dumb enough to do stupid things like that all on their own. It's easier to blame someone else."

"Do we really have to talk about this now?" If Sara needed to take her wrath out on Colton, so be it. It wouldn't be the first time.

He'd been a smart-ass with a chip on his shoulder for anyone who'd had all the benefits and opportunities he'd never had. Yes, he'd called her Brain and teased her for being smart and nerdy and uncool. But once when one of his football buddies tripped her on purpose and her glasses went flying, he'd rescued them. And noticed for the first time she had the most vivid green eyes, even if she had turned as red as the town's new fire truck when he handed her glasses back. But after she'd thanked him, in typical Sara fashion she then delivered a lecture on why he shouldn't hang around with assholes.

That's how it had always been with them. She'd always been able to grind down to the raw bone to irritate him. That hadn't changed in all these years.

But she'd certainly looked good in those boxers this morning.

Cookie was still talking. "I want to see you settled. You and Sara would make such a nice couple. And I want to see great-grandchildren before I die. It's my right as your substitute mother. And your grandmother. Double reasons to get going on that."

Cookie had taken them in a few years after Colton's father, a Chicago city cop, had died in a gunfight during a bank robbery when Colton was eight years old. His mom hadn't done well without his father, going from bad job to bad job and from bad to worse men. Hannah had come along when he was twelve—they'd never known who her father was—but by then his mother was on a downward spiral. She needed a new liver after four years of pickling hers in alcohol, but despite three bouts of rehab, she couldn't stop drinking long enough to get one.

By the time his mother passed and Cookie brought them to Angel Falls, Colton had become his sister's protector. He was determined to do anything to give her the future he didn't get to pick for himself. And he was determined to give Cookie the break she'd never had because she'd spent her time raising them.

Suddenly Hannah ran out of the house, dressed in

yoga pants and a T-shirt, ready for her job as an assistant dance instructor at the ballet studio downtown.

"Thanks for the eggs, Cookie," Hannah said. "I washed up the pan. Hey, Colton, I'll see you later if you're around, OK? Or maybe not. A few of us are going out for pizza and a movie after class." She gave them both quick kisses on their cheeks, then let her gaze trail to the detached garage at the side of the house. "And wow, how long's the hottie here for?"

Colton steered her from her position staring at a shirtless Aiden's wide, tattooed shoulders as he stood on the ladder scraping paint off the side of the garage.

"His name is Aiden," Colton said, "and he's earning some extra money by helping me out." Note to self: Aiden had to put a shirt on. ASAP.

Hannah rolled her eyes in a way Colton knew only too well. As a much older sibling, he often straddled the line between big brother (which was cool) and parental figure (which was absolutely not). "I know his name, and he's very nice, and he just graduated, just like me. Not to mention he's gorgeous. And a bad boy, even hotter. But you must like him to bring him here to work, huh?"

"It doesn't matter if I like him. He's here to work and stay out of trouble. That means no fraternizing. This one's got 'Stay away from me' written all over him." As soon as the words left his mouth, he regretted them.

"Hmm," she said with a smile. "Intriguing."

"Don't you have to get going to work?" he asked, steering Hannah along the driveway to her car.

"Geez, you're such a killjoy. I'm allowed to look at

boys. Maybe someday I can even date them like normal girls whose brothers don't do background checks on them before they can come within a five-mile radius."

Colton frowned. As was so often the case with his sister, words failed him. He owed her parental guidance because a) he was responsible for her and b) he didn't think Cookie would be blunt enough. But every time he tried, his tongue got tied up in knots. "I want you to be safe. Date someone nice." Actually, not dating at all would be his preference.

"Geez, Colt, do you think I'm going to be a virgin forever?"

He blanched. "Maybe just until you're thirty." He tried to smile, but to him it wasn't really a joke. "Have a nice day at work. Don't talk to any boys."

She saluted. "Aye, aye, Chief." But her eyes slid back to Aiden.

Aiden was ripped, he'd give him that. He was tanned and muscled, and he wore a ball cap backward as he worked. Exotic tattoos covered his shirtless chest, back, and arms and disappeared beneath the waistband of his jeans. He was also destined for trouble unless someone intervened. He'd been busted for smoking pot with his deadbeat buddies, most of whom already had criminal records. His dad was a drunk and his mother was gone. Colton had first noticed him doing his community service hours at the park, picking up litter. The kid had filled five large trash bags in a half hour while the other kids were whining and complaining it was too hot.

Colton had decided to give him a chance, just as Chief McGregor, the former police chief, had given

Colton a chance when he was an insolent, angry kid all those years ago. He'd taken a parked car for a joyride on a dare and gotten busted for it. The chief had made him do a hundred community service hours, but more than that, he'd taken Colton under his wing.

"Run along, Hannah," he said, giving his sister a gentle tug toward her car.

"No fair, Colton." She pushed out her lower lip like she'd done when she was three. "I'm enjoying the view."

"Time to go teach those little girls how to do pirouettes," Colton said, opening her car door. *And to stop noticing ripped guys with tattoos.*

"Bye, Cookie." She waved to her grandmother and blew Colton a kiss. "Love you both!" she called as she drove down the driveway.

"That girl's going to be the death of me," he said, clutching his stomach. Judging from the little jabs of pain he was experiencing, maybe he was getting an ulcer.

"You've got to let her grow up, Colton," his grandmother said. "She's going to be living on her own in just a few months." Hannah would be starting college at Ohio State in the fall. Wasn't it yesterday that she'd been a sweet, big-eyed toddler with chocolate ice cream dripping all down her chin?

"How do you know she's going to make good decisions?"

"You don't. You just pray a lot and hope what we've taught her sticks."

He cracked a little smile. "Did you worry about me like that?"

Cookie shook her head and laughed. "A thousand times worse."

He wrapped his grandmother up in a hug. It couldn't have been easy, taking in a thirteen-year-old boy and a one-year-old baby. He'd been argumentative. Disrespectful. And so angry over his mother's succumbing to the addiction that had taken over her life after his father was killed. How had his grandmother ever dealt with him?

Cookie patted him on the back. "But look how far you've come. Your father would be so proud, do you know that?"

He drew back from his grandmother's embrace. "I don't know what my father would think about me being a small-town cop. Maybe he'd be disappointed." Aw hell, he shouldn't have said that. Cookie would think he was fishing for praise.

"Nonsense. Don't even think like that." Of course she would say that. Cookie was Colton's biggest fan.

"Have I ever thanked you for everything you did for me?" he asked.

"Sweetheart, you thank me every day by letting me see what a good man you've become. And as far as your job, no person should ever underestimate their influence. You'll know if you're in the right place. Your heart will tell you. Just like it will when you've found the right girl."

"Yada, yada," Colton said, starting to walk toward the house.

"Where are you going?"

"I'm going to go tell this kid to get a shirt on. Especially when Hannah's around."

"I'm off to book club. If you're hungry, there are bagels on the counter."

He gave a wave to his grandmother and approached Aiden, who was down from the ladder and taking a swig from his water bottle. "How's it going?" he asked the kid, extending his hand for a fist bump.

"Great," Aiden said. "I've been here since eight, but it was raining, so I went and bought the paint. And I've got most of this side scraped."

"Looks great. Hey, why don't you pack it up for the night? It's already seven."

"I want to get a little more done before it starts to get dark. I've got to work at the discount warehouse tonight so I might not get back here until noon tomorrow."

Colt knew Aiden stocked shelves at night and parked cars on the weekends for events at a big hotel in downtown Cleveland. The kid was a worker, he'd give him that.

"So, have you given any thought to your plans for the fall?" Colton asked.

"If you mean college, it's not for me."

"I thought you wanted to be an electrician." He owed it to the kid to press him, just as Chief McGregor had gotten on Colton's case when he was a kid. The chief had been his dad's best friend, and his investment in Colton had made all the difference.

"I missed the deadline for applying to the program at the technical college."

"No excuses." Colt crossed his arms, knowing it made him look a little intimidating.

"Give me a break, Chief," Aiden said. "The deadline was around the time I got in trouble last spring." He glanced downward. "Plus I don't have money for school."

"Well, there's loans and scholarships and—"

"Those are for people with better grades than me. I'm not—"

"Good enough? Look, you're not going to get anywhere if you talk like that. And I actually made a call to the technical college. They admit people if someone drops out. So get your application in so you can get on the waiting list. You never know what can happen." Plus Colt had a buddy who taught at the college and said he'd look into what he could do for the kid. Colt didn't tell Aiden that, though.

"It was easier for you because you came from a good family."

Colton sighed. He really hated telling his story, because it was still painful in a way. But this kid needed to hear it. "My parents both died before I went to high school. I was an all-state wide receiver with a full ride to a D1 school until I blew my ACL in the last game of the season. I had to give up my scholarship and my dream of playing football. Even though I rehabbed that knee for a year, I never got back to my prior form. But people lent me a hand and I got through it. You can too."

He'd become a cop because his dream had gotten shot all to hell, and because the Angel Falls force, who had known his father well when he'd worked here as a rookie cop, took care of their own.

Not that he'd deserved their help. He'd been an arrogant SOB and hadn't wanted anyone's help. But they'd offered him a job cleaning toilets and emptying the city's trash cans, then helping out at different events like the traffic camp for little kids, and they'd shown him a cop's life. It had changed his outlook, given him another purpose, and he'd discovered he wanted to be a cop.

After college and the police academy, Chief McGregor offered him a job, and he came home to take care of Cookie and Hannah. He might've had grander dreams, but family was family, and Angel Falls was where he'd ended up, for better or for worse. Not that he didn't like his job—he did, a lot. He just wondered sometimes if he should be somewhere he could make a real difference instead of rescuing people's dogs and giving out parking tickets.

"The way I see it, you can accept you're not going to get anywhere and have a shitty life or fight like hell to pull yourself up." He slapped Aiden on the back. "Bring your application by the station and I'll go over it with you."

"Yes, sir," Aiden said.

"And Aiden?"

"Yes, Chief?"

"You should put your shirt on so you don't sunburn and get skin cancer."

"Aw, don't worry about me, Chief. I'm wearing sunblock."

"I'm sure you are. But my grandmother can see you and it might be too much excitement for her."

"Aw, Chief, your grandmother's not going to care if…"

Colt interrupted. "It's not just my grandma I'm worried about, if you get my meaning."

Aiden rubbed the back of his neck.

"Just keep the shirt on, got it?"

"Yes, sir," he said cautiously.

Colton nodded. As he turned to walk to the house, a dog bounded over to them from across the grass.

A bull terrier with brown ears and a big pirate patch over his left eye.

Rocket.

As he looked up from petting the dog, sure enough, there was Sara's grandmother coming up the driveway, a little out of breath. She was dressed in turquoise pants, a sweater, and white orthopedic walking shoes, and she was carrying Rocket's leash. She didn't look disheveled at all, but he recognized a certain look of panic in her eyes.

"Oh, Colton, I'm so glad to see you!" she said, clutching his arm. "Hello," she said politely to Aiden.

Colton patted her hand. "Is something wrong, Rose? How can I help you?"

"Oh, you're a dear. Maybe you can help me. This isn't my street. I—can you tell me where Glenwillow Lane is? I was taking Rocket for a walk, but I was so busy daydreaming I wandered off course a little bit."

Wandered off course. Ever since her dementia diagnosis, he'd been keeping an extra eye out, but she'd never done this before. His cell phone went off at his hip before he could reach for it to call Rafe.

"Hey, Colty, you big hunk of love," said Carmen, his dispatcher, the pleasant lilt of her Puerto Rican accent familiar and friendly. She was sassy and flirty and really good at her job. Plus at sixty, she didn't take crap from anyone, even him.

"Hey, Carmen, what's up?" Worry instantly pricked Colton's neck. Carmen fiercely guarded his time off. She never called unless it was important.

"I know you're off duty, but I just got a call from Sara Langdon that her sweet old *abuela*'s gone missing. I thought I'd catch you on your cell because you might be somewhere around the 'hood. Unless you're with a lady friend or something, in which case I do *not* want to know."

Colton ignored the lady comment. Carmen was always trying to find out details about his love life. "You have great instincts, because Rose just walked into my grandmother's yard."

"I always have great instincts as far as you're concerned, babe." Carmen paused. "Sara's worried about Rocket too. You got Rocket there?"

Colton bent down to scratch the dog behind the ears. He promptly went belly up for more. "Rocket's present and accounted for. Thanks, Carmen." Rocket started bathing his hand with his tongue in a gesture of gratitude. Colton stood up. He and Rocket were pals, but he drew the line at being coated with doggy saliva. "Hey, will you call Sara right away and tell her everything's under control? And will you give me her number, please?"

He'd call her and tell her he was driving Rose home. As a public service, of course.

"Bold move, Chief. How much is it worth to you?" his smart-ass dispatcher said.

Oh, for God's sake. "Just text me the number, Carmen."

"Okeydokey, Colty. And you show that girl what a gem you are, baby. Make her forget all about that no-good ex-fiancé of hers."

"Bye already, Carmen."

He guided Rose up to the back patio. She wound her arm through his, placing her thin, veined hand on his forearm as they walked through the grass. "Come sit down a minute, and then I'll drive you home." He wanted to make sure she was all right. Offer her some water or something. And call Sara.

"It was the strangest thing, Colton. All of a sudden I looked around and I didn't see anything I recognized. Until I saw you." She patted his hand. The fear in her eyes twisted his gut. What kind of disease was this that hijacked a person's life, made someone who'd lived here her whole life forget her own damn neighborhood? He felt bad for Rose. And for Sara, who must be panicking.

Speaking of Sara, suddenly there she was, running down the sidewalk, waving.

Just then Cookie came out the back door. She was dressed for book club in white pants and pumps and a bright floral blouse, but when she saw him sitting with Sara's grandmother, she tossed her purse on a chair and walked over.

"Hi, Rose, dear," Cookie said, giving her a hug, then stooping to pet Rocket. "I just made some lemonade. Can you stay and chat for a few minutes?" She looked over at Aiden, who was carrying a bucket to the hose. "Aiden, you too. Come have a drink." She winked at Colton, and he nodded. Thirty years as a kindergarten teacher had made Cookie an excellent multitasker, always ready to jump into action.

Colton met Sara halfway down the driveway, took her by the elbow, and guided her to his cruiser. She was clutching a hand to her chest, a look of alarm on her face.

"She's fine," he said, holding on to her arms and looking her in the eye until he was certain that registered. Her eyes instantly filled with tears, and she clamped a hand over her mouth.

"Oh, Colton. Thank God. Carmen called me, and I just took off running down here."

He rubbed her arms, which wasn't very professional, but she was clearly upset. "You OK?"

"Just upset with myself. I told Nonna I'd go for a walk with her and went up to find shoes and then she was just . . . gone. Like she'd forgotten I was coming with her, maybe? Anyway, I panicked and called the station."

"You did the right thing," he said in the most calming voice he could muster. "Rose saw me out in the yard and walked over. She was a little panicked. Said she didn't know how to get back to her street."

"Oh God." She took a step toward her grandmother, but Colton stopped her.

"I don't think it would help her if you're upset. Maybe take another minute before you go over there."

She nodded. "I was supposed to be keeping an eye

on her. That's the whole point of my coming back home to live with her."

Ah. He'd wondered why Sara had come back home. "Don't blame yourself. Everything's fine. She didn't go far, and she knew to ask for help."

Sara nodded, but he could tell by her expression it wasn't fine at all.

She turned those piercing green eyes on him, and he nearly melted. "Thank you for taking care of her."

"Not a problem. I'm happy to help anytime you need me." And, strangely enough, he meant it.

He released her, and together they walked over to the back patio. Aiden was standing with the older women, giving them a tour of the numerous tattoos inked all over his arms and chest while they watched, enraptured. "This one is the Chinese symbol for 'gentle but strong' and this is my dog's name, Sparky. He died last year."

Colton made sure not to roll his eyes. He wasn't sure if he should be horrified or pleased. The kid was certainly friendly. But he still had his damn shirt off.

Rose saw Sara and broke into a smile. "Oh, there you are, dear." She held out her hand, which Sara immediately grabbed. To Sara's credit, she didn't get emotional or freak out. "I was just taking Rocket out for a walk," Rose said, "and look who we ran into. Colton and Cookie invited me to sit down for a drink, wasn't that nice?"

"Help yourself to a brownie, dear," Cookie said, pointing to the table. "And some lemonade."

Sara hugged Cookie and thanked her, then sat next to her grandmother and made small talk. Rocket came and sprawled at her feet, resting his head on her tennis shoe.

Colton sat down too. Sara was telling a story that made the ladies laugh about a kid she'd treated in her residency. She was animated, using her hands, her eyes lighting up with laughter.

That started Cookie off telling school stories. At one point Colton caught Sara looking at him. Or maybe she caught him looking at her, he wasn't sure which. But she shot him a grateful look and mouthed *Thank you.*

It was strange seeing this side of her. He was used to the wound-too-tight Sara, the one who was a perfectionist above all else and expected the same from everyone else around her. When she chatted and laughed, she looked like a normal person. A pretty person. One whose phone number he had in his phone.

Where had *that* thought come from? He'd never call her. No way. Out of the question.

His thoughts were distracted, fortunately, by Hannah's car pulling back up the driveway. She got out, clearly in a hurry, not bothering to close her car door. "I forgot my dance bag!" she called in their direction, waving to everyone gathered on the porch.

She stopped suddenly on her way into the house. "Oh my gosh, Sara, what are you doing here? Hi, Mrs. F. Rocket! There's my good boy! How are you?" Rocket came bounding over, thumping his tail against the patio stone and leaning against Sara's leg in admiration. "Oh, I've missed you so much," she crooned, petting him. "My mean brother took Champ with him when he moved out and I'm totally doggy deprived." She looked up at Sara. "What's going on?"

"We were just passing by on a walk," Sara said. Hannah stole a look at Colt as if to say, *What alternate universe is this?* But Colt kept his expression neutral.

"I'm glad you're back in town," Hannah said to Sara. "Talk to you soon, K?"

"Let's have coffee and catch up," Sara said.

"Sounds great. I gotta go!" She bolted into the house. A few seconds later she ran out the door with more quick waves.

"Hey, no rushing," Colton said in his cop voice. "Wouldn't want you getting in an accident."

"I won't. Bye!" she said, running back to her car. But not before she took a long hard look at tattoo boy.

Even worse, Aiden turned as she passed and unabashedly checked out her ass.

As a cop Colton was trained to notice things, but he sure wished he hadn't noticed that.

Chapter 6

♥

Good morning," Sara said cheerfully, walking into her father's office bright and early Monday morning. His two longtime employees, Leonore and Glinda, were already there. She could see them through the big glass window that separated the reception area from the waiting room. Opening the door and walking into the back office, she placed a coffee cake on the Formica counter.

Yes, a coffee cake. She'd sucked up her aversion and made one as a gesture to get started on the right foot.

"Good morning, sweetheart," Leonore said, getting up from her workstation, where she had been leafing through a *People* magazine and drinking from an Eddie Redmayne coffee mug. Leonore looked like the world's most perfect grandma—plump and pleasant looking, with nearly white hair and boxy glasses that magnified her eyes and always made her look a little surprised. She was also a hardcore knitter and every item on her desk was enclosed in cases of all colors of the rainbow she'd made herself—a cup cosy, a cylindrical holder for pens, a rectangular one for her iPhone.

"Oh, here, I made you something," she said, thrusting a tiny brightly wrapped square in Sara's direction.

"Oh, Leonore, you shouldn't have." Sara was a little nervous, as the last gift from Leonore had been a winter hat with floppy dog ears on it, a little embarrassing to wear in public. She ripped open the package. It contained a multicolored knit pouch with a long string attached in a big loop. Hmm. Something to wear around your neck for loose change? Breath mints? Emergency tampon?

"It's a little case for your phone or whatever that you can wear around your neck," Leonore said. "It'll be convenient for the office."

"They're so handy," Glinda called from the exam room hallway, holding up a white version that she wore around her own neck, no doubt to match the starched white nursing uniform she wore every single day. "Especially on the days when you don't have pockets."

Indeed. "Thank you," Sara said, walking through the little half door that separated the behind-the-desk area from the rest of the office to give Leonore a hug. She placed the bright knit square around her neck. "I can't wait to use it." Come to think of it, she hated wearing a white coat. They made kids cry and always had to be laundered and pressed, even if they did have tons of pockets. So maybe the pouch wasn't such a bad idea after all. Especially the emergency tampon part. Besides, she was constantly misplacing her pens. Was it scary that she was already thinking of so many uses for this thing?

Glinda approached the reception counter. "Oh, coffee cake! What a treat from our new doctor. Did you make it from scratch? Come have a piece too." Glinda adjusted her vintage nurse cap over her blonde hair that she'd been teasing into a bouffant since 1960 at least.

Yes, Sara had made it from scratch, because she knew they loved coffee cake. Even though it looked really good, she couldn't bear to have a bite herself.

Leonore brought over the coffeepot and some ceramic mugs, each of which bore a different drug company's slogan. "Of course she did, Glinda. Would you expect anything less from our little Sara? We're so proud of you, sweetie. You've come such a long way since we caught you in the back studying your father's anatomy books."

Sara felt the first blush of the day spreading across her cheekbones. She'd been thirteen, and they'd found her reading one of her dad's heavy illustrated anatomy atlases—the one about the reproductive system. Well, a girl's got to learn somehow, right? Those years between her mom's death and her dad's marriage to Rachel had been a little short on trusted womanly influence, so she'd filled in the gaps in her knowledge by doing her own research.

Glinda patted her back. "And you've come a long way since your marriage mishap last year."

Here came blush number two. And it wasn't even eight o'clock yet.

"I never liked that Taggart," Leonore said, cutting a large slice of cake. "He always struck me as hoity-toity, you know why? Whenever I ran into him around town and had my grandkids with me, he never even so much as said hi to them. What kind of father would a man like that make?"

"Seriously," Glinda agreed, putting her much smaller piece on a paper plate. "Doctor told us you won't eat cake anymore. Does that include coffee cake too?"

Sara waved her hand dismissively. "Oh, it's not a problem, really. I mean, it's not the cake's fault, right?" She'd never admit it, but it *was* a problem, and it was all cake. Coffee cake, ice cream cake, any cake in the world.

"I was the one who took your beautiful wedding cake to the homeless shelter," Leonore said solemnly.

Sara's stomach churned. It was getting really difficult to keep this smile plastered on her face. Just then the office door opened, and Mr. Humphries, the bank manager, walked in. "Ladies, good morning," he said, waving through the glass partition and taking a seat in the waiting room. At seven forty-five, he was early for the first appointment of the day, which typically began at eight thirty.

No one jumped to get him signed in and ready. "Yep," Leonore continued. "Doctor called me and said, 'Leonore, would you mind getting this thing the heck out of my house because it's making my

daughter cry' and I said 'No problem, boss, I'll
be right over.' It was a Saturday, and I was still
dressed in my pj's." Ah yes. The cake had been delivered to her parents' house by accident, after the
wedding was called off. Bless her dad, thinking of
the shelter. At least someone had gotten some pleasure out of it.

"I'm so excited to be working here, ladies," Sara
said, smiling her cheeriest smile and hoping to leave
the topic of her beautiful failed wedding in the dust.
"I know my dad will teach me so much, but I'm also
hoping to help the office make some adjustments to
move us more into state-of-the-art patient care." At
least she *prayed* she could do that, but she knew it
wasn't going to be easy.

"Well, we're all about state-of-the-art patient care,"
Glinda said. "Your father's the best doc in town, but
let's face it, this place needs a face-lift." She straightened the frame on the iconic Norman Rockwell print
of the doctor giving the little boy a shot in the butt. It
made Sara think instantly of Colton. She wondered if
he'd been cute with a buzz cut like the boy in the painting. Actually, he was cute with a buzz cut *now*, in a
whole different way.

Ugh, why had she just thought that?

"What kinds of adjustments, dear?" Leonore asked,
the slightest furrow forming between her brows.

"My dad's going to get penalized by Medicare if
he doesn't turn his charts electronic, so I said I'd
get us started on that. Plus we talked about getting
new computers for the reception desk and electronic

tablets to bring into the exam rooms. And painting the office. Getting a new EKG machine. That kind of stuff."

"I like everything but the electronic records," Leonore said. "That sounds a little scary."

"Don't be afraid, Leonore," Glinda said. "It means a better computer. You'll be able to play Words with Friends even faster."

"Well, we'll all be learning together," Sara said. "I also had some ideas about streamlining the day so we can get out of here earlier."

Leonore patted her on the back. "You do that, honey. All my grandkids play sports, and I never get out of here on time."

"I'm sure Sara will have kids one day too," Glinda said. "I mean, when you meet someone, that is." She blushed, knowing the topic was a sensitive one. "And when you do, you'll want to get home too."

"Glinda, I want to get home before seven now, even though I don't have a boyfriend *or* kids."

"Look, we love your dad," Leonore said. "He's a kind man and a wonderful doctor. But the man can talk. He knows everyone and he'll help anyone with any problem. But sometimes you just need to get to business and get home, you know what I mean?"

Sara knew her dad loved to talk to people. It was what made him beloved in the community and also what made him chronically behind schedule. It would improve everyone's life to make a few changes.

Just then her dad walked in, gave her a quick squeeze, and went for a piece of coffee cake. "Welcome to your first day," he said. "Did you see what's on your office door?"

"What? No, I-I haven't been back there yet." A few weeks ago, Sara had helped clean out a little room down the hall that had been used for supplies but was now her office. When she walked back, she saw a wooden engraved plaque attached to her door that read "Sara Langdon, MD."

"Oh, Dad," she said, getting teary.

Leonore slipped her iPhone out of its vibrant multi-colored case as Sara rejoined them. "OK, you two, smile now. First-day picture!"

Her father wrapped his arm around Sara and pressed his cheek against hers, grinning widely. She couldn't help but grin too. "That's my girl," he said proudly as he let go. "Glad to have you here, sweetheart."

"Aw, that's so sweet," Leonore said, looking at the picture. "I'm going to frame this and hang it next to the picture behind your desk of Sara running around the Christmas tree in her diaper. Won't that be so cute?"

Sara pretended not to hear that. She was still smiling at what her dad had said. For a moment her heart reached out to grab everything in its path—his approval, the fact that he'd just basically said that he wanted her here with him, as his partner. That maybe it was all right not to be in an academic fellowship far away from family, doing research and presenting papers at Harvard. That she might belong right here at home after all.

Leonore showed her the photo. "We should put this on the practice website, Dad," Sara said.

"Do we have a website?" Glinda asked.

"Well, we probably should have one," her dad said. "But by the time we get it up there, Sara will probably be gone."

Sara tried not to let her expression fall. *Gone?* Despite the plaque and his kind words, her dad clearly still expected her to move on to bigger and better things.

"I can see Mr. Humphries," she offered. Best to get busy. Show her dad she was gung ho about starting and that she believed in efficiency.

Glinda checked her watch. "It's only eight-oh-five, sweetie," she said. "We don't start with the patients until eight thirty."

But he'd been here for twenty minutes, and Sara could use a distraction. "Well, maybe we could see him early today so he could get back to work." And keep traffic in the office flowing, which seemed to be a novel idea.

"Oh, all right," Glinda said. "Sure. I can put him in a room."

Leonore took her dad aside a moment to confer about something before she returned to her desk. Sara had just moved to pick up the patient's chart when her dad appeared at her side, clearing his throat and putting a hand on her arm. "Um, I'll see George," he said. "Longtime patient, you know?" He lowered his voice. "It will be a lot easier for me to just take this one."

Sara frowned. "Did he—did he insist on seeing you?"

"Well, you know how it is, sweetheart...people have their certain problems and they feel most comfortable with who's been listening to them for years. You understand that, don't you?"

"Right. Of course." She forced a smile.

"Don't worry," her dad said, giving her another squeeze. "You'll be plenty busy all day. It's not even eight thirty yet."

Sara fought against the awful sinking feeling in her abdomen. Her dad had a personal relationship with *all* his patients. He truly cared about them, and they adored him in return. It looked like neither her dad nor the patients were going to be able to give that up easily.

Resolutely she walked back to her office to stare at her blank white walls and her too-tidy desk. She stuck a pack of gum and a pen into her new knit kangaroo pouch. It was early yet…the first hour. But she had a feeling it was going to be a long day.

* * *

"So what are you doing here so late anyway?" Sara asked her best friend, Kaitlyn, that evening at the Bean, the coffee shop Kaitlyn had inherited from her grandfather. "Don't you have something to do with that hunky high school football coach you're dating?"

Kaitlyn was scrubbing coffee carafes in the big industrial sink while Sara sat at the steel kitchen counter sorting sugar and Splenda packets. "You may as well know," Kaitlyn said, "I broke up with him."

Sara looked up. "You broke up with Steve? Why didn't you tell me?"

"You've had a lot on your mind, what with moving back and starting work…and flirting with Colton." Kaitlyn attempted a smile.

Sara chose to ignore the Colton remark. On second thought, she would address it immediately. "You mean fighting, not flirting. And have I been that unavailable that you couldn't even tell me that? If I have been, I'm a shitty friend and I'm sorry."

Kaitlyn pushed back a strand of hair that had fallen out of her ponytail and kept scrubbing a carafe. Steam drifted up, curling Kaitlyn's already wavy blonde hair. She turned off the water and pulled off her rubber gloves. "Truthfully, Sara, I haven't felt like talking about it. I'd really rather talk about your life. It's more exciting. Speaking of which, how'd your first day working with your dad go?"

Sara smiled. "Hardly exciting. And speaking of not wanting to talk about it…" She laughed. "Seriously, it was all right. I'm optimistic. And more importantly, I'm really glad I took this time to come home and be with my nonna. And closer to you. I've really regretted being so far away. Come sit down and talk with me."

"OK, fine. I'm done here anyway." Her smile was genuine this time as she gestured for Sara to follow her as she took a seat at one of the cute tables in the coffee shop proper. "What can I get you to drink? Or I have leftover muffins if you're hungry."

"My dad and Rachel are having Nonna for dinner tonight, so I'm free. Want to order a pizza?" Sara asked. "Like the old days?"

"Anchovies and onions? I don't think so."

"Oh, come on. I'll even splurge for the Cherry Coke."

"Blech, you're making me sick. I can do a veggie

pizza with a two-liter of Diet. And a salad. If you make the call."

"Deal." Sara ordered the pizza from Lou's, their favorite local pizza restaurant and bar. "Twenty minutes until pickup," she announced.

Kaitlyn got them each a glass of water and sat down. "I'm tired."

"You must be. You start at like four a.m., don't you? And you're still here. That's worse than my dad's hours."

"The business is going great. What I mean is, I'm tired of pretending I'm in love. Steve's a great guy, but I don't love him. That's why I broke it off. I tried my best, but it just didn't happen."

"Oh, Kaitlyn. I'm sorry." Sara squeezed her hand. She worried about Kaitlyn, who kept dating guys but none of them stuck. When they were younger Sara had blamed that on Kaitlyn's having a hopeless crush on Rafe. Now she wasn't so sure.

"There's no reason to be sorry. Now Steve has the chance to meet and fall in love with someone he really loves. And I do too."

Well, that sounded positive, but Kaitlyn didn't look like she felt very positive. "You've dated a lot of guys," Sara said. "At least you've got the experience of knowing what you want."

"Well, mostly what I don't want." She played with a Splenda packet in the center of the table. "My mother would say I'm too picky. Is it too picky to want a gentleman, someone who's polite and considerate, has a good job, is kind to animals, and can cook?"

Oh well, Rafe definitely couldn't cook...much. So maybe Kaitlyn was safe. Plus she did look sad about Steve. So hopefully Rafe was out of the picture. On second thought, Rafe had brought a really good salad to dinner last weekend.

There was a sudden knock at the big plate glass window. Sara turned to see her brother's face plastered against it. Kaitlyn laughed, suddenly animated at seeing Rafe.

Rafe popped his head in the door. "Hey, Sara, Katesters." Sara didn't miss that Rafe's glance lingered on her best friend. Or that he called her that goofy name. "Anything new in coffee world? Hey, I need another bag of that Red Bull coffee you sold me a couple of weeks ago."

"You mean the Himalayan high altitude mix?" Kaitlyn asked.

"Yeah, that's it. The guys at the station love that stuff for when we're up all night."

"Rafe, did you really come by to buy coffee now?" Sara asked. "We're having girl talk. Besides, the Bean is closed and Kaitlyn is off the clock."

"Want to know the truth?" Rafe asked. "I figured if I offered to pick up your pizza, maybe you'd let me stay and eat a slice."

"Or ten," Kaitlyn added. "How did you know we just ordered?"

"Because I just called for one too, and Lou told me. I'll be back in a few."

"Here, let me get some money," Kaitlyn said, already halfway out of her chair.

"Don't bother," Rafe said with a killer smile. "You

get it next time, Katie Scarlett." Then he was gone, disappearing back onto Main Street, the bell above the door tinkling in his wake and Kaitlyn's face as crimson as the nickname Rafe had just called her.

Katie Scarlett? As in *O'Hara*? What was going on with the cute little endearments? "Since when did you get so chummy with my brother?" Sara asked.

Kaitlyn shrugged. "We've always been friends." She paused a long time. "That's the problem."

"No, Kaitlyn! Not Rafe. He's the worst kind of commitmentphobe. He will break your heart. Guaranteed. Do you hear me? *Guaranteed.*"

"It's my heart to break, Sara. I want it all, the whole package—the rapid pulse, the swoony kisses, the feeling that you know when he's in the room because your whole body reacts to his presence. That's how I feel around Rafe."

Sara disguised her horror because Kaitlyn looked so...passionate. "Are you going to tell him?"

"I don't know what I'm going to do. Because right now we *are* friends. We hang out sometimes."

"I heard you've been to Nonna's for dinner."

"A couple of times. Her lasagna is *amazing*." She rubbed her stomach. "One day, your brother is going to wake up and discover he's in love with me too. I just know it."

Kaitlyn got up from the table before Sara could roll her eyes. "Where are you going?" Sara asked, holding back her panic.

"I have leftover muffins for Rafe to bring to the guys at the station."

"No. Do not give my brother your muffins!"

"He can have my muffins if he wants them."

Oh God, were they really talking about muffins? "You're too kind and generous. He will stomp all over your muffins and break your heart, because that's what Rafe does, without even knowing it."

"Someone's going to get through to him, Sara. Maybe it could be me."

"I just care about you. I want you to be happy."

"And I appreciate it. Not to change the subject, but...Gabby and I want you to be happy too. So we've, um...found you a date."

"No, Kaitlyn." This was going from bad to worse. "I'm not ready yet."

"You said yourself you're sick of everyone talking about last year. People will forget all about it if you get back on the horse. Besides, the guy is a doctor, and he's cute. My aunt Millie tried to set him up with me, but he's not my type."

"Of course not. Because you think Rafe is your type."

Kaitlyn shrugged. Then she looked up, a huge grin spreading across her face. Sara turned around to see that Rafe had entered through the back way, carrying a big pizza box. Geez, she had it bad.

"I haven't been on a first date for thirteen years," Sara mumbled, mostly to herself because Kaitlyn was so preoccupied.

Kaitlyn tore her gaze from Rafe long enough to flash Sara a smile. "Well, that's going to change on Friday. And Gabby and I are going to help you."

Chapter 7

♥

The next Friday night, Sara walked into Lou's Pizza only to find Hannah working the hostess stand. She hadn't been to Lou's in ages, but it felt the same—crowded red booths with people talking and laughing, black-and-white photos all over the walls of Lou's family making pizzas in Italy in the very old days, and the smell of the best pizza this side of Cleveland. The smack of pool balls resonated from the pool and Ping-Pong tables in the back, where the teenagers usually hung out. Not the most romantic place to meet a blind date, but definitely a popular one.

"Hi, sweetie," Sara said, giving Hannah a hug. "You look pretty tonight." Since their grandmothers were friends, she'd known Hannah since she was a baby. And she'd been Hannah's counselor at the local day camp during her summers in college. Hannah had been one of her favorite campers, notwithstanding the fact that Colton was her brother.

"Hi, Sara," Hannah said, pulling out a menu from

behind a wooden stand. "Your sister and Kaitlyn are already here."

Sara scanned the restaurant until she caught sight of Gabby and Kaitlyn sitting together in a booth near the windows.

Hannah looked her over, no doubt noticing that she was dressed up and had makeup on. "You look really nice. Do you have a date?"

"Actually yeah, I do." She held out her hands. "I even got my nails done." Gabby's idea. It had taken a whole hour, but it had been kind of fun. Sara fingered a blue stone Hannah wore on a leather cord around her neck. "Cute."

"I made it in a jewelry-making class at the community center. Want me to make you one? Better yet, you should come to class with me. It's on Monday nights."

Sara tried hard to imagine herself taking a Monday night off to make jewelry. Yet this was her new life, and she was determined to make an effort to do normal things, for Nonna's sake and, tonight, thanks to Gabby, for her own sake. Hence the blind date. And the nails. And the fact that she was wearing Gabby's top. It was part of the new Sara. Open to new experiences, not working all the time. Moving on from Tagg, which in this town was a feat, as her patients mentioned her breakup multiple times a day. "That sounds like fun," Sara said.

Hannah seemed to genuinely brighten at that. She had the same striking eyes as Colton, only hers were hazel, not blue. Dark-brown hair like his too, but hers was straight and shiny and pulled back in a ponytail.

"Hey, congrats on OSU," Sara said. "Is your summer going OK?"

"It would be better if my brother didn't hang out here." She gestured toward the back. "He's lurking over there."

Oh no. Colton was *here*? Sure enough, there he was in the back, holding a pool cue and leaning his long frame against the wall, talking to a couple of guys she hadn't seen since high school. As Hannah led her to the table, she made certain not to look in his direction, focusing on not tripping in her high-heeled sandals (also Gabby's).

"I don't think this is a good place to meet a date," Sara said to Gabby and Kaitlyn as she sat down. "Too noisy," she added, nodding toward the back. And too close to Colton.

"Wow," Kaitlyn said. "Is that you?"

"Gee, thanks for the vote of confidence," Sara said.

"No, I mean—wow. You look different. Kind of…hot." Easy for Kaitlyn to say. She was blonde and blue-eyed, with a sweet smile and all kinds of guys drooling at her feet.

"OK, that's it. I'm leaving," Sara said, moving to escape the booth.

"Don't let the fact that Colton's here bother you," Gabby said, reaching out to pull her back. "Besides, you said he was really good about everything last Sunday when Nonna got lost."

"Yes, he was. Like a normal compassionate human." She knew she wasn't exactly being fair. He'd seemed genuinely concerned and…kind.

"You're just meeting Ken here for a drink," Kaitlyn said. "He's a nice guy, a microbiologist, and really smart, according to my aunt Millie." Yes, it had taken Kaitlyn's aunt Millie, a medical technologist, to find her a date in this town. That should've said it all. "Then you're going to a nice restaurant."

Sara rolled her eyes. "I'm really grateful to you both for setting this up and supporting me, but I don't need date coaching. I'm thirty years old!" They'd insisted she meet them here so they could help her relax before her date.

"You've been with the same guy for a hundred years," Gabby said. "Trust me, you need date coaching."

Why had she agreed to this? The sound of pool balls breaking made her turn. Colton had just made a shot and happened to glance up at the same time she happened to be looking at him. He did a double take. Oh God. She looked quickly away and nervously pulled up the halter part of her blouse. It was cute, but her boobs just didn't fill it out like Gabby's.

"Stop fidgeting," Gabby said. "Your boobs look great."

Sara took a sip of Gabby's drink. What was he even doing here on a Friday night? Shouldn't he be out revolving some poor unsuspecting female? Oh, why hadn't she insisted on meeting her date anywhere but in Angel Falls?

"You're out of practice," Gabby said. "We just want to go over a few things." She pulled out a list.

"You have a *list*?" How pathetic was she?

"Yes. First, you look very nice." She was wearing the outfit Gabby had told her to wear, a black V-neck sleeveless top that had a halter back and showed some skin and a little black skirt and heels.

"You look terrific," Kaitlyn said. "Girly."

She didn't want to look girly. She wanted to be curled up with a good book on Nonna's couch in her flannel pj's.

"We should be fixing *you* up, Kaitlyn," Sara said. If only to get Kaitlyn's mind off Rafe.

"Don't try to distract us," Gabby said. "Rule number one. Don't talk about work."

Sara frowned. "This guy is a doctor too, right? Maybe he won't mind that."

"Don't do it," Kaitlyn said. "Show him you've got other interests." She paused. "You *do* have interests outside of work, don't you?"

Sara swallowed hard. She used to—but lately? Hmmm.

"What shows have you binge watched lately?" Gabby asked.

"Seen any movies?" Kaitlyn asked.

"What's the last book you've read?"

"Volunteer work. Done any of that?"

Sara bit down on her lip. "Um, I've been busy?" she said.

Her friends stared at her.

"All right, I haven't been that busy. I guess I mostly did what Tagg wanted. And this past year...was hard. I was a little off balance." She had managed to watch all ten seasons of *Friends*. Did that count?

"OK," Gabby said. "You're going to have to make some stuff up until you get a life."

"At least she got her nails done today," Kaitlyn said. "That's a start."

Sara looked at her nails. They were a shiny dark maroon. She had to admit they were pretty. "Look, you guys," she said. "I just want you to know how much I appreciate this. I really want to start over with a fresh slate. Give people other things to talk about than my sad past, you know what I mean?"

"That's exactly what we're going to help you to do. Don't forget to sit up straight. Good posture. Think sexy." Gabby rattled off more items from her list.

Sara missed her comfy scrubs and beloved Danskos. She was worried that her skirt was too short and her heels were a little on the slutty side. But when Gabby telegraphed her the evil eye, she threw her shoulders back and sat up straight just to get her off her case.

"The important thing is to be relaxed. And show him you've got a great sense of humor," Kaitlyn said. "Don't forget to smile. And let's order you a glass of wine while you're waiting. We'll celebrate your making it through your first week." Kaitlyn signaled the waiter while Sara racked her brain to think of a humorous anecdote she could relay in a relaxed, smiling way.

The last funny thing had happened today in the office when her father got down on the floor of the waiting room to read a story to a toddler while his mom was with Sara for her annual gynecologic exam. Sara walked past the waiting room to see her dad and the toddler eating cookies and leafing through a picture book. Her dad was unconventional and sometimes old-fashioned, but he was a great doctor. But that didn't seem like the kind of story that would exactly have a new date rolling on the floor.

Oh God, she was out of practice and in trouble. Panic welled up to lodge in her throat. Her hands felt cold and clammy. She choked down a few sips of wine. Not much help. She hadn't had a new boyfriend since she was *eighteen*. That was almost thirteen years ago! She didn't even remember what to say on a first date— the last time it had been things like "Algebra sucks" and "I hope I pass my driver's test."

Gabby glanced at her watch. "Rachel's picking Nonna up from the senior center, so I've got to go. I've got Nonna covered tonight. Just have fun. Let loose a little. Everything will be fine."

"Don't do anything I wouldn't do," Kaitlyn said, squeezing Sara's arm.

Gabby kissed her cheek. "See ya later," she said with a wink.

OK, there was no reason to panic. Sara fiddled with the stem of her wineglass. It was just a date. She could handle it. And she would get herself a life. Her friends were right, she spent too much time working. Now that she was out of residency, she'd have time to do the things she used to enjoy. Funny she couldn't quite remember what those were. When she was dating Tagg, they used to see artsy films, go to lacrosse games, have dinner at expensive restaurants. She'd gone along with what he wanted. Where had she lost herself in the process?

She must've been deep in thought, because she looked up to suddenly find Colton standing next to her booth. "Hey, Red. What brings you here tonight?" he asked, leaning casually on his pool stick. He took in her sexy black top, her nails, her makeup.

Sara felt a hot blush creep into her cheeks.

"I have a date," she said.

"Is that right?" The corner of his mouth twitched a little. "Funny, because this restaurant is only rated four stars, not five."

"I'm sure it'll be just fine."

"Well, I'm glad to see you can let your hair down. A bit of advice—just be sure not to scare the guy with a bunch of talk about work. I know you probably think it's a turn-on, but...not so much."

He was still needling her, just like back in the day, when he'd teased her mercilessly. What was his deal, anyway? "Colton, why don't you just go back there and play pool like you've been doing every Friday night since high school? Geez." Apparently the nice cop who'd been kind to her grandmother had left town.

Suddenly a teenager with a crew cut barreled into Colton, wrapping his arms around him. It was Stevie Cox, one of her Down syndrome patients, whom she'd just seen in the office that morning. "Hi, Chief!" he said exuberantly. "Are you ready to play Ping-Pong with us? I'm going to win tonight." Stevie looked around and saw Sara. Pointing at her, he said, "She's my doctor. Hi, Dr. Sara."

Before she could respond, he engulfed her in a Stevie-size hug too. Looking over his shoulders, she saw a group of gangly teenage boys gathering near the pool tables.

"I didn't know you played Ping-Pong," she said to Stevie.

"I'm really good at it too. I'm going to beat Chief. Right, Colton?"

"Oh, I don't know about that, Steve. I feel pretty lucky tonight." Colton rotated his arm at the shoulder like he was seriously warming it up and smiled.

And that smile. Sincere, not laced with sarcasm— just a simple, honest smile. And you know what? Seeing it wrecked her, down to her toes. It showed the countenance of a decent man. A man capable of spending time hanging out with teenage boys who probably needed a good influence, and it was in sharp contrast to the smart-mouthed wise guy he seemed to reserve only for her.

"The guys are waiting," Stevie said, pointing a thumb toward the back.

"Why don't you start warming up?" Colton said. "I'll be right over."

"OK. I'll tell everybody you're coming." Stevie turned to Sara before taking off. "Bye, Dr. Sara!"

"Bye, Stevie," she said. "Have fun."

"See ya around, Red," Colton said to Sara, turning to go himself. "Gotta get back to my lame Friday night. Enjoy your date."

That was it? Before she knew what she was doing, she got up from the booth and followed him a few feet. "Look. I—I'm sorry I made fun of you." He stopped in his tracks. "But you don't always have to be so insulting."

He turned back to her slowly. "How am I insulting?" His stare burned a hole through her.

She swallowed. "You treat me like I'm...a snob. Unable to let loose. Like I'm...frigid. And you seem to thrive on making me think you're a jerk until I suddenly find out you're...not. I was wrong about you. Maybe you're wrong about me too." Oh, why had she even bothered going after him? What was the point?

His gaze drifted downward, to the hem of her short skirt, to her bare legs and heels, then swept back up to her face. The intensity of the look he shot her made her suck in a quick breath. A memory, jogged into the present, suddenly hit her full force. He'd kissed her once, long ago. Back in college, during the one and only time she and Tagg had broken up.

She squeezed her eyes shut, not wanting to remember, but the memory surfaced anyway.

Spring of freshman year, they'd shared a ride home from school—he'd driven, and for the first time things had been...different. For one thing, Tagg wasn't with them, and his absence seemed to have unleashed a completely different Colton.

They'd laughed and joked and actually talked for the first time. She'd ended up going with him that evening to his sister's dance recital, where she'd sat between him and Cookie. It was odd to see him act fun and teasing to Cookie, and be a loving and supportive brother to seven-year-old Hannah. And it was clear by Hannah's adoring looks that he was the moon and the stars to her.

Sara begged off before the family pictures. She was

glad to leave the stuffy auditorium and clear her head of thoughts she shouldn't be having. With that dark, too-long hair hanging over his collar and falling adorably over his forehead, Colton was handsome in a dangerous way. *Too* handsome.

Besides, she was still upset over the breakup with Tagg. After over a year of dating, she still hadn't slept with him. Oh, they'd done plenty of other stuff, but as for sex—real sex—she'd held off. And he was getting upset with her. She didn't know why she was so hesitant—she loved him. She'd known him a long time. But something held her back. Maybe it was that falling-in-love feeling that she missed, which had faded since the time he'd first noticed her, the first boy who thought she was pretty and appreciated her smarts and ambition.

But those feelings weren't supposed to last, were they? What was important was the fact that they had similar interests, similar goals and backgrounds. That was the stuff that made for a lasting relationship, right?

But Tagg was getting irritated, frustrated. Looking at other girls. And they'd broken up. *Fine*, she'd said. *Go date someone else.*

She'd gotten a quarter of a block away from the high school auditorium when she heard steps beating on the pavement.

"Hey," Colton said, catching up with her, barely out of breath, "how about some company?"

Her pulse skipped again at the sight of him. Tall, just as recklessly teen-idol handsome, yet...different. Edgier. And very, very appealing.

It was a gorgeous spring evening, unseasonably warm. It had rained earlier, so the smell of rain on top of growing things and spring blossoms was heady and fresh. Tiny pink petals and helicopters from the maple trees were stuck to the pavement as they walked along the old uneven sidewalks. The clouds were clearing, revealing a big yellow three-quarters-full moon, like a big peach with a bite out of it.

Soon they approached the bridge, the showcase of the main street of town. At its entrance was a large brass sculpture of two angels leaning toward one another so that their bodies and arms together formed a heart. An endless photo opportunity for people who spent the day in town shopping, or came for one of the art shows or programs on the green below the bridge, or to attend the local theater or a speaker program at the popular independent bookstore downtown.

Colton slowed his pace at the center of the bridge. Old-fashioned iron streetlamps flanked its sides. In summer the city hung baskets of flowers from them, but now, in early spring, they were bare. He fingered the decorative iron safety railing that rose up from the concrete. There were three padlocks attached to one of the iron posts. They had names written on them in permanent marker: Jon and Allison, Christopher and Heather, Matthew and Sigrid.

"People are always doing weird shit like that," he said.

"What do you mean?"

"They hook locks all over the bridge, then the fire department saws them off and tosses them."

"Why don't they just let them be? It's a cute idea."

"In Paris they had to saw all the locks off because they weighed more than forty-five tons. They made the bridge too heavy. Love is dangerous," he said. Then he looked at her.

Oh God, *he* was dangerous. The shadows of the setting sun brought out the strong lines of his face—his square jaw, his strong cheekbones. She'd always thought his looks were raw in a hard, mean way, but lately...lately he seemed different. Softer. Gentler.

"And then there's the stuff they throw into the river," Colton said, curling his fingers around the rails and leaning over.

"You mean like coins?"

He laughed. "When I worked for the police department last summer, I had to put on a diving suit and scoop them all out. Three hundred fifty dollars' worth. But you wouldn't believe the other stuff I found down there."

"Like what?"

"Boots. A stuffed animal. A muddy wedding dress. But the best thing was a time capsule."

"What was in it?"

"A love letter."

"No!"

"To a lost love. Someone who died fifty years earlier. People think this angel stuff is magic."

"Angel Falls needs a museum."

"You could be the curator. Every year you can dive in and find new exhibits."

"Ha ha. Very funny."

"That would be a different job."

"Well, I guess I've always been a little different." Oh God, she'd said that out loud. *How dumb.*

"That's a good thing," he was quick to say.

OK, now she felt like she was living in an alternate universe. "Colton, I'm surprised you'd say that. Because for as long as I can remember, you've been giving me shit for just about everything."

"I used to think you were spoiled. That you grew up having everything you wanted, didn't have to struggle for things."

She knew his father had died on the police force in Chicago. The rumor was that his mother had drunk herself to death, but who knew. He never talked about that.

"Do you want me to apologize for my family?"

"No." He'd turned and was staring at her. A slow steady hum buzzed through her limbs like an electrical current, making her weak and unsteady. All her senses were telling her to flee, but she couldn't seem to move, so she just stood there and stared back at him.

"I was an idiot in high school," he said.

His gaze dropped to her lips. Wait—was he going to—oh no.

"For what it's worth, I don't think you're an idiot now." Her voice sounded funny. Hoarse. A whisper.

He turned back to the falls. The cheery sound of water splashed in the background, like nothing was amiss. Like Colton Walker hadn't just apologized.

"What will you do—after college?" he asked.

"Go to med school, hopefully. And after that...I don't know."

"You could go anywhere. Do anything you want."

"So could you."

He shook his head. "My knee ruined any chance of that."

"I'm sorry." She was sorry. What else could she say?

He tossed her a brief glance. To see if she meant it? But then he was back to looking at the water. "Don't be. I'll be coming back to take care of my grandma and Hannah. Maybe on the police force. If I can time it right and get a job in town, that is."

He had burdens she couldn't even fathom. And he was right, her freedom was limitless compared to his. She'd once thought he was shallow, but she was coming to understand things were far more complex.

"So I guess I'll be a townie forever."

"I love our town. That's not necessarily a bad thing."

She looked down at the falls too but suddenly felt his gaze on her, intense and as palpable as a touch.

Then he leaned over and kissed her. His lips were soft and careful on hers, the pressure gentle but steady. That simple, chaste kiss made her heart squeeze, her breath catch. The world spun dizzily as her knees threatened to collapse beneath her, making her grasp his arms to steady herself.

Colton pulled back, an unspoken question in his eyes. She answered it by standing on tiptoe, curling her hand around his neck, and kissing him back, her lips moving against his, feeling the softness of his mouth, the contrasting rasp of stubble. He cupped her face in his hand, tangled his fingers in her hair, and tugged her against his hard body.

She went hot and cold. A noise squeaked out from her throat. She opened to him, their tongues tangling together, their mouths fitting together perfectly. That kiss, it was the most erotic thing she'd ever experienced. The way his mouth moved over hers, the way he held her tight against him, the way she could feel he trembled too.

He tasted...wonderful. He smelled like plain soap and leftover sunshine from the warm day. And he kissed like...like no one had ever kissed her before. Like she'd imagined being kissed in a dream.

Suddenly there was a flashlight shining on them, even though the sun hadn't yet set. The first thing Sara thought was, *What if it's the cops?* Then her family would know, Tagg would know...

Tagg. Oh, what was she doing? She'd forgotten all about him. About *them.*

The flashlight belonged to old Mrs. Mulligan, who was walking her dachshund Georgie.

"Oh, just look at you two kids," she said. "So cute. How about a picture?"

That was the thing. Everyone was always taking pictures in front of the angels. Couples especially. Rumor had it that if you had your picture taken there and tossed money into the water, your love would last forever.

"For good luck," she said.

Surprisingly, Colton got ready to pose. "Thanks, Mrs. M.," he said.

The old lady snapped the picture while Colton held on to Sara's waist, her panic climbing the mercury scale, high and higher.

Mrs. Mulligan moved on, Colton let go. He still had that dreamy look in his eyes, like he would've been perfectly happy to get back to whatever it was they were doing before they were interrupted.

"I-I have to go," she said. Guilt tore at her conscience.

He held her back with his arm. "Wait." His gaze locked on to her like a tractor beam, forcing her to stare into the pure, deep blue of his eyes. "Come with me to the art museum next Friday. They always have music in the courtyard. It'll be a nice break from studying for exams."

She was speechless. She should say no, but the words wouldn't form.

"Give me your phone."

She did, God knew why, and he punched in his number. "Promise me you'll think about it."

"Colton," she said, and it was as if she'd said his name for the first time.

He raised his head. He had a look on his face. Hopeful. Anticipatory.

"OK," she found herself saying. "I'll do it. I'll see you Friday."

He broke into a smile. Held her hand and insisted on walking her home. But not before he reached into his pocket and tossed some coins into the falls.

Guilt and confusion warred within her. As well as shock that Colton Walker had given her the most amazing kiss of her life. He was so different from the cool, standoffish persona he projected so well. She'd had him pegged all wrong.

In the back of the restaurant, the sound of kids cheering jolted Sara back to reality. Stevie had won a point or a game, she wasn't sure which, but he was holding up two Ping-Pong paddles with a triumphant expression on his face while the other boys slapped him on the back.

Her date with Colton so long ago had never happened because he'd stood her up. When she'd sought him out at his dorm room, he'd answered the door shirtless, female laughter echoing in the background. At that moment she'd known everything had been a joke. All these years later, that thought *still* made her sick to her stomach. She'd learned unequivocally from that experience that Colton couldn't be trusted, and he'd proven over and over through the years that that was the case.

She warned herself to heed that advice now. Colton stood there, not speaking, that same blue gaze drilling through her with an intensity that caused gooseflesh to rise on her arms. She wasn't sure if she'd stunned him by her confrontation or if he simply intended not to say anything. Just as he opened his mouth to finally speak, a tall, thin man appeared at her side.

"Are you Sara Langdon? I'm Ken. Dr. Ken Houseman, from the microbiology lab at the hospital. I'm sorry I was running a bit late. Lots going on at work, you know?" He glanced at Colton. "Am I interrupting something?"

"No. Not at all," Colton said, still staring. "See you

around, Doctors." He gave Sara a little salute and walked back to join the kids.

Her date sat down across from her and ordered a scotch. She downed the rest of her wine. It was difficult to concentrate on the small talk he was making. "You're Ivy League trained, aren't you? So am I. Princeton. I study mutant bacteria. Ones that aren't susceptible to any antibiotics. I always wonder what would happen if we accidentally poured some down the sewer and started a killer epidemic, you know?"

Sara tried to focus on what he was saying, but frankly, she wasn't into killer germs or the creepy way he'd just casually mentioned the possibility of a deadly epidemic. Honestly, he could've announced he'd found a cure for cancer for all she would've cared. Out of the corner of her eye, she watched Colton play Ping-Pong, laughing and joking with the boys.

Thing was, she was seeing a completely different side to Colton. First with her grandmother, and now with these boys. Heck, even in the way he'd treated her when she was distraught the other day. But every time they had an opportunity to get closer, he seemed to draw a line in the sand, doing something to push her away.

Chapter 8

♥

At eleven a.m. the next Friday, Colton pulled up in Cookie's driveway. This was Cookie's morning to volunteer at the Salvation Army store downtown, and he knew Hannah wasn't scheduled to work until the dinner shift today, so he was hoping she'd be home...sort of. Meaning he needed to talk with her but was dreading it about as much as a testicular exam.

He walked into the kitchen to find her sitting at the breakfast bar in a T-shirt and pj bottoms, her long hair pulled up in that complicated messy bun only girls knew how to do with a few flicks of the wrist and a rubber band. She was doing something on her phone and eating a bowl of Cap'n Crunch, her favorite cereal since she was three.

Dammit, he *wished* she were three. Then he wouldn't have to have this discussion with her. "Do you have something you want to tell me?" he asked, instantly realizing that he'd started this off all wrong. He hated being a quasi parent. He didn't know what the hell he was doing.

"Good morning?" She had no makeup on, and she looked so young and innocent his stomach hurt.

He crossed his arms, more to make himself believe he was tough than because he felt that way. "Anything else?"

"No, Colton, nothing else. I'm just a normal teenage girl trying to lead a normal teenage life, if my brother would just get off my case." She let go of her spoon, which clattered against the side of her cereal bowl. He'd done it now, managed to irritate her with two sentences. Fuck.

"I had coffee with Lou this morning."

She bit her cuticle, her usual tell, and glanced at her phone again, which was buzzing with texts from her million friends. So, she *was* a little nervous about what he was about to say.

"I haven't missed a shift since I started working there. What's the problem?"

"You were there past midnight last Saturday night."

"I'm allowed to go out with my friends."

"Not this particular friend."

Her phone dropped, and she bent to pick it up. When she popped her head up again, he could tell she was biting the insides of her cheeks, but still she didn't say anything.

She looked so much like their mother. Slight build, pretty heart-shaped face. But where their mother had had blue eyes like Colton, Hannah had big hazel eyes that he'd always thought were honest with him. Until now. Where his mother had been flighty, whimsical, and anxious, Hannah was in general calm and even-keeled.

But she had her moments. Moments that made him worry. He didn't want her going down the same pathway as their mother. It was his job to ensure that. But first he'd have to stop pissing her off as soon as he walked through the door.

He tried a different tack, sitting down across from her on a stool. It was her turn to cross her arms and give him the evil eye. "Why didn't you tell me you were seeing Aiden?"

"It was a little hard considering the first words out of your mouth about him were *Stay away*."

Colton sighed. "I said that for a reason. The guy has a troubled past. His family life sucks. He's already been in trouble once with the law."

"But you're trying to help him. He deserves a chance, Colton."

Suddenly a weird thing happened. Colt heard Sara's voice in his head. He saw an image of her in Lou's the other night when she'd run after him. *I was wrong about you. Maybe you're wrong about me too.*

Maybe he did tend to leap to conclusions about people. But this kid…He was bad news. He didn't want Aiden anywhere near his sister.

"Look, Hannah. You're bright and smart and beautiful. Your future is in front of you, and it's a great one. I don't want anything to derail that, do you understand?"

He had to say things that he did not want to say. That were his obligation to say. But the back of his neck and his palms were starting to sweat. He wanted her to have a good life. A *great* life. He didn't want her to get dragged down like their mother after his father died—

with bad men, one after another. Hannah was compassionate like their mother. She saw the best in people. That had been part of their mother's downfall. She'd trusted people who didn't deserve her trust.

He couldn't lose Hannah like they'd lost their mother. He *had* to make sure she made the right choices. But he was at a complete loss as to how to do that.

Hannah looked at him as if he were speaking Greek. As if he were the most clueless person on the planet.

He decided to try one more time. "The people you hang out with impact your life and your future. You've got to pick your friends wisely. You can't let yourself get dragged down by other people's problems."

Aiden's family was a train wreck. He'd had a terrible childhood. Colton had no idea how that neglect and chaos had imprinted itself upon his personality, but with everything he saw daily, he could believe it had had some bad effects. Effects he did not want his sister hanging around.

"Look," Colton said. "Lou saw you and Aiden making out, and from the looks of it, you two were just getting started."

Hannah glared at him like he'd just crawled out of a sewer. But he held his ground. If, God forbid, Hannah and Aiden were having sex, he needed to make sure that she was protected against an unplanned pregnancy. Hannah wasn't saying a thing, but she didn't have to—her hostile stare said it all. He opened his mouth to say something, but nothing came out. "Don't have sex" didn't sound like a good opening. Or the more gentle

"Abstinence is important," or the more blunt "Are you having sex?"

"Are we done here?" Hannah asked, sliding off the bar stool and grabbing her phone. "Because I have to take a shower before work."

"We're done," he said, putting up his arms in surrender.

That went well. They were done, for now, but he knew he had to do something to make sure Hannah was safe. He wasn't about to let her future get screwed up or her choices get taken away like his had been.

* * *

Colton walked into the Bean around noon, and the first thing he saw was Sara with her forehead pressed against the glass bakery cabinet, rolling her head back and forth.

"Take a deep breath," Kaitlyn said, working the espresso machine. "Your coffee'll be ready in a sec. Breathe."

"Remind me why I came back here again."

Kaitlyn took a rag and wiped down the counter. "Because your nonna needs you. She's what matters the most."

"My father is so set in his ways. He doesn't want any change. He watches over me like I'm a med student and questions every test I order. And every patient but one this morning mentioned my wedding. Or lack of one, that is."

"Which one didn't?"

"His name was James Pollard, and he was a new-born. And his mom was too nervous about bringing him in to care about my love life. But everyone else did."

Colton edged a little closer to the door. He didn't want to open it or the bell would go off and out him for sure.

"Don't make me go back there," Sara said.

"Sara," Kaitlyn said, "this is only your second week. It's a big adjustment for everyone. Give it some time. A little bit of caffeine and you'll feel like a million bucks."

"Now I know why my father didn't have a partner all these years. He doesn't *want* a partner. He doesn't want an interloper in his practice."

"Your dad's got to know you're an awesome doctor." Kaitlyn banged something around behind the counter that indicated she was making some kind of fancy drink. "You even got that fancy award last year for being the most outstanding resident before you grad-uated. What was that called again? The Doppelganger Award or something?"

"Hopplebauer Award. And it doesn't matter. No award in the world can prove my worth to my father."

"So melodramatic," Kaitlyn said. She looked over Sara's shoulder. "Oh, hi, Colton," Kaitlyn said brightly, outing him for good. "Your usual?"

Sara's head bolted upright.

"The usual's great, thanks," he said. No use pretend-ing he hadn't just heard everything. He turned to Sara. "Rough morning?"

"Go on. Just...say it," she said. "Hit me with it."

"With what?"

"Some snide remark. Some snippy comment. Remind me of all my faults and inadequacies. I'm ready."

"I was just going to say that you're a good doctor and...and it's going to be OK."

"No advice? Platitudes? An I-told-you-so or a You-better-go-back-to-your-Ivy-League-world?"

He wasn't going to do that. Or do something to get her spine prickled, like ask her how that loser date had been last weekend. Because he already knew. Rafe had told him all about the microbiologist and his fascination with killer bacteria.

This time, Colton dug down deep and tried to be something he hadn't been so far. A friend. Call him crazy, but when she'd come after him at Lou's and accused him of being insulting...Well. Maybe she was right. He could tone it down a little.

"Your dad's really respected around here. People say he takes the time to talk to them, unlike all the docs who are watching the clock and try to get in and out like seeing patients is some kind of race. It's just that anyone who's been at a job for that long is going to have certain...ideas that are resistant to change."

"Like ingrown toenails," Kaitlyn said. "Completely embedded."

"Thanks for the gross visual," Sara said.

"Hey, you're the doctor," Kaitlyn said, passing Colton a big cup of coffee with a lid on it. "I was just trying to use an example you can relate to."

Sara threw up her hands. "My dad's still using paper records. And manual blood pressure cuffs. The EKG machine has one strip, like a grocery store cash register receipt. And they might still be killing rabbits for the pregnancy tests for all I know."

Kaitlyn's eyes went wide. "They used to do that?"

"Yeah. In 1960," Sara said.

"Here you go," Kaitlyn said, handing Sara her coffee. "I put an extra shot of espresso in that, by the way."

"I love you," Sara said. Her phone went off with a text, and she set down her cup on the counter to pull it out of her purse. "I have to run. See you later. Thanks for the help. I think." Sara blew Kaitlyn a kiss, gave Colton a quick wave, and left.

Well. The first interaction in a week where she hadn't threatened to kill him. Things were looking up.

"It'll get better," Kaitlyn said, pulling a big tray of freshly iced cinnamon buns off a shelf behind her.

He leaned his arm against the bakery case. "Yeah. New-job problems."

Kaitlyn held out the tray of cinnamon buns. "Actually, I was talking about you, Colty. These are still warm, by the way. Want one?"

The scent of warm cinnamon rolls was already permeating the whole shop, making his mouth water. Colton took one. "If you don't call me that, sure, I'd love one. But I'm not sure I'm following you."

Kaitlyn shrugged. "Any bad blood between you two is none of my business. But don't think I can't see that I-want-to-eat-you-for-breakfast way you look at her. Plus it's getting exhausting pretending I hate you too."

Colton narrowed his eyes. "Why are you suddenly on my side?"

"I happen to know you're a nice guy. Not that you

used to be, though. Of course, Sara hasn't forgotten that."

No, she hadn't. He wasn't the same jerk he'd been in high school, but she still thought he was, and it seemed at times he couldn't help feeding into that. It was just that Sara seemed to be able to push all his buttons. Remind him that he was a small-town cop in the same town where he'd lived for half his life. He didn't have her grand aspirations and dreams—mostly because he'd had an obligation to do what was right, take care of his family. Work to give Hannah the choices he'd never gotten. But it niggled—had he settled?

"Oh, look. It's your lucky day," Kaitlyn said, nudging her head toward the top of the bakery case.

"Why's that?"

"Sara forgot her coffee. And if anyone needs coffee today, it's her, right?"

He took the cup. "I'm going that way anyway. See you around, Kaitlyn."

"Hey, ladies," Colton said a few minutes later, resting his elbows on the windowsill in the Langdons' office and peering at Leonore and Glinda through the glass. "How's it going?" No sign of Sara. Looked like she was already back at work. He should just leave the cup and go, but that perverse part of him that seemed to totally enjoy getting himself into trouble spoke up.

"How's Sara getting along?"

"Oh, hello, Chief," Glinda said, sliding open the window. "Well, she's a sweetheart, always has been. But Doctor's set in his ways. It's hard for him, after working alone all these years."

Leonore pulled off her giant earphones. "Whew-y! That Sara sure talks a lot when she dictates her charts. Lord, my fingers are going to fall off from all this transcribing."

Glinda laughed. "That's because Doctor barely says anything at all, just 'normal exam.'"

"Well, Dr. Sara includes every body part in her physicals. And the tests she orders! I haven't heard of half of 'em!"

Colton smiled. "Sounds like Sara's just what this office needs. Like getting a big gust of fresh air in here."

"Why Chief Walker, are you sweet on her?" Leonore asked.

"Absolutely not." He shoved the coffee cup closer to the window. "Sara forgot this at the Bean. And I'm—um—here to get my stitches out. Sara told me I could just stop by sometime and I've been so busy I keep forgetting. But if now's not a good time—" Oh, hell, what was he doing? He hadn't intended to get his stitches out right now. Guess he'd panicked a little. He certainly didn't want them to think he'd gone out of his way on Sara's account.

Glinda immediately disappeared into the back, then reappeared a minute later to open the door to the waiting room. "Come on back, sweetie. Doctor can see you now. He said no need to wait for Sara. He's got a couple of minutes."

A strange wave of disappointment washed over Colton, which he quickly brushed off as he made his way to an exam room. Had he actually been looking forward to sparring with her over his suture removal?

Her father would be the saner choice. Plus he wouldn't have to worry about getting another shot in the ass.

"Well, hello there, son." Dr. Langdon said, pulling his bifocals down his nose and rolling a stool up to the exam table where Colton sat. "Let's have a look." The older doctor inspected his arm. "Sara did a nice job with these. Everything looks well healed."

"Yes, sir." As the doctor tore open the suture removal kit, Colton asked, "What's it like having your daughter here working with you?" *Why don't you just keep your mouth shut and get your sutures out?* a voice in his head said. He was never good at listening to voices of authority anyway.

"Oh, it's fantastic. I'm so proud of her," Dr. Langdon said as he snipped a suture. "I just fear we may not have her here with us for very long. She's destined for things more prestigious than a family medical practice in a tiny town like ours."

Tiny town. Right. Sara wouldn't be hanging around here for very long, that was for sure. "You ever tell her that—how proud you are of her?"

He paused with his instruments in midair. "Excuse me, son?"

Oh boy, he was really overstepping now, yet he couldn't seem to stop his mouth. "Oh, just that maybe she needs to hear that. I mean, I imagine working with your dad is a great thing, but it can be a little stressful too, especially in the beginning. Everyone has to be a little flexible, which is hard after doing things the same way for so long—and everybody needs to know they're wanted, right?"

Dr. Langdon raised a thick gray brow. "Yes, well, sure. Are you implying that my daughter doesn't feel that she's wanted here?"

"No, sir, I'm not saying that. It's just that I could understand how she might feel you might not want a partner to interfere with your way of doing things."

Dr. Langdon chuckled. "Sara's made a decision I don't necessarily agree with. I respect her wanting to come back home to be with her grandmother, but I disagree with her delaying her fellowship training to do it. She's meant to do greater things than Angel Falls can offer."

The doctor sat back and cleared away his instruments. "There you go, Chief, good as new."

"Thank you." OK, this discussion was done and Colton had clearly overstepped his bounds. Plus Dr. Langdon had just echoed what he'd known all along— Sara wasn't here to stay. This town was just a tiny pit stop in a life full of bigger things. Harvard, Mayo Clinic—who knew what would be next? He jumped down off the table, inspecting his arm. "Oh, I was talking to the firefighters," he said. "We'd like to have a medical person come in and talk to both departments about our protocols for Narcan use during our drug overdose runs. Would you be able to help us out?"

They walked together out of the room, stopping beside the reception area. "I think that might be something Sara would jump at the chance to do."

"Did you just sign me up for something?" Sara asked as she flew by. She halted in her tracks just in front of Colton. "Colton! What are you doing here?"

"He brought your coffee," Leonore said, putting her cup up on the counter. "Wasn't that a sweet gesture?"

"Sweet," Sara said, looking at him with a puzzled expression. She was standing close enough that he could see the light smattering of freckles she'd tried to cover with makeup but hadn't quite succeeded. Her scent wafted over to him, a fresh, light vanilla, like a cupcake straight from the oven. All that wondrous hair of hers was pulled back in a no-nonsense ponytail, which left an expanse of creamy white skin exposed on her neck. Pretty. He had a sudden urge to reach over and place his lips on it.

No, no, no. "You forgot it," he said. "At the coffee shop."

"Oh, thank you." She took a sip and smiled. He must've been an idiot all these years, making her frown instead of flash that smile.

"Your dad took my stitches out," he said, holding out his arm. "All healed." Now he was acting like an idiot. "Anyway, have a nice day."

"Thanks. You too." As Colton turned to leave, he heard Sara ask, "What happened to Larry Crosby, Leonore? I swear he was in the waiting room a minute ago."

"Oh, we were a little backed up, so I told him he could run and get his hair cut, as long as he came back in about a half hour."

Sara's gaze drifted over to his. He caught her incredulous look and worked hard to suppress a chuckle. She grabbed her coffee and took a big swig. When she looked up, her mouth was turned up in the tiniest smile, like they'd just shared a private joke. "Thanks again for the coffee, Colton," she said.

"Hey, no problem," he said. But inside he had a growing feeling that it was.

* * *

Yep, she'd really needed that coffee. And Colton had delivered it, with a smile. Without a gotcha. Yet.

Sara realized she'd been standing near the reception desk, staring at the closed door.

Leonore cleared her throat, making Sara snap to attention.

Glinda inclined her head toward the exam rooms. "I heard Chief Walker in there just now talking to your father. He was *defending* you."

"Defending me?" What on earth…?

"Yeah. He said your dad should tell you how proud he is of you because people need to hear that. Isn't that sweet?"

Sara blanched. What was worse, she wondered, the fact that the staff was eavesdropping on private patient conversations or the fact that Colton had felt a need to intervene with her father? She wasn't going to earn her father's respect by having someone else fight her battles.

And why on earth would Colton suddenly stick up for her, anyway? It was unnatural. Like just now, when he hadn't even drilled her with his usual smart-ass comment. Just grinned that unholy grin and sauntered out. Leaving her with cappuccino and a dumb smile on her face.

"I hate to say it," Leonore said solemnly, "but I think Chief's got a crush on you."

"What?" Sara said. "No way. That's ridiculous."

"Yep," Leonore said. "He brought your coffee. And he didn't even have an appointment to get those stitches out."

"He's like the boy in grade school who pulls the little girl's braids," Glinda said. "She thinks he doesn't like her, but it's just the opposite."

"It had better *not* be the opposite," Sara's father said, suddenly materializing at the counter. "That boy's a good police chief, but he's not marriage material. Now don't we have some patients to see, ladies?"

Sara winced for what felt like the thirtieth time that day. She had enough problems—she could not let runaway speculation about Colton or her personal life be one of them. Grabbing a chart and heading to a room, she was more than happy to get back to work.

Several hours later, she felt a hand on her shoulder— her dad's. "Hey, pumpkin, it's quitting time. You've officially made it through your first two weeks."

Sara looked at the clock. Nearly seven. Seven o'clock! No one here seemed to think an eleven-hour workday was unusual.

"Rachel just called," her dad said. "Gabby's friend Malcolm is in town. She wants us all to meet for dinner at Giuseppe's. Can you come? Say around eight-ish? You can ride with us."

Giuseppe's was the world's most wonderful restaurant, the place where the family often celebrated big events, but Sara was dead on her feet. "I'm going to stop at home," she told her dad. "I'll meet you at the restaurant." She said good night to the ladies and walked out into the golden summer evening. Except her steps didn't walk her toward home.

She couldn't have the ladies in the office gossiping about the possibility of a romance between her and Colton. People would overhear and it would be all around town faster than you could say *happy hour specials at Lou's*. And she didn't want Colton interfering in her business with her father—no matter that he was actually being nice for once, for God's sake.

There was no time like the present to shut this rumor mill down quick. The irony was not lost on her that now that Colton had finally done something nice, she was going to tell him to back off.

Chapter 9

♥

Sara walked into the main room of the tidy white-brick police station where the full-time deputy, Evan Marshall, was talking on the phone. "Chief Walker's off duty now, Mrs. Robertson, but I'm happy to come by. So Mr. Clinton's dog pooped on your lawn again?"

Evan looked up and waved. He was an eager twenty-three-year-old, but to her he still looked like the freckled little kid she used to babysit. Except he never had outgrown that gun fetish of his. He was sitting behind one of three desks and a console with more blinking lights than the starship *Enterprise*. She made out a police radio, two printers, and a big black scanner with red lights scrolling maniacally back and forth.

Just then Colton leaned into the room, stretching his arms over his head on the door frame between the main room and his office and suppressing a yawn. He had dark circles under his eyes. His gray uniform shirt was a little rumpled, and there was a giant grass stain on the thigh of his uniform pants. (How did a person even get a grass stain there?) All of which led her to believe maybe he'd had sort of a not-great day too. Which suddenly made her feel awful about coming here to give him grief about being *nice* to her.

Evan covered the phone receiver with his palm and spoke to Colton. "Louise Robertson's insisting on talking with you."

"Tell her I'll stop by on my way home," Colton said.

"I can take care of this, Chief. It's just dog poop, and you were supposed to be out of here an hour and a half ago."

Colton shook his head. "Harry Clinton needs to step up his game. When's he going to learn that having his dog poop in the yard of the widow he wants to ask out on a date isn't going to get him anywhere?"

He chuckled. That small bit of laughter changed his entire face, took it from simply ho-hum handsome to please-be-the-father-of-my-children devastating. Sara's stomach catapulted. Heat spread through her abdomen, rushed into her cheeks, weakened her knees.

Settle down, ovaries. It was just the Colton Effect. Which was impacting her due to the fact that it had been a year since she'd had any physical contact with a man. So there.

The moment he saw her, his hands dropped from the door frame and he stood up straight, cracking his knuckles—nervously? Nah, Colton Walker didn't do nervous. She was the one who was struggling to keep it together right now.

"Sara, what are you doing here? Is something wrong?" He sounded—concerned.

In fact, he'd sounded concerned a lot lately. Starting when her grandmother got lost and continuing through today at the coffee shop. And again at the office.

A ball of guilt suddenly lodged in her throat.

She swallowed it down. Reminded herself that he was the same person who'd sat in speech class sophomore year during her inspirational speech on finding your passion and mimicked everything she'd said; who'd been kissing Stacey Prescott in the hallway and said to Sara, who must've been staring, "Like what you see, Langdon?" And laughed. Who'd kissed her one time—*once*—and never spoken of it again. And literally looked at her in annoyance and disgust for years afterward.

Why was she even thinking about that now?

She had to get things straight with him if they were going to coexist in the same town. She wasn't going to back down now.

"No, I just—I wondered if we could have a word in private?" she said.

"Sure," he said, waving a hand toward his office.

She walked in, and what she saw surprised her. He'd clearly inherited Chief McGregor's massive glass-topped desk, and it was covered with stacks of papers. But in the deep windowsill behind the desk there were…plants. A philodendron climbing all around the window frame and headed to a nearby bookshelf. Palms and other houseplants and even a cactus.

A blue-and-black-striped rug sat tidily under his

desk and the walls were painted a light blue. A cluster
of framed photos hung on the wall near the desk, including one of Chief McGregor linking arms with three
smiling cop buddies, arms around each other's shoulders. A German shepherd lying in a dog bed in the
corner perked up his ears as soon as she walked in.

"Police dog?" she asked.

He nodded. "Champ's working," he said, his mouth
lifting at the corners.

"I see." She nodded as the dog trotted over for affection. "Can I—pet him?" The dog nudged his nose
against her palm until she did, taking that decision off
the table.

"Actually, he fell a little short of passing the K9 exams as a puppy," Colton said. "He's my dog now. I
bring him to work with me most days."

"You're a handsome boy," Sara said as she scratched
behind the dog's dark ears. The dog sniffed her hair and
licked her face. "And ferocious, I see." She took a seat in
one of the simple navy upholstered chairs on the other
side of his desk. "Look, I came here to get something
straight between us. Leonore overheard what you said
to my dad this afternoon about—about maybe being a
little more—flexible—and I—maybe you were trying to
help, but…"

Well, she was quite articulate, wasn't she? She
thought of all those years when Colton had definitely
not ever tried to help her. Why on earth he'd be interested in doing so now she couldn't fathom. The Colton
Walker she'd seen over the past two weeks seemed like
someone she'd never met before.

She tried again. "I appreciate what you were trying to do, but I have to handle my dad on my own. If it looks like I need help to do that, I'll never gain anyone's respect. Plus Leonore and Glinda are convinced you're sweet on me, and that is not only insane but the last thing I need to contend with in the office—or in town, because if that gets around, neither of us will have any peace."

When she'd been a teenager with braces and pimples, she'd had no words. She'd been completely and utterly tongue-tied in front of him, intimidated by both his good looks and by whatever mean things he could utter. But now the playing field between them had been leveled. And Tagg was no longer in the middle. It was just the two of them.

A peculiar feeling slid through her. That they were both different people now. That this was a completely different ball game, and she wasn't sure of the rules.

He leaned forward a little. A desk lamp was on, shining a blue-white beam over all the paperwork and the dozen sticky notes marching in a neat row down his desk. It also highlighted his great bone structure— his strong jaw, that five o'clock shadow already well on its way to becoming a full beard. He stared at her, mulling over his reply.

"For what it's worth, *I* respect you." He paused to let that sink in. "Since I've been chief, I've become a problem solver. It's what I do. I was just trying to be helpful. I'm sorry if I did the wrong thing." He tapped a pencil on his desk, which worked his forearm muscles, which were . . . impressive. Plus he was tanned. And he had nice hands. He used to have great hair too, but it was short now, no nonsense. Like he'd shaved all his vanity off.

Sara sucked in a breath. That was it? She'd expected...resistance. Anger. At least sarcasm. But an apology?

She was completely thrown.

"Another thing, Red, I know you're eager to get your dad's office up to snuff and running efficiently but you might just want to...relax a little. This isn't Columbia. Not that some things don't need changing around here but big adjustments take time, you know what I mean? Just my two cents." He didn't say it in a know-it-all way. In fact, he sounded concerned. Like a friend. Except the feelings coursing around inside her right now weren't exactly giving off a friends vibe.

"I get it. Rome wasn't built in a day and all that." She cringed. God, could she babble any worse?

He leaned back in his chair. "I have something else to ask you too, while you're here."

"OK, what is it?" He seemed so calm. When it felt like a flock of geese had suddenly overtaken her stomach.

"It's my sister. She needs a physical before she starts college."

A simple enough request. "Oh, sure, of course. There's still time to get her scheduled for that."

He cleared his throat. "I want to make sure she has...all the facts. Before she goes off to school."

"Facts?" What he was really asking suddenly dawned. He wanted her to make sure Hannah was informed about sex. "Oh, *facts*. Of course. Sure, I'd be happy to see Hannah. Just have her call the office."

"Great. Thanks. Anything else we have to talk about?"

He stood and walked around his desk until he was mere feet away. She stood too, but she still had to look up—way up—to see him, a definite disadvantage. And God, he was tall. Even though he was a little disheveled at the end of the day, he looked devastatingly handsome. And—something she'd never noticed before—he had beautiful, full lips. Plus he smelled good, a light, barely there scent that reminded her of the woods after a rain. She took a step back, trying to escape his pheromone field, but he moved a step closer, spearing her with that deep-blue gaze. She opened her mouth to speak, but the words got stuck somewhere. Hot and cold flushed through her, and her heart suddenly felt like it was trying to beat itself right out of her chest. "Colton, I—"

That was all she managed. His mouth turned up in the slightest quirk. He was amused! Oh God, who would've known a simple apology could be so...arousing?

She shook her head. Swallowed hard and backed up with a step so big she knocked into one of the navy chairs.

How could she allow herself to be so flummoxed over him? It suddenly dawned on her that maybe all his nice behavior was a reaction to something else—his behavior last year. The bachelor party. "Look, you don't have to make up for—"

He frowned. "For what?"

All those years of torment? Culminating in that awful bachelor party that got so, so out of control? Maybe his trying to help her out today had been a result of his guilt over that.

"For the past."

His eyes narrowed a little. "What about the past?" he asked.

"Maybe you're trying to help me because you feel bad about things that have happened."

"What are you talking about?" He looked completely clueless.

She sighed. Might as well come out with it. "The bachelor party."

"Wait a minute." He stepped back, almost as if startled. "You think I'm being nice to you because I feel bad about the bachelor party?"

Sara put her hands up in defense. "I don't blame you for what happened. But maybe you're trying to make up for that by trying to...help me."

"I think you *do* blame me for what happened, if you think I'm trying to make up for something."

"Well, things clearly got out of control. And maybe you feel guilty for that." She slid her gaze over to his, which was lit up with anger.

"Guilty? You think I feel guilty for Tagg acting like an idiot? Maybe you need to ask him what happened instead of always assuming the worst about me."

Fine. Except Tagg, that bastard, had never had the courage to explain his behavior. He'd just done this desperate, severing act to get out of their marriage. What other explanation did she really need? So Colton was technically right, Tagg was the idiot. Except now

Colton was pissed, and he wasn't going to tell her anything either. And maybe Tagg was a nitwit, but it sure seemed that Colton was still loyal to him. "Looks like you and I are back to square one, Chief Walker." Sara turned to go, but Colton held her back.

"No. No, we're not. I want you to know." He took a deep breath, and she had no idea what he could possibly say next. "I took Tagg home after the bachelor party and put him to bed. That's how I left him. I should've stayed with him. Made sure he was OK. Made sure *you'd* be OK. I am sorry for that. And I never hired Val. She came with the cake. I had no idea."

Her eyes filled with tears, even though she willed them not to. Took Tagg home? Put him to bed? And he'd still found Val. Sara closed her eyes. This shouldn't be painful anymore, but the hard truth always was.

"I'm sorry, Sara."

"You're right," she said, "I did assume the worst about you. I didn't think you took anything seriously. I figured you sat by and watched things get out of control."

"I should've cut him off. I wish I would have."

She shook her head. "It wasn't a bachelor party mistake. He didn't want to marry me. I knew as much. But thank you for telling me the truth." She took a big breath and swiped at her eyes. "I'm late for dinner out with my family. I'd better be going." She had no idea what time it was; all she knew was she had to get out of there.

"Let me give you a ride home."

She shrugged away from his touch. "No, I—walking

will be good, thanks." Which made no sense if she was really late. She headed for the door, and frankly, she couldn't get out of there fast enough.

* * *

"How's work going, sweetheart?" Rachel asked as the family settled around a large table on the patio at Giuseppe's, where Sara's family celebrated every graduation, birthday, and family event. Tagg and Sara had announced their engagement here, right on this very patio under the lovely wooden arbor covered with grapevines. The fact that he'd stood up to make a toast and smacked his head on a low-hanging branch should have been a sign that things would not go well for them.

Sara took a sip of her wine. "It's going great," she said. "Thanks for asking."

Sara had learned long ago with Rachel to simply say things were just fine. While Rachel was kind, and they always got along, their relationship had never really deepened into something more. Maybe because of the simple fact that Rachel was not her mother. By the time her dad remarried, Sara was eighteen, and she and her sisters had become a tight network of support, together mothering Rafe. They'd learned not to need a mother anymore.

"Oh, that's wonderful," Rachel said with her usual enthusiasm. "Your dad is so thrilled to have you in the office." And did she mention that Rachel also tended to speak for her father?

"We had a pretty good day today, eh, Dad?" She elbowed her dad playfully.

Sara decided to make the best of the evening. She was with family (except for Rafe, who was working, and Nonna, who was at her twice-monthly bingo night with her girlfriends), and it was a gorgeous night, the summer evening sweet smelling and warm, flowers overflowing from boxes rimming the patio, and tiny white lights twinkling everywhere.

Funny, though. She wasn't really fretting about all the office issues she wanted to work on that had been at the forefront of her mind. Instead she had an image stuck in her mind of Colton in his cop uniform, bending down to pet his dog. That navy uniform showing off those baby blues, that muscle peeking out from his sleeves, those competent-looking hands.

Dear God, he'd taken Tagg home and put him to bed and still felt guilty he hadn't done more. Yet she'd accused him of inciting things, riling things up. She'd thought the worst of him.

She rubbed her chest. It suddenly felt funny in there. Oh, Rachel was looking at her strangely. Probably wondering why she was staring off into space.

"Rachel, how's the shop lately?" Sara asked. "One of these days we'll have to have lunch." If there was ever time for lunch. By noon the office was already backlogged, and today, like most days, she and her dad had both worked straight through the lunch hour.

"Oh, I'd love that. The shop is great. In fact, it's going to be featured in the Lifestyle section of the *Plain*

Dealer next month. Because of my trip to Italy and all the Renaissance antiques I brought back."

"That's really cool, Rach," her sister Evie said. "I'm glad the shop's doing so well." She looked at Joe. "I love being home with the kids, but I miss working sometimes." The fact that the rent on her studio at the art space had gone up too high for her to justify the expense of a sitter had factored into her decision to stay home with the kids, but Sara knew Evie really missed her pottery wheel.

Joe grabbed his wife's hand. "I was thinking maybe we should turn the garage into a little studio for you."

"A kiln is expensive," she said.

"You should do it, Evie," Sara said. "You're so talented. Plus it would be good stress relief." Evie threw everything she had into being an amazing mom, and Sara knew she loved being home with her kids. But she'd really loved being an artist too.

"I'm plenty busy with the kids right now, but…maybe." She smiled at her husband and he winked back. Aww. They always were the perfect couple.

Which reminded her. "Don't forget I'm babysitting next week for the Fourth," Sara said.

"Oh, thank you," Evie said. "The kids are already getting excited for the fireworks."

"I am too."

"OK, just so you know, Michael sometimes pees his pants when he gets excited, so nothing too thrilling."

"Gotcha," she said. Now that she was back home, she was really looking forward to being able to spend more time with her niece and nephew. She couldn't wait to spoil them rotten.

Just then Gabby arrived with Malcolm, who looked like he just stepped off the cover of a Billionaire romance novel. Sara smiled politely and greeted them. It was obviously important to Gabby that he meet the family, so Sara owed it to her sister to try and keep an open mind.

"You all remember Malcolm, right?" Gabby said. "He's a partner at his hedge fund group now."

It was no accident Gabby shot a look at their father. That Malcolm was a hedge fund manager was sure to press a couple of acceptable-spouse buttons in their father's mind. Seemed Sara wasn't the only one of them to seek their father's approval.

"Tell us, son, what kinds of funds do you manage?" her dad asked as he got up and leaned across the table to shake Malcolm's hand.

"Only the lucrative kind, sir," Malcolm said, slicking his hair back in a gesture that bespoke vanity. "I work for Wernor and Vescott downtown. We're doing quite well. So rest assured, I can keep Gabriella in the style to which she's accustomed."

Sara took another sip of her wine. What the hell did that mean? Her sister made a great income on her own. Plus she hung out in sweats and flip-flops. She wasn't "accustomed" to a life of wealth or leisure. Sara had forgotten a lot about Malcolm in the years since Gabby had broken up with him, but she was beginning to remember why she'd disliked him so much.

After the waiter brought more wine and poured

some into everyone's glass, Gabby cleared her throat. "Now that our drinks are finally here, I can tell you all the good news." She paused. "We're getting married."

Sara choked on her wine, which promptly spilled down the front of her brand new cream-colored romper. She hurriedly dipped her napkin in water to try to flood the stain as exclamations went up around the table.

Gabby hadn't even hinted about this to Sara in their conversations, which created a new wave of guilt. Maybe Sara had been too wrapped up with her own problems lately to really listen.

"How long have you two been dating?" her father asked, frowning. Rachel gently put her hand over his.

"We reconnected six weeks ago, Dad," Gabby said. "But you only knew our mom that long, right?" She beamed at Malcolm. "We knew right away it was love."

Malcolm beamed right back, which was a little reassuring. He was very Italian looking, tanned and toned, with a head of hair whose thickness rivaled John Stamos's. His custom-tailored suit clung to his muscular frame like a wet suit, and his very nice haircut had probably cost more than their dinner. Sara could understand lust, maybe. But *love*?

She tried to reconcile this Malcolm with the guy she dimly remembered from Gabby's college years. That Malcolm had worn seersucker pants and brightly colored polos with the collars lifted up. This Malcolm dressed better but was still showing signs of trying too hard to flaunt his wealth and status. But wait—just then he took Gabby's hand and stared lovingly into her eyes before he addressed her father and Rachel. If

Sara wasn't mistaken, his eyes were a little teary. "I love your daughter, Dr. and Mrs. Langdon. More than anything." Gabby blushed prettily.

"Well," her father said judiciously, "congratulations." Turning to Malcolm, he said, "If my daughter loves you, we will too. Welcome to our family."

As everyone hugged and congratulated the happy couple, Sara thought it was a good thing Rafe wasn't there. He wouldn't be as accepting, at least outwardly, as their father. But she couldn't help thinking their father was right. They owed it to Gabby to give him a chance.

"Let's show them your ring, honey," Malcolm said, holding up Gabby's hand, which she'd been subtly hiding under the table. A diamond the size of a small snow globe gleamed and sparkled on her ring finger. Gabby had never wanted a snow globe. She'd wanted something out of the box, unique. Vintage, maybe. But flashy and enormous? Sara just couldn't see it.

Sara chided herself. Maybe she was just being bitter and envious because of her own broken plans. She'd never been jealous of her sister, but maybe being back home was stirring up all her own conflicted emotions—and, let's face it, loneliness. She could do better. Be more positive. For Gabby's sake. Still, she couldn't shake the unsettled feeling that shifted through her.

"I bought it at Tiffany's," Malcolm said. In case they had any doubt it wasn't the best.

While everyone was oohing and aahing over the ring, Malcolm's phone went off. "Excuse me. I have to move my Tesla. I'll be right back."

As soon as he left, Evie, never one to stay silent, spoke. "Gabby, six weeks? That's not very much time."

"It's not like we just met," Gabby countered. "Really, Evie, can't you just be happy for me for once?"

"We are happy for you, Gabs," Sara said quickly. "We just don't want you to rush into anything, you know?"

"I'm not rushing. I love Malcolm. And I'm old enough to know this time. I wish you all would have faith in me." *He's not perfect, but maybe he's as close as I'm going to come.* Gabby's words from the attic echoed in Sara's brain. Her stomach churned sickly.

"We do," Rachel said, ever the peacemaker. "Now, we want to hear all about the proposal, right, girls?"

Malcolm returned, and talk turned to his proposal on the observation deck of the Empire State Building with a violin quartet nearby. "Because Gabby loves *Sleepless in Seattle*," Malcolm said.

That seemed very thoughtful. Maybe he *had* changed. Maybe he did love her sister. That thought, and the fact that everyone in the entire restaurant seemed to be paired up over candlelit tables on this beautiful summer evening, made Sara feel a little weepy. A picture invaded her brain of Colton on such a night, sitting across from her at a candlelit table. Laughing, casually taking her hand and bringing it slowly to his lips, where he would plant a tiny lingering kiss, promises of many more to come, while looking sexy as sin.

Wait, what was she doing? How had she made that leap from annoying and awful to a decent man, and then suddenly to this? The Revolver didn't do candlelit dinners or monogamy. Maybe he *was* a decent guy, but he was *not* boyfriend material, as even her own father had noted.

After the main course was finished, Sara headed to the ladies' room. Under the bright fluorescent lights, the stain down the front of her brand-new romper looked hideous, like she'd spilled an entire bottle of pinot noir instead of a small sip. In a stall she had to unzip one zipper on the back and another on the side and shimmy out of the entire garment. She usually didn't wear such complicated clothing, but the romper had a crocheted neckline and was summery and cute.

She *was* feeling a little weepy, and she wasn't sure exactly why. She was happy for Gabby...but also worried. Was she a little jealous? Definitely not of the Tesla. Or the ring...Well, on second thought, maybe a snow globe wasn't such a bad thing after all.

But still Sara couldn't help but reflect upon her own situation. She'd chosen unwisely, and look where she was now, back in a town where everyone knew everyone's business, and where there were no eligible men for miles. Except for Colton, and he didn't count.

With that she stood and shimmied the romper back up, then threaded her arms through the arm holes. The back zipper went up just fine, but the side zipper got stuck halfway up. She yanked and pulled in vain. Sara left the stall and went out into the main part of the bathroom where there was more light and tried to tug the zipper down and then back up. No luck.

Exposed to the air conditioning was a good hunk of pale white flesh over her left hip and—horrors—more than a little of her granny panties. Why had she worn the comfortable undies today? On second thought, maybe she should be grateful that she had extra material to stretch upward to cover her exposed skin.

A stall door opened. "Oh, hi, Sara," came a voice from behind her.

Sara stopped wrestling with her zipper and turned. There, striking and beautiful, her lips coated with a bold sheen of red lipstick, was Valerie Blake, aka Cake Girl. Tagg's girlfriend. She wore a flowing, sleeveless black maxi dress and jeweled black sandals. No jelly roll around her waist to get skirt zippers stuck in, no sirree.

Sara yanked up on the zipper so hard she heard a rip. Oh God. One glance down told her the fabric had separated from the zipper. That was strike three for the poor romper. She covered the gaping hole with her hand. "Valerie! Hi! How are you?"

Frankly, she didn't care how Valerie was. She just did not want Tagg to see her like this. She was certain he was out there somewhere, looking like his usual handsome self, while she was literally falling apart at the seams.

Why did she always think of really bad jokes at the worst times?

"Oh, I'm great. Tagg and I just got back from Greece." Val smiled a blinding white smile and flipped back her long, silky hair. "You can probably tell from my tan."

She did look beautiful. In fact, she looked like a Grecian goddess, wearing that beautiful black dress with beads that sparkled from the fringe at the hem. She had some kind of smoky eye thing going on, and dangly earrings, and her neckline was low and showcased her perfect boobs. She was hot, she was sexy, and Tagg *loved* her.

And that thought made tears burn behind Sara's eyes.

"Tagg and I are so happy," Val said. "It was like it was meant to be. I wanted you to know that—that it's not some quick thing with us. It's *forever*."

Sara forced a smile, but words seemed to get caught in the sudden clog that had lodged in her throat. Forever. With Tagg, her boyfriend of ten-plus years, whom Sara'd thought she'd known inside and out. True love initiated by a sudden pitch face forward into a cake, while she'd been oblivious at home, carefully laying out her wedding clothes and dreaming of her future. Maybe Colton was right. Maybe she needed to start placing blame where blame was due. "Is Tagg—here?" *Please God, say no. Please please please. Not tonight.* Not when she was bursting out of her clothing and looked like a sad drunk on a binge.

"He's meeting me here in a little bit. We'll come find you, OK?" Val at long last made her way to the door, while Sara kept smiling her frozen smile and tried to keep herself covered. "I'm sure he'd love to say hi." Did this woman have no clue at all that Sara might possibly be affected by the fact that Valerie had *stolen her fiancé*? Did she really believe that they could all visit like civilized people when Sara hadn't seen or spoken to Tagg since *last summer*?

Sara lurched out of the bathroom like she had a bad hip, because keeping both hands plastered over her wardrobe malfunction took work. Finally she made it outside to the table. "Family, I love you, but I've got a migraine coming on and I think I'm going to say good-bye." She kissed Gabby, hugged her new future brother-in-law awkwardly with one arm, and blew kisses to everyone else.

"Sara, what's wrong?" Rachel asked, trailing behind her to the door.

Rachel looked so concerned, she decided to tell her the truth. "I ran into Val in the bathroom. My zipper got stuck and when I tried to fix it, it ripped." She flashed Rachel a bit of skin, as well as more than a little of her granny panties. "And Tagg's here somewhere and I *really* don't want to run into him like this."

"How about I drive you home?" she offered. "You've had a long day."

"Rachel, they need you at dinner. I feel awful leaving, but…God, Rachel, what is Gabby thinking? Or am I just a bitter old hag, jealous of my sister's happiness?"

Rachel shook her head. "I think you're more of a good sister with legitimate concerns. But Gabby's grown up a lot since college. We can give him a chance, for her sake."

"Right." Sara thought about her dad's philosophy about people, having watched most of the town grow up as they came and went through his office. Personality was part of who you were, and most people didn't change much over time. Fatalistic, perhaps, as Rafe would say, but true? She wasn't sure.

Sara kissed Rachel goodbye and hobbled out to her car. She'd had enough of this day. She couldn't wait to get home and go to bed and let it end.

Chapter 10

♥

"Hannah, you can't go out to the lake now with a bunch of idiots. It's too late." Colton glanced at his watch, which was lit up by his dashboard. Ten p.m. on a Friday night, and he'd been driving around for hours, Champ snoozing in the back seat of his cruiser. He'd even helped Mrs. Jennings get her cat out of a tree, which Champ hadn't exactly appreciated. Not the usual way he'd spend an evening off. But he couldn't relax. Couldn't get thoughts of Sara out of his mind. And now he was back to dealing with Hannah and walking on thin ice to try not to mess up, but he was going to fall through anyway.

"I knew I shouldn't have even told you what I was doing," she said, the familiar tone of irritation evident in her voice.

"I'm glad you did, but you still can't go." *Be calm*, Colt's inner voice said. *Be reasonable*. Both things he was not feeling.

"I'm going to be in college in less than a month, doing whatever I want." He winced. "You can't boss me. You're not our mom or dad."

Colton bent his head and pinched the bridge of his nose. No, he certainly was not. He was just a guy who'd had a long workweek who wanted some peace and quiet. Except he kept seeing visions of a certain redhead in front of him. One who'd always assumed the worst about him and still did, despite his efforts to prove her wrong. And that irritated the hell out of him.

"Colton. Colton, did you just hear me?"

"Sorry, what did you say?"

"I said I promise to be back by midnight. It's just the lake. All my friends are going."

"Hannah, the lake on a Friday night this late means nothing but trouble." Kids smoking weed, drinking, doing God knows what else. She was not. Going. "Don't you have to work in the morning?"

"Yeah, but I told you, I won't stay long. It's summer, Colton. My friends and I don't have much time to be together before we all leave and go off in separate directions. Don't you trust me?"

Of course he didn't, because he was a teenager once himself. Plus what if she was sneaking around with Aiden? But he didn't even get a chance to formulate a response.

"I don't have to listen to you. You're just my brother." The line went dead. Colton tossed his cell onto the passenger seat and stared at it until the lights went out like it was a living thing. What was it with women in his life steamrollering him before he could even get his thoughts across? Wait. Since when was Sara a "woman in his life"? Jesus.

She thought he was an arrogant ass and a know-it-all. He'd encouraged her to believe the worst about him. He wanted to believe she was ultra type A, Dr. High Achiever, hell-bent on changing the world, but the thing was, she was so much more than that. She adored her grandmother. She was hardworking. She had a vulnerable side. His sister loved her. She had amazing legs.

When she'd grabbed his arm that night in Lou's and told him, *You don't always have to be insulting*, she'd been right. He *had* been insulting through much of their teenage years, yes, but that was because he'd been an idiot. Now he knew better.

How much of his teasing now was because he hated that she'd accomplished so much and he was stuck here, leading a small-town life? A life he hadn't really chosen? She was destined for bigger things. Why did that rankle him so much? Why did he use the teasing to push her away, keep her at arm's length? And why was all of this bothering him so much?

He should have spoken to her, not about the bachelor party but about *them*. What it was that made him act like an idiot. About how he didn't want it to be like that anymore between them.

A Honda Civic with a taillight out passed him and pulled him out of his thoughts. His heart rate accelerated a little. Because Sara had a Civic, and Evan had stopped her a few days ago about the light. Without having a clue what he was about to do, he started his car and pulled out onto the road.

* * *

Sara left the restaurant in her old but reliable Honda Civic and had just reached the Angel Falls town limits when she saw a flash of red and blue lights in her rearview mirror. A glance at her dash showed she was going thirty-five in a thirty-five zone. There were no other cars on the deserted road that wound through a dark stretch of wooded park.

The police vehicle accelerated until it was directly behind her. No question it was on her tail. She had no choice but to pull over. Being on the border of Angel Falls and Richardson, she had no idea which police department was responding. It brought her a sense of relief to know it wouldn't be Colton, who'd definitely be off duty by now.

The relief was short lived. Her heart tripped as she considered she was alone in the middle of the woods. What if she was about to be maimed and beaten by a cop poser? It was pitch-black, and the opportunities to stow a body would be endless.

Footsteps fell on gravel, and a bright light shone in her face. "Your taillight is out, ma'am," said a too-familiar voice.

Colton. What was worse—a cop-posing killer or him?

Lord, would this day never end? Hadn't she had enough of him for one day?

She held her hands in front of her face to shield her eyes. "I thought you were off tonight," she said.

"Technically, I am," he said.

"So you're out in your car during your time off cruising around, looking for trouble?"

"And it looks like I've found her."

He put his hands on the car window and bent over close enough that she could smell the zingy scent of that woodsy cologne he wore. And feel his body heat—and the intensity of his gaze as it swept over her. She shivered a little—but it was just from the evening air. Surely.

"So. The taillight," he said, pulling out his tablet to write her up.

With everything else going on this week, she'd forgotten all about it. Surely he wasn't really going to write her up, was he? Well, it was Colton, so anything was possible. "I'll get it fixed this weekend, OK?"

"This is your second warning," he said. "Evan told me he stopped you a couple days ago."

"You must be really bored tonight if you're lying in wait in the woods for people on your night off. Why don't you go pull some cats out of trees or something?"

"The law's the law. And actually, I just spent an hour doing just that."

"Well, I'm sure you have to go write up a report about it. So how about letting me go home?"

He inhaled deeply. His mouth twitched. "Have you been drinking?"

He shone his beam into the car. His gaze flickered from her bare legs to her wine-stained cleavage. Suddenly remembering the gaping patch of flesh on her side, she slid her hand down to cover it.

"I had one glass of wine, and most of it's on my top."

"Are you sure you didn't have more than one glass

and that's why you spilled it? With your rough first couple of weeks and all, I wouldn't want you drinking and driving."

"I'm a doctor. I don't drink and drive." What was with this guy?

"Calm down, I believe you. Hey, I need to ask you something. Will you come sit in my car for a minute?"

"Because you're going to write me up for a ticket? Your grandma would be ashamed. Absolutely ashamed."

"I'm not going to write you up for a ticket." He leaned over the driver's window, his arm muscles taut, and stared directly at her. "Champ's in my back seat and he's getting all worked up. But the real reason is I just need to talk with you. Please."

Oh. Just like that, her anger deflated. The fact that Champ was there would've probably gotten her to move, but the *please* definitely did it. "OK, I'll come," she said, then opened her car door. Because maybe it was finally time to stop assuming the worst about Colton Walker.

* * *

Colton knew he should stop this and allow her to go on her way and go back to his calm, quiet life. But he couldn't. Because it seemed to him that since she'd come back, calm and quiet had fled on foot screaming. Plus he had things to say that were sitting there festering, especially since their conversation earlier. Things he couldn't stop thinking about.

He opened the passenger door of his cruiser and waited for her to get in. His gaze flicked quickly up and down her. Her hair was down, and her outfit and heels showcased her pretty legs. She stirred him, as always, against his will.

"Why are you walking like that?" he asked.

"Like what?" she asked. She held both hands over her left hip and lurched a little in her heels. "Not used to the heels," she mumbled.

She sat down in the seat. Champ stuck his nose through the bars. She rubbed his snuff with her index finger, which made him push against the bars even more and bark. Even the dog wanted more of her attention.

Sara looked nervous, glancing up and down the street for traffic. "No one can see us talking," Colton said, "if that's what you're worried about."

"Colton, you've lived in this town a long time, just like I have. When has anyone not seen everything?"

"That time I kissed you," he said quietly. "No one saw that."

That quieted her fast. He could hardly believe he'd said it himself. The silence hung over them, palpable as a heartbeat.

Sara leaned closer, close enough that he could see the little golden flecks in her green eyes. Her eyes had always fascinated him, but he'd never given in to the temptation to look for too long, first because of Tagg and now... well, she'd mostly been too angry at him for any civilized discussion.

"No, no one saw, except Mrs. Mulligan." She shifted

her weight. "But even that turned out to be a big joke to you. Like everything else."

He tightened his hands on the steering wheel. "Let's get one thing straight. That kiss wasn't a joke."

"Oh yes, it was." She pointed a finger at him accusingly. "You never even showed for our date the next week."

He shook his head adamantly. "You don't even remember that *you're* the one who stood *me* up."

"I didn't stand you up! I waited at the museum in the dark until eight that night. Then I came to your dorm." She shook her head back and forth, like she was trying to fling the memory out of her head.

His heart lurched. Jolted. He stared at her in disbelief. "You went to the museum?"

"Of course I went. I-I was excited about it. I thought you meant it. I didn't know you were just playing a joke on me."

He gazed out the windshield, breathing heavily. Trying to get his shit together. Gripping the wheel like it was his last hold on reality. Because what she'd said...It couldn't be true. Because that would change...everything.

He finally turned to face her. "Tagg told me you'd gotten back together. That's why I didn't show. When you knocked on my door that night, I figured you were just coming to tell me what I already knew, that you were back with him."

"Tagg told you..."

"Tagg was my best friend. I'd felt guilty enough for kissing you. But when he said you two had made up...there was nothing I could do but accept that. So I got drunk and slept with Tiffany Downing." Because he'd been nineteen and stupid and heartsick.

Silence filled his cruiser, thick and dense, like an invisible fog. Even Champ lay quietly on the back seat, surely sensing that something grave was going on. Colt had done it now. Spilled his guts. What had he been thinking, pulling her over like this? And how the hell had he never known that they could've actually had a chance together?

Jesus.

Sara rubbed her temple. She looked...upset.

Oh God. One kiss. One lie. One missed opportunity from ten years ago.

"I stayed away after that." He'd pretended it didn't matter, that there were plenty of other fish in the sea, and a hell of a lot of them wanted him.

He tried to push his feelings down, somewhere deep and dark where he'd pushed everything regarding Sara for years. "I told myself I hated you. You chose Tagg. He was everything I wasn't."

She was sitting forward now, hands resting on the armrest between the seats. Champ had given up on getting any attention and had fallen asleep with his paws up in the air. Colton had an urge to curl his hand over one of hers, but he didn't dare. He'd already crossed enough lines tonight.

Her face was tilted upward, her eyes big and round. She looked stunned and upset, things he had little idea how to deal with in the context of relationships. He understood sex. Wanting. Desire. But not this.

He sat back in his seat and blew out a breath. Closed his eyes.

After all this time, he couldn't deny his feelings. He could tell himself she was the most annoying woman on the planet, that she was uptight and anal. But she was so much more in ways he was just beginning to discover. Truth was, those long-buried feelings from years ago still mattered. They still fucking mattered.

* * *

Sara was aware of Colton's big body, ramrod straight, the tension rolling off him in waves, his long fingers curled around the steering wheel. For a moment their gazes locked, and for the first time she wondered if there had been a toll for him all these years.

Had it hurt him when Tagg and she got back together? Had he thought of her, of what could have been? Or had he simply moved on over time? Everything about him suggested the latter, except the way he was looking at her now.

His gaze was...piercing. Electrifying. As if he saw straight through her. And it did things to her, made heat flare through her in big, unwelcome waves.

"You're nothing like Tagg," she whispered. She was coming to believe Colton wasn't anything like what she'd thought he was.

He cracked a little smile. "I take it that's a good thing?"

"Tagg and I weren't right for each other. What happened was for the better."

For the first time in a year, she was able to say that. It still hurt, but not the way it had.

"You're still pretty torn up about it? Your breakup with him? I mean, it's only been a year, and that would be natural after all those years together..."

"I'm not in love with Tagg anymore, if that's what you're asking."

She wasn't sure exactly what he was asking, but he seemed to look relieved.

She should be focused on what he was saying, but she didn't want to talk about Tagg. Instead her mind went back to their past. She'd known he'd slept with Tiffany What's-Her-Name that long-ago night, and she'd been repulsed. Angry. She'd stood there humiliated, feeling again like that nerdy teenage girl he'd poked fun at. She'd vowed never to trust him again. Instead she'd gone back to Tagg, accepted his assurances that he loved her and believed his promises of a happily ever after.

Yet Tagg had been the one who'd lied. Not Colton. Tagg.

Colton got out of the car and opened her door. Watched her walk out in silence, his gaze drilling into her back.

She felt like she should do *something*...Say thank you? Or run the hell out of here as fast as her legs could carry her?

Should she tell him she was sorry for misjudging him all these years? It hadn't really sunk in, any of it. That the wild, carefree persona he played so well was not who he was at all.

Things suddenly got awkward. For one thing he was still staring at her, and God knew what he was thinking. Hopefully not about the gaping hole in her clothing, which she'd forgotten to cover, which she tried to rectify now.

"How about we start again," he said, his jaw so tight she could bounce a quarter off it. He didn't seem to be focused on the zipper at all, thank goodness. What a gentleman.

"Start again?"

"Yeah. A fresh start. A new beginning." He extended his hand for her to shake. "Friends," he tacked on.

Friends? A handshake? Not what she'd been expecting. But what *had* she been expecting? She glanced from his face to his hand. He looked...hopeful. Or maybe she was just imagining that. After all these years of his I-don't-give-a-shit attitude, how could he look like he cared what she thought? What she did?

Finally she awkwardly stuck out her hand. To be polite, of course.

He wrapped his big hand around hers. It was warm, and his grip was strong and no nonsense. The grip of a man you could count on. She stared at him incredulously—suddenly the impassive eyes, the perfect posture had returned, and she realized he'd gone back to being the cop on duty.

She was beginning to see how he was able to wear a mask to hide his feelings. It occurred to her that he might be waiting for a sign from her.

But she was still shocked by what he'd said. Still trying to reconcile who the real Colton Walker was.

Their hands were still locked together, and had been for far longer than a normal handshake. His nearness was making her shaky, giddy, confused.

She broke away and walked to her car, but he jogged ahead and got there first to open the door. She moved to get in, then stopped. Impulsively she stood on tiptoe and kissed him on the cheek. It was rough and raspy in a very sensual, masculine way.

For a second he didn't move or look at her. She was kicking herself for the reckless gesture when his radio went off.

"Hey, sweet pea," Carmen the dispatcher said. "You big hunk of love, we've got a 314 on Elm Street."

Colton pulled his radio off his belt. "I'm sorry Pete's exposing himself again, Carmen, but I'm off duty."

"Evan has a migraine, and besides, I know where you are from the Find My Friends app on my cell. You want me to call him or you want to take the call?"

"I'll take it, Carmen," he said into his radio, but his gaze had swung to Sara. "Tell Pete to keep his pants on." Sara ducked down into the car, not wanting to keep him from his work. And anxious to get the hell out of there.

"Hey," he said. The tiniest smile turned up his lips. "You OK?"

His voice was low, easy, rough at the edges, and it reverberated clear through her taut nerves. "Yeah. I'm fine." She smiled. "Thanks for not giving me a ticket."

"I won't give you a ticket, but I hope you don't mind my giving a bit of advice."

"Sure. What is it?"

"Next time a cop pulls you over, don't pull your zipper down to try and get out of the ticket."

"I would *never* do that. My zipper broke!"

He winked. "And those high-waisted white bloomers. Really sexy."

Now she was going to die. She knocked her head against the steering wheel.

He placed his hand over hers on the steering wheel. Just covered it lightly, giving it a small squeeze. She looked up in time to see him nod, close her door, then head off to do his job.

And despite herself, hope, dangerous and headstrong, bloomed within her.

Chapter 11

♥

OK, Nonna, I've got everything ready," Sara said, standing in her grandmother's kitchen after work the next Friday. Strawberries, raspberries, blueberries, blackberries, check. Lemon juice, check. Butter, check. Vanilla ice cream, double check.

She was making pie. Not just any pie, her mother's mixed berry pie, though the recipe had come originally from Nonna. She was killing two birds with one stone with this one. Nonna was showing her how to make it, so she would learn her mom's secrets, and...she was making it for Colton's birthday.

She'd found out from Carmen, whom she'd seen at the Bean today, that he was on duty until ten tonight, so that didn't leave much time for celebrating. But she thought she'd call him over for a piece of pie. A gesture of friendship. Except maybe she should've made cake...yes, maybe she should've. But her mother's berry pie was the bomb.

"Put that butter back in the fridge until just before

you're ready for it," Nonna said in a commanding grandma tone, and Sara instantly obeyed. "Everything's got to stay as cold as possible for a good crust."

"Yes, ma'am," Sara said.

"Who are you making this for?" Nonna asked, looking her over carefully.

"I'm just really craving pie," she said. "Doesn't that sound delicious tonight before bed? Warm berry pie with ice cream melting all over it?"

Nonna had just taken a pitcher of sun tea from the yard and was making lemonade to mix with it for her favorite summertime drink. She narrowed her eyes and gave Sara the once-over. "Yes, but you hate baking, Sara Jane. I know you."

"Fine, it's for Colton's birthday."

Nonna clapped her hands. "Oh, you're making him pie for his birthday. This is serious. You know what your grandfather always used to say."

"Um, you find your way to a man's heart through cooking?"

"No. Of course not. 'Kissin' don't last, but cookin' does.' And truthfully, the kissin' can last too. But it sure helps if you can cook." Nonna chuckled at her own joke.

"OK, Nonna, what next?" Sara asked, waving the measuring cup to bring her grandmother's attention back to the recipe. Actually, it was a relief to have her make bad jokes. "How much flour?"

"Four cups," she said. Four seemed like a lot, but Sara dutifully dumped that amount in a large bowl. "Got it. Now what?"

"Put some of this in," Nonna said, shoving the sugar bag over. "You know how to do it."

Sugar, in the crust? Sara was no expert, but that didn't seem right. She'd just pulled out her phone to Google how to make a piecrust when Nonna thrust a tin of Crisco on the counter.

"Oh, I've already got the two sticks of butter ready," Sara said.

"But it needs Crisco," Nonna said. "That's the secret ingredient."

"I did want to kill Colton, Nonna, but not by giving him a heart attack."

Just then there was a rap on the back door, and Rachel walked in.

"Hi, Sara, hi, Nonna," she said, giving them both a kiss. "What's cooking?"

"We're making a berry pie my mom used to make a lot," Sara said. "Nonna's teaching me." Sara hugged her grandma. Although she was convinced the piecrust was a bust. Maybe Evie knew the recipe. Or maybe she should dump everything and just go buy a pie at the bakery. She tried not to be disappointed that her grandmother could no longer make the family recipe she loved so much, and cursed herself for having been gone for so many years. She'd been so wrapped up in her own life. She hadn't cared about piecrusts at all, and now it was too late.

"You finish now, dear," Nonna said, patting her arm. "I'm going to take my drink and sit down. Rachel, how about some tea and lemonade?"

"Thanks, Nonna, I'd love some." Rachel came to

stand next to Sara at the counter and surveyed the work in progress.

She hoped Rachel didn't see the sadness in her eyes. No, not disappointment. Heavyheartedness. First off, Nonna never sat down. Ever. She was a powerhouse of energy. The old Nonna would've snatched the ingredients up and had them all blended and mixed and would be champing at the bit to show her *exactly* how it was done.

Rachel gave her a squeeze and smiled and was her usual undaunted self. "So you cut the butter into the flour"—she looked into the bowl—"except that looks like a lot. There shouldn't be more than two cups in there. And you add ice water by the tablespoon until it turns into dough. And there's a secret ingredient— lemon juice. Got any of that?" Rachel began moving things on the counter and rustling around for a new bowl.

Sara stepped back while Rachel became a whirlwind of reorganization. She'd never even thought Rachel would know how to make this recipe. Never even thought to ask her. And that shook her to her core.

"What's with the sudden urge to make pie?" Rachel asked, as Nonna sat outside the back door on her little deck watching the birds at the feeder.

"It's for Colton's birthday." Maybe she shouldn't've said that, but frankly it was a relief to tell someone.

"Oh," Rachel said judiciously. Her careful tone spoke volumes.

"We're just friends," Sara added hurriedly.

"I see."

"We had a talk. Got a few things straightened out."

"Is that right." Rachel cut the butter into the flour with a fork.

"I would never want to do him—I mean *date* him. *Date* him!" *Oh my God.* "It's just that he's working late on his birthday today and I thought he might like some pie. A gesture of friendship, you know?"

Rachel stopped and looked at her until Sara met her gaze. "Sara. Sweetheart. It's OK. It's just pie."

The *sweetheart* kind of melted her.

"I mean, I'm totally not ready to start anything with anybody. Especially someone who lives in the same town. After all those years with Tagg, I mean, come on. I need to meet lots of different men, right? Nothing serious for me, no sirree. And let's face it, Colton would never get serious about anyone. He's not that kind of guy. In fact, he's the kind of man most sensible women stay away from."

Ramble, ramble, ramble. She needed to shut up already.

Rachel's mouth twitched. "Oh, I don't know about that. Maybe he just hasn't found the right one."

Sara got busy collecting dirty dishes and wiping the flour off the counter.

Rachel touched her shoulder. "Sara, it's OK to explore your feelings. Besides, I like Colton. It's Malcolm we have to worry about."

Sara looked up. "He's still awful, isn't he?"

This time Rachel outright laughed. "Why are we the only ones who know this?"

"What are we going to do?"

"I don't know. But something pretty quick."

As Sara considered that, she put dishes in the sink and started washing them. Rachel added tablespoons of ice water to the flour mixture. It was actually starting to look like dough. "Nonna used to be able to make pie crust in her sleep," Sara said.

"I'm sorry, sweetie. You know, I've got her signed up at the senior center for some activities there."

"You mean senior day care?"

"Yes. The director is your dad's patient. Apparently it's quite a nice community, and they offer lots of options. We're going to check it out next week. And remember Claudia Gaines? Her husband died recently and she said she can come be with Nonna a few days each week. Take her places, grocery shopping, to get her hair done, that kind of thing."

Sara nodded, although her heart was twisting. Her grandmother couldn't be alone anymore. They'd talked about all these things, but it was so hard to accept.

"We've all agreed to keep her at home for as long as we can. I think between all of us, we can make it work. One day at a time, right?"

"Girls, come out here, quickly!" Nonna said. "There's the cutest little chipmunk and he's eating all the birdseed. I wish I had a camera!"

Rachel guided Sara toward the door. "Don't miss the chipmunk. Oh, one more thing. Over the years, Nonna's given me a lot of your mom's recipes. I'm working on assembling them all for you girls and making keepsake books. So if you need anything, just ask me, OK?"

"Oh. Thank you, Rachel." She hugged her stepmother, tears gathering in her eyes. In part from relief that the recipes weren't lost. But mostly over Rachel's thoughtfulness. Somehow it had never occurred to Sara that Rachel would want to be a protector of her mother's legacy.

Sara walked outside to see Nonna enraptured by the antics of two chipmunks who were chasing each other around the patio near the bird feeder.

"Aren't they the cutest things?" she said, chuckling.

Sara sat down next to Nonna. She remembered all the times her grandmother had gotten excited about little things like birds, or the color of one of her roses, or some little anecdote she'd heard. She had a simple excitement about things that had always been contagious.

Somewhere along the line, Sara feared she herself had lost the ability to enjoy—or even notice—simple things. When was the last time she'd sat like this on a porch? Or taken time to notice the flowers? She couldn't even remember. Life had gotten too busy.

But not today. Today she would hold her Nonna's hand and sip iced tea and lemonade, and watch the chipmunks chase each other across the lawn.

* * *

Colton had just spent the past two hours settling a domestic dispute. Elias Riegler, who lived in a rental whose front yard resembled a garage sale in progress, had thrown a bottle that barely missed his wife's head. His fist, however, made contact just fine. The man wasn't drunk, and being an idiot wasn't good enough reason to bring him in when his wife refused to press charges.

She'd said it was her fault she made him mad.

Elias was the family's only income source, so with five kids, the woman was terrified to toss him in jail. Or maybe she was afraid of what he'd do to her once he got out. So Colton left without an arrest. It wasn't the first time he'd been called out there either.

Colton had no problem with his job when he could help people, but when his hands were tied . . . Well. Let's just say it wasn't exactly the kind of call he wanted to respond to on his birthday. Or any day, for that matter.

Thinking about Sara on his drive back to the station was far more pleasant, but a little uncomfortable too. He hadn't spoken to her since last weekend, just waved to her across the street one time while he was helping ninety-year-old Moira Perkins navigate the curb on her way into the library and Sara was walking out of the antique shop.

It wasn't like him to avoid anyone. In this town it wasn't possible to do that. But Sara . . . something had shifted between them. And he wasn't quite sure what to do about it.

Thing was, he couldn't stop thinking about their talk last weekend. The part, specifically, when she'd stood on tiptoe and kissed him on the cheek.

Her hands had rested for that brief moment on his chest, and he'd wondered if she could feel his heart practically beating out of it like a trapped bird. Or the sudden way his breath caught. Because it was all he could do to keep himself from wrapping his arms around her and pulling her flush against him, turning his head so that his lips met hers, not his damn cheek.

Instead he'd stood still as a statue while her lips made contact. While her pretty scent surrounded him and her hair tickled his neck. She'd worn it down for once, all that thick red hair spun through with gold. He'd never in his life seen hair like that, and the urge to drag his fingers through it and pull her lips to his had him fisting his hands at his sides.

He'd be a fool to read anything more into that kiss besides a truce, a gesture of friendship. They'd spent ten years nearly despising each other. Why couldn't he just be grateful that was over? After all, he'd been the one who'd stuck his hand out like an idiot and suggested friendship in the first place. *Good one, Einstein.* He could no more be her friend than he could be her enemy anymore.

Ten years of crossed wires. Who knew what could've happened between them if it weren't for one simple lie?

Who knew what still could?

That kiss had opened a floodgate of possibility. Thing was, he had no idea what to do next. Pray the attraction would pass? Hope it was just temporary insanity brought on by an old memory best left forgotten? Certainly getting involved with her was a bad idea in a small town where they had to face each other nearly every day. Not to mention how that would complicate his relationship with Tagg.

Besides, he didn't really do relationships. He liked keeping things casual and fun, without attachments.

He'd had a few steady girlfriends—none of them from town—but he didn't want to be shackled to anyone. Yes, his buddies called him the Revolver in jest, but it was true in that he didn't care to have any of them stick.

Colton checked his watch. One more hour on duty, then it was the weekend. The Fourth of July was tomorrow, and besides some paperwork in the morning, he was finally getting some time off.

His phone buzzed just as he finished his last cruise through town for the night.

Can u stop by on your way home? the text read. It was from Sara. How had she gotten his number? He'd wager from Carmen.

Sure, he typed back. Everything OK? His first thought was that maybe something had happened with her grandmother.

Nothing wrong. See u soon.

Those last three words triggered a flurry of emotions. Puzzlement. A little trepidation. And yes, excitement. He'd missed her. Although he wasn't quite sure what to do after that heart-to-heart. Maybe he needed a good run-in with her to show him how annoying she was and prove to him why thinking of her romantically was a very bad idea.

When Colton pulled up to her grandma's little bungalow, Sara was sitting on the swing, the porch lit only by a couple of outdoor candles—the kind that kept the bugs away. She motioned for him to hurry up.

As he got out of his car and climbed up to the porch, he saw a solitary birthday candle planted in the middle of a pie sitting on the low table. She sat there in a gray Indians T-shirt and cutoffs, smiling. The candle-light flickered on her hair and her face, casting all her features in a warm glow that nearly stopped him in his tracks.

Rocket was cuddled close to her side, snoring.

"Nonna believes in recycling candles," Sara said with a sheepish smile. "This is the only one in the house, and it's down to a stub. Make a wish fast."

His brain finally put two and two together. How had she remembered? "You got me a pie for my birthday?" Suddenly the simple act of drawing in air became complicated, like he'd somehow forgotten how to do it. He dragged his gaze from her to the pie so she wouldn't see what was surely on his face.

How touched he was.

"Nope." She shook her head. "I didn't get you a pie. I *made* you a pie."

Words clogged up in his throat. Her eyes were dancing in the low light, and he could see the golden highlights in her hair. Forget the damn pie. He wanted to taste *her*.

Whoa there, Colton. Friends, friends, friends, he repeated to himself. What had happened to all that animosity between them? The desire to tease her, to make her blush? To keep her at a distance, which was what all that bickering had done. Now he found he did want to make her blush. But for a completely different reason.

"Did you celebrate today?" she asked.

"Carmen made cupcakes. I'll have dinner with Cookie and Hannah this weekend."

She patted the swing beside her and he took her up on the invitation, staking out a spot on the other side of

Rocket, who sniffed him discerningly, then leaned back against Sara. His uniform grazed her leg, and his gun banged awkwardly against the swing.

"Better hurry and wish before it fizzles," she said, gesturing to the candle, which really did seem to be on its way to flickering out.

Oh, he wished all right, while she did a speedy rendition of "Happy Birthday." She couldn't hold a tune to save her life, but he loved it just the same. Then he blew out the candle.

As it sat there smoldering, a thin wisp of smoke curling elegantly into the wooden slats of the porch ceiling, Sara jumped up. "Do you like warm pie? I'm going to nuke some pieces and put ice cream on them, is that OK? I've been waiting for this all ni—"

Before he knew what he was doing he reached up for her arm, tugged her back down beside him, and planted his lips on hers. Then he curled his hand around her neck and pulled her in deeper.

Her lips were soft, and she tasted amazing, sweet like the pie, and sure enough, she was kissing him back, parting her lips, resting her hand lightly against his chest. Over his heart, where he was certain she could feel its wild rhythm as his entire body responded to the thunder of that kiss.

Caught up in the feel of her, soft and warm in his arms, he lost track of time and his sense, and for once he didn't even care if half the damn town drove by and saw their chief not being chiefly.

When he finally wrenched himself back, he was shaking a little.

"You're awfully grateful for birthday pie," she said. She was breathless too, he was pleased to note. Her hair was mussed, and she looked a little stunned. And so beautiful he knew he'd remember this moment forever.

"I am so grateful," he said. God, he sounded like an idiot. Before he could think better of it, he kissed her again. She made a sweet little noise deep in her throat. Her hands slid up his back, curving around his shoulders, and she grabbed on, tugging herself flush against him.

The woman was driving him mad. She wasn't uptight or tense or any of the type A adjectives he'd once accused her of being. She was just soft and lovely, and she fit perfectly in his arms.

The dog, clearly offended at being left out, insinuated himself between them and started licking his arm. At the same time, a voice calling out from the house made them suddenly break apart.

"Is that Colton's car parked in the driveway?" Nonna asked.

"I was just wishing Colton a happy birthday," Sara said, her lips curved into a little smile.

"Well, happy birthday, Colton," Nonna said. "I'd come out, but I've got my curlers in."

"Thanks, Mrs. Faranaccio," Colton said, but he was looking at Sara. Her pretty blush. Her slightly dazed expression. All he knew was that he wanted to kiss her again.

"Come have some pie with us," Sara called out. "We don't mind the curlers."

"Thanks, sweetie, but I'm headed to bed. Happy birthday again, Colton."

Nonna waved from the screen door and disappeared into the house. "I'll be right back," Sara said as she got up, scooped up the pie, and disappeared into the house, leaving him with the dog, who stretched out on the swing and went belly up for more love.

Best. Birthday. Ever.

* * *

Oh my God. She'd kissed Colton. Well, technically he'd started it, but she'd fully taken part. Why had she done that, kissed someone she used to hate—well, OK, *hate* was a strong word—disliked intensely up until a few days ago? And she'd liked it. So, so much. She reached up to touch her lips. Dear God, he was a fantastic kisser.

Sara never remembered having this feeling of being electrified, on fire, hot and cold, weak and ready to dissolve into a boneless pile, panting and restless.

"Need help in there?" Colton called from the porch.

She was standing at the kitchen counter, staring at the fridge, panic surging through her veins. Kissing Colton Walker? What had she been thinking? *Well, that's what happens when you bake a man a birthday pie. He gets ideas.* Well, and she clearly had ideas too. Friendship ideas, like he'd suggested. Friends she could handle. Then where had that lip lock come from?

They were opposites in every way. He was chill, she was high-strung. He laughed easily and was beloved by everyone. She . . . Well, she wasn't sure where she quite fit in, but she knew she definitely didn't have the type of personality that made teachers forget their reprimands and every woman within fifty yards feel faint and giddy. And she didn't have dimples. Definitely no dimples.

Most important of all, he was Tagg's friend. And that reason, above all, was enough to warn a sensible person away forever. And yes, Sara reminded herself, she was a sensible person. She had to handle this...attraction. It was there, but she could rein it in. She didn't have to act on it. Plus he was the Revolver. God, what was she thinking!

She was back outside a few minutes later, handing him a warm bowl loaded with berry pie, ice cream sliding down over the top like the snow atop a mountain. "Here you go, Colton. Happy birthday." She cleared her throat, which suddenly felt like it was stuffed with a massive ball of cat hair. She nudged Rocket down off the swing and scooted a healthy distance away from Colton. The dog gave her an offended look and crawled beneath the swing.

Colton took a healthy bite. "Amazing," he said, but he was looking at her.

"My mom's recipe," she said, dropping her gaze to the table, the floor, anywhere not to make contact with those blue eyes that were signaling something very, very dangerous. Blatant desire. Wanting. She took a small bite, but it caught in her throat. She put down her fork, forcing a swallow. "You don't mind pie, do you?"

"Why would I? It's terrific." He looked confused. Understandably, since cake was her issue, not his.

She fidgeted her fingers in her lap, suddenly not

knowing where to put them. "I really haven't had cake since before...the wedding."

"Sorry to hear that," he said.

"The bakery delivered the cake to our house, did you know that? This gorgeous thing, covered with perfect fondant icing and tiny edible pearls. I was the one who opened the door."

He shook his head. "I'm sorry, Sara." That was two *sorry*s in under a minute. She had to signal to him in no uncertain terms that there would be no. More. Kissing. Kissing was bad. Off-limits. Too dangerous.

"It's OK." She smiled stiffly. She barely knew what to say, but from the expression on his face, she could see he'd gotten the hint.

He set down his bowl. They both stood up, awkward now.

"No one's ever baked me a pie before. I mean, besides Cookie." He assessed her in that thorough way of his, a slight frown forming.

"Listen, Colton," she said, suddenly looking straight at him. "I—don't think anything more than being friends is a good idea for us. I'm totally not ready for a relationship and—um, well, we both work in the same town and all. Things could just get really...awkward, you know?"

Something flickered in his eyes. Disappointment, maybe? She couldn't tell. He was very quiet.

"I hope you understand it's nothing personal," she said. "Just that I think it's better for us to keep it platonic, you know?"

Not better. *Safer.* Much, much safer.

"Well," he said quietly. He looked confused, maybe even a little stunned. "All right then. Thanks again for the pie. It was delicious."

"Have a great birthday celebration," she said, too cheerily.

She watched him walk down the driveway at last, carrying the pie she'd made him take.

The pie that she'd been so excited about. Well, that had certainly taken a bad turn.

She could not start something with him. She could not subject herself to that awful scrutiny again—the embarrassment, the humiliation, which surely would happen once things ended because, you know, it was *Colton*. She would chalk this up to temporary insanity. Rework things in her mind to adjust to their being friends, and be a lot more careful about doing things that might send him the wrong signals. Starting with no more kissing!

It would be all right. She could do this. She would be cordial and friendly and carry on as they'd planned, as friends. It was the right thing to do.

As he drove off, he waved. She stood there for a long time, watching his car disappear, touching her lips.

Chapter 12

♥

The next day was the Fourth of July. Colton had spent the morning catching up on paperwork and now sat on the freshly painted bench outside the police station having lunch with Rafe. He'd packed a turkey-and-cheese sandwich with an apple. Rafe was eating spaghetti and meatballs, and his lunch looked a lot better.

"You make that?" Colton asked.

"Yep. Made the sauce from scratch too."

Colton scowled. What with Cookie planning to snowbird in Florida come winter and Hannah leaving for college, he was going to be in trouble. "You taught yourself to cook like that?"

"I've learned a few things at the station." He leaned over to check out the contents of a plastic Tupperware container. "What's in there?"

Colton had packed a healthy slab of his birthday pie. He took a plastic knife and cut it in half, then slid it onto a plastic lid near Rafe. "I brought extra. Have some."

Rafe took a bite. "Oh, wow. This tastes just like my mom's berry pie."

"It *is* your mom's berry pie," Colton said. Rafe raised a brow. "Your sister made it." He and Rafe were good friends. He wasn't about to lie.

"Evie made you pie?" Rafe asked. "Wow, what'd you do, rescue her cat or one of her kids or something?"

"Sara made it." There, it was out. Rafe would be touchy if he knew Colton had kissed his sister, and he saw no reason to discuss that, but the truth was the truth. Not like there was anything scandalous in making someone a pie, anyway.

Rafe looked him over carefully. "Is there something you're not telling me?"

Colton snorted. "No." Rafe telegraphed him a glare. "Not at all," he said more adamantly.

Apparently Rafe didn't buy that. "Wait…no…not you and Sara. She hates you, man."

Colton suppressed a groan. What had he been thinking? He definitely should've lied about the pie. "She doesn't hate me," he said, a little irritated. "She just doesn't more than like me."

He'd kissed a lot of women, but none of them had affected him like Sara. None of them had the ability to piss him off like she could either, that was for sure. But last night he'd barely slept, and his mind kept circling back to how amazing it had been to kiss her again. Even better than he'd remembered from way back when, and that was saying a lot. Those soft lips, those little sounds she made in the back of her throat as she kissed him back, the way her body melted into his. He could swear she'd been as eager as he'd been.

He hadn't meant to kiss her. It had just...happened. Then she'd pulled the friend card on him and shut him down, just like that. To be fair, he'd been the one who'd played that card first. Idiot.

"She must like you plenty if she's baking you pie," Rafe said, brows pulled down in a staunch frown. "My sister hates to cook." He took another bite. "Wait a minute. What about the bachelor party? You two come to terms with that?"

"What happened after that bachelor party was not my fault. You *know* that. Geez." He stuffed his half-eaten sandwich back in his bag.

Rafe studied him. "Look, Colton, I mean, Sara's had a rough year. I love you, bro, but you're not exactly a relationship kind of guy. And I don't want you thinking you can use my sister as—"

"Forget I said anything, Rafe, OK? And it's not like that. At all. Besides, I have a date tonight."

Colton had asked Hannah if she'd like to go to the fireworks in the park with him, but she'd said she was going with some friends. Even Cookie was going with the book club ladies. So when Everly Peterson, who was in charge of the little theater company in town, had asked him this morning if he'd like to go with her, he'd been just peeved enough at Sara to say yes. Going out on a rare night off would be a distraction. It would remind him in case he was in danger of forgetting that he was single and it was never a good idea to get stuck on one woman. Especially a woman like Sara who wouldn't be hanging around Angel Falls for long. Besides, Everly had been trying to get him to go out all summer.

"Here. Have the rest," Colton said, handing the container over to Rafe.

He was done with the pie. He was going to move on. Starting tonight.

* * *

"I want cotton candy," Sara's five-year-old niece Julia said as they walked across the green in the middle of downtown, where everyone was setting up chairs and spreading blankets for the Fourth of July fireworks. It was nine thirty, the horizon still glowing with a rim of deep indigo where the sun had just set. "Can we get some, Aunt Sara? Please?"

"Of course we can," Sara said, eager to finally get the opportunity to spoil Julia and her three-year-old brother Michael. Gabby, minus Malcolm, who was working, was holding Michael's hand as they walked across the grass. Kaitlyn brought up the back of their little group, carrying a giant waterproof blanket. She'd decided at the last minute to tag along instead of staying home and fretting about her breakup, which Sara thought was a positive thing. Sara was hoping to find some time to really talk to her about it, because so far she'd been avoiding the topic.

"How about here, ladies? And boy," Sara said, bending to plant a kiss on the top of her nephew's sweet blond head. She'd found an empty space in the middle of the green, which was dotted with a veritable patch-work quilt of multicolored blankets, each occupied by a little cluster of family or friends.

She loved the town's Fourth of July celebrations. The parade, the picnics, the fireworks—yet today she couldn't help but feel that something—someone—was missing. Every dark-haired, broad-shouldered guy who walked with a noticeably confident stride made her think of Colton.

She hadn't heard from him since last night, which was hardly cause for alarm, but she knew deep down that he wasn't going to call or text her. She'd given him a message, and he'd gotten it, loud and clear.

In her mind she kept seeing the expression on his face when she'd handed him that pie. He'd seemed truly touched.

She'd be out of her mind to even consider getting involved with him. As far as she knew, he'd never had a girlfriend for longer than a lunar cycle. It would be crazy to think that someone like her, Sara Jane the Brain, could break that streak.

He'd always been the cocky, too-handsome boy who was completely out of her league. Yet she didn't feel like that nerdy high school girl around him anymore. When he looked at her, she felt the absolute heat of his gaze. The way his eyes lingered on her told her he wanted her. The way he'd kissed her, so suddenly and unexpect-edly, had taken her completely by surprise, but the way they'd fit together, and the heat of their kisses, wild and unrestrained, told her a lot more could've happened be-tween them if she hadn't put on the brakes.

Not that she'd kissed a lot of guys, but she knew what it was like to have a kiss travel south so fast it made your toes curl. And heat up other places along the way.

"Here come Colton and Rafe," Gabby said, and Sara almost choked on the lemonade she was sipping.

Sure enough, the two guys were walking toward them, both of them out of uniform. Colton was wearing a black short-sleeved polo and gray shorts. He looked tanned and lean, his biceps flexing under his shirt. It was disconcerting to see him dressed like a normal person. And to find he looked just as hot out of uniform as in it.

Rafe said hi to Kaitlyn and tossed his niece and nephew up in the air, his usual riling-up activity that would leave them totally wired for at least the next half hour.

"Hi," Sara said, avoiding Colton's gaze. He wore a dark expression, his brows knit down low, adding to his sexy vibe but also disconcerting her even more. She had to steel herself not to look at him because…muscles. Serious ones. And really nice legs. He was wearing athletic flip-flops and even his toes were really nice. Geez. She needed help.

"Excuse me a second," Colton said before Sara could get her head back on straight. He called after a boy of around ten who was running past with another boy. Curious, Sara watched Colton out of the corner of her eye while Gabby and Kaitlyn made small talk with Rafe. Colton reached for his wallet and handed a bill to one of the boys. "Go to the concessions and grab a hot dog, OK?" she heard him say.

"Their dad's sick and their mom's working two jobs," Rafe said quietly to Sara. "Colton tries to make sure they get to do something fun once in a while."

Sara looked up at her brother and blushed. Not so much because he'd caught her eavesdropping as because she'd just witnessed another example of Colton's proving that she'd been completely wrong about him.

"Want to join us?" she asked Rafe casually as Colton jogged back to the group. There went those fine, fine muscles again.

"We can't," he said. "I've got to get to work soon and Colty here has a date." He gave Colton a playful slap on the back.

"A date?" Sara echoed. Her gaze wandered over to Colton, who suddenly seemed to find the grass really fascinating.

Just then a pretty blonde walked up, threw her arms around him, and gave him a big kiss on the cheek. "There you are," she said. "It's so crowded I was afraid I'd never find you."

Well, Colton certainly hadn't wasted any time fretting over Sara's rejection, had he? She recognized the woman as Everly Peterson, from their high school class. She'd moved to New York to become an actress. Evie had told her she'd returned last year divorced from her plastic surgeon husband, but with boobs three times their previous size. Sara didn't like to make judgments about anybody, especially since high school had been a long time ago. Everly had come back to run the town's little nonprofit theater. Maybe she'd changed and wasn't the attention-seeking drama queen she'd been back then.

"Oh, cute kids!" Everly said, tugging down her already low-cut T-shirt so it showcased her boobs. She checked out Julia and Michael, who were currently running around Rafe's legs as he pretended to be a monster, growling and moaning and tickling them as they passed. "They yours, Sara?"

"My sister's. I promised them cotton candy before the fireworks start." With that she turned to Kaitlyn and Gabby. "Want anything from the concessions?"

"Oh, I'd love some cotton candy!" Everly said.

"No problem," Colton said. "Sara, I'm happy to get your stuff too."

"No thanks," she said. She could get the kids their cotton candy herself, thank you very much. He went off, and she grabbed her purse from the blanket.

"Hurry up," Gabby said. "Fireworks are going to start any minute."

Of course she ended up in the line right behind Colton. She tapped her foot anxiously against the grass. There was no reason to be angry. She was going to be calm and dignified about this. Everly was beautiful in a way Sara would never be. More importantly, Everly was Colton's type of woman—beautiful and buxom. She even had this giddy little laugh. Clearly she was fun.

In line, three separate people said hi to Colton. An elderly woman thanked him for hauling her Christmas tree down from the attic for her Christmas-in-July celebration, a father thanked him for talking to his son after he'd gotten caught spray painting graffiti under the bridge, and Mr. Langotti, who owned one of the cafés downtown, thanked him for keeping an eye on his house when he'd been on vacation the week before.

It appeared everyone in the entire town was in love with him. Finally the last person left. Sara poked Colton in the back.

"Nice night for a date," Sara said. She knew full well she sounded catty but couldn't seem to help herself.

"It is," he replied, though he didn't turn around.

"Leave it to you to date the prettiest girl in town." Again with the catty. She needed to just keep her mouth shut.

"Not only is she pretty, she knows how to have fun too."

Ouch. "My pie must've not been very tasty, because it only took you twenty-four hours to get over it." *Why couldn't she stop?*

Finally he turned to look at her, and his gaze was steely. "A pie is just a pie, sweetheart."

And with that he turned back to the concession counter and handed her a Coke and two cotton candies. She took them, mollified and confused. His expression was business as usual. "Thank you," she said. "You didn't have to—"

"I wanted to."

Why did he always have to do something nice? She wanted—no, needed—to stay pissed at him. She tasted the Coke. Diet. "How did you know I drink diet?"

He shrugged. "Good guess." His gaze seared through her, leaving a burning trail of heat in its path. It burned through her insides and bloomed on her face in a crimson blush. "I've got to get back to Everly," Colton said. "Enjoy the fireworks."

He turned to walk back to his date, leaving her alone. The brief walk back to the blanket didn't improve her mood. She gave the kids a couple pulls of the cotton candy, even ate a bite herself, but she couldn't relax. The excitement she'd felt about bringing the kids here had faded.

"What's wrong?" Gabby asked her while Kaitlyn entertained the kids.

"Nothing's wrong. I'm just waiting for the fireworks to start." She sneaked a glance over at Colton and Everly, who of course had chosen to sit about ten feet away. She could see them chatting and Everly playfully pushing his shoulder. A time or two she heard his laugh, deep and sonorous. Everly must be very clever to get him to laugh like that. Sara didn't think anyone had ever laughed that way with her. And she wondered if anyone ever would. "Just that Everly's acting like the Eveready sex bunny."

"Sara! That's not like you."

"Well, maybe I'm not feeling like myself tonight. Am I fun?"

"Right now you're not, but you can be. You've got feelings for Colton, don't you?"

"No! Of course not. Why would I have feelings for him?"

"Because he's a nice guy. And because he might have feelings for you too."

"Colton doesn't do relationships. I'd be humiliated all over again, and the whole town would start gossiping. I could never subject myself to that again, believe me."

"You're scared!" Gabby wagged her index finger at Sara. "That's why you're running from your feelings."

"I made him a pie and he kissed me. But then I shut him down. And that was just last night and look who he's with today. End of story."

"You probably hurt his feelings."

She snorted. "I doubt it. If I did, he certainly recovered quickly."

The fireworks had begun, lighting up the sky with bursts of white light and loud rat-a-tatting noises that Sara felt reverberate clear through her chest. It had always been a fantasy of hers to watch fireworks with someone who kissed her as the *boom-boom-boom* of the explosions filled the night sky. Tagg had hated fireworks, so they'd rarely gone, plus he hated showing affection in public. Oh well, guess she was going to have to wait for another Fourth for a man who could make her see stars. Because she'd totally blown it this year.

She tried to take joy in her niece and nephew, but Michael was a little frightened and kept holding his hands over his ears. Sara tried to hold his ears for him and make a joke, but he wasn't buying it.

"I haveta pee," he said. Evie had warned her that he meant what he said. But where was she going to take him? The public bathroom was quite a hike away.

"Auntie Sara," he said more urgently. "I haveta pee *now*."

"C'mon, I'll take you," she said, scooping him up and heading to the back of the crowd. A patch of woods surrounded the baseball field, and in high school kids used to go in there to make out and smoke weed. She just hoped no one was in there now doing that or other worse things she didn't want to see. She walked about a foot into the woods and said, "Pee on that big rock."

He lifted his little face. "*Outside?*"

"Yeah. Um, Spider-Man pees outside when he has to, and this is an emergency." He liked Spider-Man as well as Barbies, didn't he?

"A 'mergency," he said, grinning. Then pulled down his pants and got the deed done.

"That was awesome!" she said as she carried him back to the field. "Don't tell your mom, though, OK?"

"I'm telling," he said, grinning and wrapping his little hand around her neck. His mother's son all the way.

On the way back to the blanket, Sara couldn't help but notice Colton and Everly again, but this time she did a double take because Everly was leaning over on the blanket, cleavage in plain view, feeding him cotton candy.

"Aunt Sara, why did you stop?" Michael asked.

Sara shook her head. "Oh, sorry, Mikey," she murmured. The intensity of her unkind, murderous feelings for Everly shocked her so much she'd stopped walking. And those same feelings bubbled up for Colton. How could he let Everly feed him cotton candy when yesterday he'd eaten Sara's *pie*?

She became aware Michael was tugging on her shorts. "What is it, sweetie?" she asked.

"You stopped again."

She scooped Michael up and kissed him and carried

him through the crowd back to their blanket, forcing herself to stay in the moment. But in the back of her brain, something niggled. The overt jealousy she felt at seeing Colton with another woman appeared to be above and beyond what she'd feel for someone she was merely attracted to. She couldn't possibly have real feelings for Colton.

Or could she?

Chapter 13

♥

Well, Sara had certainly acted jealous about Colton's date. And he had to admit that made him really...happy. He'd enjoyed sticking it to her too, and had taken a perverse pleasure in seeing her all riled up. Could it be possible she *was* interested in him, even after that just-friends speech?

"Colt, why are you chuckling to yourself?" Everly asked, scooting up close to him on their blanket. Instinctively, he leaned away from her overpowering perfume. He'd gone along with her feeding him cotton candy because he'd seen Sara walking toward them with Michael, and dammit, he wanted to make her jealous, but now that the fireworks were almost over he just wanted to go home.

He shook his head, as if it were easy to shake thoughts of Sara out of it. "I'm just thinking what a nice evening it is." He was spending way too much time thinking about Sara. Maybe he was losing it, because since when did he prefer someone who'd rejected him over a beautiful woman who was right next to him? Everly was close and getting closer. He could tell from the looks she was telegraphing him, from the way she kept showing him her cleavage, from her subtle little touches, that she'd be more than delighted to join him in bed tonight. Trouble was, he just couldn't work up the excitement for it—for her.

Geez. Ruined by a smart, pretty type A woman who'd turned him on by baking him a birthday pie. Maybe he really *was* losing it.

Everly linked her arm through his. Fireworks lit up the sky, booming and bursting.

But Colton barely noticed—the fireworks or Everly. He was thinking of how cute Sara looked in shorts and a T-shirt, her hair up in a ponytail. Out of the corner of his eye, he could see her holding her nephew and pointing up at the sky. The little boy was leaning back against her and watching the display with a look of awe, and Sara was laughing.

His eyes wandered in her direction, only to find she was looking right back at him. So she *was* staring at him. Interesting. Maybe she was running scared. She'd spent a lot of years with Tagg and had been through a lot this past year. Maybe she was a little nervous about jumping into something.

"It is a beautiful night," Everly said after the fireworks ended. "And it doesn't have to end." She gave him a pointed look meant to telegraph her meaning.

"Gee, thanks, Everly, it's been a lot of fun, but I've got to get home. Early day tomorrow, you know?"

Colton drove Everly home, then parked his cruiser

at the station and walked the short distance downtown. The shops were lit up. One or two people walked their dog, and there were a few stragglers from the fireworks, but the place was pretty dead. He kept walking to the bridge.

The angel statue greeted him as it had every day since he'd moved here.

"Don't look at me like that," he said to the angels. "She told me to get lost. Well, not in those words, but she friend-zoned me." He leaned over the bridge to look at the falls cascading over the rocks. The green was mostly deserted now.

"I'm the one that friend-zones people," he mumbled. "I'm the one who likes to date around. This is a good thing." Except even though Everly was beautiful and willing, he had no desire to go out with her. There was no challenge there. What was wrong with him?

Sara was able to raise his blood pressure like no other woman, that was for sure. And admittedly, he did sometimes take a perverse pleasure in baiting her, in watching her outrage rise in a pretty blush up her face. "I don't know why I do it," he told the angels. "In fact, I don't know why I'm attracted to someone I can't help sparring with half the time."

He had to let this go. But as he stood there on the bridge, the memory of that early spring evening came to him, with the blossoms blowing across the bridge, their sweet scent intoxicating and heady. He'd shared one hell of a kiss with Sara that evening. A kiss so full of promise that he could barely sleep the entire week.

That attraction was still there, regardless of her years

with Tagg, regardless of the fact that their date had never happened. It buzzed between them like bugs around a flame, and there was no denying it. Until he saw it through, he would always have questions that nagged at him. That kiss hadn't been the end of something. It had been a beginning.

* * *

In a small town like Angel Falls, the fireworks display didn't last that long. Thank God, because Sara had a splitting headache. Julia was tired and whiny, her small hand literally stuck to Sara's like syrup on a pancake, and Michael had fallen asleep, his head wobbling a little on Gabby's shoulder. Kaitlyn had taken off with Steve to have a big relationship talk, so Sara and Gabby headed with the kids toward home.

"Remind me of why we decided to walk again?" Gabby asked, adjusting Michael's dead-to-the-world weight in her arms.

Sara peeled her hand carefully away from Julia's. It made a sound like a zipper unzipping. "Oh my gosh, Julia, here, sweetie, stick to Aunt Gabby for a bit while I take Michael." She chuckled, but Julia just responded with an "I'm tired" and rubbed her eyes, getting more sticky stuff on her face, which was already coated with a sparkly layer of cotton candy sugar.

Sara traded glances with Gabby. She saw the glint of desperation plain as day. Gabby pointed to the picnic bench on the far edge of the park, which stood on the grass a few feet ahead. It would be their last pit stop before hauling the kids another half a mile home. Which wasn't that much, but it now seemed as impossible as a trip on foot across the Sahara with no water.

"Why is it children weigh twice as much when asleep than awake?" Gabby said as they sat. A soft snore emanated from Julia, whose mouth had dropped open in a soft little *O*.

Sara laughed. "I don't know, but I'm sorry I've been such a pill tonight."

Gabby patted her on the knee. "I forgive you. If it's any consolation, Colton kept looking over at you."

Sara shook her head. "I doubt Colton was looking at me when he had Everly to ogle."

"Oh my God, Sara. That man wants to do you, and you drove him into the arms of that horrible woman."

Sara rolled her eyes. "I didn't drive him into anybody's arms. I mean, it took him less than twenty-four hours to find someone else! Who does that?"

"An angry alpha male? Who maybe wanted to make you a little jealous? Or who wanted to try and forget you, but of course he can't because he's fallen deeply in love with you. Or maybe he's always been."

"My God, Gabby, you should write romance novels. Really."

"I'm just saying, I personally wouldn't write him off just because you're scared."

"I'm not scared!"

"Come on, Sara. I mean, if that were me, I'd be a little nervous too of someone whose nickname is the Revolver."

"I've only been with Tagg."

"Having only been with one person isn't the problem here. The trouble is, he wasn't the *right* person. And you've hinted to me before that maybe the sex with Tagg wasn't that great. A man like Colton has got to know what he's doing in bed. Maybe it would be... you know, a little fun to find out?"

"Gabby!" She looked down to check that the little ones were still asleep.

Her sister raised her brows in a *Well, I'm just sayin'* expression.

Sex with Tagg had been pleasantly predictable at its best... and, to be honest, generally lacking. She'd always covered up those feelings, thinking that that was the way it went when you were with someone for a long time, or blamed it on her own lack of experience. Thought that maybe if she tried new things, read *Cosmo* more, whatever, the sex would be better. After all, that's who she was at her core. Try Harder Sara. Out to please. Out to win everyone's approval.

"Thank you for being my sister," Sara said. "And I'm sorry everything's been about me lately. I was shocked when you announced your engagement. I felt bad. Like I'd been so wrapped up in my own troubles, I never even saw that coming."

"You didn't see it coming because I didn't see it coming. It had nothing to do with the fact that you just moved, started a new job, and are understandably stressed."

Sara picked her words carefully. "Are you happy with him?"

Gabby sighed and adjusted Julia's head on her shoulder. "What's happiness? If happiness is having a family one day, then yes, I'm happy, because I want that more than anything."

Oh God, that was not the right answer. "Gabby, you're young. You're talking like this is your last shot at marriage and a family."

"Let's get real, Sara. I'm twenty-nine, I have a job I dislike, and time is ticking away. I know Malcolm's not perfect, but he's smart, adventurous, and he's got a great job. Not to mention he's cute. Sometimes we don't get exactly what we want. We have to make do, or we miss out entirely."

"It's not like you to compromise for something so important. You're the romantic of the family."

"Maybe for once I'm a realist."

She tapped her sister's shin with her foot. "Don't settle, Gabs. I almost did. If Tagg hadn't been stupid, who knows how long I would've kept telling myself I loved him, trying to make it work, despite knowing in my gut there had to be more? I thought Tagg leaving me was awful, but now I see it in an entirely different light. It's a second chance for me."

A second chance with Colton. Which she'd blown.

Suddenly Sara began to laugh.

"What?" Gabby asked. "What is it?"

"We are never going to be able to carry these kids home. I mean…look at them." Michael was asleep with his cheek on Sara's shoulder, drooling, bless his heart. Julia was snoring, her head leaning back wantonly on Gabby's arm.

"I suppose we could call Joe and Evie to come get

us," Gabby said. She nodded in the direction of the road over Sara's shoulder. "Or . . . we could just get into Colton's cop car."

"Colton's . . ." Sara turned to see a car drive slowly down the road and stop directly in front of the park bench. Colton rolled down the passenger window and leaned over the seat. "Care for a ride home?" he asked. No one else appeared to be with him, including pretty buxom females who were cute and bubbly. Thank God.

"Yes!" Gabby said without compunction. She didn't even acknowledge Sara's glare. Fine. They were desperate. She'd take the ride.

Colton lifted Julia and carried her to the car, handing her to Gabby once she climbed into the back seat. Then he came back for Michael. "I've got him, thanks," Sara said, struggling to get up from the bench with a sleeping three-year-old who suddenly appeared to weigh as much as a sleeping elephant. Colton reached over and took Michael anyway, flashing Sara a don't-be-stupid glare.

"We don't have car seats," Sara announced from the back seat once they were all settled in.

She found her gaze level with Colton's in the rearview mirror. "Oh, you're right, Doc. Maybe you two should walk then."

"Now, Sara," Gabby said quickly, "it's only a few blocks, and Colton will drive really carefully, right, Colton? And we're so grateful for the ride, aren't we?" Sara felt a smack on her thigh. "Aren't we, Sara?"

"Yes, fine, Gabby, we're grateful. Very grateful."

"That's what I like to hear, ladies," he said, pulling

away from the curb. Sara didn't miss his grin in the mirror. "I promise I'll drive carefully."

They drove the short distance to Evie's with Gabby chatting exuberantly with Colton about cotton candy, the kids' antics, and the people she'd seen at the park. Which was fine with Sara, who couldn't wait to get out of the car. Evie and Joe met them in the driveway and carried their sticky sleeping angels to their beds.

When Colton offered to drive Gabby and Sara to Nonna's, Gabby wouldn't let Sara protest. As soon as they got out of the police cruiser, Gabby yawned loudly and stretched. "Those kids really wore me out, man oh man. Think I'll go in and check on Nonna. And Sara, you can just, you know, take as long as you want. Even all night, if you know what I mean. I've got things covered."

Gabby gave her a wink, jogged up the porch steps, and disappeared through the screen door before Sara could murder her.

She was ready to bolt up the stairs herself when Colton's hand on her arm held her back.

"It's a nice night," he said, his gaze steady and calm, his touch soft but insistent. "How about we take a walk?"

She scanned his eyes. He was looking at her in a way that seared clear through her like a lightning bolt, burning her to ash.

Why was she angry with him, again? Oh, Everly. But deep inside, she knew Everly posed no threat. The threat she worried about was much closer than Everly and her new boobs. It was inside Sara's own heart.

Colton seemed to have an uncanny ability to see her inside and out, X-ray vision kind of seeing. He constantly called her out on all her noise: her drive for perfection, going a million miles an hour, and trying so hard to achieve. Somehow she sensed that with him it might be OK to just *be*.

He took her hand as they walked down the tree-lined street. The moon was a bright crescent, and the sky looked like some magical fairies had tossed a bucket of glitter all over a backdrop of black velvet. It was one of those warm, wonderful midsummer nights when you didn't even need a sweater. Golden lights from inside the century-old houses made everything look picture-book perfect, and Colton strolled along as calmly as if they were old friends out for a walk.

Maybe she wasn't ready for this, for him, for any man. The past year had been so full of pain. The rejection she'd felt last summer at being passed over for someone who'd appeared on a whim still hurt. It made her question everything about herself, who she thought she was, what she thought she wanted, where she even belonged in the world. Being back home had just added to the unsettled feeling, since working with her dad seemed like a temporary stop along the way.

But Colton, he belonged somewhere, all right. As perfect a fit as a puzzle piece. He had that magic kind of personality that attracted people—he always had. Everyone loved him. He was woven into the fabric of their town, while she would always be the outsider looking in.

"I always like to imagine when I'm doing my rounds

and I see lights on in a house, a family is tucked in for the night," Colton said. "It makes me feel..."

She laughed, thankful to be dragged from her maudlin musings. "Like a voyeur?"

"Ha ha," he said. "I was going to say peaceful."

"When I was younger and I was walking home at night, I always looked into lit-up houses and imagined a family sitting around a table, the kids doing homework, the mom and dad supervising. Sort of like the fantasy family I was missing after my mom died."

He gave her hand a sympathetic squeeze. "I know the feeling."

Sara stopped on the sidewalk and faced Colton. He was so handsome, standing there in the glow of a nearby streetlight, the shadows highlighting his defined cheekbones, his strong jaw.

Was it possible that the two of them could be much more alike than different? Each of them had grown up missing a parent and longing to belong to a "normal" family, if there was really any such thing. They'd both ended up back here in Angel Falls for reasons not of their own choosing.

Sara took a deep breath. "Colton. I told you I wanted to be *friends* because you scare me to death."

"Yeah, I tend to have that effect on people," he said, chuckling a little, but she could tell it was a nervous laugh.

"I've been with one guy my whole life. I'm not ready for a relationship. I—"

He cut her off. "I don't care about any of that. I don't care about the past anymore, not our past or your past with Tagg. It's time to take a new course. For both of us."

Colton tugged her hand up very slowly to his mouth. His warm, masculine grip encased it as he slowly kissed her knuckles, one by one. A simple and easy gesture, but her pulse was doing the Indy 500 thing and it was making her dizzy.

"I'm sorry I brought Everly tonight," Colt said. "I was angry at you. Look, Sara, I don't want anyone but you. I can't eat or sleep, and all I do is think about how you'd feel in my arms. God knows why, because you're a real pain in the—"

She put a finger over his full lips. "Stop while you're ahead, big guy." Couldn't eat? Couldn't sleep? How she'd feel *in his arms*? Oh, wow. He'd had her at *Let's take a walk*.

His mouth curled up in the slightest smile. Then he kissed her finger.

The silly yet touching gesture melted her. He lowered her hand slowly from his mouth. The heat and fire of his gaze raised goose bumps up and down her arms despite the warm evening. "I want you, Sara. Every second of every—"

Sara cut him off, wrapping her arms around his neck and cutting off his words with her lips. He circled his big arms around her and kissed her back, deeply and urgently, pressing his body against hers. *He wanted her.* She could feel it down to her marrow, in the way he held her, tightly and possessively, the thorough way his lips moved over hers.

"How about we go back to my place and sit on my balcony?" he asked.

She crinkled up her nose. "That might sound a little like a line."

He stroked her cheek, and her knees almost caved. "It is a line," he said, his lips twitching. "But come anyway."

She sucked in a breath. Was he asking her to... Well, yes. Yes, he was. It wasn't like she'd never been propositioned before, but it had always been by semidrunk guys in bars. Usually with Tagg nearby to fend them off.

She glanced up at him, past the spinning, heady feeling, past her heart throbbing in her throat and every nerve standing on end. Once she saw the way he looked back at her, tenderly and calmly, her panic halted. He had a way of quieting her soul at the same time he filled her with anticipation and excitement, which seemed impossible but was the only way she could describe his effect on her.

"OK," she whispered, smiling. She gave him her hand and let him lead the way.

Chapter 14

♥

Colton led the way up the stairs and into his apartment, where he managed, a little shakily, to turn on a lamp. Around him stood his token bachelor living room, comprised of a leather couch, a La-Z-Boy, and a bunch of electronics along one wall.

"Nice TV," Sara said stiffly, looking around. She'd turned quiet during the last block, and dead silent on the way up the stairs.

"Thanks." God, he hadn't been this nervous since he had to read aloud in front of the class in third grade. He must *really* be losing his touch if he was thinking about that when he had a beautiful woman in his apartment.

Not just any beautiful woman. One who challenged him, and who brought out the best and the worst in him. A woman he could not stop wanting.

"I mean, there are no wires," she continued. "Some people have all those tangled wires." She made jumbled-up motions with her hands. "Not you though, nope. Tidy as can be."

"Do you want a drink?" he asked. His voice sounded a little higher than usual, their normal conversation having been replaced by Sara's waxing poetic about the quality of his TV setup. Her hands were shaking a little. He wanted to tell her his were too, but feared that would make her even more nervous.

She cleared her throat. "Water would be nice. I'll get it myself. I need to wash my hands." She held up her palms, which had a few blue streaks of cotton candy on them. He'd been thinking more in terms of a good, stiff shot of Jack Daniel's.

She walked into his kitchen and turned on the water while he poured a glass of ice water from the fridge and handed it to her.

"Thanks," she said politely, taking a few sips. "Are you nervous?" she asked over the top of the glass.

They were finally alone in a place where they could do something about it, and he could not blow this. Nervous? More like completely off the bell curve. "No," he said.

Sara, usually ready with some kind of retort designed to make his blood pressure skyrocket, was oddly silent. That was one thing about getting into it with her: they always had something to say. Getting *along* was a lot harder. He placed his hand lightly over hers, which was oddly cold. That little sign of cold, clammy vulnerability, plus the fact that she alternated between jittery small talk and complete silence, made him feel strangely tender.

"Red, I—" He wanted to tell her not to worry, but he faltered. Up close, he was drawn to all the multicolored flecks in her pretty green eyes—some dark, some honey colored—a beautiful unique mixture that took his breath—and his words—away.

"I—saw you giving money to those boys tonight," she said, filling in his awkward silence. "That was...sweet."

He looked down, not wanting to discuss how "sweet" he was. "Look," he said, rubbing the back of his neck, "don't make me out to be a hero. If I can do little things to help, I try to do them. Mainly because growing up, I understood what it was like—not to have stuff. Not to have fun."

She placed a hand over his chest. "You're very kind-hearted."

"I'm a small-town cop just doing my job." Why were they talking about his job when he wanted to be kissing her?

"I heard all those people who came up to you in line. Pulling down Christmas trees for elderly ladies and talking to kids and keeping an eye on people's houses when they're gone."

"Like I said, it's my job."

She shook her head. "It's more than that. Everyone in this town loves you. You look out for people—just like you look out for your family."

He sighed. Gently he took her glass and set it down. Then he lifted her up and set her on the counter next to the stove, stepping carefully between her legs.

She swallowed. He leaned his hands on the counter-top beside her, caging her in. "How do I get you to stop talking?" he asked, biting back a smile.

Gingerly she reached out and patted one of his biceps, as if she were examining it. Another avoidance technique, not a good sign. He massaged her shoulders. Yep, tense as a live wire. That made him back up a little and gesture toward the living room. "Come on. Let's watch TV. You can check out my sound system."

She laughed at that. But when he turned to go, she tugged on his sleeve, keeping him in place. "It's the over-ten-year thing," she blurted. "With Tagg. And no one else. Particularly the *no one else* part. Whereas you, on the other hand—"

With one swift move, he took her in his arms and pulled her close. She was soft and warm and he didn't know a damn thing about flowers but her scent reminded him of summer—warm sunshine and sweetness. "Sara," he said, smoothing wisps of hair back from her face. God, she was pretty. "I don't care about any of that. Unless, of course, you still want Tagg."

Her gaze met his. "I want you."

His heart was thundering crazily in his chest. He ached to touch her, but he needed to make certain she was all in on this. Wanted everything to be just right.

He took her smile as a good sign. So he bent closer to capture her mouth.

She held out a hand and pressed it against his chest. "I-I just want to make it clear, I'm in no position for a relationship. I—this is just for fun, right? I want us to be on the same page."

That surprised him, mostly because that was usually *his* line. He tried to figure out why it disappointed him a little too. Colton understood a woman like Sara wasn't likely to hang out for long with a guy like him anyway, no matter how people praised him ad nauseam for his good deeds.

All he knew was that he wanted her. And he'd take whatever she would give him. "Gotcha. Loud and clear."

Then he kissed her. Which, he was relieved to find, finally stopped all the talking. A funny thing happened when his lips met hers. Everything—the apartment, the hum of the fridge, the fireworks kids were setting off in the streets, the background humming of his nerves, ceased to be. There were just the two of them and his mouth on hers, their arms circling tight around each other.

Sara kissed him back, their tongues tangling, their lips searching, their bodies flush. She tasted like cotton candy and a sweetness he'd been missing for years. She fit perfectly in his arms, all curvy softness. With that kiss all the years of animosity disintegrated, and he thought he must've been an idiot to ever bother arguing with her about *anything*.

"You're beautiful," he murmured, running his hand under her shirt, over the warm, smooth skin of her back.

She blushed and shook her head, smiling.

"If you're forcing me to take compliments, I'm going to make you do it too," he said.

"Just kiss me," she said, curling her hand around the nape of his neck and kissing him deeply. A whimper escaped from her throat. When he pulled back to look at her, her eyes were dreamy, and, he thought, full of the same hunger he felt coursing through him. No nerves. A tidal wave of relief bowled through him.

"Sara, I—" Words lingered on his lips, the need to tell her something honest. But her words stayed with him: *just for fun.* So he traced his finger along her cheek instead. His hand was shaking a little, and he moved it before she could see.

When there was no sarcasm left between them, what was there? He wasn't sure, but it didn't feel like anything he'd ever experienced before. He tucked a strand behind her ear. "I always wanted to do that. Touch your hair."

"Take me to your bed now, Colt," she said, her mouth curving upward. "I don't want us to do it next to the coffee maker."

The magic words. "Whatever you say," he said, lifting her up, loving the way she wrapped herself sweetly around him. He carried her to his bedroom, kissing her all the way.

* * *

Good thing Colton carried her, because Sara's legs felt like marshmallows, weak and offering no support. She was trembling all over. Warm lava was pumping through her veins, and she thought she might be having a stroke, based on the hot and cold, the weakness, the leaden pounding of her heart. Whatever disease this was, she didn't want to get over it.

And oh my God, the man could kiss. She could spend *hours* kissing those beautiful, skilled lips.

He laid her unceremoniously on the bed and shucked

off his shirt and shorts in typical guy fashion, then stood there in all his male perfection, confidence flowing in spades. He was all sculpted hills and valleys, all tight muscle and golden skin. Then he was over her, their legs tangling, his erection pressing against the throbbing, aching pulse between her legs.

"Colton," she said. He was kissing her neck, behind her ear, tangling his hands in her hair, kissing her like she'd never been kissed, carefully, slowly, then suddenly demanding, consuming her, burning her up in flames. Somehow her blouse got undone and tossed off, her shorts pitched to the floor. He whispered sweet things, how beautiful she was, how happy he was that she was here with him, how he loved making love with her. She'd pegged him for a quiet man, not demonstrative at all, but again he'd surprised her. She'd never heard such words before, words that made her feel...treasured.

He unhitched her bra effortlessly, and then his mouth was on her breast and he was using his tongue in wicked ways. Heat built in her core and flashed all through her as he kissed and suckled, her body tensing and tightening and readying for him as her fevered need for him rose. When a moan escaped her, she felt him smile against her skin.

She drew her arms around him, up the sinewy cords of his back, fascinated by the hard muscle and contrasting softness of his skin. She slid her hand under his briefs, smoothing it over the taut muscle of his butt. "How's your tetanus shot these days?" she murmured as she stroked him.

"That's my girl," he said. "I was waiting for you to

mention that. I'm sorry, but I'm going to have to dole out some payback for that."

"No payback," she managed to say.

"Oh, don't worry. I think you might like it." He peeled off her scrap of panty and slipped a finger into her slick wetness, stroking her swollen flesh, kissing her long and slow and deep.

"Colton," she said, her voice urgent, grasping his arms, tugging him over her.

He put on a condom and she guided him into her body, clutching at his back while he entered her carefully, steadily, filling her, moving her. For a moment their gazes locked. Honesty, earnestness, connection—it all shook her. She met his gaze full on, tamping down an underlying sense of terror that somehow this man was different from any other, and she would never come out of this the same.

Waves of pleasure rolled mercilessly through her, every muscle tightening. She could tell from the way his muscles were tensing that he was very close to release too.

He kissed her mouth and began moving inside her, starting a rhythm that sent the little waves cascading into bigger, hotter ones, rolling through her one by one like a warm, languid summer tide. She opened to him, wrapped herself around him, embraced him with all her strength.

"Sara," he cried out, and then he let go, taking her with him. And she clung to him as they both plunged over the edge.

* * *

Colton was not a cuddler or a spooner, but he reached
for Sara and pulled her to him, smoothing out her
amazing hair as it fell against his neck. He inhaled its
sweet scent, felt its silken weight run through his fingers.
Around now was the time when he'd typically mention
he had to get started early tomorrow, and the woman
in question would take the hint and leave. A part of
him had been hoping that once they'd made love, he
would see Sara was like any other woman, that it was
just sex, yada yada. Instead he'd found himself experiencing another feeling he had no real understanding
of—contentment.

She surprised him by talking first. "Tomorrow's Sunday. I've got to get up early to help Nonna get ready for
family dinner." She paused. "You should come sometime. To family dinner. I mean, you're good friends
with Rafe, and Nonna loves you, so it's not like anyone
would wonder why you're there."

He hesitated more than the usual time, finally de-
ciding to be honest. "Thanks, but family dinners...just
not my thing." It wasn't his thing. He didn't consider
that maybe she'd be the exception to his rule, because
she'd said she was in this for fun. There was no point in
pretending otherwise.

"Oh, OK." Disappointment resonated in her voice.

"It's nothing personal. Just that...you know,
it's...family." Great, that was making a lot of sense.
"What I mean is..."

She kissed him quickly. "Sounds like we're both on

the same page. We'll keep this light. I'm not offended."
She still looked a little disappointed, maybe. He did
know her family's Sunday dinner was a big deal. Something he'd never show up to casually. And he knew her
family would never interpret his being there as a casual
thing.

She moved to get up. Impulsively he put a hand on
her arm to hold her back. "I said I didn't do family
dinners. Not that I wanted you to go." If she were anyone else, he'd encourage her to leave and get a good
night's rest. But he didn't want her to go. So he tightened his hold and draped a hand around her waist. She
gave in and lay back against him, resting a hand lightly
on his forearm. It looked pale and creamy—delicate—
compared to his much darker coloring.

"What are you thinking about?" he asked. Also new
for him. When had he ever asked *that*?

She smiled. "What we just did. How I still can't even
believe it. When I think about you and me in high
school—"

"I don't even want to talk about how I was in high
school."

"Why not? You were handsome and popular. You
had everything I wanted. Popularity, friends. I was just
an ugly little duckling."

"I was a jerk." He paused. "And I never thought you
were ugly."

"Oh, come on. It's all right. I had pimples and thick
glasses and braces until I was a sophomore."

He shrugged. "Everyone has an awkward phase."

"Except you."

He nuzzled her neck a little. God, she smelled good. "I almost asked you to homecoming senior year."

"What?" She propped herself up on one elbow, giving him a view of her pretty shoulders—and her cleavage, which she'd covered loosely with the sheet. "You did not."

"Remember when I'd hurt my knee and was hobbling around on crutches, and you'd sprained your ankle and were in an AirCast?"

"Oh yeah. I sprained it working at Outerspace Burgers while I was on those awful roller skates they made us wear."

"Yeah, well, we were sitting together at an assembly in the handicapped seats. Remember that?"

"I remember being nervous sitting next to you. Because you were so handsome. And I felt bad for you—it was right after you'd blown out your knee. The whole school was talking about it."

"Everyone was telling me I'd be fine, I was a great player, I'd come back. Basically blowing smoke up my butt when the doctors told me from the beginning it was bad news. You didn't say any of that. You just said, *I'm sorry*. That meant something to me. I think I understood deep inside my football career was over. I never thought I'd even make it to college without my scholarship."

She rubbed his shoulder. "That must've been a hard time for you."

"Honestly, I was more worried about the college part than the football part. I had to provide for Hannah. I couldn't do that without a decent job."

"You had a lot of responsibility for such a young man." Suddenly she grinned.

"What is it?"

"So what's the part about me? And homecoming. I can't wait to hear this." Her eyes were lit up in anticipation of what he was about to say. He couldn't help thinking he'd never seen this side of her, expectant as a little kid, her guard totally down.

"So you sat with me and we talked and I got to thinking you were pretty nice. That I'd been wrong about you."

"But I went with Tagg to homecoming that year."

"He uninvited you, remember? After you screwed up your ankle." Tagg had been an asshat—thinking she'd ruin his fun being on crutches. He'd eventually felt bad about it, but it had taken him long enough. "I was about to suggest we go together, as fellow invalids."

"Why didn't you?"

"Just then, Tagg came by and sat down with us. I was angry he did that to you. But he was my best friend, I couldn't move in on him."

"We never would've lasted back then anyway," she said with an exaggerated sigh.

"Why not?" He heard the hurt in his voice and silently cursed himself.

She smiled. "Because I always had my heart set on dating a professional athlete, and you clearly disappointed."

"Yeah, but I just might be professional at something else." He lifted his brows to let her know what it was.

She rolled her eyes and laughed. A snorty kind of

laugh he'd never heard from her before, and he loved it. This was the real Sara, and he liked her. A lot.

In response he rolled her over and kissed her until her laughter faded and was replaced by an entirely different kind of fun.

* * *

Judging by the gray light behind the shades, Sara guessed it was around five a.m. She knew because the summer light was always early, and the dark turned to gray long before the sun came up. It was one of the things she loved about summer.

Next to her, Colton was sleeping on his side, facing her. His long lashes made him look boyish, but the muscle of his arm traveling under his pillow, and the plains and valleys of his chest clearly visible above the sheet, were all man.

Consciousness fully dawned, and with it a surge of pure adrenaline hit her, jolting her fully awake, and suddenly she was completely freaked out. What had she been thinking, to fall asleep with him? To stay *all night*? That smacked of...relationship. Something she knew full well the Revolver wasn't interested in.

And while he might be very well acquainted with the "just fun" kind of thing they were embarking on, this was all new territory to her. She didn't know the first thing about navigating a fling, but she did know that last night with Colton had been too perfect, their lovemaking easy and natural, how they'd fallen asleep wrapped up in each other's arms. And she was pretty certain that thinking this way could only lead to heartache.

Panic hit her in bursts, each one bigger than the last. Suddenly she couldn't breathe, couldn't take in enough oxygen. She had to get out of here. She was not ready to face him in the light of day. Somehow, she had to find some sense of control.

Very cautiously she slid from the bed and found her bra, T-shirt, and shorts. God only knew where her panties had gone.

She slipped on her clothes in the living room and had just picked up her sandals near the door and placed her hand carefully on the knob when she met resistance.

In the form of a six-foot-two cop wearing nothing but navy boxer briefs, leaning over her with his hand on the door.

"Good morning," he said, his voice a little gravelly, the shadow of beard growth on his face sexy as sin. He moved to prop his hip up against the door and cross his arms.

"I—um—have an emergency." The emergency was that she was panicking and having a heart attack and she needed to get out of here. Fast.

"That right?" he said, one brow raised. "Funny, but I didn't see you with your beeper. And I seem to recall your saying you were off all weekend."

"Why could you not be a heavier sleeper?"

"Cop reflexes." He paused and let that sink in. "Don't leave. Stay."

"You should be glad I'm leaving. Isn't that what guys want? A woman who's not clingy and knows when to leave?"

"Stay," he said again, putting his arms on either side of her against the door, caging her in, which was sexy as hell. "Please."

Still she stayed strong. "We just *did it*! Like, three times. Aren't you exhausted?" *Three* times. And each time had been so, so good. Like walking-on-air kind of unbelievably good. Tagg clearly needed some lessons, because this man...

He bent to kiss her neck, and she shuddered. "Stay because I like you being here," he said. "And I'll make you breakfast." He was nuzzling her neck, and it was getting hard to think, with whatever he was doing with his lips between her neck and collarbone.

"Sounds like breakfast might come with a price," she said.

He smiled against her skin. She struggled to keep up the fight, trying not to smile herself, trying not to succumb to the warmth that was even now flooding through her.

Her thoughts were getting muddled, and the common sense that had led her to seek out the door was rapidly fading under the onslaught of his kisses. Sara reminded herself this was just for fun. Sex for fun did not involve hanging out for hours in bed talking and then staying for breakfast. It involved cutting loose and getting out before feelings got tangled up.

Yet his playful pleading got to her in ways she couldn't even describe. He liked her being here. He wanted to make her breakfast. He wanted her to *stay*.

He did a weird thing then. He lifted his head and hugged her. Put his arms around her and rubbed his hands up and down her back and just...held her. It was the sexiest full-body hug she'd ever had, and for a second she thought she was going to cry.

She couldn't talk. It felt like she had a Kleenex stuck in her throat. She didn't dare say it out loud but she felt it, clear through her bones. *Wanted.* She felt wanted.

He drew back and looked at her. Lord, she must be a mess. Crazed hair, wrinkled clothes, no makeup, plus she'd slept in her contacts and her eyes felt like a thousand needles were prickling them.

"I never had a woman get so emotional over the thought of breakfast." He reached over then and tilted her chin up so she had to make eye contact. The honesty in his gaze terrified her. It was as if he could see past all her bullshit. Before she could look away from that piercing blue gaze, he curled his hand around her neck very softly and gently and kissed her on the mouth.

Then, knowing full well he'd kissed all the fight out of her, he took her hand and tugged her back to his bedroom. He was irresistible. She had no choice but to push her fear aside and follow him.

Chapter 15

♥

Leonore, where's my dad?" Sara asked at work on Monday, setting a chart on the counter.

"He's still in with Mrs. O'Connor," Leonore said. "He told me to tell everyone he's running a little behind today."

A little? Sara glanced at her watch. It was ten o'clock, and the nine-thirty patient hadn't been seen yet. "I tell you what, I can see the nine thirty. But when Dad comes out, will you tell him I need to talk to him?"

"Sure thing."

Sara was already halfway down the hall when Leonore called out, "Hey, Sara... You forgot your pen, sweetie!"

"Oh! Thank you," she said, grabbing it from Leonore and making sure to stick it in the knit thingamabob around her neck, pleased to see Leonore smile.

"I told you that little thing would come in handy."

She held out another pen. "Here, stick this in there so you always have an extra." Sara had this terrible habit of forgetting pens everywhere. "Will do," she said, and ran down the hall.

She caught up with her dad after she'd seen the patient, who had a straightforward sinus infection. He was walking out into the reception area with Eva O'Connor. Her eyes looked a little puffy. She grasped Sara's hand unexpectedly.

"Hi, Mrs. O'Connor," Sara said, squeezing her hand back.

"Sara. I'm so happy you're back with us in town. We need a nice woman doctor like you. But I have to tell you, your father is a saint. Honestly, we're going through some tough times, but he made me feel so much better." She blew her nose, and Leonore pulled a few more out of a box on the counter and handed them to her. "I think I've held him up with my troubles."

Leonore patted her hand. "Oh, now, you know how Doctor is. He always has time to listen."

"Well, I am truly grateful for that, Leonore. You ladies have a good day."

Sara found her father back in his office, dictating the visit. "Patient's son is in the middle of a contentious divorce and got stopped for a DUI, her daughter's just moved back home with two little kids, and her husband just found out he's got to have back surgery." He looked up from dictating into his computer. "I'm sorry, sweetheart, for throwing off the schedule."

"Oh no, Dad. I'm really glad you made time to talk with her."

He smiled. "Me too. It's the part of my job I like the best. Sometimes people just need someone to listen."

Easy to forget that, in the hectic pace of the day. "Hey, Dad, I need to consult with you on one of your patients I just saw."

"Oh, sure," he said, walking around the desk and standing near Sara, crossing his arms. "Who is it?"

"Stacy Simmons. I know she's got irritable bowel syndrome, but she's having bad pain and her abdomen feels tight. It's concerning to me, like she might need a CT scan to make sure it's nothing worse. I thought I'd get you to take a look and see what you think."

Her dad rose from the chair. "I've been treating Stacy for years. I'm glad you asked me what I think." As he went off to see the patient, Sara couldn't help scanning his desk. Tidy piles of papers, pens with drug company logos, and a few goofy things his patients had given him, like a coffee mug that read, "I found that humerus." In the corner of the desk was a stack of charts. On the top was the name of a patient she'd seen the day before. She flipped through the stack. Yep, her entire afternoon lineup from yesterday. He was still checking them over as if she were an intern.

Just then her dad came striding back in the room. "I agree with you, her abdomen's tight. But she's really stressed, and her irritable bowel always acts up when she's overwhelmed. I told her you'd adjust her medication and to give us a call this evening if she's not better. Sound all right to you?"

Sara tucked her disappointment about the charts aside. She'd bring that matter up another time. "Yes, but it makes me nervous too. How can you be sure nothing's really wrong with her?"

He shrugged. "I can't be. I'm just willing to take the risk because I know her so well."

"But Dad—malpractice, lawsuits. Bad stuff happening to people." Sara shuddered just thinking about that.

Her dad laughed. "Yeah, yeah. That's why they call it the art of medicine. Or we'd spend all day ordering every test in the book on everybody." He pulled his beeper off his hip and squinted at it. "Say, can you help me turn on that newfangled EKG machine? It's like it has its own mind. This one asks you twenty questions before it decides to turn on. My old one just used to have a switch."

"Sure, of course I'll help you turn it on. Dad—"

"Yes, sweetheart?" He was already bolting down the hall. She caught up with him there.

"Thanks for that. It's—it's fun seeing you in action. I—hope I can be like you one day."

He rested a hand on her shoulder. "Give yourself a little time. I think you're going to be even *better* than me one day."

Wow, what? Did she just hear that out of her dad's mouth? A compliment? She took a minute to bask in the fact that her dad saw her potential. That she was doing OK, falling into a groove. Besides that, something more was happening. She was enjoying getting to know her patients, who were also her neighbors, friends, past teachers, and kids she'd babysat for. It made her feel a part of something...It made her feel like she belonged.

"Hannah Walker's in room three," Glinda said when Sara returned to the counter.

"Thanks, Glinda," Sara said, taking Hannah's chart and knocking on the door. She was a little nervous about seeing Hannah as a patient. Of course she would keep Hannah's concerns private, as she was obliged to do, but she wasn't quite sure if Colton would like that or not. Hopefully he'd be relieved that Hannah had gotten all the info she needed and be grateful to be spared the details.

Hannah's chart said she was here for a physical. A meningitis shot before college. And Sara couldn't forget about the sex talk. Part of her job. An important part, she reminded herself, whether it was a little uncomfortable or not.

"How's your summer?" Sara asked as she took a seat on the stool and put Hannah's chart off to the side.

"Fabulous. But it'll be coming to an end. I'm a little sad about that."

Hannah's tone was chatty, as always, the only evidence of nerves the fact that as she sat she twirled her long braid in one hand. "Are you nervous about college?"

"No, not really. Excited." She dropped her hands into her lap but fidgeted them a little. "Except I met someone. A boy."

Sara raised a brow. "A nice boy?"

"He's awesome, Sara. Kind and sweet and really handsome."

God, she loved this kid. Mentioning *kind* and *sweet* before *handsome*. Mature beyond her age. Colton would be so proud.

"My brother found out I was seeing him." Hannah looked Sara directly in the eye, which also impressed her. "You won't tell him any of this, will you?"

She wanted to make certain Hannah understood she had her trust. "Anything we discuss in this office is private."

"Aiden happens to be my brother's latest project."

"Project?"

"Yeah, you know. The cops helped Colton when he was a wild teenager or something and now he feels like it's his mission on earth to do the same for other kids. And he picked Aiden. He's painting Cookie's house, of all things."

"Have you had a talk with your brother about this?"

"Well, he confronted me because he found out I was hanging out with Aiden. And he basically went ballistic."

Colton going ballistic? Hard to imagine. On second thought, maybe not so hard, knowing how much he loved his sister. "Why's that?"

"Because Aiden doesn't come from a nice family—he's not going to college, and he wants to be an electrician. And he got in trouble last spring, but that was an accident. But he works three jobs and he's amazing."

"Three jobs. That *is* amazing." Sara made small talk but knew she had to somehow professionally broach the topic of sex while making the transition as natural as possible. She was just trying to figure out how to do that when Hannah spoke.

"I already know about the birds and the bees, if that's

what you're wondering. And no, I'm not having sex with him. Not yet. But I have a few questions."

"Well, I'd love to help you with whatever questions you have. Not just here in the office but anytime, right?"

"This isn't a fling. I love Aiden. But Colt will be so upset."

"Well, I know one thing—your brother adores you. He wants nothing but the best for you."

"My brother is stubborn. He can't see beyond Aiden's past. Geez, he practically broke out in hives when he found out I was seeing him." She grinned and waved her hands near her face. "I mean it, Sara, his face got all blotchy and he looked like he was going to pass out or something."

Sara couldn't help but chuckle. "My advice is to talk with your brother. And go slowly. Sometimes we think we're in love, but it's just infatuation."

"And sometimes it's love," she insisted.

"I'm just saying waiting to have sex might be a good thing. Slow things down a little. Really get to know one another. Proceed with caution." She certainly hadn't done that with Colton. But she was old enough to realize the starry-eyed feeling she felt around him was not love. She would not allow herself to get burned by that again.

Hannah was sitting there, her long dancer's legs dangling off the exam table, pretending to listen. Sara knew the look. Hannah was being respectful, but it looked as if she'd already made up her mind.

As Sara went on talking, educating, and informing, she thought about how dearly Colton loved his little sister and how she had to do right by him but also do right by Hannah. However that balancing act tipped, one side was bound not to be as happy as the other. But she had to do her job first.

*   *   *

"Hey," Colton said as he walked into Sara's office at twelve fifteen and found her writing up a chart at the counter. "Have time for lunch?"

"Yep. I'm done and I'm starving," Sara said, closing the chart and beaming a bright smile that told him she was happy to see him. He couldn't help grinning back like a smitten teenager, and bit down on his cheeks to control it. What was it about her that made him feel like he wasn't in control at all?

"I'm starving too," he said, giving her a look that let her know exactly what he was starving for.

She blushed at his comment, a fact that did not go unnoticed by Leonore and Glinda, who gave each other a knowing look.

He leaned through the open reception window. "Ladies," he said. "How goes it?"

"Great, Chief," Leonore said with a wave.

Sara hung her lab coat on the hook and walked into the waiting room. As they headed for the outside door, Glinda said, "Lord, I am having a hot flash. Did you see the way that man looks at her?"

"Like he's a sailor home after a six-month voyage," Glinda said. Colton held the door for Sara and gave her the most indecent look he could muster, which wasn't hard at all. As soon as they got outside, Colton swung her up against the side of the building and kissed her. "Ahoy there, matey," he murmured against her neck.

She giggled. "They said a *sailor*, not a *pirate*."

"I like the pirate better. Shiver me timbers, lass."

She groaned at his bad impression, but kissed him back just as eagerly, wrapping her hands around his waist and gazing at him with those stunning green eyes. In the cool shade by the door, under the old lilacs, he wished he could keep kissing her forever. "I hope you didn't mind I came in?" He grinned—again. He really had to stop with all the grinning. "I missed you."

She laughed. "But you just saw me yesterday morning."

He shrugged. "I know, but I missed you last night." Dammit, he shouldn't have said that. He knew she had commitments to her grandmother. Plus he was supposed to be treating this as casual and instead he was acting stalker-ish. What had gotten into him?

But then she grabbed him by the shirt and went in for another kiss. She tasted wonderful, felt so good in his arms. He skimmed her jaw with kisses, then trailed them down her neck.

She arched her neck to give him better access. "Maybe we should go to your place for lunch?"

"Can't," he said. "I have to be in court in Richardson by one. But I do have lunch for us in my car. And I thought I'd take you somewhere special to eat it."

She raised an elegant brow. "Somewhere special?"

"Yeah," he said. "You'll see." His gaze skimmed lightly over her. She was wearing a flowered dress and red sandals, and her hair, up in its usual ponytail, was catching golden highlights in the sun. *Gorgeous woman. Mine*, something primal cried out inside him. He started walking around the back of the building to his car before he could say something stupid. Sara was stirring feelings in him he had no business feeling. Ones he'd made it a point not to feel with women, and especially not her. Yet he couldn't seem to rein them in.

Just then they saw an older woman walking toward them with a cane. It was Mary Mulligan, the angel photographer. She must've seen them kissing outside the door in broad daylight. He uttered a curse under his breath. What had he been thinking? Did he really want the whole town knowing about them?

"Oh, hello, Chief, Dr. Sara," Mrs. Mulligan said. "Seems I always catch you two kissing."

Colton felt his face flush, a rare occurrence. He was suddenly at a loss for words. Fortunately Sara chimed in.

"Hi, Mary," Sara said, shooting a glance at Colton. "Headed to see my dad?"

"Yes, my stupid arthritis is acting up." She stopped and rummaged in her purse, then pulled out her iPhone. "Say cheese," she said, suddenly snapping their picture. "You two are such a cute couple. Are you headed out to lunch? It's such a lovely summer day."

A sense of apprehension spread through Colton. Terms like *couple* and *catch you two kissing* were the kinds of words that were apt to give him hives.

Mary replaced her phone, and Colton offered her his arm as she walked over to the office door.

"Have a nice day, Mary," Colton said.

"You too." She turned around at the top stair, grabbing on to the door frame for support. "It's nice to finally see you both together. But those angels are certainly taking their time with you two."

Colton waved to Mary and steered Sara to his car, reminding himself that this was only a summer fling. No big deal. It was only lunch. He couldn't allow himself to think further than that.

* * *

"Are you OK?" Sara asked as Colton drove them downtown and turned up a side street right after the falls. "You're not letting that angel stuff get to you, are you?"

"No, of course not," he said. But frankly it had, a little, and he wasn't quite sure why. Sara had said she wanted to keep things casual, which was exactly what he wanted too. What she'd said just now seemed to confirm that. Then what was his problem?

He'd decided on impulse this morning to show Sara his plot of land. But now he was having second thoughts. Maybe it was too personal. Half of him wanted to show her everything, tell her everything on his mind because his heart was bursting like a damn teenager's, but the other half told him he was a fool. A relationship wasn't what she wanted. Or what he wanted, right?

One more turn, and they were suddenly traveling up a gravel driveway surrounded on both sides by trees. He felt a little nervous about what she would think, but didn't want to even think about why that was important to him.

"Someone lives back here?" Sara asked.

He laughed. "Well, they used to." The car crunched along the road, which wound through a patch of woods and over a tiny stone bridge where a creek gurgled below.

"It's like a park back here," Sara said.

"It's next to the park. Pretty hidden, isn't it?" He felt the same peace come over him that he always felt making this climb. As if he'd left his world of problems back on the main road.

They continued through a clearing, and that's where Colton killed the motor. He got out of the car and grabbed a bag of food from the back seat and a blanket from the trunk.

"We're eating lunch in the field?" Sara asked.

He quirked a smile and signaled her to keep walking.

Suddenly, past the weedy field, a view opened up of a house that at one time used to be a showstopper but was now crippled with age. It was a big rectangular colonial, the bottom half covered in brown stone. The top half was made of wood and had been painted white, but the paint was now gray, chipped, and peeling. The front steps were crumbling, and a big tree alongside the house was growing through the roof.

"So who owns this decrepit old house?" Sara asked as Colton led her over to the tree and laid out the blanket. She seemed fascinated by the tree limb climbing through the window and popping out the roof. "I've never seen a tree do that before."

"I own the land, up to the house."

"You own this?" She squinted at him in the sunshine. "How could I not even know about this place?"

He shrugged. "Believe me, kids know about it, and sometimes they come out here and cause trouble. An elderly couple lived here, but it's been abandoned for years. Their grandchildren are finally selling it. They intend to knock down the house and sell this piece of land off too." Colton reached into the bag and pulled out two wrapped sandwiches. "Want to eat?" But she was already taking off toward the house, so he set down the food and followed her.

She climbed onto the porch, stepping around the crumbling stone steps, and peeked in one of the windows.

"Hey, be careful, Red. It's not safe. Plus it looks like *Hoarders* in there."

That of course made her peek in all the windows. "Oh, wow. I see all kinds of furniture. Newspapers, magazines. Lots and lots of stuff." When she turned, it surprised him to see excitement on her face. "So what made you buy the land?"

"Sometimes being police chief makes me feel like I'm in a fishbowl. I wasn't really ready for it with Hannah's college expenses, but sometimes you just know when something's right." He winced. That seemed to reflect some other feelings he might be having too. Ones he did not want to assess that deeply right now.

"So what are you going to do about the house? You have to buy it, or you'll have neighbors."

"The family asked me if I want it, but I said no. Too big for me. Not to mention it's a train wreck."

"It might not be too big if you have a family one day. Do you like old houses?"

A sudden picture popped into his head. Kids running around this field playing, dogs running right alongside. Some of the kids had red hair. *Oh geez.* He shook his head and made himself focus on the front door, which was coming off its hinges. "I'm not sure this one's worth saving."

She sighed. "There's something to be said about a house that's quirky and one of a kind. Have you been inside?"

He laughed. And remembered Tagg complaining when he and Sara had house hunted that she'd been drawn to houses precisely like this one. "There's not an inch of space in there not covered with junk. Plus it smells like mouse pee and other bad things. I know a lot of guys in the trades who can help me build a nice house from the bottom up. I've been clearing the field on my days off."

"Oh, c'mon, Colt," Sara said with a wink. "You're not afraid of a little challenge, are you?"

"No, but I'm also not crazy. Thanks for the pep talk, though." Then he kissed her, nice and long and slow, and it was the perfect kiss, on the most perfect day imaginable, being out here in the warm sunshine, the birds singing, the smell of summer grasses and growing things thick in the air.

"Can you stay over tonight?" he asked. He missed her in his arms, in his bed. If they'd had more time he would've made use of that blanket he'd brought, just sitting under that shady tree.

"I've got to stay with Nonna tonight."

"I understand. Disappointed, but I understand."

Impulsively she kissed him again, standing on tiptoe, tugging on his shirt to bring him closer.

"Woman, you are bewitching me," he murmured against her lips. Definitely not a safe thing to say, but nothing with her seemed to be following the rules.

"I tend to have that effect on men," she said, smiling against his lips. "Thanks for showing me this place. It was fun." Her phone went off with a text, and she looked at it. "Oh, how about that," she said incredulously.

"What is it?"

"It's from a friend of mine at Columbia. Looks like there's going to be a sudden opening in the type of fellowship I almost started last year. They're taking applications, and they want to fill the vacancy by Christmas."

Dread tore through him. "So you're going to apply?" he asked, hoping he kept a positive expression on his face.

"My dad assumes I'll just pick up where I left off last year and go back to doing research and working at a big hospital. I'm not sure he believes I'm cut out to be a family doctor."

"What is it you want?"

For a heartbeat, her gaze searched his. "I don't know."

He had no idea what to say. He wanted to cry out, *Don't go*, but who was he to hold her back? Or imply there would be commitments of any kind? He'd always known she wasn't long for Angel Falls, and this just confirmed it.

They ate lunch, but Colton had lost his appetite.

This reinforced what he felt in his gut: he did not want rumors to spread about them dating. He shouldn't have been so reckless as to kiss her outside her father's office. And it was of questionable judgment to be sharing his land with her too. The more he thought about it, the more he realized it was a bad idea to go too public with this—whatever it was. It was fantastic and amazing, but as far as he was concerned, it was too good to be real. Even if she didn't take that fellowship, she'd soon tire of him, a small-town cop still stuck in the same old place they'd grown up in. He'd just be happy for each day and stick to his rules—that he didn't get serious. Or do family dinners. Whatever it took to avoid a broken heart.

Because he could read the writing on the wall. Sara would be off soon, on to a big city, a big hospital, something much bigger than the life he had here. Keeping it casual would make it easier to say goodbye.

He dropped her off at her office. "Bye," she said, kissing him and lightly running her hand down his cheek. "Your land is awesome. Thanks for sharing that with me." She gave a little smile before she closed the door and walked away.

Leaving him more confused than ever.

Chapter 16

♥

Colton was working out at home that evening when Sara's text came through. OK to come over? He'd just set down his free weights and decided to hit the shower when his doorbell rang. He opened the door to find her standing there, holding her phone, wearing a gray T-shirt, leggings, and a long gray sweater with flip-flops. A flowery little overnight bag was slung over her shoulder. If she'd been in a gorgeous gown and heels, he wouldn't have wanted her any more.

"Surprise," she said.

His heart rolled over and surrendered right there. It struck him that it was an ordinary evening—he was sweaty from his workout, he still had earbuds in his ears from the audiobook he'd been listening to—and there she was, looking like everything he'd ever wanted.

He reached out and took her hand and guided her across the threshold, a little afraid he'd better do it quick before she vanished into the night. Champ bolted over, wagging his tail a mile a minute and nudging his nose into her hand. She laughed and cooed to him and stroked his back. Lucky dog.

"What happened with Nonna?" he asked, closing the door and tugging her away from his dog.

"Gabby understood how badly I wanted to come and shooed me out. Is it…all right? I hope you don't mind, but I brought my stuff for work tomorrow. I mean, just in case. Not that I have to stay that long, I just thought—"

"I want you to stay."

"Tagg told me once you don't care to have women leaving their toothbrushes and things around everywhere—"

He winced. "Tagg hasn't really known me for quite a while." He didn't want to talk about other women. Or about Tagg. "For what it's worth, you're the only woman I've ever had over here."

"Oh. That sounds like a compliment."

"It is." He slid the bag off her shoulder and leaned in to kiss her, then suddenly pulled back. "I forgot. I just finished working out and I need to hit the shower."

"Oh, go right ahead. Champ and I can hang out." He was about to suggest she join him, but no sooner did she sit down on the couch than Champ hopped up and settled right next to her, his head on her knee, giving him the eyeball. Fine, the dog won that round. But Colton could shower quick.

He was in the shower when he felt a gust of cool air. He turned to see her step in beside him.

His breath hitched. God, she was beautiful. He wasted no time pulling her into his arms. "What made you change your mind?" he asked, kissing the hollow between her neck and shoulder. "Champ didn't have gas again, did he?"

"No, but your country-western singing is terrible. This was the only way I could think of to shut you up." She waved something in front of him—a condom packet—and placed it on the high tile ledge.

He kissed her as they stood under the warm spray, steam fogging up the doors. Lathered up his hands with soap, then slid them all over her body, loving the feel of her, the satiny, slippery wetness.

He whispered sweet dirty things in her ear that made her blush and laugh, until she finally shut him up with kisses. After tracing a trail of kisses down her neck, he laved a sweet nipple with his tongue, then paid homage to the other, loving the way she writhed under his touch, the little sounds of pleasure that escaped her throat, and the way her hands roamed greedily all along his back, his hips, his ass.

For the moment all his worries had fled, and he decided right then and there that he would enjoy every moment he had with her. His mouth found hers again, tongues tangling and sliding, and his arms tightened around her waist as they stood pressed together.

He dropped a hand between her legs, slipped two fingers inside her, stroked her at her core until she arched under his touch. She slid her soapy hands up and down his length until he nearly lost his sense and his balance. She was driving him wild, and the heat was tearing through him like flames.

He put on the condom and managed to sit down on

the tiled shower seat. She hovered over him and slowly took in his length, took him inside her inch by inch. Her gaze was calm, direct, never deviating, her green eyes bright and intense in the misty shower. He never stopped looking at her either.

A shudder passed through him. He couldn't tell where his trembling stopped and hers began. Some kind of connection, intense, final, absolute, passed between them despite no words being spoken at all. They started a rhythm, at first slow, then more intense, as he moved inside her until she got dreamy eyed and a tiny frown creased her forehead. He was right with her, coming at the same time, driving into her, feeling her muscles clench around him. They came like that, in the hot, steamy shower, mist swirling around them, their lips melded, their arms wrapped around each other tight, her body tightening around him as they moved together to climax, his lips finally releasing a guttural cry.

For a while they didn't move, until the lukewarm water started to feel chilly. Colton was a little shaky as he stepped out and handed her a clean towel, wrapping it around her, then grabbing one for himself and tying it around his waist.

He tried to collect his sanity as he tumbled into bed. Good Lord, what was happening to him? He wasn't one to wax sentimental, but the words of every sappy love poem he'd ever heard were on the tip of his tongue.

Sara came out of the bathroom in a gray nightshirt that came down to her knees and had a cat on it or something. It looked old and well-worn and comfortable. And she had her glasses on. Her hand flew up to adjust them, and he knew she was self-conscious about them. He pretended he didn't even notice, and got up to let Champ out for the last time, then turned out all the lights before climbing into bed beside her.

On impulse he reached over and took off her glasses, then set them down gently on the nightstand and kissed her good and hard. Then he pulled her into him and wrapped himself around her before Champ had an opportunity to sneak in himself. Mindlessly he fingered a curl of her wet hair, felt its silky texture, how it sprang back softly from his touch.

"Not too bad for a work night," she said, her hand draped over his. "We're even in bed on time. This isn't disruptive at all."

He kissed the top of her head. "Yeah. Not too bad for a work night." Except that being next to her was getting him aroused. He tried to focus on other things, like that he had to stop at the bank tomorrow and get an oil change for his car, and what would happen if he got awakened by a call in the middle of the night, but nothing was working. He hoped she wouldn't notice.

She'd definitely noticed and was reaching back and touching the evidence, stroking him gently with her hand. Oh God, there he went again. All it took from her was a couple of touches and he was hard as granite.

"Don't fan the fire unless you want to use the flame," he said, kissing her neck.

"In your case, it's not taking much fanning," she said, laughing. She turned around in his arms and kissed him, pulling herself flush against him, and before they knew it, playful, short kisses gave way to deep, long, wet ones, and hands started roaming. They just fell into it, plain and simple, and he could no more hold himself back than he could stop himself from breathing.

They lay there for a long time afterward, her head nestled between his chest and his shoulder, he softly stroking her arm. Finally she slid her nightshirt on over her head and snuggled back in next to him until this time they both fell asleep.

* * *

Sara slept like the dead until three a.m., when Colton's phone went off. "OK," she heard him say in a sleep-heavy voice. "He's drunk again? Be right there." He hung up and jumped from the bed, then tossed on his briefs and walked over to a chair where his uniform shirt, pants, and shoes were carefully laid out. She was fine until she saw him strap on the bulletproof vest. And the gun holster. He must've noticed her awake and staring at him because he said, "I'm backup on a 911 call. Got to fly."

Sitting upright, she watched him tug on his pants and tie his shoes. He opened his top dresser drawer and took out his gun, shoved it in his holster, and flew out the bedroom door.

She ran to the front door and opened it for him. "Be careful," was all she was able to get out as he gave her a quick peck on the cheek and was gone.

Sara closed the door and leaned against it, a new understanding of Colton's job fully sinking in.

Of course it had been a fantasy to think that his

job was all traffic patrol and lecturing kids about drugs and stopping to have breakfast with the locals at the downtown diner. Their town was quaint and lovely and friendly, but that didn't mean it didn't have a dark side, a side that Colton had to deal with on a regular basis. He could be going to a car accident, or a drunken brawl, or to confront a crazed lunatic with a gun.

In her world there were emergencies, but they were what she and her colleagues often joked were the "tucked-in kind": the EMTs had usually taken vitals, administered IVs, and begun the assessment process, so by the time the patients got to the ER, things were already under some degree of control.

Not like the situations Colton walked into. The complete unknown. He was a first responder. Anything could happen.

Sara didn't even try to go back to sleep. As she paced the apartment, Champ followed right behind her. She made coffee. Tried to watch TV. Prayed. Paced some more.

At five a.m. her cell went off. Her heart sank to her feet when she saw it was her father.

"Dad. What's wrong?" she asked.

"Hi, Sara," he said, his voice calm and soothing as always. "Everything's fine, but I'm working the ER tonight and Colton was just brought in by the squad. He's a little banged up, but he'll be OK."

Terror curled its limbs around her and squeezed, stole away her breath and her voice. "Dad," she managed in a raspy whisper. "What do you mean...banged up?"

"We've got George Carver stitching up his forehead, and he's got a black eye and a broken nose and a little concussion, but I think that's the extent of it. Disarmed a drunk with a knife but got punched out."

The words all ran together, *knife, black eye, broken nose*. Oh my God, a *little* concussion, what the hell was that? Tears flooded her eyes, the grateful and the frightened kind both.

George was the local plastic surgeon, who was often called in to suture up important places on bodies that most people didn't want to risk scarring, like faces. "I'm coming down." She paused. "Did you call Cookie?"

"Rafe suggested I start with you." Leave it to her dad to keep talking in the same calm voice. No evidence of surprise or even shock that his daughter was involved with the man she'd practically hated just a short time ago.

Explaining about her love life would have to wait. "Does Colton know you're calling me?"

"No. He went right to CT and I decided to call you myself."

"I'll be there in ten minutes."

"OK, sweetheart. Don't speed."

"Thanks—for calling me." She had no idea what her dad knew. Probably everything after talking to Rafe.

She wasn't sure how Colton would handle having her at his side. She didn't want to barge in and embarrass him, especially since they weren't officially a couple—in fact, she wasn't sure quite what they were. All she knew was she had to be with him. She couldn't bear not being there.

Sara put on her work outfit for morning, a simple print dress, brought her big gray sweater because the ER was always freezing, and brushed her hair back into a ponytail. She tried to calm down. Her dad had said Colton would be all right, but her doctor's brain kept imagining the worst.

Hearing upsetting news was an almost-daily part of her job. She understood how important it was to remain calm and objective when bad things were going on. But one look in the mirror showed that she was pale and shaking. What if he wasn't OK? A concussion was serious. Plus someone had blackened his eye and broken his nose. Just thinking that he'd been the recipient of that type of violence made her tear up.

Sara took a deep breath. Blew her nose and tried to hold it together. Where Colton was concerned, she was anything but calm and objective. And, she was coming to realize, he was anything but a fling.

* * *

"Since you're not next of kin," Sara's dad said when she arrived at the ER, "I can only give you the CT results if Colton allows it. You know that."

Sara rolled her eyes. "I slept with him, Dad. Please just tell me if something's wrong."

Besides the arch of a single brow, her father kept his same calm demeanor. Sighing deeply, he said, "OK, fine. As one physician to another, I can tell you it's just a concussion. He's got to take a week off. The rest you already know."

It was her turn to sigh. "He's going to hate that."

"I know he prides himself on never missing work." Her dad paused. "Maybe he won't give me such a hard time if you go in first."

She would've taken off if he hadn't grabbed hold of her arm. "He doesn't know I called you. Just warning you. And Sara—"

She was already walking toward the ER bay where Colton was resting when she heard her name and halted.

"Yes, Dad?"

He steered her away from the desk to an area where they could talk quietly. "Being a cop is a dangerous job, no matter how many Fourth of July parades you police or school talks on drugs you give or drivers' ed classes you help teach. The hours are terrible and you never know what you're going to walk into. Which means anyone who falls for a cop worries a lot. It's part of the package."

"I don't understand. Are you warning me away from him?"

"At this point I'm just trying to tell you to not go in there upset."

Oh, she was upset, all right. As much by the fact that he was hurt as by the fact that she'd been kidding herself. The moment her dad had called and told her Colton was hurt, she'd known that her feelings ran way deeper than she'd ever admitted to herself, and now there was no turning back.

She understood the subtle message her father was trying to convey. That if she walked past that bright-yellow

ER curtain into the room where Colton was lying, she had an obligation to respect his job. Not to fall to pieces. She tried to slow her heart down to the normal range and stuff down the panic. For Colton's sake.

* * *

"Someone's here to see you, Chief," said Sandy Feldon, the head nurse, rolling back the curtain, which opened with a satisfying *whoosh*. Colton looked up from the gurney with his one good eye, saw Sara standing there, and bit back the curse that threatened to roll off his lips.

Dammit, no. Not Sara. Not here. He didn't want her to see him like this. Wounded, weakened, looking like shit.

Her face said it all. Judging from that, he must look pretty damn bad.

Yeah, probably something like Rocky after a fight, bloodied and swollen. He'd sustained a lot of bruises and bumps in his time. Par for the course. Part of his job. But he'd never felt as helpless and uncomfortable as he felt now.

She was assessing the damage critically. The Frankenstein stitches on his forehead. His probably-still-bloody nose that they'd had to pack with gauze, and the gash on his arm from wrestling the knife from the guy. His nose and head hurt the worst.

"What are you doing here?" he asked. Not meanly, he just wanted to know who'd ratted him out. "What I mean is, they shouldn't have bothered you." His attempt to soften things didn't sound much better.

Her cheeks flared with color. And something worse happened—her eyes welled up with tears. *Shit.* He didn't want her shedding tears over him. That felt too—real. His mom had done plenty of that with his dad.

"Sara, no, don't—"

She sat down next to him on the bed and clutched his hand, hard. She was shaking. Her reaction took him by surprise—for someone used to seeing sick and bloody and injured people, she was taking it hard. For a woman who'd vowed to keep things casual, she seemed awfully upset.

His impulse was to hold her and tell her it was going to be OK. But another part of him wanted to tell her to just go and leave him be.

He reminded himself that this was his job. The job that had taken his father and made his mother go to pieces. It was a big reason why he kept things light with women. Why he needed to keep things light with her.

"You look terrible," she said.

"The other guy looks worse." He tried to smirk, but his lip was swollen and it hurt too.

"I bet he does."

"Who called you?"

"My dad. Rafe heard the call come in."

Just then her father walked in, looking distinguished as always with his gray hair and white coat. Colton dropped Sara's hand and sat up a little straighter.

Dr. Langdon scanned the room. To his credit, he didn't even raise a brow on seeing his daughter sitting on the bed. "Hey, sweetheart," he said. "Colton." He pushed his glasses down his nose and examined

Colton's forehead. "George said it took twelve stitches. I would've done it myself, but I like to leave stitching faces to the experts. I didn't think you'd want a reminder of your fight with a mean drunk the rest of your life."

"Thanks," Colton said.

Her dad rolled a wheeled stool over to Colton's other side and sat down. "Your face will be fine in no time. Your nose will require resetting in a few days when the swelling goes down. I could do it, but again, I think we'll send you to the folks who do this sort of thing every day. In the meantime you're going to need to take at least a week off because you have a concussion."

A week? Holy shit. Absolutely not. Colton shook his head. He tried to take a breath to calm down, but he couldn't breathe through his nose. "I can't miss work. There's not enough backup, sir."

"Well, here's where you get a little overridden, son. You just saved a woman from her drunken husband and protected all of us from his wrath, should he have gotten loose to wander our town. Or stepped into a car, God forbid. But you hit the concrete hard and you were out for a while. That earns you a week out minimum. No sports, video games, TV, no"—he cleared his throat—"no sex—until the neurologist tells you otherwise. And definitely no work."

Colton didn't miss Sara's head-to-toe blush. He was pretty sure her father didn't either. He looked at Dr. Langdon. "I've been in worse brawls than this back in college, sir, if you'll excuse my saying."

"Your head hurt?" Dr. Langdon asked.

"Yes, of course, but—"

"You were pretty stunned when you woke up, a little confused in front of the EMTs, and your balance was off."

If his head was hurting before, it was literally pounding like a bongo drum now. "I'm the only show in town." He looked up at Dr. Langdon and pleaded, "Please don't do this."

The doctor rested his hand on Colton's shoulder in that way he had, friendly but persistent. "Think of it this way. If you go back to work like this, some thug could take advantage of you in your weakened condition. So you wouldn't be able to protect your citizens like you usually can. None of us is indispensable. Surely you can get the sheriff's office to send a few days' coverage?"

"I'll work on it," Colton said, straining to be polite.

"Also, I didn't call your grandmother. I thought I'd leave that up to you. Didn't see the point of waking her up and scaring her half to death. It's best to stay with her a few days, son, where you can be watched and rest up." He patted Colton's leg, meaning their conversation was about through. "We'll get you those discharge papers and you can go home."

"My cruiser—"

"Is parked at the station. I might have forgotten to say no driving either."

Great. Sounded like all he was going to be able to do was stare at the walls for a week.

Just then Sandy the nurse walked back in. "Are we all ready for discharge here?"

Sara's dad gave Colton one final pat on the shoulder.

"I'm glad you're all right, son. You'll be back to work in no time."

"Thanks, Doc, for everything," he said, shaking his hand.

"See you later, Dad," Sara said, giving him a quick kiss as he left. She stayed at Colton's side. He couldn't help but notice Sandy glancing up from her paperwork, her gaze shifting between Colton and Sara.

"Just sign here," she said. "You're going to need a ride home, right?"

He really wanted to drive himself. Enough with the fussing already.

"I can drive you home," Sara said cheerily. "I'll go pull up my car."

"Sounds great," Sandy said. "I just have to run and get a wheelchair, and you'll be all set."

He knew the rules. But he hated them. Everyone would see him getting wheeled out. It wasn't good for his job, to have people know the chief was in a weak state.

Sandy handed Colton a copy of his discharge instructions. He sensed what she was about to say. "So you two. I had no idea you were a couple. I mean—"

"Sara and I are friends, Sandy," Colton said, cutting her off. "Thanks for the instructions."

Out of the corner of his eye, he saw Sara flinch. What was up with that? She couldn't think . . . Nah. She'd told him from the beginning she wanted to keep things light, and so did he. She was going to leave Angel Falls and find someone else who had an MD or some kind of Ivy League pedigree. He'd be left with only his pride, and he had to do anything possible to spare that. And to spare himself the humiliation of his whole community knowing that he was a fool to get things started up with her.

"Oh, OK then. Sorry. I'll go get that chair. Nice to see you, Sara."

Sara smiled. "See you around, Sandy." She turned to Colton, the same calm expression on her face. "I'll go get my car. Unless, of course, you'd like to call another *friend*?" Before he could answer, she gathered up her purse and walked out.

What the hell? Could it be possible she'd changed her mind? Did he *want* her to change her mind? Granted, he felt things with her he'd never felt with anyone else. Everything with her was different. But now that he'd had this scare, all he could think of was that look on her face when she'd first seen him. The same horrified face his mother had worn for his dad. The nights of worry, the stress of wondering every single day if it was going to be just another day shooting the bull in the coffee shop or something like this, only with even worse consequences.

It didn't matter anyway. Sara wasn't going to be around long, and he was going to stay the course. It was the only thing that made sense.

* * *

Colton's head might have been spinning, but Sara would bet not as much as hers, which was reeling over that *just friends* remark. Yeah, she knew that's what she'd told him at the beginning, but how could he say that after how amazing everything had been between them? Maybe he was protecting her from town gossip by saying that in front of Sandy, quelling rumors, that kind of thing. She'd been so afraid of that, but now that someone close to her—her dad—knew about her and Colton, it wasn't so bad.

She wasn't so afraid anymore of what her dad thought of her choices. Hell, she wasn't so afraid of her choices herself. Maybe she really did want more with Colton. Was she even staying in town? Could this be her actual home again?

The two minutes it took to wheel Colton out felt like two hours. All the ER staff stopped to look at his messed-up face and wish him well. He smiled and waved at everyone, including the cop at the ER doors who opened the car door for him, but he drew the line at being helped into the car. He winced when he bent his head to get in.

One look at him and she knew for certain she couldn't pretend anymore that what she felt for him was casual. She'd never felt so comfortable with someone. So *herself*. And he'd seemed genuinely thrilled to see her, and have her stay with him, and he'd even said she was the only woman he'd invited into his home. Was that all in the name of *friends*?

But he'd certainly hated seeing her emotional over his wounds. And seemed to hate the fact that she'd shown up at the hospital. She wondered if she was really the only one feeling that this was something more. Perhaps she was off base, as she'd been with Tagg, thinking he'd loved her. She'd pushed away all her uncomfortable feelings, frightened to bring them out into the open. She'd vowed not to be like that anymore.

This time, she wasn't going to sit by unquestioning. This time, she knew what she wanted, and she was going to let Colton know, regardless of the consequences to her heart.

Colton breathed a heavy sigh as Sara finally pulled away from the curb, and Sara knew he must be exhausted and in pain. Not the best time for a relationship talk. They drove in silence the ten minutes to Cookie's house. The sun was coming up over the green hills and the forests just outside of town, the first light of another glorious summer morning.

Sara pulled into Cookie's little gravel driveway. "I let Champ out before I left, but I didn't feed him. How about I go do that now and bring him over?"

He turned to her, as much as he could with the stiffness. It looked as if his neck was hurting too, and who knew what other body parts. He assessed her through his one good eye.

"Sara, turn off the car for a sec, please?"

She cut the engine. "Colton, I'm sorry I showed up. I'm sorry I embarrassed you," she said before he could continue. "We can talk about this when you feel better. Just go in and rest, OK?" She managed a tight smile.

He took hold of her right hand, which was resting on the steering wheel.

"It's not good for citizens to see their police chief injured. I don't like people seeing me like that."

His words struck her as odd. "Like what—being a human?"

"Weak. Helpless."

"Human beings get hurt, Colton." What was he trying to tell her?

He swallowed and spoke again. "I hated seeing you cry over me."

He looked very vulnerable, upset even. "I didn't think I was going to cry," she said. "I thought I could handle it. But I took one look at you and I—"

Oh, hell, she felt like she was going to start crying again. "Part of the reason I don't like to get serious with anybody is I don't want anyone doing that," he said.

Oh dear, this was taking a turn. "Doing what?" she asked, her tone carrying a definite edge now. "Caring?"

Even in the dark, she could see something flash in his eyes.

"Look, sometimes my job is scary, and I don't know how I feel about letting anyone in on that." He shifted uncomfortably in his seat. "I mean, we did say we were going to keep it casual, you know?"

Oh God, she was tearing up. She didn't want to do that, and she didn't want to stress him any further. But she was afraid she'd lose her nerve if she didn't tell him now. "What we have…it doesn't feel casual to me." There, she'd said it. "I told you I didn't want a relationship because I've only dated Tagg. After his rejection, I was afraid to put myself out there again. But what's between us, I mean—" She swallowed and forced herself to continue. "What I'm trying to say is, to me, what we have is special. I care about you. Whatever's going on with you, I want you to know that."

The silence was getting deadly when he finally spoke.

"Thanks for driving me home," he said evenly, like she hadn't just spilled her guts. "And for coming to see me." He paused. "I just—I just don't want anyone worrying about me."

Well, that went well. Still a little stunned, Sara watched as Colton got slowly out of the car and righted himself. Somehow she managed to start it and put it in reverse. Before she pulled away, she turned and looked at him, still standing stiffly by the passenger door, his gaze impassive, his jaw stiff as granite. Her eyes were watery and her voice cracked a little with emotion. "You big fool," she said. "Don't you know it's too late for that?"

Chapter 17

♥

"You're super cranky," Hannah said as she passed through Cookie's living room with her car keys in her hand. She lingered near the couch, where Colton was sprawled out for the fourth day—and going stir-crazy. "Is that because you hit your head?"

He gave her a nasty look and went back to watching TV. Champ, who was sprawled on the floor, was handling his enforced rest well, more than happy to have Colton lying by his side all day.

Hannah went to grab the remote, which was lying on Colton's chest, but he was too quick, grabbing it instead. He could see out of his eye now, and nothing was wrong with his reflexes. And he was still a little dizzy and headachy but getting better each day. The only problem was that he was dying of boredom. And stupidity, considering how he'd treated Sara.

"Cookie," Hannah called. "Colton's watching TV again."

"Hannah, I swear—" He couldn't get away with anything around here.

"You know what the doctor said," Hannah said. "No TV, no texting, no computer, no paperwork..." At Hannah's scolding tone, Champ drooped his ears, ready to take the blame for Colton's indiscretions.

"Don't you have to go to work or something?" he asked his sister.

Cookie walked in, took the remote from his hands, and turned the TV off. "You know what the doctor said. No TV, nothing that strains your brain."

"I'll just lie here and stare at the ceiling all day." That was not a way to shut off his brain, just a way to make him insane. It also made it way easier to think of Sara. All. Day. Long. And how she'd said she cared about him. How she believed what they had was special. And how he'd pushed her away.

God, he'd screwed up. And the pain of missing her was worse than the pain in his head and his boredom combined.

He winced.

"Head still hurting?" Cookie asked. "Do you want some more Advil?"

"No, I'm fine," he said, trying not to sound irritated. He wanted to kick himself.

"Sara's grandmother brought us some chocolate chip cookies," Hannah said.

"That would make most people pretty happy," said Cookie.

"Don't you two have places to go? Geez." The hovering. The concern. He could do without both. Being left to wallow in his frustration and boredom sucked, but it was better than this.

"OK, fine then. I'm going to work," Hannah said. "I'd kiss you on the cheek, but I'm afraid you might bite me." She bent down and kissed him anyway, and gave Champ a pat, which turned into a belly rub.

"Thanks, squirt," he said.

"I'll be home at eight after dance class," Hannah told Cookie. "Oh, I forgot my keys in the kitchen."

Hannah ran into the kitchen, and Cookie sat down at the end of the couch. Colt moved his feet to make room for her.

"Your business isn't that private, you know. I ran into Sandy Feldon at the grocery store. She told me she'd seen Sara sit with you in the ER in the middle of the night and asked me if you and Sara were dating. She told me you said that the two of you were just friends. But she didn't believe it, by the way."

"Colton, you did not," came a voice from the kitchen. Hannah popped her head through the doorway. "Why would you do that?"

"Quit eavesdropping," he said. "Get to work already."

"I could be a few minutes late."

Colton sent her a glare.

"OK, OK, I'm going. But don't screw this up. I like Sara too much."

Hannah's phone buzzed, as it did a thousand times a day, and then she was tapping vigorously on it, sending a selfie, and running out the door. "Gotta go, good luck, love you."

When the dust settled, it was a little too quiet in the room.

"Thanks for worrying about me, Cookie, but I'm fine. You can get on with your day."

Instead of getting up, she crossed her arms and settled back into the couch. "I'm not going anywhere. Maybe Sara doesn't want to come around and upset you because of your head problem, but frankly I don't have a problem doing it. What's wrong?"

He felt like he was thirteen again, being stubborn and sullen and Cookie was telling him to snap out of it. "Nothing's wrong. Sara and I *are* friends. I'm just having a hard time doing nothing all week. It's all fine."

"Well, when I saw her yesterday she looked about as unhappy as you do. I'm old, and my clock is ticking. That means I have a low threshold for bullshit. What's going on?"

He was close to Cookie, and they'd sat here on this couch many a time throughout his growing-up years. Except now his troubles were a lot different. He didn't normally discuss his love life with her, and he felt at a loss.

"I know you feel you have to be the man of the house and take care of us all the time, but I can see you're hurting now."

Colton sighed. "I *have* been seeing Sara, but don't get your hopes up. She came right down to the ER the other night. Rafe called her dad and her dad called her and then...there she was, at my bedside. She took one look at me and..." He squeezed his eyes shut. It hurt to remember the look on her face when she'd seen him. He pinched the bridge of his nose. He didn't want to remember it.

"She was upset," Cookie offered.

He nodded. "I don't want to hurt her. Nothing good comes from a relationship with a cop. Families end up getting hurt. We all know that."

Cookie fell silent. She patted his calf before she spoke again. "Colton, you remind me so much of your father. You look like him. You have his big heart. You're handsome like him. But mostly you're stubborn as a mule. Just like him too."

"I'm not being stubborn, I'm being smart. She told me she's not ready for anything serious. So I don't know why she got so upset seeing me in the ER, or why she's upset I introduced her as my friend." Oh, he knew why. His gut was telling him why, with all its churning and pitching like a small vessel at sea. It was because their casual arrangement had gone to shit. For both of them.

"What happened with your father was a terrible tragedy," Cookie said. "And it led to other bad things. You were forced to act like an adult when you were only a child. You lost your father and your mother way too young. That's a lot of loss for a young boy."

"It is what it is, Cookie. We got through it."

"You're not understanding what I'm trying to say. This isn't about your getting beat up on the job and being afraid to upset Sara. It's about you being afraid of getting hurt yourself. You're not worried about Sara. You're worried about *yourself*."

Colton jolted upright. Champ startled awake, his dog tags jingling. "That's ridiculous," he said, but even he was beginning to see through himself. "I just wouldn't want to put anyone through a cop's life is all."

"Nonsense. You were all by yourself, as it were, taking care of Hannah when your mother couldn't be counted on. Your parents were both gone by the time you were a teenager. And so you protect yourself against more loss by not getting close to anyone. It's no wonder you're afraid to pull the trigger."

He shot her an incredulous look. "Afraid to pull the trigger?"

"Well, they call you the Revolver, don't they?"

"Geez, Cookie. Where'd you hear that?"

"The ladies at the beauty shop talk, Colton." She sighed. "Out of love for you, sometimes you need to hear things. I hope you understand that. Plus there is my need for great-grandchildren."

"Sara's not going to stay around here. She's meant for bigger things."

She shrugged, turning her palms up to the ceiling. "Well then, I guess there's no use in trying. Or asking her what *she* wants." She got up from the couch but didn't turn away. "I know you were sweet on her in high school, but you deferred to Tagg. But Tagg's out of the picture now. The only thing stopping you is yourself."

Was Cookie right? Had he been protecting himself? "I'll think about what you said."

She smiled and patted his calf again. "Well, you have plenty of time to do just that, don't you?"

* * *

Just Sara's luck. Of course she would get the job of chopping onions for the salad the night of the big family dinner, which happened to be at Dad and Rachel's house this week. And pungent onions they were, making her eyes leak and her nose run as she sat at the big kitchen island.

Rachel passed by on her way to the stove and squeezed her shoulder. "You OK?" she asked.

"Killer onions," Sara responded with a watery smile. Yep, her tears were all the fault of the onions. Not at all due to a certain cop who had friend-zoned her. Revolved her. Because that's what he did.

"Where's Malcolm, by the way?" Evie asked Gabby, who was tossing the salad. Through the big paned window, they could see their dad grilling his specialty salmon while Rafe and Joe played ball with the kids.

"He's lying down upstairs," Gabby said. "He had a sinus headache and needed a little quiet time."

Sara hoped he'd find it now, because once they were all around the table, quiet was going to go right out the window.

"Who's Malcolm?" Nonna asked. She sat at the island slicing strawberries for the top of the Jell-O salad.

"That's Gabby's sweetie, Nonna," Evie said, sneaking a strawberry. She turned to Sara. "Speaking of sweeties, how's Colton?"

"He's not my sweetie," Sara said, chopping more vigorously.

"You do know you're chopping the onions into microscopic pieces, don't you?" Evie asked.

"Oh! Sorry!" Sara set down the knife.

Gabby brought Sara a beer. "Everything all right?"

She smiled and took the beer. "I'm fine. Thanks,

Gabs." Or at least she would be, once she stopped thinking about *him*. It had been a week since she'd poured out her heart and he'd handed it back to her.

A loud siren bleat suddenly sounded from outside the house. Then another and another. It sounded like all the rescue vehicles the town owned had come to a stop in their driveway.

"Colton's here," Rachel announced as they rushed into the dining room to see what the commotion was all about. "And every other emergency services person in town."

Colton's here. The words hardly registered. Sara pulled back the dining room curtain only to find an EMS unit, a police car, and a fire engine, lights flashing. Dear God. She looked around, sniffed the air. Just the smells of a delicious dinner cooking. Was the house on fire and they didn't even know it?

"I saw Nonna pick up the phone a few minutes ago," Gabby said. "You don't think she could've..."

Oh Lord. Dialed 911. Nonna?

Nonna was at Rachel's side, innocently peering out the window. "Here comes Colton," she said. "My, that man is good-looking, even without his uniform on. And look, he's carrying flowers!"

"Flowers? To an emergency?" Rafe said, coming in from the backyard with the other men and the kids. Everyone gathered around the windows as if Sara were sixteen and getting picked up for a date. Except for the sirens wailing.

"Oh, I wanted him to come," Nonna said. "I called 911."

Evie rushed to Nonna's side. "You're kidding, aren't you, Nonna?"

Maybe Nonna didn't hear over all the commotion because all she said was, "I haven't seen a fire engine this close up in a long time."

It didn't appear that the house was burning down, Colton was here, and he had flowers. Anticipation fizzed up and bubbled over inside Sara like too much soft drink in a glass. She tried to tamp it down, and then finally just bypassed everyone and opened the damn door.

And there he was, looking amazing in a dark polo and khaki pants. And a suit coat, even though it was eighty-five degrees. "Everybody OK in here?" Colton asked, surveying the foyer. Sara couldn't help wondering what they all must look like, standing there gawking at him.

Nonna ran up to Colton, took the beautiful bouquet of flowers, and put them to her nose. "Oh, they're lovely! Just like the ones you brought Sara for homecoming."

Colton let that crazy comment pass and flashed a smile at Nonna. "Glad you approve, Mrs. F." His gaze scanned the foyer. "So we've got a report of a 911 call coming from this location."

"Nonna may have accidentally done it," Sara said quietly, so Nonna wouldn't hear. She rubbed her temple, where a massive headache was forming, despite the fact that dinner hadn't even begun. Sirens, trucks, flowers, Colton. Her entire family now staring at her.

A big burly firefighter appeared behind Colton, whom Sara recognized as Randall Ames, one of Rafe's friends. "OK if I go in and check around, Chief?" he asked.

"Have at it, Randy." Colt turned to Sara and smiled a big, wide smile, looking at her with an intensity that almost made her forget why they'd fought. "I think I better go out there and talk with the guys."

"Oh yes. Of course." She moved aside to let him do his job, staving the wave of disappointment that rolled over her. What was she expecting? An apology during a 911 run?

"I'll come with you," Rafe said, moving to the door.

"Just a sec," Colton said, pulling Sara aside. He dropped his voice. "I've been an ass. Forgive me." He raised her hand briefly to his lips and kissed it. "Talk later?"

Words caught in her throat. A shiver ran through her despite the warm day. Around her, her family became oddly quiet. "Um, sure," she managed.

"Oh, I almost forgot," he said, reaching into his suit coat and pulling out a long thin box. She recognized it immediately as being from the upscale candy shop downtown. "For you. Hope they're not melted."

Chocolate coconut nests. Her favorite. Stupidly, her eyes teared up, as if the chocolates were as precious as a diamond ring. "Thank you," she said, her voice sounding a little raspy and choked up.

He gave her a wink, then ran out the door to disperse the EMS people. As soon as the door shut behind him, her sisters swarmed.

"Oh, wow. He knows your favorite candy," Gabby said. "This is serious."

"He knows because he asked me," Evie said, reaching over her shoulder to steal a piece.

"So he really was coming for dinner," Rachel said. "Not just for the—um—emergency."

"I guess so," Sara said incredulously.

"Can I have one?" Nonna asked, nearing the chocolates.

"Hmm...I wonder what it means that he decided to surprise you and come to family dinner after all?" Evie said, with a little groan of pleasure over the chocolate.

"It means Sara has a boyfriend," Nonna said.

Evie reached over and tugged the apron tie at the back of Sara's neck. "Not that you don't look beautiful, but maybe you should take this off." She pulled off the apron and rolled it up in a ball.

"What's going on?" Malcolm asked, running into the foyer from upstairs.

"We had a misdialed 911 call," Gabby said quietly, nodding in Nonna's direction and putting a finger to her lips.

"Grandma did it?"

"Rachel, may I put these in a vase?" Nonna asked, holding up the bouquet.

Rachel smiled. "That would be lovely, Nonna."

"I'll help you," Gabby said, taking Nonna's hand and leading her into the kitchen. "C'mon, Malcolm, you can keep us company."

A few minutes later, Colton and Rafe walked into the kitchen, where the women were finishing up the meal preparations. Malcolm was perched on a stool at the island sipping wine, watching them work.

"Is everything OK?" Rachel asked.

"The crews were having a slow day anyway," Rafe said. "They enjoyed the excitement."

"Everything's under control," Colton said. "And the kids are loving the vehicles." He shook Rachel's hand and said, "Mrs. Langdon, hope you don't mind I showed up for dinner." He glanced at Sara. "Sara invited me off the cuff."

Sara raised a brow. Oh well, she supposed that was sort of true. But how had he even known dinner was here this week instead of at Nonna's?

"I don't know," Rafe said with mock seriousness, patting Colton's stomach. "He eats a lot, Rach. I may have to go to the store for more salmon."

"Oh, Rafe," Rachel said, chuckling. She turned to Colton. "Ignore him."

"Yeah, really. We usually do," Evie said, passing by and ruffling Rafe's hair. He scowled and smoothed it back down.

"Please, call me Rachel." Rachel took Colton by the elbow and steered him to a seat at the island. "And thanks for the flowers. We're thrilled you could join us. Your head is better?"

"Back to work tomorrow for a full day," Colton said. "Can't wait."

"Some cities charge big fines for false 911 calls," Malcolm said. "What does Angel Falls do? I mean, Grandma must've told them the house was burning down to get an engine out here."

Colton shrugged. "We have a pretty good sense of humor for accidents," he said. "A real nuisance call would be treated differently."

"Isn't anyone going to talk to her about that?" Malcolm asked. "I mean, old ladies can't just go around summoning every EMS vehicle in the county on a whim."

"Malcolm, it was an accident," Gabby said. "Chill, OK?" She turned to Colton. "It was my fault. I should have kept a better eye out. I saw Nonna hang up the phone. I didn't even think—"

"No one's to blame," Colton said. "On a positive note, the kids got to meet some firefighters and paramedics."

"I want to be a fireman," Michael said. "I wanna ride in the truck."

"I'll take you for a ride in the back of my police car after dinner, OK, Mikey?" Colton said, rubbing his head. "With your car seat, of course," he said with a wink at Evie.

"Hey," Rafe said. "Why would you want to ride in a tiny little police car when you can ride on the big engine?"

Michael jumped up and down. "I wanna go on both."

"Atta boy," Colton said.

"Maybe Michael would like to fly in my company jet," Malcolm said. "If you go to Wharton business school you could fly on a private jet one day too."

Sara didn't miss the subtle look Rafe and Colton exchanged before Michael spoke up. "No!," he said. "I want to go in the police car *and* the fire truck!"

Good boy, Mikey, Sara said to herself. She handed Colton a beer. "Are you on duty?"

"I'm on backup starting at midnight," he said.

"Then take it." She lowered her voice. "You might need it to get through this dinner." She tugged on his jacket. "Let me—um—take your coat."

"You sure I shouldn't keep it on?"

"Well, you can. But if you do, Rafe will never let you hear the end of it."

He took the beer and leaned over to whisper in her ear. "Did I tell you—you look pretty tonight."

She laughed. "You don't look so bad yourself. What made you come?"

"I missed you." He let that sink in. And oh, it did. The absolute intensity in his eyes told her he meant it. She felt it down to the marrow. Those simple words made her heart skitter and her usual redhead total body flush go into full-blown mode.

"I missed you too," she replied.

Then Rachel was calling everyone for dinner. Sara held Colton back. "Wait—how did you know dinner was here this week?"

"I didn't," he said, his lips curved up in a smile. "I was headed to Nonna's when the 911 call came in. I got lucky."

She shook her head in disbelief.

"You're important to me, Sara. I know how important this dinner is to you, and I wanted to show up."

"I'm glad you did," she said.

They all took their seats at a long outdoor table set with pretty blue dishes and matching napkins, Rachel's elegant doing. It was definitely a step above a normal backyard barbecue. OK, maybe a couple of steps. The patio was surrounded by antique statues and water features, gorgeous flowers blooming in spades. And of course her father's precious tomato plants, which he took every opportunity to explain in great detail.

"Rafe, you're the only one here without a date," Nonna said as everyone began eating. "You do like girls, don't you?" She took a sip of her wine. "I mean, it's OK if you don't. But who's going to carry on the family name if you don't, because there are no other boys in the family?"

"Grandma, rest assured," Sara said, patting Rafe on the back. "He likes girls."

"I don't need a date, Nonna," he said, wrapping an arm around Nonna. "Because I get to sit next to you." This made his siblings groan.

"Dinner's very good," Colton said, saving Rafe's ass. And gave him a look that told him so.

"Yes, dinner's fantastic," Malcolm said. "I took Gabby to a private chef tasting in New York City last month. It was around two hundred fifty bucks a head, wasn't it, babe? Every course was served in a little box, like a present you had to open. And when you'd open the box, smoke from the dry ice would waft out. Very elegant."

"Little boxes?" Nonna said. "It doesn't sound like there was much food."

"I was so hungry after that dinner, I ordered a pizza at midnight, Gran," Gabby said from Nonna's other side.

"Well, it was all about the presentation, the taste experience." Malcolm poured himself more wine—from Sara's count, his third glass. Not that she should be counting, but the more wine he consumed, the looser his tongue got.

After dinner Rafe left the table and came back with a football. "Would you boys like to play some catch?" he asked.

"Sure," Colton said. Sara tried not to give him a worried stare, but she must have, because he reached over and squeezed her hand. "It's only catch," he said and grinned.

"That's what I'm worried about. The men in this family are very competitive."

Her dad slid his chair back. "We'll keep it noncontact, sweetheart."

"Dad, not you too!" she said.

"Hey," Rafe said, smacking Colton in the stomach, "we can't have our police chief getting soft from all this sitting around."

Rafe, Colton, Malcolm, and her dad went out into the backyard and began tossing the ball while Rachel made coffee.

"So," Rachel said, giving Sara a conspiratorial look, "Gabby, sweetheart, tell us how things are going with Malcolm."

"Well," she said, "I know Malcolm can be a little direct and tell things like they are, but underneath that he's got a heart of gold. He's actually a lot of fun, and very spontaneous. He'll wake up on a Saturday and say, 'Let's drive to the beach,' and off we'll go on a wild adventure. He believes in not wasting a single second of time. He's always bringing me flowers or little gifts, and he's very affectionate in public."

That was an impressive laundry list, Sara had to admit. Seemed to her that Gabby, in her quest to get the life she wanted, was trying hard to focus on the positives and completely ignore the negatives. But Sara knew her sister deserved more than just to settle.

"Owww!" They heard a yelp of pain from the yard. Sara's first thought was that Colton had hit his head again. She was out of her seat and in the yard in an instant, but no one was on the ground. But Malcolm was standing beside the patio cursing a blue streak and holding a very bloody nose. Rachel arrived with a box of Kleenex she'd grabbed from the kitchen. "I sent Gabby for paper towels," she said to Sara. "What else do we need?"

"Maybe an ice pack," Sara said as she moved to inspect the damage.

"I threw him a pass, and it hit him in the face," Colton said sheepishly.

"Yeah, thanks a lot, Colton," Malcolm said loudly. "I think my nose is broken."

Chapter 18

♥

Colton understood that bloodying Gabby's fiancé's nose had probably not been the best way to make an impression. Between the 911 call and Malcolm's inappropriate comments, it had been a not-to-be-missed dinner.

All he'd wanted to do was make up to Sara for pushing her away. Cookie had made him face up to some uncomfortable truths he hadn't wanted to face, but Colton was no coward. And Sara was more important to him than his fears. So he'd decided to show up at her family dinner, and with a little help from Nonna's 911 call, he'd made it. But the evening was degenerating fast.

"It wasn't your fault," Rafe said after Gabby and Sara led Malcolm away to ice his nose. "The jerk started to talk about what a great football player he was in the middle of the pass. He looked away."

"Did you hear how he talks about Gabby?" Joe said. "'I've been trying to get her to lift weights to tone up and lose those ten extra pounds.' I mean, who talks about their fiancée like that? You should've taken him out completely, Colton. Would've been better for everyone concerned."

"We cannot let Gabby marry this guy," Rafe said.

"Now, boys," Dr. Langdon said, catching up with them as they walked toward the perfectly manicured hill leading up to the house. "Let's not forget to be charitable." He paused. "Wait a minute. He said that about Gabby's weight? I may have to take him out myself."

"So Colton, how's your head?" Dr. Langdon asked after Rafe and Joe went to grab another beer. Colton refrained. He wanted to be clearheaded in case he got called out later.

"Much better, sir. I'm looking forward to getting back to doing everything I enjoy." Oh, hell, that came out wrong. "Like sports and stuff," he added hurriedly.

"You've got a tough job, son. You're on call more than we docs are. The worst thing I have to fear most days is a kid puking on me. I never give a thought to physical harm."

Colton shrugged. "This is my town and I'm responsible for protecting and serving every citizen in it. It's a privilege to do it, so I don't mind the hours. As for never knowing what you're going to walk into—well, I'm sure it's like that for you too. Medical emergencies are unpredictable too. I guess I don't spend too much energy thinking about that, just try to be as prepared as I can. In those situations, instinct tends to take over."

"You're a brave man. But you've chosen a tough life in which to raise a family. Hard on the wife and kids."

This conversation was taking a turn. Sounded like Dr.

Langdon was subtly warning him away from his daughter. Colton didn't know what to say. Because he'd lived that life firsthand ever since he was born. Everything Dr. Langdon was saying was the truth; he couldn't deny it.

Dr. Langdon's comments reminded him that he'd come here to make things right with Sara. That meant being honest with her—about his job, and about how he felt about her.

He was grateful when Sara interrupted their conversation. "Dad, Nonna's tired. I'm going to take her home."

Colton stood. "I'll come with you."

He liked and respected Sara's father, and understood he wanted the best for his daughter. Tagg had always spoken fondly of him. He used to tell Colton about how they'd golf together, talk about patients, and attend medical conferences. Dr. Langdon certainly hadn't found anything to disapprove of about Tagg's job.

Colton got up and shook Dr. Langdon's hand and thanked Rachel for dinner. Family dinner hadn't been so bad. Yet he couldn't quite help wondering if Dr. Langdon would prefer for his daughter a guy who wrote prescriptions and not tickets.

* * *

Colton waited on the porch swing with Rocket while Sara helped her grandmother to bed. She was a little breathless when she finally came back outside and sat down next to him.

"You made us coffee?" she asked, noting the cups set out on the little table.

"It's decaf." He handed her a cup. "Cream only, right?" She looked pleased about the coffee. Good, because he wanted to please her and let her know he was trying to be the man she needed. But he also needed her to understand a few things.

"Perfect, thanks." She took a sip. "Thank you for coming to dinner tonight," she said.

"No problem. It was... exciting. At least the 911 part was." He fell into silence, intent on balancing his coffee cup on his knee, but really working up the courage to tell her what was on his mind.

"I need to tell you something," they both said at the same time.

He set down his cup. "Can I go first?"

"Sure. Go ahead."

He took up her hands, half facing her on the swing. Gently, he rubbed his thumbs over the soft flesh of her palm. "My father was a city cop. You know that, right?"

"Yes, I remember Nonna told me you'd lost him a long time ago."

He kept holding on to her hand. "My mom used to worry about him a lot. She would stay up all hours of the night smoking cigarettes at the kitchen table, waiting for him to come home. Once he got hurt and she had to drag me out of bed in the middle of the night to go with her to the hospital. When I finally got to see my dad, he had an arm cast and his face was banged up. I was a little kid, and I guess I started crying, because he hugged me. I'll never forget what he said to me."

"Tell me," Sara said, sitting close to him, resting their joined hands on the swing.

"He said, 'Sometimes police officers get hurt so other people won't.' I think that's when I knew I wanted to be one too." He paused. "I was eight when he was killed on the job."

"Colton, I'm so sorry."

"It was during a bank robbery. He saved eight hostages."

"He was a hero." Sara's eyes were teary.

Colton smiled a little. His dad *was* a hero. Colton just wished the hero part hadn't kept him from actually having a dad. "The point is, small-town life isn't the big city. Most of my job is just being around, getting to know everyone, patrolling, keeping an eye on things. But not everyone is nice, Sara. You never know when a call's going to come that's going to take you way out of your comfort zone. It's a risk I have to live with as part of my job."

That made her tear up more. She reached out and touched the area around his stitches. "It was awful, seeing you hurt like that."

"The other night in the hospital, I thought I could push you away. I didn't want you to see me like that. I didn't want to put anybody through the kind of pain I saw my mom go through. It brought back too many bad memories."

"Colton, I couldn't not come." Her voice was low and hoarse. "When my dad called, I had to be with you. Seeing you was all I could think of."

Yeah, he got that—how upset she was, how much she cared. She'd worn it all over her face that night, and he could see the tenderness now in her eyes. He owed her more, the whole truth, so he forced himself to go on.

"Truth is, I told Sandy we were just friends because I was afraid."

"Afraid of what?" Her eyes were big and round.

He held her by the shoulders. Tucked a strand of hair behind her ear. "Of how I feel about you. I want to be more than friends, Sara. I want to give this a real shot. And I want to ask you if you'd be my girlfriend."

There, he'd said it, and oh God, she was really tearing up now. He held her face in his hands, wiped away her tears with his thumbs.

He moved his hands along her jawline, angled her face, and kissed her, slowly and tenderly. Her lips were soft—hell, she was soft and sweet in his arms and he got lost in the simple act of kissing her, of exploring every inch of her mouth, of holding her in his arms. Nothing had ever felt so absolutely right.

"What happens if I say yes to the girlfriend thing?" she murmured.

"You get more kisses," he said with a grin. Their lips met again, more thoroughly, more insistently. God, he'd missed her. It had been a week since he'd kissed her, but it had felt like a year. He moved his hands through the silky thickness of her hair and tugged her closer while she slid her arms around his waist.

He was just contemplating the pros and cons of doing her under the porch swing when he became suddenly aware of headlights spotlighting them. Rafe's truck pulled up the drive, the wheels spitting out gravel. He got out and walked up to the porch.

"Rafe, what's wrong?" Sara asked.

"I came to spend the night with Nonna."

Oh my God, Colton loved this guy. "You sure you don't have a date or something?" Colton asked.

"Nope. So I can sleep here, right? That's all I have to do? And when I get up in the morning, if I'm lucky she'll make me breakfast?"

"Something like that," Sara said.

Colton stood up and pulled him in with a bro handshake. "Thanks."

Rafe lowered his voice. "You know I love you, but if you hurt my sister you're a dead man."

"Got it," Colton said.

"See you tomorrow, Sis."

Sara hugged her brother. "Thanks, Rafe."

* * *

Sara followed Colton into his apartment. Champ was happy to see her but even more happy to go outside with Colton to relieve himself. Sara had just enough time to dash into Colton's bathroom and use his mouthwash. OK, so she'd managed to relax quite a bit, but she still couldn't help having some type A moments.

Colton found her on the couch, leafing through a *Time* magazine she was pretending to read. Champ came bounding over, grabbing a tennis ball from somewhere and depositing the wet slimy thing in her lap. She petted his glossy black coat. "Well, hello there, handsome. You're in the mood to play, aren't you?"

Colton sat down next to her and threw the ball for his dog, who tore off across the living room chasing it. He looked at her with an unholy gaze that sent a shiver racing down her spine. This time, when Champ dropped the ball into her lap, Colton tossed it as far away as he could. "Champ can wait," he said, his mouth curving into a smile.

Then he was kissing her, toppling her to the couch, his delicious weight over her. He kissed her thoroughly, his hands roving everywhere, murmuring wonderful things like how much he'd missed her and how lucky he felt to be with her. This was her crack, this love talk, which, she was discovering, he used quite frequently. He could mumble his grocery list like that and she'd surely melt just as easily into his arms.

Speaking of arms, somehow his shirt was off, and she found herself encased by a pair of rock-solid biceps. She wrapped her arms around his lean waist, slid them up his back, feeling the hills and valleys of muscle, the soft skin over the flexing, sculpted firmness.

Of course the dog trotted back, tennis ball in his teeth, nudging both of them with it. Colton turned to Champ and patted him on the head. "Sorry, buddy. Go in your bed."

The dog crossed the room, tail between his legs, and slunk into his bed. No surprise he listened. Who wasn't under this man's spell?

Colton smiled from above her on the couch. He had such full lips for a man, and skillful too, running them along her stomach, using one hand to open her bra with one quick flick. Then his mouth was on her breast, and she was arching and reaching for him, and somehow in the shedding of the clothes they ended up on the floor. Sensation spilled over her in waves, and all she knew was how he was touching her, kissing her, using his clever mouth to bring her to a place where words couldn't form, where there were only the two of them and nothing and no one else. She marveled at how perfectly they fit together, how they moved, how everything felt so...effortlessly right.

"Sara, I...Now. OK?" She smiled at his lost words, the struggle for control. In the fever pitch of the moment, all she could do was nod. He reached for a condom and before he entered her, he looked at her. No, not just looked—he *saw* her in a way no one had ever seen her before. That one resounding moment shattered her and she knew—just knew—this was it. *He* was it. She wrapped herself around him and clung to him, telling him with her body what she could not say. How could she say it? His coming to family dinner was a big deal. It had been difficult for him just to ask her to be in a relationship. Mentioning the L word would surely send him running for the hills.

Then he was inside her, moving, starting a rhythm that swept all thought away. And there was just him, his body, his lips, the clean scent of him that was so familiar and comforting, the confident way he moved and touched her—it was all him, only him.

They came together, shattering quickly and absolutely, and when it was done they lay there on the floor, tangled up in each other. Colton drew her into him so that her head was resting on his shoulder, his big arms wrapped around her perfectly. They were both a little sweaty. He smoothed her hair back from her face. She curled an arm around his waist, and they lay there together, their breathing slowing.

He kissed the top of her head.

"Was this our first makeup sex?" she asked, running

her hand along his chest, over the soft, light coating of hair that lined his muscles.

"Um, I think so. Why?"

"Because if it is, I mean—wow. Maybe we should disagree more often."

"Or maybe I should come to family dinner more often." He chuckled. And then he kissed her again.

* * *

Colton found her on his couch at four in the morning, writing on a legal pad and glancing at her laptop, and took a seat beside her. He kissed her cheek, then asked, "What are you doing awake?" They should both be sleeping like the dead, in his opinion.

"I'm a little excited. We've got a decorator coming to the office tomorrow who wants our input about paint, and we're ordering new waiting room furniture and some paintings to hang on the walls. And I had an idea about how we could actually schedule my dad more half-hour visits so he could spend time with his more complicated patients and still keep the office moving. My goal is to actually have us all leave the office by five p.m. I've already got us starting a little earlier, and I even blocked a half hour out for lunch."

She seemed happier and more relaxed than he'd ever seen her. Well, except during their lovemaking. She definitely seemed happy and relaxed then. "Sounds like things at the office are going better."

"I'm learning tips from my dad, like how to focus down on the immediate problem. He's got so much experience. Plus he knows any rash this side of the Mississippi. And he's been asking me about new treatment options he's not as familiar with. It's...I don't know. I feel like it's starting to work."

"That's great. Sounds like a real partnership."

She looked at him and smiled. Her hair was mussed. She was wearing one of his T-shirts and a pair of his boxers, and she looked like the sweetest thing he'd ever seen. "Yeah. I hope so."

"I'm really happy for you," he said, gently nudging the laptop from her hands and shutting it. Then he nuzzled her neck.

"Well, it's getting there. And I'm really getting to know people again. Guess who I saw yesterday? Mr. Campanella."

He continued to kiss her neck. This time she extended it, giving him better access. "Our trig teacher?"

"Yep. He retired, did you know that? I'm starting to feel like I'm becoming part of the community. Or at least I hope so. I keep working towards that."

"Sara, all you have to do is be yourself and I'm certain you will." She liked her job, she liked Angel Falls. Music to his ears. "Besides, I'd certainly love it if you stayed. And I've been thinking."

She blushed, which he took as a good sign. "About what?"

"I have a few new ideas I'd like to discuss with you too."

"Oh, is that right?"

He took the pen out of her hand. Placed the legal pad on the coffee table. And proceeded to show her exactly what he meant.

Chapter 19

♥

Sara went into the office early Monday morning to catch up on paperwork, entering through the staff entrance in the back. At 8:10, she remembered the meeting with the decorator about the waiting room redo. As she walked into the hallway from her office, she heard voices from beyond the reception window. She was on her way to join everyone when she saw that the green flag had been lifted in front of one of the exam room doors, which meant the room was occupied. Sure enough, a chart was in the door.

She walked around the counter and peeked into the waiting room to ask her dad if it was one of his patients, but everyone was excitedly weighing in on fabric swatches.

"Burnt sienna is really popular right now," the decorator, Claire Hutton, was saying. "We could do that in a vinyl on the waiting room chairs and alternate with aqua chairs. And I've got this fun pattern here that we could mix and match in between the other two. What do you think?"

Her dad pulled his bifocals down on his nose, deep in contemplation.

"I think after thirty years anything's an improvement," Leonore said, catching Sara's eye through the window and winking.

Sara decided not to bother them and go see the patient for herself. She'd just pulled the chart from the slot and turned the doorknob when Leonore came bursting into the back office. "Sara, wait!" she said excitedly, waving her arms. "He insisted on seeing your father as a sick visit. Don't go in there!"

Too late. She'd already opened the door. There, sitting with his long legs dangling off the exam table, was Tagg.

Tagg. After an entire year. She didn't trust herself to close the door behind her. She might murder him, and with the door open, maybe someone could stop her before it was too late. On the other hand, she didn't want anyone hearing whatever he had to say. Closing the door won, after she'd signaled to poor Leonore that everything was OK. Maybe.

"Tagg," she said on an exhalation, trying to suck in deep, calming breaths as she approached him. "How did you get in here?" She'd known that sooner or later their paths would cross, although he seemed to be making every effort to ensure that that didn't happen. Except for the paperwork she'd had to fill out to give him her half of their house, she hadn't heard a peep from him. So why was he here, masquerading as a patient?

His big brown eyes swiveled over to her. She used to love those dark, mysterious eyes—used to think they were honest eyes. His shiny ink-black hair and full lips were so familiar to her, yet knowing him seemed like a lifetime ago.

She thought of all the times she'd looked at that face. Loved that face. They'd shared a lot together, over ten-plus years of life, there was no denying. For just a moment, it was as if none of the ugliness had happened and it was just another day, when he'd somehow come to joke around and say hey before his own workday began.

But Tagg's face wasn't the same innocent face she'd once loved. He wasn't the person she'd once thought he was.

"What are you doing here?" she asked.

"I had to see you, Sara. I'm dying." He placed his hands over his chest.

He was sitting there calm as could be. Definitely not in any distress. "Quit clowning around."

"I'm not clowning around. Look at my chart." He pointed with a fine, long-fingered hand to the manila folder resting near the sink.

She did. It read, simply, "Chest pain."

Chest pain? A nagging feeling in her gut told her something was up. Even if he was serious, she wasn't about to collect his medical history. And she certainly wasn't going to examine him.

"I can't see you as a patient." She walked to the door and put a hand on the doorknob. "Let me get my dad."

"Wait," he called out. "Why can't you just see me? I'll cooperate, I promise."

Who cared if he cooperated? She was too annoyed

to see him, and the fact that she was truly irritated with him filled her with relief. That pining feeling, that yearning she'd felt in spite of herself for much of the last year was…gone. In the past year she'd often imagined meeting him again, and the thought had filled her with dread. She'd pictured running into him and his girl-friend on the street, maybe even seeing them strolling an adorable, drooly baby, Valerie wearing a diamond the size of a golf ball and proclaiming their love. And the same feelings would overtake her, that she simply hadn't been enough. She'd been the woman someone could bail on two days before their wedding and never think of again.

But strangely, she didn't feel like that lonely, dis-placed person, the object of pity. She felt no sadness, no dread, no longing. Her heart wasn't racing. Nor were her thoughts. She just wanted to move on with her day.

Colton had already sent her a pic of Champ looking adoringly into his phone, captioned We both miss you already. And just then, as if she'd conjured him, her phone vibrated. Is Tagg in there? read the text. I see his car out front.

Of course Tagg had probably parked his Popsicle-red Porsche on the street, with its license plate TAGG IM IT. Conspicuous consumption at its finest, that was Tagg.

She ignored the text for now. She doubted Tagg was having a heart attack, but if he was, she didn't want it to be on her conscience that she'd botched the diagnosis. Although it was tempting to do just that.

"Just a minute," she said, and walked out into the hall. She avoided the reception area, instead going to the only other exam room with a closed door and knocking.

Her dad poked his head out.

"Dad, how long will you be in there?" she asked.

"I'm seeing Clara Ridgeway."

Oh God. A lonely senior who was also a hypochondriac. That meant a half hour at least.

"Anything I can help you with, honey?"

"It can wait until after you're through."

Her phone vibrated again. Are you OK? She shoved it into her Leonore-pouch and reentered the exam room.

"Are you having chest pain now?" she asked.

"Yes, yes I am." He splayed his fingers over his chest and grimaced.

She glanced at her watch. Chest pain could be a complicated diagnosis, but the workup was fairly straightforward. Tagg was also a smart guy—and a doctor. If something were seriously wrong, he would have taken himself to the ER. This whole situation smelled like bad cheese.

"Maybe you should head over to the ER," Sara said.

"No," he said, quite adamantly. "I came to see you. I-I want to discuss my problem with you."

"Where does it hurt?"

He moved the palm of his hand over his chest. "All over."

"How often and how long does it last? And does it happen during activity or at rest? Any fever or shortness of breath?"

"It's come and gone for about a year now, but it's been nearly constant for the past month."

"How severe is it, and any radiation down your arm?"

"No radiation. But it nearly doubles me over sometimes."

"Palpitations, skipped beats, strange rhythms?" She ran through all the usual questions, although the hair on the back of her neck was prickling. Nothing was adding up, but at the same time she didn't want to ignore a weird or unusual problem that needed to be dealt with ASAP.

She unwound her stethoscope from her neck and approached him. "Let me have a listen and then we'll do an office EKG, OK?" She took his wrist and timed his pulse. "It's steady, and you're not tachycardic."

Suddenly he grabbed her hand. The abrupt movement startled her.

"Sara," he said, looking her in the eye, "I screwed up. Bad. I'm so sorry. My life's been hell without you."

Sara pulled her hand away. "Tagg, what are you thinking? I'm at work. There are people who are *sick* here, for God's sake."

"I didn't think you'd talk to me any other way."

"You were right." Her boldness shocked her a little, and her heart thumped hard in her chest. But she wasn't backing down. This time she was going to say what she should've said long ago. "It's been a year, Tagg. One whole year. Surely you've had other opportunities to contact me."

He at least had the decency to look sheepish. "I was embarrassed. With every day that passed, I felt more and more ashamed about what I'd done." She shook her head and backed up, but he grabbed her elbow. She used to love that he'd always been a little touchy-feely, but not anymore.

"Look," he continued. "We dated for such a long time. As it got closer and closer to our wedding, I kept thinking I never got to sow my wild oats. It was like I had this monster inside of me, always wondering what it would be like to date someone else because I never did."

She crossed her arms. "You'd think you'd have come to that conclusion sooner than two days before our wedding."

"I panicked. Maybe there's even something admirable about that, wanting to get that out of my system, not committing because I wasn't ready. I mean, what if we'd gone through with it? Imagine starting a marriage feeling like that."

The look in his eyes told her he believed what he was saying. Although she had an entirely different word for him, and it wasn't *admirable*.

"I know I embarrassed you and you're right to be angry with me, but I understand myself so much better now. And I've come to understand there's no one like you, Sara. No one. You're beautiful and good and kind, and you were the best thing that ever happened to me. I was a huge fool. I hate myself every day for what I did to you. I hope you can forgive me."

"Where's Valerie?" Sara asked. "Is she in the waiting room?"

"We...broke up." He looked embarrassed. "OK, she left me. But that was because I kept comparing her to you."

He was the picture of earnestness. Sara knew him well enough to know he was in pain. But she also understood what had happened to them so much better now. Tagg hadn't admitted to himself that he hadn't loved her the way he needed to until he'd done something really stupid. And she hadn't had the courage to leave their relationship because it had been too damn comfortable.

As with so many other things in her life, she'd gone with the flow to live up to other people's expectations. Getting A's, going to the best schools, achieving, achieving, achieving. Staying with Tagg because he was the "right" kind of guy, one who lived up to her dad's expectations. Not that the achieving part had been a bad thing, but why had she been so afraid to rebel a little? Choose what *she* wanted?

"Tagg, you're forgiven," she said, placing her hand over his. She meant it too. She now saw the whole embarrassing event as a relief, an opportunity to start over that she would've missed. She would have missed *Colton*, and never known what the possibility of true happiness looked like.

Speaking of Colton, her phone vibrated again in her pocket.

Tagg stood and took both her hands. Maybe it was the blue gown that made him seem extra vulnerable, but she did feel sorry for him. "I hope you can see it in your heart to give me another chance. If you do, I promise I'll be faithful to you until the day I die."

"Tagg, you were my first boyfriend. My first everything. We supported each other through those really tough med school years. We believed in each other's dreams. But the rest of it... it wasn't right. *We* weren't right. I'm sorry." She dropped her hands and walked over to the door.

He followed her. "I want to prove to you I've changed. Give me another chance, Sara. Please."

She felt really... bad for him. But his feelings weren't her concern anymore. It was Colton she needed to check in with, which meant responding to his texts ASAP. "I'm sorry, Tagg." Then she opened the door and left.

In the hall it was so quiet you could've heard someone slice cake. She walked through the office to the reception desk. Leonore and Glinda were staring at her, wide-eyed. Her father was leaning on the counter, writing up a chart, and to his credit, he didn't even look up. Behind the open reception window was Colton, standing there quietly.

Thank God. She didn't want him worrying, and now she could put his mind at ease in person.

The exam room door opened, and Tagg stepped out into the hall, tucking in his shirt.

"Dr. Langdon! A pleasure to see you, sir." Tagg extended a hand. For a long second, her father stared down his nose over the top of his bifocals in that way he had of quietly assessing everyone he met.

"Hey, Colt! How's it going?" Tagg asked, giving Colton a wave. Colton nodded back, his jaw spring-loaded like a mouse trap, ready to crush and kill.

"Taggart," her dad said cautiously. "What brings you back to town?"

"I came to beg Sara for forgiveness," he said, his eyes darting around at everyone. Judging by the looks on their faces, Leonore and Glinda were definitely thinking this was better than Netflix. As were the handful of people in the waiting room. Leonore sat at the reception desk, arms folded staunchly across her ample chest. Glinda held a syringe in her hand, ready to inject at a moment's notice.

"And you've got it," Sara said, her face turning its usual fifty shades of red. Now would he just leave already?

"But I want more than that. I want you. And I want everyone to know. Complete honesty from here on out."

"Isn't it a little too late for that?" Colton asked. He was frowning, and his steely gaze was boring a hole through Tagg.

"Oh my," her dad said. His gaze swung back and forth between Tagg and Colton, but he didn't say anything, just cleared his throat. Maybe he'd decided not to touch that one with a ten-foot pole.

In the old days her dad would have made small talk, or hugged Tagg, or at least given him a friendly slap on the back. Not so today—thank you, Daddy. He did, however, turn to Colton. "Have a nice day, son," he said, giving him a wave before he left to see his next patient.

Colton, in true cop form, scanned all the players, nodded at her father, and addressed Sara. "How are you?"

"Oh, good. Thanks for asking." She couldn't help

the near-hysterical giggle that bubbled up her throat. God, she just needed Tagg to leave already.

Colt eyed her carefully. Then his gaze flitted to Tagg, his eyes narrowing a little. It struck Sara that this was how he might look during target practice.

"Colton," Tagg said, walking past Sara and out into the waiting room to embrace his friend. "Long time no see. What are you doing here?"

Colton's gaze landed on Sara, who held her breath while waiting for what he was about to say.

"I saw your car out front," he said casually. "Came in to say hello."

"I was just leaving. Walk out with me?"

"I have a minute, sure."

Tagg actually walked back into the reception area and kissed Sara on the cheek. "We'll talk more later, OK?"

Ugh, that was just like him. What had she not made clear? After a year, did he actually think simply waltzing in and apologizing would bring everything back to the way it had been?

Oh man, Colton's jaw was so tight you could bounce a quarter off it, and a muscle at his temple was twitching. Maybe she should have shut Tagg down immediately by telling him about Colton. But she didn't want drama in front of the entire office. Colton would understand and no doubt tell Tagg himself.

"Take care, folks," Colton said a little stiffly. "Have a good morning, Sara," he said, as he and Tagg walked out the door.

Her morning schedule was on the counter. First up

was Troy Cummings, a two-year-old whose mother Holly worried endlessly about every sniffle. Holly's own mother had passed away shortly before Troy was born, and she needed lots of reassurance. Sara would also be seeing an elderly patient from the nursing home with diabetes, a bad heart, and lung problems, and a recent widower, Mr. Stevens, whose bunions were bothering him for the second time in a week but who probably just needed a little TLC.

Despite all the turmoil this morning, Sara was really looking forward to her day. Seeing her patients. Plus she felt that a huge weight she'd been dragging behind her for a year had been cut free.

"You OK, sweetheart?" her dad asked in a quiet voice. "If I would have known it was that pea brain, I would have taken care of him myself. You should've told me."

God love her dad. He never said an unkind word about anyone, but calling Tagg a pea brain was about the most wonderful thing anyone could say to her right now. She even teared up a little.

"Dad, I always thought you liked Tagg."

Her dad took off his glasses and eyeballed her. "No, honey, *you* always liked Tagg. I just supported your choice, like I've supported whatever you wanted in life."

Sara blanched. Could she really have gotten it so wrong all these years? "But I always thought you thought he was the perfect guy for me."

"I appreciated his ambition, but I always felt he had his eye on anything and everything beyond his reach. The most prestigious job, better cars, better fiancées, that kind of thing. He was never one to be happy with what he had. But then, he didn't really show his true colors until last year, did he?"

"How could I not know you felt this way?"

"I try to think the best of people. Sometimes I'm wrong, of course. But you're an adult now. You can figure out what you want for yourself."

What else had she been wrong about? Her dad's constant push to have her succeed—his hints about her continuing the fellowship she would've started last year—how did he really feel about that? And hadn't he just told her now it mattered more what she wanted for herself than what he wanted?

Well, she finally knew what she wanted. Colton.

* * *

Colton turned over in his brain what he'd just seen and heard. Tagg was going to talk to Sara later? He'd kissed her on the cheek and she'd said...nothing?

Jesus, Colton's stomach was churning as he walked outside with Tagg.

It was a bright morning, but clouds were building, making the sun look a little watery.

"It's great to see you, man," Tagg said, slapping him on the back. "And Sara. God, I've missed her."

The acid feeling in Colton's stomach crept up to his esophagus. He was definitely going to have to break out the Tums.

"I've been such an idiot." Tagg paused and leveled his gaze at Colton.

"Things not working out with Val?" Colton asked. Shocker if they weren't.

"I knew Val and I weren't going to last forever. It just ran its course. But being with her helped me understand how much I'm really in love with Sara. Thank God she's still single." Tagg smiled and Colton clenched his fists.

"A year's a long time. Anything could happen."

Tagg didn't seem to hear. "The one good thing that came of this was that I finally cut myself free and got to explore who I really was. After ten years of dating one woman I felt entitled to that."

Yes, entitled. Something Colton had come to realize was part of Tagg's character. He'd never really noticed it before. Or he'd ignored it. Now Colton felt entitled to pick him up by his skinny neck and shake him, but somehow refrained.

"I screwed up, Colton. I'll do anything to get Sara back. I heard you two are on good terms now. I may need you to go to bat for me, to tell her this was just a crazy phase."

A crazy phase, canceling your wedding to the woman you were supposed to love on a whim and moving in with someone you barely knew?

Colton was reminded of the times he'd deferred to Tagg, because Tagg and his family had done so much for him. They'd given him a real family as an example, and Tagg's dad had helped Colton stay on the straight and narrow, and for that he'd always be grateful. For years he'd had Tagg's enduring loyalty—Tagg had always thought Colton was cool, and Colton had liked that. It had made him feel important.

He didn't need to feel important anymore. Tagg had lied and had potentially cost Colton years with Sara. Water under the bridge, but still. Once upon a time, his dedication to Tagg had known no bounds, but maybe it was time to consider that debt repaid in full.

More important, he wanted to tell Tagg to stay the hell away from Sara. *Mine* was the word that kept drumming through his head. But something stopped him. His own fear, maybe, that Sara might possibly want Tagg back? She'd certainly tolerated that kiss on the cheek. And the fact that she was going to talk to him later? He didn't know. She'd looked a little shocked, a little confused. All he knew was he needed to talk to her.

"I want to ask Dr. Langdon to set up a meeting for me with the new neurology group in town. And hopefully he'll drop a bug in their ear that I'm a hometown son and a perfect future candidate for their practice. Dr. Langdon golfs with them, and I'm pretty sure he'll put in a good word for me."

Colton wasn't so sure that Sara's father would put in a good word for the guy who'd broken his daughter's heart. "So you're planning on moving back to town?" Colton asked. Tagg lived about an hour away, nearer to his job.

"I want to be closer to Sara. She forgave me, even though I can tell she's still angry. I know I hurt her. Part of me was rebelling against my parents pushing so hard for our marriage, but now I understand why they love Sara so much. She's the best. I'll never find anyone better. I don't know how you've done it, going from woman to woman all these years. It's exhausting. All I want is my old life back."

Save it for your shrink, buddy, a voice in Colton's head said.

Colton wanted to hit something. A punching bag, Tagg's pristine face. Both decent-size targets. He clenched his fists repeatedly to try to knead out some of the tension. Wasn't working.

He'd heard this same speech from Tagg in one form or another for years, the gist being that he'd always wondered what else was out there. He'd always defaulted to Sara, though, until the bachelor party. As far as Colt knew, Tagg had never cheated on Sara before then. Colton had never said anything to Sara—hadn't felt it was his place—but maybe he should have.

The difference this time, despite the subtle dig about Colton's love life, was that maybe Tagg really *had* learned his lesson. This time he seemed dead serious, and when Tagg set his mind to something, he usually got it. What if Sara wanted him back too?

As Colton's mind wandered, he noticed a white blur moving in the shrubbery next to the office. Sure enough, there was a little white dog peeing in the boxwood. On closer inspection he saw it wasn't just any dog, but a poodle, a super-groomed one, with painted toenails and bright pink bows in its hair.

"Dolly?" he called. The dog stopped peeing and froze.

Tagg's beeper went off. "I've got to get this. I've got a head trauma patient in the unit who's really sick. Hello," he said into his phone while Colton walked toward the dog. "His intracranial pressure's increasing? Let's give him more Solu-Medrol and call neurosurgery to schedule him for craniotomy, OK? I'll be there as soon as I can."

Colton bent down and pulled out the emergency dog biscuit he always kept in his shirt pocket. "Come here, Dolly. We'll find your mama, OK? Come get a cookie." He looked up and down the street. No one running down the street frantically panicking...yet.

At the sound of *cookie*, the dog practically leaped onto the biscuit, making it easy for Colton to scoop her right into his arms.

"What the hell?" Tagg said, laughing, as he looked at the dog, who was now sniffing Colton's pocket for another biscuit.

"Mrs. Nelson's dog," Colton said.

Just then Maggie Nelson, who ran Angelfood, the gourmet chocolate place, and Cindy Madison, the dog groomer, came running down the street, exclaiming over Dolly's misbehavior.

"Gotta go, buddy," Tagg said, climbing behind the wheel of his car. "Let's have dinner one night soon."

Colton stood there holding the poodle, who was now licking his face. Tagg was off saving critically ill people while he was here nipping an overgroomed poodle's dream of freedom in the bud. The question was, which guy would Sara prefer?

Chapter 20

♥

Later that afternoon, Colton was standing on a stepladder working on his grandmother's porch roof trying not to think about upsetting things, like Tagg wanting Sara back. Aiden had told him he'd seen a loose downspout, and Colton thought he'd give it a quick fix before he met Sara for dinner at Fallside, the popular multideck restaurant downtown that sat practically on top of the falls.

Logic told him Sara cared for him, a lot. But Tagg could be persuasive and charming, and he and Sara had a long history together. Plus they had similar backgrounds and their parents belonged to the same social circles. The list of how they were alike and he and Sara were different seemed a mile long.

Tonight was his first real date with Sara. But he wasn't really in the mood for it. He'd kept thinking of Tagg all day, wondering about Sara's reaction. There'd been no time to talk with her this afternoon, and it was eating him alive.

That was probably why he cut himself on the jagged rim of the disconnected spout. Nothing serious, but his thumb started bleeding.

He stopped in the kitchen to run water over his cut and wrapped it in a paper towel while he hunted for a Band-Aid. No luck in the kitchen or the downstairs bathroom, so he ran up to the bathroom at the top of the stairs, the one Hannah had appropriated. The narrow sink was lined with bottles of stuff he didn't recognize and a curling iron that looked ready to fall into the sink. He'd have to warn her about that hazard. He opened the medicine cabinet above the sink.

He found the Band-Aids, all right. Right behind a little pink wheel of birth control pills.

He forgot all about his bleeding finger and stared at the thing. Picked it up, even though he knew it wasn't his business. Some of the pills were popped out of the foil backing. He flipped it over. There was a pharmacy label. "Sara Langdon, MD, Langdon Family Practice."

With fumbling fingers, he replaced the wheel and shut the cabinet. Leaned over the sink. He felt a little sick. One, because his sister was taking the pill. Having sex. With the guy he'd brought to the house, a kid he'd tried to help get into electrician school. Two, and worse, because Sara had prescribed them.

He forced himself to calm down enough to wrap a damn Band-Aid around his finger, but it took him two tries.

Colton leaned over the sink and heaved a big sigh, avoiding his reflection, which looked panicky. He was the father figure in Hannah's life, and sometimes the boundary between that and being her big brother got blurred. But he was responsible for her. It was his job to protect her future, to make sure she had a great life. That meant sending her to college and making sure she was free to make choices he'd never been free to make. That didn't include something like this. A guy who was wrong for her, who could alter her future plans. A guy she was having sex with at eighteen!

Dammit, why hadn't he talked to her himself? He'd trusted Sara to do the right thing.

This was not the right thing. This was disaster.

* * *

Sara hadn't minded at all when Colton suggested they cancel their dinner reservations and pick up Chinese instead. In fact, she told him he was welcome to bring the food to Nonna's, since Nonna was with Rachel at the big senior center Italian meatball cook-off.

She couldn't wait to see him. Tell him all about the stupid things Tagg had done in the office. Mostly she just wanted to feel his arms around her. Be reassured that what they had was real and good and so different from what she'd had with Tagg.

As soon as Colton's cruiser pulled into Nonna's driveway, Sara ran to the driver's side and bent down to kiss him on the cheek. "Hi!" she said. An enthusiastic greeting, because she was starving—for food and for him. A couple of brown bags of takeout sat on the passenger side. The smell of ginger, sesame oil, and soy sauce wafted up, and her stomach grumbled.

As soon as Colton looked up, Sara sensed something was off. He was too quiet. Not smiling, his mouth drawn in a tight line. His brow was furrowed, and a muscle twitched in his jaw. Plus he had a white-knuckle grip on the wheel.

"What's wrong?" She was learning that cops often kept a lot of things to themselves, things that would be upsetting to those that they loved. Maybe he'd had a terrible day at work.

He met her gaze briefly but didn't smile like he usually did, or try to kiss her back. "I thought we might eat first, but I'm a little too upset." He was staring straight ahead out the car window, and that unnerved her. It wasn't like him not to look at her. My God, what was wrong?

"Do you want to come sit on the porch?"

"OK." He walked up the porch steps and set the takeout bags on the table.

She took a seat on the edge of the swing while he stood against the porch railing, glancing out over the backyard.

He sighed heavily. Turned to face her. "I found Hannah's birth control pills. The ones you prescribed for her."

"You're angry?" she asked.

He snorted. Well, that answered that.

"I sent her to you for information and you gave her license to fool around." The anger in his eyes wasn't what slayed her, but rather the hurt. He felt betrayed. By her. She could see it, all over his handsome face, and it devastated her.

She chose her words carefully. "Regardless of how I counseled her, she's old enough to make her own decisions."

"Why couldn't you have told me?"

"She's my patient. I couldn't discuss what she told me in private."

"Did you not think I had a right to know?"

"God, Colton, it has nothing to do with that. Look, I gave her all the facts, including my opinion on waiting. It was never my intention to encourage her to run off and have sex—just to protect her."

Another heavy sigh.

He didn't believe her, and that broke her heart.

The sound of a car idling down the road made her turn. A red Porsche was pulling up in front of the house. She saw that idiotic license plate, TAGG IM IT.

"Looks like your fiancé couldn't stay away."

"Ex-fiancé," she said. This was getting worse by the minute. "Oh, come on, Colton." She folded her arms. He could *not* be serious.

"You didn't tell him about us this morning."

"I was in the middle of my office. He was…emotional." She paused. "You're his oldest friend. Did *you* tell him?"

"Maybe there's nothing to tell."

Really? He was actually doing this? "Are you really going there? Before we do, let's make it clear—is this about Hannah or Tagg?" Tagg got out of his sports car, shut the door, and took off his sunglasses. He was going to be up on the porch in a minute.

"It's about everything. It's about us and how different we are. Our families, our education, our backgrounds—*different*."

She'd looked on their differences as complementary. Apparently he thought they were insurmountable.

"Colton, I'm sorry you're angry. If you just talk with your sister—"

"This isn't working," Colton said, still staring out over the backyards where next door, a couple of kids chased each other around, laughing and playing.

"What's not working?" Sara sucked in a breath. He was angry. Furious, even, about her interference with his sister. But was he so angry he wanted to *break up*?

"*We're* not working."

"We—us? Wait—are you breaking up with me?" Oh God. He couldn't be serious. This was their first fight about something other than their relationship. How could it be their *last*?

Her heart was drumming inside her chest as if she were having a heart attack. She felt sick. And angry. He was being obstinate. And she had no defense. She'd done what she felt she'd needed to do for Hannah.

Tagg was striding up the lawn. "Hey, babe," he said, approaching her and giving her a side hug, which she quickly stepped out of.

She did not need this now, not ever.

"Babe, huh?" Colton said, clearing his throat. He rolled his eyes, his fists balled into a death grip at his sides.

Jealous. Could he be jealous of Tagg? His comment about their differences, about calling Tagg her fiancé…it was all making sense now.

"I stopped by so we could continue that discussion we started in the office," Tagg said. "Guess what? Turns out my dad's friends with the head of the neurology department at Falls Hospital and he's arranged to have lunch with me. I'm really excited."

Sara glanced at Colton, who seemed...shut down. Distant. She wanted to shake him.

"Tagg, this is a bad time," Sara said.

"Hey, I'm glad you're here, Colt," Tagg said. "Maybe you can tell Sara how much I missed her. How sorry I am. How much I—"

"I meant what I said this morning," Sara said to Tagg. "I'm not getting back together with you. I—I'm seeing someone else." She looked pointedly at Colton, who seemed very busy checking his radio.

Tagg stared at her. At least that had temporarily shut him up. Unfortunately Colton didn't say a thing.

"I love somebody else." She looked at Colton, but he still wouldn't make eye contact. God, the man was impossible. She frowned at him, but inside she was starting to panic. "So that's it?" she finally said. "You're not going to say anything?"

This time he turned cool blue eyes on her. Emotionless. "I need some time to think."

"You're really breaking up with me?" Her voice was shaky now.

Tagg had gone silent but suddenly began to sputter. "Wait a minute...You two...?"

"I love you," Sara said softly to Colton. Oh God. Look what she'd done. The words had slipped out at the worst time. They came out sounding like a desperate attempt to keep him, a statement of outrage instead of a tender profession. As if she were really saying, *I love you, how could you possibly break up with me?*

He looked at her then, his gaze detached and level. "I'm not sure that's enough, Sara."

"Of course it's enough," she said, starting to cry. How could it not be enough?

"I—I've got to go." He barely glanced at her as he walked down the porch stairs and to his car, leaving her standing on the porch with Tagg.

Sara wanted to escape into the house and get away from Tagg, but her muscles were paralyzed. She stood frozen, arms wrapped around herself. She was afraid if she moved she might fall to pieces.

"You've been dating Colton while I was gone?" Tagg asked, irritation tingeing his voice.

"Tagg, go home, OK?" Tears rolled uncontrollably down her face. She needed to move. If only her legs would obey. She didn't care about Tagg or his unjustified outrage. She just wanted to get inside before the whole damn neighborhood caught her outside bawling.

"I can't believe it. I mean, you two hated each other."

OK, that was it. All the anger she'd kept bottled up inside for the past year finally burst out. "Maybe Colton and I wouldn't have hated each other if you hadn't lied."

"What are you talking about?"

"That time you and I broke up in college, I made a date with him. You made sure it didn't happen."

For a second his eyes widened. "Oh, come on, Sara, that was years ago. I've always loved you. You can't blame me for trying to hold on to you."

"Tagg, you've always *thought* you loved me. What did we know of love? We were kids."

His voice got quiet. "I know what love is now, Sara. You have to believe me. I've learned my lesson."

Sara frowned. "Does this have something to do with the fact that you and Val broke up?" Of course it did.

His brows knit down. "Of course not."

"I don't know, why else are you suddenly here after an entire year?" He looked a little uncomfortable, but what did she know? And you know what, she didn't really care. Tagg was not her problem anymore. "Maybe you need to stop searching for the right woman and try living with yourself for a while."

"I've found the right woman. And she's standing right here."

"It was never right between us, Tagg, but I didn't see it. Thank God things happened the way they did. Because you'll always be looking over your shoulder, looking for something—some*one*—other than me."

His mouth dropped open. He looked hurt and maybe even a little shocked. The Sara she'd been a year ago would never have made that speech. It was her only consolation now when she was aching, body and soul.

Sara turned and walked into the house. She couldn't help but be reminded of the day before the wedding last year, when Tagg had shown up at her parents' and told her he'd slept with Valerie. How devastated she'd been.

She'd hated being rejected, hated the cheap way it had happened, with Tagg sleeping with Cake Girl instead of having the guts to tell her to her face that he didn't love her enough to marry her.

But now she felt only relief. Thank God she hadn't married him! Who knew how long she would've kept telling herself she loved him, kept trying to make it work, despite the nagging in her soul that surely there must be more.

With Colton she felt love the way it was meant to be. He knew her so well, her vulnerabilities and her strengths, and he wasn't afraid to call her out on either. But now he was rejecting her too.

* * *

Colton found the door to Hannah's room closed. On it was a little magnet board covered with pictures of her and her friends and some goofy signs her friends had made for her eighteenth birthday. Typical teenager stuff.

The photo that caught his eye was of Hannah hugging a scraggly teddy bear whose left eye hung a little lower than his right. Elmer. Colton had sewed that eye back on when he was sixteen, after they'd all hunted for it for over an hour on Cookie's front lawn.

He remembered how Hannah had cried about that lost eye, big, heaving sobs that had made him vow he'd search high and low all night if he had to, until the thing was found.

Where had the years gone? And why couldn't today's problems be as simple to fix as yesterday's? Sewing on a teddy bear eye was nothing compared to worrying about the consequences of bad choices.

He hated that Hannah was growing up. He *really*

hated the thought of her getting serious with someone. Someone who was a tattooed troublemaker, who would probably dump her for some other girl in a heartbeat. Someone who could get her pregnant and narrow her choices and alter the course of her life forever.

He rubbed the heel of his hand over his forehead. It was no secret that he had a difficult time talking about feelings. Add the birds and the bees into the discussion and he felt beyond helpless. But now he had no choice. Hannah's life was too important to him. He wanted her to have the best life ever—full of love and happiness and fulfillment. Every choice that had been taken away from him—through his parents' deaths, his heaped-on responsibilities, his blown-out knee—he wanted to be hers for the asking. He'd been a coward to depend on someone else to do what he should've done himself.

He knocked on the door.

No answer, but he was pretty sure she was in there, so he knocked louder.

"Come in," Hannah said. "Is it Cookie?"

"Colton."

He opened the door to find her sitting on her bed in a jumble of blankets, talking into her laptop. Elmer stared at him with his uneven, oddly suspicious gaze from her side.

"I'm FaceTiming Sydney," she said, laughing at something. "What's up?"

"I wanted to talk with you. Can you call her back?"

"Hey, Syd, I gotta go. I'll text you later, K?" She closed the computer.

There were clothes tossed all over the floor, makeup

strewn across her dresser top, some smudged into the carpet. Photos lined her vanity mirror on both sides, mostly of her and her friends hamming it up for the camera. A lacy purple bra dangled off the edge of the mirror. He was really, really glad he never came in here.

He headed for the desk chair. "Can I sit here?" She jumped off the bed and moved the clothes that hung over the back of the chair. "I wanted to talk to you about something I probably should have brought up a long time ago."

Hannah bit back a smile. "I've already had my period, Colton. It's all good."

"Ha ha. Look, I'm just going to come out and say it, OK? I found some pills in the cabinet when I was searching for a Band-Aid. I-I wondered if you'd talk to me about that."

"About why I'm on the pill?"

He nodded. His hands were clenched so tightly on his knees he was pretty sure he'd leave bruises, and his jaw was stiff from clenching. But he had to stay the course on this, or he'd never forgive himself.

"Wait—no," he said. "It's not really about that. I feel like I've let you down as a brother."

"What are you talking about? Most boys are terrified to ask me out because you're so scary." She was smiling.

That was the idea, but clearly Aiden hadn't gotten the *scary* memo. And Colton didn't feel very intimidating now.

Who the hell was he to give a sex talk anyway? He hadn't had a serious relationship in his life. He'd cultivated that lifestyle on purpose. Carefree, easygoing

Colt, who had enough responsibilities at home. Who didn't want to be tied down to anyone.

Until now. Until Sara. And now he'd wrecked that.

"I screwed up because I was afraid to talk to you about what's important because it made me uncomfortable. Because I told myself it was easier to send you to someone else who could help you."

"That was great advice. I love Sara. By the way, she said she'd take me to the Young Adult Bookfest in Coventry next weekend. My favorite author's going to be there and there's food and a street party. Wanna come?"

"Maybe. The point is, I passed something off on Sara that I should have done myself. Should have *said* myself." He took a deep breath. "Don't have sex just to have sex. Or because a boy is pressuring you. Do it because you love someone."

"I haven't had sex, Colton."

His exhalation was audible. "You haven't?"

"No. And I'm not going to have sex with randos or just to hook up."

"If you aren't having sex...then why are you taking those pills?"

"Because I've been seeing Aiden since March. I love him. And I'm *thinking* of having sex with him."

March? Jesus, it was July. He'd had no idea.

"I'm sorry I hid it from you," she said. "I was afraid you'd go ballistic."

"Look, Hannah, Aiden has a lot of things to overcome. He's already gotten into trouble and my whole reason for bringing him here was to..."

"I know, Colton. Get him on the straight and narrow. He appreciates it. He knows he screwed up with the pot, but he's a good guy. And very driven. His dream is to own his own company one day."

"Hannah, there are lots of guys out there. Ones with intact families who don't have all that turmoil at home and lots of stuff to overcome."

"*We* come from a family with a lot of turmoil and lots of stuff to overcome, and look how we turned out. Well, you can speak for yourself, but I'm personally planning on being terrific."

Colton cracked a smile. God, he loved this kid. "Hannah, you *are* terrific. And you've got your whole life ahead of you. Decisions like sex can lead to permanent consequences—babies." There, he'd said it. "I want you to have every choice, every opportunity you dream of. I don't want something like an unplanned pregnancy or a boyfriend that ties you down to this town to make you alter your dreams. So I still wish you'd wait."

"Sara told me the same thing. She told me to talk to you because she said you'd probably be afraid to bring it up. She said you weren't going to like that I was starting the pill, but it was my decision. And she told me how to be safe. I really like her, Colton. Honestly, you'd be an idiot if you didn't marry her."

Sara told her the same thing. Yet he'd been so angry, accusing her of dispensing birth control with little thought. And of course she'd told Hannah to talk to him because she herself could not.

God, he was an ass.

He stood up and went over to the bed. Hannah's phone with the pink sparkly case was next to her, pinging every few minutes. He remembered when she wore pink sparkly tutus and pink sparkly ballet slippers and pink sparkly everything. Not everything had changed, apparently.

He put his arm around her and hugged her. "I'm really proud of you. You have a lot of good sense. I love you."

She wrapped her arms around him. "Oh, Colty, I love you too." After a few seconds, he heard sniffing.

"What is it?" he asked, drawing back to look at her.

"It's just—sometimes you're a kick-ass brother. I want you to know that. You've taken good care of me and Cookie."

Sometimes. He'd take that as a compliment. He smiled against her hair. "I still don't want you to have sex. Ever."

She hugged him back. "I'll take it under advisement. Now what about you? Don't screw things up with Sara, OK?"

Don't screw things up. Yeah, he was pretty sure he'd already done that.

Chapter 21

♥

There were times when not having your own place was a very bad thing. Like now, for instance, when Sara sat numbly on her grandmother's old sofa, Rocket lodged next to her hip. Gabby, Rachel, her dad, and Nonna were due back any minute from the senior center meatball competition. She didn't want to see anybody. She just wanted to watch *The Notebook* and ugly cry.

She checked her phone every ten seconds, but there were no texts from Colton saying he was sorry for being an ass and couldn't live without her. Dammit.

She was rummaging through the cupboards looking for Nonna's Christmas Eve bottle of Crown Royal when Gabby walked in. "Nonna won the sauce contest and Rachel and Dad took her for ice cream to celebrate. And I stopped at the liquor store because Dad told me Tagg's back and causing trouble—" Gabby took a good, hard look at Sara. "Geez, you look terrible."

"Colton broke up with me," she said, her voice cracking. She gave up on the liquor search and poked around in the freezer. Through the blur of tears, she saw a bunch of things wrapped up in tinfoil and labeled with masking tape with dates on it. A quick perusal showed random packages marked "2013" and "2014." No ice cream. She shut the door.

"Did you say liquor store?"

Gabby held up a brown bag. Sara didn't care what was in it. She'd take it.

"Oh, Sara. Maybe he just needs time—"

"He hasn't called me to make up." Gabby pried her phone out of her hand and set it on the kitchen table. "He's not going to, Gabs. He broke up with me. Done. *Finito*. Kaput."

"What happened?"

She took the bag from Gabby and pulled out a bottle of wine. "I could tell you, but then I'd have to kill you."

"What are you talking about?"

"I saw his sister in the office at his request and . . . and I can't really talk about it but he's upset with me."

"You gave her the sex talk?"

She nodded. "And other things."

"He should be thanking you."

"Well, he's pissed." She rolled the cold bottom of the wine bottle against her forehead. "Really pissed. And then Tagg was here, being an idiot, and it just snowballed. And then Colton said he wanted to call it quits. Said we're too different. Just like that."

"Have you had dinner?"

Sara's eyes suddenly filled with tears. "I don't want dinner, Gabby. I want Colton."

Gabby guided her over to Nonna's table and pulled

out a chair. As Sara glanced out the big bay window, she saw the old oak tree, steadfast and solid, but somehow it didn't provide her with any of its usual comfort.

"Sit here," Gabby said. "I'm going to make you something to eat, OK?"

They'd gotten used to taking care of each other after their mother died, depended on each other for comfort and confidences. Gabby's mothering was familiar and welcome.

Gabby opened the wine and poured them each a glass in one of the many plastic cups in every color of the rainbow that filled Nonna's cupboards.

Her sister handed her a cup, and Sara took it gratefully. Gabby had just started to crack eggs into a bowl when they heard voices coming up the walkway.

"Oh, they're home," Gabby said.

"Don't say anything." Sara wiped her eyes and blew her nose.

The door opened, and Nonna, her dad, and Rachel walked in. Nonna was clutching an old iron pot with a blue-and-white-speckled lid to her chest.

"I won first prize in the meatball contest," she said.

"The best meatballs this side of the Mississippi," her dad said, giving Nonna a hug.

"And there were ten other contestants," Rachel said, looking elegant as usual in jeans and a sleeveless black blouse.

"Oh, Nonna, that's wonderful," Sara said, a note of false cheer in her voice. Rachel, always intuitive, looked at her a little strangely, but kept a smile on her face.

"I got a gift certificate to Giuseppe's. So it can be my

treat next time we all go." Nonna looked at Gabby, who was beating the eggs. "Who are those for?"

"Sara. She's feeling a little low and hasn't had any dinner yet."

Nonna shooed her away and took over the cooking in that way she always had. "Go, go, sit down. Sara, want some mushrooms in your omelet?"

"Anything you want, Nonna," Sara said. She wanted nothing but Colton. That big stubborn jackass.

"Why are you feeling low?" Rachel asked, narrowing her eyes.

"Colton and I broke up." There, she'd said it. They might as well know.

"Damn that Taggart," her dad said. "Thinking he can come home with his tail between his legs like that and stir trouble. You're not taking him back, are you?"

"No, of course not."

"Oh, honey," Rachel said. "I'm so sorry."

"Colton's jealous," her father said. "That's got to be it. He certainly didn't appreciate Tagg showing up in the office today."

"I have no idea why he'd feel threatened. I don't love Tagg anymore. I don't *want* Tagg anymore. I love Colton."

"Did you tell him that?" Rachel asked.

"I tried to, but he was too busy being angry with me about seeing his sister in the office to listen."

"I know about that visit," her dad said, frowning a little. "The pharmacy called me about the prescription."

She nodded. She thought her father would understand the difficulties of seeing Hannah in the office, even if they couldn't really talk about it now in front of everyone.

He patted her knee as if she were twelve again. Kissed her forehead. "Hang in there, sweetheart."

She attempted a smile. "Thanks, Dad."

Rachel hugged her. "I'm sorry, sweetie."

She squeezed Rachel's hand. "Thanks, Rach."

After her dad and Rachel left, Nonna served her up a perfect mushroom-and-onion omelet, and made one for Gabby too, but Sara was barely able to stomach a bite. Then they all sat on the couch, Nonna in the middle covered up with her favorite crocheted afghan, and turned on an episode of *Friends*, which Nonna loved.

Nonna wrapped her arm around Sara's shoulders and Sara leaned her head against Nonna's shoulder. She smelled like baby powder and spaghetti sauce, not a bad combination, actually.

"Nonna, where are our mom's journals?" Gabby asked during a commercial. She tended to ask every once in a while. *You never know when Nonna's memory could be triggered*, she'd say. "We've combed through every box in the attic."

"In my bedroom closet," Nonna said. "Want a meatball?"

Gabby got up and came back into the room a few minutes later with a box.

Sara saw the elated expression on Gabby's face and threw back the afghan. "Oh my God."

"What is that?" Nonna asked.

"It's a box of Mom's things. I found it exactly where you said it would be."

Gabby set the box down and knelt on the floor to rummage through it. It was filled with bundles of computer-printed paper rubber-banded together.

"These aren't journals," Gabby said excitedly. "They're stories. Typed out."

"Oh, your mother was always writing stories, from the time she was in third grade," Nonna said.

Gabby pulled out a fat bundle. "What kind of stories did she write, Nonna?"

"Oh, adventures with animals mostly. Kid stuff. She always did have an amazing imagination. She stopped writing once she got married, but after Rafe was born, she got back to it. She even had a writers' group. I think she may have been writing a romance novel. You know, like that one about the girl falling in love with the priest."

"Good God, Mom was writing a *Thorn Birds* story?" Sara said. "Maybe you don't want to read that. There might be *love scenes*." She made a silly gagging gesture for Gabby's benefit.

Gabby was completely enthralled, leafing through the bundles and the notebooks. "Nonna, is it OK for me to have this? Sara, it's all right with you, isn't it?"

"Oh, have at it," Sara said. It felt good to see Gabby happy. Excited about something other than Malcolm.

"Well, this was a lovely surprise," Nonna said.

"I know!" Gabby said, grinning.

Despite her pain, Sara couldn't help but be happy for her sister. She put a hand on her shoulder. "You always loved to write. Maybe it will give you some inspiration." Now if only it gave Gabby some inspiration to dump that idiot Malcolm. But Sara didn't want to ruin things by saying that.

"Just knowing Mom did this inspires me. I don't even need to read what she wrote, although I will. Every word."

Gabby emptied all the papers out until they were piled all around her. Then she tipped the box toward herself and reached into the bottom. "Oh my God, Sara."

"What is it?"

She pulled out a small rectangular box wrapped in pretty pink-and-green paper, with a silver bow.

Under the bow was a tag.

Gabby exchanged glances with Sara. Sara knew Gabby was thinking the same thing she was.

Her long-lost birthday present from so long ago. Somewhere deep inside, she knew it. Even more fitting, because tomorrow was her birthday. Her eyes filled with tears yet again.

Aw, hell. As if there hadn't been enough crying today.

Gabby handed it over. She was getting teary too.

"Open it, sweetheart," Nonna said.

Sara flipped over the tag. Her name was written in her mother's beautiful script, with the usual flourishes and swirls she'd used for special occasions.

"Better late than never," Nonna, always the practical one, said.

Sara studied the perfectly wrapped package meant for her thirteen-year-old self. She was never one to carefully unwrap a present, but this one made her hesitate.

"Hurry up, I can't stand it!" Gabby said.

Sara smiled a little. If Evie were here, she'd make Sara wait until the whole family was present, but there was no way she was doing that. She put her finger under a seam to start tearing the paper but stopped herself. Like a piece in a museum, this package seemed almost as if it shouldn't be touched. And certainly shouldn't be ruined.

She carefully pulled up the tape without tearing the paper. Almost immediately she could tell it was a book.

Her vision blurred. Then, without thinking, she ripped into the rest of the paper. Her mother wouldn't have wanted her to treat it like a museum piece.

It was a copy of *Pride and Prejudice*. A collector's copy, the kind with gilt edges. A special edition that had the original text on one side of every page and footnotes explaining all kinds of things on the other.

Her mom had known how much that book meant to her. She'd bought her a copy that would allow her to fully learn every last detail. The perfect gift.

"Open it," Gabby said.

Sara stilled with her hand on the cover. She knew what she'd find when she opened it. Every book their mother had given them had been inscribed by her at the front.

"My sweet girl," the inscription read. "Welcome to your teenage years! A wonderful, scary time. Just a warning, there will probably be a Wickham or two to deal with before Darcy comes along. My wish for you is to know the difference. Love always, Mom."

Oh, Mom. A landslide of tears hit her, not just for

the beautiful gift but also because her mother's message seemed so spot-on in an eerie way. She wanted to cry out to her mother that she did know the difference! It had taken her over ten years, but by God, she knew. Too bad that when she'd finally figured it out, her Darcy had flown the coop.

"Colton's your Darcy," Gabby said.

"You're *such* a romantic," Sara said, rolling her eyes.

"He's liked you for a long time, Sara," Nonna said.

"You're thinking of Tagg, Nonna," Gabby said gently. "We're talking about Colton."

"I love Colton," Nonna said with a sigh. "Such a nice man."

Sara felt tears coming on again. He *was* a nice man. He took care of Nonna and his own grandmother and everyone in town. He'd stood up for her to her dad and shown up at her family dinner and handled all the craziness really well. She thought of how he'd taken off her glasses so carefully, setting them on the nightstand, and kissing her. Yeah, he'd loved her for who she was, all right. Or at least she'd thought it was love.

And she loved him in a way she'd never loved Tagg. Tagg had given her validation that being smart was OK. He'd been a shield of sorts for her to hide behind during those years when she wasn't confident enough in herself. But he wasn't the one. Not the *right* one.

No, the right one was a man who at the beginning couldn't have been more wrong. She'd gone from hating him to loving him. What a fine line that was, between love and hate.

"Are you all right?" Gabby asked, because sure enough, Sara's eyes were leaking again.

"Gabby," Sara said, wiping her eyes and leaning forward so Gabby would know what she was about to say was important. Her words came out shaky. "Don't marry a man who doesn't treat you like you're the best damn thing that's ever happened to him. Because if I learned one thing from all of this, it was that Tagg could always take me or leave me. But with Colton, I thought...Well. I clearly don't have it all figured out, but..."

"I get it," Gabby said, putting her hands up. "I get what you're saying."

"Don't ever marry a man who doesn't look at you like you're chocolate ice cream," Nonna said out of nowhere.

"Chocolate ice cream," Sara said, smiling through her tears.

"Perfect," Gabby said, laughing.

"I wish I had some of that," Nonna said.

Gabby rose from the floor and stepped around all the piles of paper. "I'm going to run and get us some."

"Get the half-gallon size," Sara called after her.

"Hurry back so we can watch more of the *Friends*," Nonna said.

Sara leaned back against the couch and linked her arm with Nonna's. Maybe Nonna didn't always get the facts right, but she was still very, very wise.

* * *

"Hey, babycakes." Carmen's voice blasting through the police radio on Colton's desk startled him awake. "I'm coming in there."

Colton bolted upright. His neck had a crick, his back ached, and his left leg was asleep. Champ's tags jingled as he shook himself awake too. The smell of police station coffee, strong and a little burnt, reached him through the door. He rubbed his neck and tried to pretend he hadn't spent the entire night at his desk.

Carmen walked in, holding a cup of coffee in one hand and a box of chocolates in the other. She was wearing a bright-orange sleeveless blouse, print pants with yellow pineapples on them, and hot pink pumps. It was hard not to be wide awake after looking at her.

"Carmen, what are you doing here? I thought you were supposed to be dispatching from the sheriff's office today."

"First, Maggie Nelson brought these in to say thank you for rescuing Dolly the other day." She waved them under his nose. "They're delicious, by the way. Second, I went out of my way to tell you to your sweet baby face personally that you're making a big mistake with Sara and to get your head out of your ass."

"How do you know anything about my personal life?"

"Tagg's mother told everyone what happened at the Angel Statue Preservation Society meeting this morning. Apparently she's rooting for her son to get back together with Sara."

He sighed. "Thank you, Carmen. You can go to work now."

"Did you sleep in those clothes? You look terrible."

He sent her a glare. The best he could do right now. Maybe if he didn't talk much she'd go the hell away.

Wishful thinking, because she parked her butt in one of the chairs in front of his desk. "I watched you grow from a cocky kid who was angry at everybody to a kind, gentle guy who watches out for every single citizen in this town. You hold your head high, Chief." Her voice cracked a little. She shook her finger at him emphatically, her bright-fuchsia polish sparkling. "Don't you let someone move in on your life who doesn't have half the integrity you do. Even if he does have double the degrees."

"And a better car," Evan said from the other room.

Colton scrubbed a hand over his head. "When did everybody get to be Dear Abby around here?" Still, he felt a warm little tightening in his chest.

Evan appeared in the doorway. "Hey, someone's here to see you, Chief." He lowered his voice. "It's that kid you gave the painting job to."

Carmen leaned over, grabbed Colton's chin, and shook it. "Think about what I said. Sara's too good to let her get away."

"Thanks, Mom," he said as she headed out the door. He was only half kidding. "Hey, Carmen," he called after her.

"Yes?" she asked, turning around.

"Seriously, thanks. I...appreciate your concern."

She grinned. "No problem, boss." She blew him a kiss as she left and patted Aiden on the shoulder as she passed him in the doorway.

Colton managed to grab a slug of his coffee before he told the kid to take a seat.

"So, Aiden," he said, leaning back in his seat and tenting his fingers. Where to begin? *The paint job looks terrific. Now get the hell away from my sister.*

Aiden had taken a ball cap off his head and was holding it to his chest. He looked contrite and humble—and nervous. But Colton didn't fall for that kind of thing easily.

As soon as the kid plopped into a chair, Colton said, "Look, Aiden, I'm glad you're here. Let's get a few things straight." He was going to get the upper hand on this. Attack the problem head-on. Make it clear where he stood in terms of Hannah. Which was, he didn't really want him near her but it was clear he wasn't going to be able to stop them. But he could scare the shit out of Aiden. That might help. It would at least make him feel better.

Colton felt a sudden burning in his chest. Heartburn. He choked it down with a slug of coffee, probably not the best remedy.

"Before you start, I want to tell you I'm grateful for what you've done for me, Chief," the kid said. "And I came to show you this."

Colton wondered if the kid was being a kiss-ass. Aiden was smart enough to know when he was in trouble and clever enough to wheedle his way out of it. Colton might have tried the same back in the day. One look in Aiden's eyes as he handed over a long envelope showed Colton otherwise. The kid looked eager. Proud. He was also shifting nervously in the chair. What in the world?

Colton pulled out an official-looking piece of paper. He took a minute to skim it. It was a letter of acceptance to the electrician program at the local technical college.

Well, I'll be. The kid had followed through. Applied and gotten in. And looked damn proud of it.

"I start in the fall," Aiden said. Despite his tough appearance, he was practically beaming.

Colton sat forward. The kid was grinning broadly. Colton couldn't help breaking into a grin too.

"Congratulations," Colton said. "Wow. I mean, this is great."

"I owe it all to you, Chief."

"You got the grades, Aiden. You got yourself in."

"When I interviewed, the guy told me you'd personally put in a good word for me. I'll never forget how you helped me."

Aw, geez. This was killing him. The kid really meant it.

He stood up. "Look, Hannah told me you were upset about us. I didn't tell you about me and Hannah because I knew you wouldn't approve. I want you to know I'd never hurt her or mistreat her. I-I love her, sir. Hannah's…amazing."

There went his heartburn again. But somehow, the pain wasn't so bad. He couldn't not like this kid, who reminded him so much of himself. Who had so much potential. Who'd been dealt a shitty hand but was trying to overcome that. All he needed was a little bit of help.

"I'll always be grateful for what you did for me. I'm going to do good, you'll see."

Colton put down the letter. He pinched the bridge of his nose, trying to find the right words.

"I expect you to keep working until your community service hours are done," Colton said. "That will take the rest of the summer."

"Will do."

"And I expect you to turn in all your grades to me from school—as part of your court supervision, of course. No slacking, right?"

"Absolutely." The kid was grinning widely now.

"And if you ever hurt my sister I will personally kick your ass, understood?"

"Yes, sir."

He knit his brows down low. "And if you ever encourage her to get a tattoo I will come find you, is that clear?"

"Yes, sir."

He escorted the kid out, wrapping his arm around him and squeezing his shoulder. "I'm proud of you, son," he said. It suddenly occurred to him that this was the first time he'd ever called anyone *son*. It reminded him oddly of Chief McGregor, who had seemed ancient when Colton was a teenager but who probably hadn't been much older than he was at the time.

The kid flushed and shook his head, a little embarrassed. Colton slapped his back and sent him on his way.

As he walked back to his desk, his eye caught the framed picture of Chief McGregor with his three buddies that hung on the wall. The buddy in the middle was his dad, whose smiling face looked up at him through time.

Colton wasn't his dad. He had to live his own life his own way. But he liked to think his dad would be proud that he'd become an officer and was serving their hometown.

Colton hadn't exactly chosen this job, but it suited him. Every once in a while, he was able to do some good. Besides, he loved it. Especially on days like this when something actually went right.

So maybe he wasn't saving lives, not the way Sara and Tagg did, anyway, but he'd built himself a place here, a life. Made a few people smile. Listened to their complaints. Tried to alleviate their worries and make their town safe. Saved their dogs when they were roaming loose. Not such a bad job after all.

He'd messed up with Sara. And he hadn't spoken honestly with her. He'd let things get in the way, like Tagg and the feeling he'd harbored that he was somehow not as good as Tagg. He'd been afraid of her slipping out of his fingers, thinking she wouldn't want to stay here in this town, but had he actually asked her what *she* wanted?

Maybe it was time to let her know how he felt. And maybe he really was right where he belonged.

Chapter 22

♥

The next day in the office, Sara noticed her charts from the day before were missing, so she walked into her dad's office, where he was sitting behind his desk reading a medical journal on his iPad.

"How's it going, Dad?" she asked. His desk was gorgeous glass-covered cherry, his office complete with all his diplomas hanging in neat rows on the wall beside his desk. She'd always loved coming in here as a child, if only to sit in the big leather swivel chair or experiment on tapping Gabby's knees with her dad's reflex hammer.

The old Sara would never have made waves, just quietly suffered in silence. Not that things had been bad in the office. She felt there was real potential for her there. But first she had to get her father to look on her as a partner. And if she kept saying nothing, nothing was going to change.

She took a seat in one of the upholstered chairs across from his desk, where over the years he'd given a myriad of patients news about their health, both good and bad. "Dad," she began, "what do you think of me coming to work here with you? I want the truth."

He looked up from his iPad. "I think you're going to be a successful physician no matter what you do."

"That's a canned answer. What do you really think of me being here? I mean personally?"

What had gotten into her? Well, a breakup would do that to someone, but she couldn't really blame her boldness on that. She'd told off Tagg, and that had felt really good. And she'd told Colton that she cared about him, and even if that didn't work out, she wasn't going to crack. So she was on a self-assertiveness roll. She waited with her arms crossed.

"You want the truth?" her dad said, folding his arms and setting his jaw in a stubborn way that reminded her of...herself. "I hate to tell you my personal feelings because I don't want it to cloud your judgment."

"What do you mean?"

"Well, I don't want you to stay because we love having you here. I want you to stay because it's the best *opportunity* for you."

"I really like seeing families. Talking to them about their concerns, educating them about health issues. I'm not going to apply for the fellowship again, Dad." She suddenly spotted a familiar pile of manila folders on the corner of his desk. "And Dad, for God's sakes, quit checking my charts every day!"

"First of all, I thought you *wanted* to go back to your fellowship. And secondly, I'm studying your charts. Not for errors. Well, maybe a little bit. Maybe. With the more complicated patients, but I must say, you have excellent clinical judgment. But I'm learning the new medicines you prescribe. I'm keeping up to date."

"You don't need to read my charts to learn that. I can teach you. More importantly, I thought you hated me doing family medicine. I thought you wanted me far away, on the East Coast somewhere."

"I would never hold you back from what you want. If opportunity takes you far away from home, I want you to feel free to take it."

"But sometimes it's hard to figure out what exactly you're thinking, you know? You just don't...say much. And you're all about academia. Reaching for the stars. Going as high as you can go. I've always wanted to please you, Dad, but I can't help thinking that I always fall a little short."

At that he took off his glasses and set them down on a pile of magazines. "Well, I'll say one thing. Your assessment of me is just wrong."

"Maybe it's because you rarely say anything. Not that I'm begging for praise, but a nice word or two goes a long way, you know?"

"Sweetheart, I couldn't be more proud of you. I've always encouraged all of you kids to reach for the stars—what kind of parent would I be if I didn't?"

"Yeah, but Dad, sometimes you're just pushy."

He raised a brow. "Well, it appears that you've learned to push back, now haven't you?"

She smiled at that. "All right then, while I'm on a roll, I'd like you to treat me like a partner. That means letting me see some of your more complicated patients—you know I'd talk over their treatment plans with you. I just don't want to be treated like a med student."

That was good, but she had one more thing to say. She took a deep breath and plunged in. "But mostly, Dad, I want you to treat me like your daughter. I want you to tell me you love me and are proud of me, because you are, aren't you? Sometimes I just feel like you can't express it or something. Or else you're deeply disappointed."

He looked at Sara and smiled in a sweet, nostalgic way that caught her off guard. "I delivered you, you know. Your eyes were green. Most newborns have blue, of course. You were wide awake with these big, round eyes, putting your tiny fist in your mouth, and I just... Well, I just fell. As purely and simply as I fell for your mother standing by the punch bowl at the senior prom. Anyway, I examined you and made sure you had all your parts, and there you were, my beautiful daughter."

Oh, that did it. Sara started to cry. Her dad got up from his chair and met her on the other side of the desk, wrapping his arms around her.

"Oh, Dad," she said, hugging him tightly and inhaling the spicy old-fashioned aftershave he'd worn for years.

"Your mother's death wrecked me, sweetheart," he said quietly. "There was a time when I didn't think I could go on. Just because I don't talk about her doesn't mean I don't still love her very much. Or you."

She mopped at her eyes. "Maybe sometime we could have lunch and you could... talk about her a little. If you wanted to. Gabby and I want to know more about her—I mean, now that we're adults."

"I can do that." He paused, and Sara noticed something she'd never noticed before. His eyes were watery. "I love you, sweetheart," he said. "I'm sorry I don't say that often enough."

"Got it, Dad," she said. "I love you too." *Open the floodgates, the whole dam just broke.* "That's all I wanted to hear."

Her dad reached over to a mahogany-covered tissue holder and handed her a Kleenex. Then he surprised her again. "You love the cop?"

"Really a lot." Oh God, there she went again. "And I think…I think you might have given him the impression he wasn't good enough for me."

"No one's good enough for my daughter."

"I think he assumed you were comparing him to Tagg."

"Tagg's an ass." Her mouth dropped open. Her dad never cursed, yet now he was up to twice in one day. "And I wouldn't be so sure the cop's done with you yet. He looks at you like you're chocolate ice cream."

He'd clearly been hanging around Nonna too long.

A loud rap sounded on the door. "Doctors, let's get the lead out," Leonore boomed. "We've got people waiting out here, you two." The firefighters probably heard her at the station two blocks down.

Her dad began walking toward the door but suddenly turned around. "I might want to go golfing on Wednesday afternoons and leave you in charge. What do you think of that?"

"You should take Wednesday afternoons off." She grinned. "But then I would get Thursday afternoons off, how's that?"

"Fair enough."

In the hallway, her father passed a longtime patient. "Hey, Bill," he said, stopping to shake his hand.

"Hey, Doc, how's it going?"

"Great. Hey, this is my daughter, Sara, and she's going to be seeing you today. She trained at Columbia, one of the finest hospitals in the country. You're gonna love her," he said, giving Sara a squeeze and beaming. "I know I do."

After Bill passed by, her father said, "By the way, I never told you this, but I got the Hopplebauer Award in my residency class too."

Sara's mouth dropped open a little. "How did I not know that?"

He shrugged. "It was your moment."

"Like father, like daughter then."

"I'm really proud of you, sweetheart," her dad said, giving her a fatherly squeeze. "And I'm so glad you came back home to work with me. We're going to make a great team."

"Got it, Dad," she said, grinning. "I love you too."

* * *

"Hi, honey," Rachel said as Sara walked into family dinner, which was at Rachel and Dad's house that evening. "Oh, I'm so glad you came!" Rachel said from where she stood working at the kitchen island. She pecked Sara's dad on the cheek. "How did you get her here?"

A corner of Dr. Langdon's mouth turned up, and he gave Sara's shoulder a squeeze. "I told her we didn't want her to be alone on her birthday."

Rachel gave her an enormous hug that made her tear up. "We're your family. We know you're hurting. But I'm so glad you're here."

Sara saw the pains Rachel had taken to make a nice birthday dinner. On the island two pies sat, half-covered with fresh whipped cream. Coconut cream, Sara would venture to guess. But she didn't have the heart to swipe a sample. She checked her phone, as she had a million times that day. Colton still hadn't called. Apparently he'd meant what he said about breaking up. OK, well, let him be like that. She'd be fine.

She wasn't fine.

Rachel moved to finish putting the topping on the pies.

"They're beautiful. Thank you." Sara was touched by the gesture, but she was starting to feel really bad about this whole pie thing. Now that she'd spoken to Tagg, her aversion to cake was dimming, and she was ready to move on from it.

"Well, you've got to eat something. Right?"

Actually, she had about as much enthusiasm for dessert as a patient post gallbladder surgery, but she didn't tell Rachel that.

"Rafe's bringing Nonna over," Rachel said. "We'll all be together." Well, that did it. She certainly wasn't going anywhere now. Who knew how many birthday celebrations she had left with her grandmother?

Her dad had gone out in the yard to pick a few tomatoes for the salad. Rachel finished topping the pie and placed the spatula in the bowl.

Sara sat down across from her at the big island. "Rachel," she said.

"What is it, honey?" Rachel asked as she slipped the bowl into the sink.

"Sit down a second." Sara patted Rachel's hand. "Look, this thing with Colton got me to thinking a lot—not just about my relationship with him but with the whole family. Sometimes I go a mile a minute and lose track of what really counts, you know? I just want to tell you you've been a sweet, wonderful stepmother to me, despite my holding you at arm's length. The only thing you did wrong was you weren't my mother. And I want to say...I'm sorry. I never allowed us to grow closer. I never gave you a chance."

"Oh, sweetheart. You were a teenager, too old to accept a mother substitute. And you were awfully independent. All you girls were. You all stuck together so tightly and mothered Rafe. If anything, I consider that strong bond a tribute to your mother."

"Those years after Mom died—we didn't know what else to do. We had to pull together. What that must've been like, to enter a house full of teenagers..."

"You had fierce loyalty to your mother. That's as it should be." She squeezed Sara's hand. "There's nothing to forgive."

"Well, you've always been kind and openhearted. I'm trying to take an example from you. And...I hope we can finally get to know each other better."

"Oh, Sara. Honey." Rachel's eyes got a little watery. Sara suddenly realized she could do a lot better. She got up from the island stool and hugged Rachel. "I love you. I just want you to know that."

"I love you too, sweetheart." Rachel squeezed her back for a long moment. Then she walked over to a built-in hutch and took out two wineglasses, grabbed a bottle from the cupboard, and poured them each a glass of red wine. "Happy birthday, Sara," she said. "May this be your year."

Sara clinked glasses and forced a smile, for Rachel's sake. She didn't think her year was exactly starting off on the right foot, but she didn't want to be any more of a killjoy on her birthday. "Any ideas about Gabby?" she asked.

"Have faith, my dear. Sometimes bad things self-destruct on their own."

"Sometimes good things do too," came out of Sara's mouth before she could censor herself.

"Oh, honey," Rachel said, giving her another hug, which Sara took gratefully. Sara brushed away a tear. "I don't know about that. Part of love is learning to iron out your differences. Don't give up yet."

Just then, Evie and Joe showed up with Julia and Michael. Rafe and Kaitlyn had ridden together and picked up Nonna and Rocket, and Gabby had actually convinced Malcolm to forego his usual late-afternoon workout and join the family, although Sara wouldn't have minded if he hadn't. Her dad had grilled chicken and vegetables tonight and thrown on some nice un-healthy brats just for Sara.

Julia shoved a little flat rectangle into her hands, wrapped in bright-pink tissue paper with lots of tape. "It's a pwesent." She grinned, showing a huge gap where one of her top teeth had recently fallen out.

"For me?" Sara asked, shaking the package. "Hmm. What could it be?"

"Open mine, open mine!" Michael said, running up and shoving another package at her.

Sara caught Evie's eye as she hugged her niece and nephew. "You better open them now, Sara. They've been driving me crazy all day."

"Hurry up, hurry up!" Michael said.

Sara unwrapped a package of sparkly hair barrettes from Julia and a pair of Spider-Man socks from Michael. "My favorite things!" Sara exclaimed as she brought both kids in for a hug. Julia was already trying to get the barrettes into her hair. "I love you both so much," Sara said, winking at Evie. "I'm so lucky to be your aunt." She wasn't kidding. The day might pretty much suck, but these kids were a huge bright spot.

"Can we have pie now?" Michael asked as his mother led him and Julia to the table. The dog followed close in tow, confident he would get food dropped, accidentally or intentionally, by the little ones.

Rafe came in at the last minute and slid into a seat beside Malcolm. "So how's business going, Mal?" he asked.

"Fantastic," Malcolm said with a wolfish grin. "Stocks are up and life is good. I'm making a killing."

"I heard on MSNBC today that Wall Street is robbing Main Street," Nonna said. "Hedge fund guys are all crooks."

Malcolm stiffened and shot Nonna a disgusted look. "Hey, watch it, Grandma. That's my job you're talking about."

"Take it easy," Gabby whispered, giving Malcolm an elbow. "She has dementia, remember?"

"This one political reporter said it," Nonna said. "I forget his name."

"You don't know what you're talking about," Malcolm said. Sara looked up. Rafe stopped serving himself potatoes. Evie frowned.

Gabby stood up. "No, Malcolm, *you* don't know what you're talking about, and I've had enough. No one talks to my Nonna like that."

Malcolm raised his hands in surrender. "Hey, I'm just defending my job."

Gabby crossed her arms. "Is it really necessary to do that? Geez!"

"Settle down, sweetheart," he said, sipping his wine. "Your grandmother just insulted my livelihood. The one that's going to make both of us very comfortable."

"Make that one of us, Malcolm." Gabby pulled the giant stone off her finger and placed it on Malcolm's plate, where it landed with a *chink*. "I think you should leave."

Malcolm made the mistake of glancing over at their father for support. Her calm, mellow father, who had welcomed anyone and everyone to their table over the years, was holding his fork with a death grip. His face was red. Maybe he was contemplating using it as a weapon. He quietly set the fork down and tossed his napkin on the table. "You heard her, Malcolm. I believe she's asking you to go."

Just then there was a knock on the door. Rafe, who had stood up and assumed the crossed-arm stance of a bouncer, complete with massive biceps, reluctantly glanced in the direction of the front door, torn between answering it and booting Malcolm out on his well-dressed rear.

Fortunately he was spared the decision. Tagg walked in, bearing a small wrapped package. Rafe took the opportunity to escort Malcolm out.

Sara moved to get up. She didn't need Rafe as her bouncer. She'd get rid of Tagg herself.

"Hi, everybody," Tagg said sheepishly. "I hope you don't mind, but I just stopped by to wish Sara a happy birthday."

Her father met Sara's gaze across the table and gave her a do-you-want-me-to-take-care-of-this look. Rafe remained on standby, ready to do the same.

Sara got up to deal with Tagg in private. And to get him out of the house, because he was definitely not staying for dinner. She tugged him by the elbow back to the front door, opened it, and went out onto the front stoop.

"I'm not here to try to make up to you," he said. She shot him a puzzled look. Was this a joke too, like the chest pain? If it was, she was definitely getting Rafe to bounce him. "I mean, I am, but not romantically. Here," he said, handing her the package. "Open it."

"Tagg, you didn't need to—" The last thing she wanted right now was a present from Tagg. Yet he stood there looking contrite. Not exactly humble, but his demeanor was different in a way that threw her.

"Please," he said. "I wanted you to have this."

She ripped open the elegantly wrapped gift. It was a Montblanc pen, black and silver and sleek. It must've cost a fortune.

"Oh, thank you," she said, fighting tears. Not because it was a sinfully expensive gift, or because she wanted such an expensive pen, but because she knew exactly why he'd chosen it for her.

He flashed her a smile. "I figured if I got you an expensive one, you'd be a little more careful about where you put it."

"For this price, I may have to wear it on a string around my neck." Which she literally had, thanks to Leonore's thingamabob.

"You like it?"

She ran her finger along its smooth wooden surface and nodded. It was too fancy for her, but he meant well.

"I thought about what you said," he said. "I've decided to try something new. I'm leaving next week to do a year of research at Stanford. Check out a whole new place. See what it's like to be alone for a while."

"That's wonderful, Tagg."

He turned his beautiful brown eyes on her. "I want you to know I'll always love you, Sara."

"I'll always love you too." She kissed him on the cheek and stepped back, amazed that Tagg was taking this so well.

"But if, in the future, you're ever up for a fresh start..."

She should've known he'd qualify that. "Tagg—"

"The only one she's starting fresh with is me."

Sara jumped. There, standing in Nonna's front yard, was Colton. Also carrying a box. But his was bakery big, a square white box. His intense blue gaze locked on to hers, and in that instant Sara saw something that stole her breath away. Their future. Babies with beautiful blue eyes. A house with a fireplace. Two toothbrushes side by side on the sink.

Maybe this birthday wasn't going to be so bad after all.

Sara's eyes flooded because, God, he was here.

Colton acknowledged Tagg with a nod, then walked right over to Sara. Behind her, in the house, the family had gotten up from the table and gathered in the foyer. She could see Gabby and Nonna straining to stick their heads out the front door.

Turning to Sara, Colton took her hands in his big, calloused ones. His hands felt warm and steady and wonderful, and she gripped them with all her strength.

"I told you he came for homecoming," Nonna said in a horrible version of a stage whisper.

He turned to Nonna. "Yes, I did, Nonna." He said to Sara, "Nonna's right. I decided that night that if Tagg wasn't going to take you to the dance, I was going to. That we'd go together, hopping along. But I was on the way up to your door when Tagg called me, feeling guilty that he hadn't taken you. And I backed down for him." He looked over at Tagg, who was standing off the porch. "I'm done doing that, by the way."

"I told you," Nonna said. "He brought such pretty flowers too. I found them in the shrubs."

"You said you almost asked me to homecoming, not

that you almost picked me up at my door," Sara said. "Geez, Colton!"

"Yeah," he said. "Funny, isn't it? Don't blame Nonna. At the time I begged her not to tell you." He turned to Tagg. "You've been a good friend to me over the years, Tagg, but I love Sara. I can't step aside anymore for you."

Tagg walked up to Colton and extended his hand. "You've been a good friend to me too. Be happy, you two." Tagg pulled Colton into a hug, and then gave Sara a longer one before heading down the driveway.

Colton pulled Sara away from the family threatening to spill out the door and led her toward a big shady maple at the side of the house.

"I overreacted about Hannah. I didn't want to accept that she's growing up. But I finally had that talk with her, one I should've had years ago. Anyway, I'm sorry for blaming you."

"I'm sorry I couldn't talk to you about it. I didn't mean for you to be blindsided."

He shrugged. "It wasn't really about Hannah. I've been in a kind of mental competition with Tagg for half my life, and in most cases he won. But I learned that life's not really a competition, is it? I didn't exactly choose my path, but it all worked out all right. I think I'm where I'm supposed to be."

"Colton, I just hope that one day I could serve the people of our town half as well as you do."

"You think you'll end up staying?"

She grinned. "I love it here."

"Oh, good. Well then, I guess you can have your

birthday gift now." He nodded toward the box in his hands.

"I'm always up for dessert."

By the time they walked into the house, the family had somehow managed to pretend they'd been sitting at the table all along, making small talk. Colton said hi to everyone and nudged the box over to Sara.

Colton's eyes twinkled mischievously. Sara couldn't help grinning wildly. She couldn't care less what was in the box, because she already had the best birthday present ever. And he was standing right in front of her.

Kaitlyn gave a little sob. Rafe handed her a birthday napkin, which she used to blow her nose.

"Don't cry, Kaitlyn," Nonna said, patting her shoulder. "It's not like it's a ring box."

"Happy birthday," Colton said.

Someone handed her a knife to slit the tape. She lifted the lid to the fragrance of chocolate and sweet icing. Inside the box sat the most beautiful chocolate cake she'd ever seen, decorated with intricate multicolored flowers, tiny gilded leaves, chocolate shavings, and "I love you, Sara" written in gorgeous pink swirls.

"Colton—it's beautiful."

"Thank Kaitlyn for that," he said, giving her a nod.

Sara looked over at her best friend. "You made this?"

"I got up early to do it this morning. Just for you, babe." She was blubbering pretty hard now. Rafe had grabbed a roll of paper towels from the kitchen and ripped one off for her.

Colton walked over to Sara and took her hands. "I

love you and I want to celebrate a lot more birthdays with you." He gave her a big, wonderful smile. "And I want to give you a reason to like cake again."

Her heart was in danger of melting right there, into a huge puddle on the braided rug. That was about the sweetest thing she'd ever heard.

"No surprises popping out of this one?" Nonna asked.

"Well, actually, I can't promise that there's no surprise in the cake," Colton said, winking at Kaitlyn.

Sara imagined one of Kaitlyn's exquisite fillings—chocolate ganache, fresh strawberries and whipped cream (her favorite), or maybe raspberry custard or amaretto.

Rachel was suddenly lighting candles. Everyone sang "Happy Birthday" and cheered.

"May I cut it?" Kaitlyn appeared at her side, taking the knife. "I know how you hate to cut cake."

"You're the professional," Sara said. "Can I take a picture of it first?"

Rafe did the honors, capturing the beautiful cake for posterity, then Kaitlyn cut it into slices and passed them all around.

"Take the first bite," Rafe said. It was a tradition they'd had since they were little kids. The birthday person always got the first bite. Except Rafe really pissed her off one year by biting into her cake before she did, and she never let him forget it.

She bit into the cake, everyone watching. "Eat, everyone, eat," she said, waving them on. "Oh my God, it's delici—"

Her teeth chomped down on something hard. She covered her mouth with her hand and ran her tongue over the hard object that had nearly broken her teeth.

And suddenly stopped chewing. Heat blazed into her face. Colton was staring at her, a very broad grin spreading across his face.

"Make sure you don't swallow that, OK?" he said, a little too seriously.

She turned her head away and spit out the bite into a napkin.

Holy shit.

A chocolate-covered…Oh, wow. She tossed it into her water glass and shook it and fished it out.

A gorgeous, shimmering diamond, none the worse for wear, surrounded by a circle of tiny diamonds, and it was the most beautiful thing she'd ever seen.

Except for the stunning, wonderful man next to her, who had dropped down on one knee. Sara's eyes misted over and everything blurred—the cake, the ring, the smiling faces of her family, and Colton, kneeling on the floor with Rocket trying to jump on him.

"Down, boy," he said. Rafe pulled the dog away as Colton looked up at her. "I love you, Sara. Will you marry me? Be my wife?"

She couldn't see very well through her tears but she could see Colton right there in front of her, and that was all she needed. "Yes, yes. Of course." Her lips found his and she kissed him with everything she had. He kissed her back, his lips sliding softly against hers, his hands reaching up to caress her cheeks, all just this side of PG-13.

"They're kissing," Julia announced. "They *love* each other."

"Yucky," Michael said, putting his hands over his mouth and giggling.

By this time all the women were crying too. The men looked awkwardly at their drinks, and Rachel was running around pouring—was that champagne? And the whole family was getting ready to toast them.

"This is the best birthday ever!" Nonna said. "Can I have more cake?"

"I have to agree with you on that, Nonna," Colton said. "The first of a lifetime of birthdays together," he said, sneaking a kiss. Then he set down his plate and kissed her again, good and hard, in front of everybody.

Nonna smiled. "Life is just too short to hate cake."

Epilogue

♥

The bachelor party took place in mid-December in the back room at Giuseppe's, which had craft beer on tap and the best sauerkraut balls in town. Rafe was there, and all of Colton's cop and firefighter buddies, and Joe and Sara's dad. Colton tried not to get drunk, but there were definitely more than a few rounds bought. But at the end of the night his friends stuffed him into an Uber and he asked to be taken to Nonna's house.

Sara met him at the front door wearing flannel pj's, thick red slipper socks with reindeer heads on them, and an old terry robe. *Perfect.*

"What are you doing here?" she asked, a little alarmed, pushing up her glasses. "It's two in the morning."

"Sorry. I just—wanted to be with you."

Her eyes softened, and she gave him a kiss. He probably smelled like booze and cigarette smoke, but she didn't say anything.

"You look pretty in flannel," he said.

She snorted. "Oh, you are a little drunk." But he'd meant it. And he couldn't wait to show her something. Then she'd never think badly of a bachelor party again.

She pulled him into the little foyer. "Did you have fun?" She was whispering, so as not to wake up her grandmother.

"Yeah. I have great friends." He paused. "Hey, can you drive us somewhere?"

"Do you mean can I take you home? Of course. Let me get my keys."

"Not exactly home." She scanned his face for clues, but he just smiled. He was a little buzzed, but it was wearing off.

"OK. Give me a sec."

She ran upstairs and came back a minute later with her phone. Then she pulled on boots and a winter coat and followed him out the door.

A few minutes later they pulled up to his plot of land. There was enough snow to cover the grass, but not so much that the car had much difficulty climbing the long gravel drive. The snow crunched under the wheels as she passed over the tiny bridge and parked at the edge of the woods as Colton instructed.

He reached in his pocket and pulled out a wool scarf. "Give me your glasses and cover your eyes with this," he said.

She eyeballed the scarf a little reluctantly. "You sure you're sober enough to make sure I don't fall in a ditch and break my leg?"

"Just put it on, Red."

"All right. Here goes." She handed him her glasses and wound the scarf around her head. He helped her out of the car and held her hand while they trudged through the snow. After a few minutes, he tugged on her arm to get her to stop walking and lifted the scarf from her head.

"Surprise," he whispered, placing her glasses into her hand.

* * *

In front of her the old, dilapidated house slowly came into focus. But it had been transformed by hundreds of tiny white Christmas lights on every window, the door, and on the awful overgrown bushes. They were wrapped tightly around the trunks and branches of the trees too.

With the blanket of snow, bluish now in the moonlight, and the softly glowing lights, the house had been transformed into a fairy tale.

She had no words. Colton was watching her, smiling.

"It's so beautiful," she said. Before her, delicate lights sparkled and twinkled.

"I think it could be, one day," he said.

"How did you..."

"Generator. Rafe helped me."

"It's spectacular." The old house, its flaws subdued by the night and the glow of the lights, looked elegant and proud.

"Come on." He pulled her by the arm, but she resisted.

He walked up to her. His breath was turning into

white puffs of steam, and his eyes were watery from the cold, but they held something irresistible in them...more than amusement. A...gravity. Whatever it was he wanted to show her, it was important. "Stop thinking of *Hoarders*, OK? You're going to have to trust me on this one."

She nodded and let him lead her up to the front of the house. Digging into his jacket pocket, he pulled out a flashlight. "Here, you'll need this."

She flicked it on. There was a wooden ramp where the crumbling steps used to be. "You do know I hate spiderwebs? Like, they completely freak me out. And I saw this old abandoned house on HGTV that looked just the same—filled to the brim with newspapers, broken furniture, raccoon poop, mouse pee..."

He cut her off by pushing the door open, scooping her up, and carrying her though the doorway. She gave a little squeak at being swept off her feet.

"Welcome to the foyer," he said, turning in a slow circle. Surprisingly the foyer was empty. And it smelled like sawdust, not mouse pee. "Here, flash that light over there." He pointed above the door. A semicircle of leaded glass panes sat above the door. Similarly paned glass sidelights with the lead in a vine pattern ran the length of the door on either side.

"Ohhh, it's beautiful," she said, curling her hand around his warm neck. She was thrilled to be in his arms, thrilled to see him so excited. And thrilled to be swept up and carried over a threshold, which made her heart race crazily. What had he done?

"I knew you'd like that." He set her down and took

the flashlight, his fingers grazing hers. When her eyes adjusted to the dim light, she noticed the house was empty. No boxes, no papers, no broken furniture, no hoarder stuff. What in the world?

He took her hand and walked to one side of the big staircase. "This is the hallway—where our dogs will come falling over each other with excitement to greet us every day."

"Have you been drinking? Oh yes, you have. Did you just say *dogs*—as in more than one?"

He shrugged. "I always wanted two. Champ could use a buddy. How many do you want?"

She laughed. "I guess two's fine. But what about some kids running to greet us?"

"Oh well, they might do that too. Until they get older and leave it to the dogs."

He pulled her through a doorway to the right. They stood in a big rectangular room with two white china cabinets built into the corners. The ceiling was rimmed by a wide and intricate crown molding. A wire dangling in the middle indicated the presence of a chandelier at one time. "This is the dining room, where we'll have big family dinners on Sundays with your family. But Cookie and Hannah will probably be there too. And Rocket, who will hang out with Champ and our new puppy. And I know Cookie will love to hold our babies. She'll tell us it's to help us have time to grab a bite to eat, but in reality she won't be able to get enough of holding them. And our kids will have a million birthdays and other celebrations here, and we'll listen to them tell us how their day was every night over dinner."

That's what started the tears. That he'd cared enough to do all this, and say all the touching things he was saying. Colt stood there, stroking her hand, his low voice echoing a little in the empty rooms.

A smoky scent suddenly drifted through the chilly air. "Is everything all right?"

"That just means Rafe has done his job," Colton said. Before she could ask what that meant, he pulled her along again. "C'mon."

The next stop was an enormous formal living room with a big fireplace, where a hearty fire was blazing and crackling. Candles burned on the mantel and on the floor surrounding an air mattress heaped with blankets. Everything looked a little blurry because she was crying down the insides of her glasses. She rubbed them against her robe. "You had Rafe do all this?"

"I set it up earlier today, but his job was to come light the fire."

"Wow," she said.

"Don't worry, he's already planning payback. I think it involves taking his truck somewhere to pick up furniture or something."

That sounded more like the Rafe she knew and loved. "Colton, I-I don't even know what to say. Everything is...amazing."

"There's no family room—yet," he said, pointing toward the back of the house. "That will have to be a future addition, but when we build it, it will be spectacular, with a view of the backyard. It overlooks the creek. Of course we'll need a fence, to keep the dogs and kids out of there. Are you OK with fences?"

"Sure, I—"

He paced a little around the room. "This is the formal living room, except I don't expect we'll be all that formal." He swept his arm around the room. "But for tonight, it's the bedroom."

Her legs just melted right there. The chill in the room was nothing against the warmth that suddenly spread through her entire body. Was this man real, or was she still asleep under the eaves at Nonna's, dreaming of a man like this, a life like this?

Colton's eyes were dancing, and she knew deep inside that she'd remember how he looked at this moment for the rest of her life—the firelight playing on his face, accentuating the dark, dangerous brows, the chiseled jawline, the full lips that quirked up in a tiny smile.

He led her closer to the fire and tugged her into his arms. Lowering his voice, he said, "Once we make love here, the house is ours, you know that, don't you?"

Sara's heart was pounding so furiously she thought surely Colton could hear it. She felt weak and dizzy and suddenly hot, but overall so, so right. Her voice came out sounding strange and muted. "No refunds, huh?"

He laughed. "Actually, the Wrights told me I could have another day to try and convince you."

"Colton, you had me at *Hoarders*."

"So you like it? Enough to live in it?"

She was really crying now. He reached over and wiped her tears with his glove. "Hush now." He cradled her face in his hands. "This was meant to be happy. And if you hate it, we'll bulldoze it. Simple as that."

She grabbed him by the arms, shaking him a little. "I am happy. Happier than I ever thought possible. And from what I can see, the house has beautiful bones. I can imagine us living here. But honestly, I'd live in a one-room shack with you if that's where you wanted to live. I love you, Colton. So, so much."

He drew her close and kissed her forehead. "I can't wait to spend my life with you. Have babies with you. Share our days over dinner and go to bed holding you and wake up with you every morning." He bent to kiss her but stopped. "Oh, I almost forgot." He grabbed a package off the built-in bookshelf next to the fireplace and handed it to her.

"Open it," he said.

"Is it a wedding gift? Because I have yours back at Nonna's." She'd made him an album of photos of them taken over the past months. Even found an old one Tagg's mother had taken of the two of them standing unhappily together during some awards ceremony for Tagg. It was a fitting reminder of how far they'd come.

"It's just something little," Colton said. "Go on."

She tore into the package. It was a framed photo. One she'd never seen before. She and Colton were standing in front of the angels on the bridge. They both looked flushed and...happy. It was the one Mrs. Mulligan had taken when they were nineteen, on the day of Hannah's dance recital. Right after he'd kissed her.

"How did you get this?"

"Mrs. Mulligan sent it to me. She swears the angels are never wrong."

She was quiet. And swiping at her eyes again.

"We could've been together all these years."

"The way I see it, you're getting a much better version of me than the one from ten years ago. Maybe things happen as they do for a reason."

She wrapped her arms around his waist and looked tenderly into his eyes. "I'm so glad they happened, Colton."

He wrapped his big arms around her, and she curled into his warmth. They stood like that for a minute.

"It's warmer by the fire," she said. "Plus there are blankets. I'd hate to waste that nice little bed you set up. I mean, since it would probably be a good idea to inaugurate our new home, don't you think?"

"I thought you'd never ask." Then he kissed her. "I love you, Sara."

"I love you, Colton. And I always will."

Acknowledgments

Many thanks to Jill Marsal, my agent, who is always in my corner. Thanks also to Amy Pierpont, my editor, who worked tirelessly to help me to realize the vision of this story.

Many of us are walking the Alzheimer's journey with a loved one. The way can be fraught with stress as families must navigate a complex medical care system and care options. This experience during the past decade with my mother-in-law has taught my own family kindness, patience, and love, and has brought us closer together, as I am certain she would have wished. A friend told me, when you have a loved one with Alzheimer's, you lose them twice. I believe this to be absolutely true.

My husband is my rock, and he also has a wicked sense of humor. If Colton has any whopping good one-liners, you can thank him. Thanks also, sweetie, for sharing with me the ups and downs of Sara and Colton's path to love. At one point I think he said, "I think I know their problems as well as you do," and that is probably true.

Thanks to my older sister, who has given me many wonderful books through the years, the same ones on Sara's mother's shelf, in fact. She has also inscribed the front of each one with a beautiful message. I'll keep all those books forever, Mar.

Writer sisters, you know who you are. We live far apart yet we are only an email or phone call away. Your friendship means everything to me.

Pride and Prejudice is one of my favorite books. The edition Sara is given as a gift with text on one side and notes on the other is actually not a fancy gilt edition. It's called *The Annotated Pride and Prejudice*, edited by David M. Shapard, and is a must for any true Austen fan.

Lastly, thank you, dear readers, for sending me messages about things in the books that made you laugh or cry. These thrill me to the core. I've said before that writing can be a lonely job and getting to the end of a book is a struggle, but you make it all worthwhile. Thank you from the bottom of my heart.

xo
Miranda

About the Author

Miranda Liasson loves to write stories about everyday people who find love despite themselves, because there's nothing like a great love story. And if there are a few laughs along the way, even better! She's a Romance Writers of America Golden Heart winner and an Amazon bestselling author whose heartwarming and humorous small–town romances have won accolades such as the Gayle Wilson Award of Excellence and have been *Harlequin Junkie* and Night Owl Reviews Top Picks.

She lives in the Midwest with her husband and three kids in a charming old neighborhood that is the inspiration for many of the homes in her books.

Miranda loves to hear from readers! Find her at mirandaliasson.com, Facebook.com/MirandaLiassonAuthor, or on Twitter @mirandaliasson. For information about new releases and other news, feel free to sign up for her newsletter at http://www.mirandaliasson.com/#mailing-list.